questions of perspective

daniel maunz

Black Rose Writing | Texas

ISBN: 978-1-68433-458-2
PUBLISHED BY BLACK ROSE WRITING
www.blackrosewriting.com

Printed in the United States of America
Suggested Retail Price (SRP) $18.95

Questions of Perspective is printed in Garamond

*As a planet-friendly publisher, Black Rose Writing does its best to eliminate unnecessary waste to reduce paper usage and energy costs, while never compromising the reading experience. As a result, the final word count vs. page count may not meet common expectations.

Cover art: Stephanie Insalaco
Copyediting: Adrienne Marie Barrios
Author photo: Irene Bello

As with just about everything positive I have contributed to the world since I met her, this book is for and because of Lynne.

acknowledgments

It would be a monumental understatement to say that I could have never finished this book without the support of many others.

First, I am indebted to my beautiful wife, Lynne. Her support and encouragement were unwavering even during those times I did not believe I had anything in me worth sharing. She patiently read (and reread … and reread …) countless drafts and never stopped pushing me to drive forward with this novel. I am blessed to have such a loving and supportive wife.

I also owe a great deal of thanks to my mother, Barbara Lush. Aside from instilling in me a love of books from the time I could first hold one, she also spent countless hours reading multiple drafts of this story, painstakingly catching my typos and all of those unfortunate instances where I inexplicably used the same adverb four times in the same paragraph.

I am also thankful for my lovely in-laws, Walter and Patricia Anderson, who supported me with kind words of encouragement over countless pizza lunches over the course of the several years I worked on this novel. They never wanted to stop hearing about how the writing was going, and I was thrilled when their interest maintained even after reading early drafts of this story.

Many others were also kind enough to sacrifice their time in reviewing early drafts of this novel and offering constructive advice or words of support that kept me from ever giving up. In this regard, I thank John Foote, Tracey Kappenberg, Eric Anderson, Daniel Cooney, Kristen Mogavero, Jules Barrueco, Brooke Skolnik, Katie Berkovich, Dana LaScala and Erin Rieu-Sicart.

Much thanks also to Rosemarie Iaconis for her invaluable advice (legal and otherwise) during the writing and publishing of this book.

This book was my first experience working with a copyeditor, and I was incredibly fortunate to end up with Adrienne Marie Barrios. She reviewed this novel with care and diligence, and her attention to detail is unmatched. The end result was a marked improvement because of Adrienne's impressive efforts.

I am also extremely thankful to Stephanie Insalaco, who took my vague idea for a cover and ran with it, exceeding my wildest expectations and creating art that I am honored to have on the front of this book.

I also owe thanks and appreciation to Reagan Rothe and everyone at Black Rose Writing, both for their hard work on this particular novel and, more generally, for giving new authors like me an opportunity to have their voices and stories heard.

My two cats, Captain and Admiral, aside from serving as the inspiration for Peaches, also routinely kept me company on those many occasions when I was writing deep into the night (and often prancing across my keyboard at the worst possible times), and I am grateful and lucky to have them in my life.

To my son Patrick: I finished this story a few weeks before you were born but I have little doubt that it would have ended up a much bleaker tale if it wasn't for the excitement and hope I felt in anticipation of your arrival. After just about two years of getting to know each other, I truly could not be prouder.

Finally, when I first started writing this story, I figured that, at worst, I would have a novel for my wife to read (and hopefully enjoy). Of course, I dreamed that this novel would someday find a wider audience. So, to all of you who took a leap of faith and picked up this book, I am extremely humble and grateful. I hope it was worth your time.

I promise I did my best.

questions of perspective

prologue

No one, let alone me, realized it at the time, but April 19, 2011, was the most important day in the history of the world. Probably of the entire universe.

As I lived it, though, the day actually kind of sucked.

My morning started in a packed courtroom in Jamaica, Queens, filled with attorneys donning cheap suits ranging from dark blue to dark gray—a rainbow for the colorblind. The day would have been considered hot in July, but it was downright inhuman for April, and many of the lawyers in the room (particularly those on the heavier side) were trying (and failing) to will themselves to stop sweating. As I waited for the judge to emerge and the calendar call to begin, I found myself wedged on a long bench in the gallery between two such attorneys. The lawyer to my right had given up any pretense of dignity and was furiously using his tie to mop his damp forehead. I squirmed in misery and glanced down at the thin file I was carrying, noting the plaintiff's name: Abramson, Jack. *At least I'll be one of the first to get called,* I thought, assuming an alphabetical call. I could have confirmed this by checking the calendar that the clerk had posted by the door to the courtroom, but that would have involved climbing over a number of attorneys to get out, and I wasn't *that* curious about where my case sat on the court's schedule.

Justice Marder, a thin, stern-looking judge who looked to be in his eighties, eventually hobbled out from his chambers to take the bench. He looked angry from the get-go; the simmering fury of a man struggling to reconcile his significant power with the fact that even he could not avoid spending the blistering morning in a non-air-conditioned room (in a clingy black robe, no less). In the silence that washed over the room as the judge limped slowly to the bench, I suddenly heard a small *plop*, followed by another. Looking down, I saw two dark spots slowly expand on the redweld folder containing my litigation file—an inadvertent gift from the dripping attorney to my left. Annoyed, I cocked my head and threw him a perpendicular glare, which he seemed to receive.

"Hot in here, right?" he whispered, chuckling nervously. I didn't respond. I had a longstanding rule of ignoring any comments made in my direction relating to temperature or the weather.

The calendar was finally and mercifully called. My case was not only *one* of the first to be announced, it was *the* first. Had I planned ahead a little better, I would have fought harder for an aisle seat. But I didn't, and, as a result, it left me with an undignified climb over ten attorneys to escape the row and make my way to the front of the courtroom. Even though it was a slightly longer route, I opted to go left, solely for the opportunity to shove my ass into the face of the attorney who had dripped all over my file.

I was surprised when the judge directed me and my adversary to approach the bench rather than take our places at the standard tables assigned for the plaintiff and the defendant. When I arrived at the bench, my adversary—a kind-looking bald man in his mid-sixties—stood waiting for me. "Kind-looking" isn't typically a profound description, but in this profession, it's a rarity. The lawyer smiled at me and actually threw me a wink, which I returned with a taut nod. Justice Marder asked us about the status of the case, and the plaintiff's attorney filled him in. As he spoke, the judge's eyes narrowed more and more until they were thin slits of pure malice aimed squarely at me. It dawned on me that this would be an unpleasant conference, and, like many other instances in my legal career, I wished I were a little more prepared than I was, which was none. None prepared.

After he had been caught up to speed, Justice Marder continued to stare at me with naked disgust. I opened my mouth to speak in my defense, but he quickly shut me up with a raised finger, and then he started to yell.

As the judge's tirade, punctuated by the occasional snicker from the rear of the courtroom, washed over me, I felt myself sliding into a familiar state of numbness that suffocated any emotional response I may have otherwise had at being publicly chastised like a child. I was no longer an active participant in the scene; I had stepped outside myself to become an audience member watching a movie involving a man who just happened to look exactly like me, and who just happened to be getting humiliated in front of a room full of strangers. I recognized, at some level, that this detachment was a byproduct of depression, but in that moment, it did not bother me at all. I'd learned to work with the tools I was given.

Even in my emotional cocoon, though, the unfairness of the situation was not lost on me. While I stared at the screaming judge, all I could think to myself, in a whiny interior monologue, was that this wasn't even *my* case.

It was like this: The prior evening, around 7:15, I was working in my cramped office, trying to finish writing a motion to dismiss that was due at week's end, when a fellow associate named Mark Foster appeared in the doorway. Mark, holding a thin file, wore a sheepish grin that I imagine he thought was charming. With his artificially whitened teeth and out-of-season tan, Mark was regarded by most in the firm as the good-natured office idiot. I happened to like him more than I liked most of the other associates I worked with, which really was not saying anything at all.

"Hey, Doctor!" Mark said. Mark had taken to calling me "Doctor" because of my name—Dave Randall—or, more specifically, my "DR" initials. As noted, Mark was not a clever boy.

"What's up, Mark?" I asked flatly. Mark seemed momentarily surprised at my ability to divine that something was indeed "up," but even a dope like him could interpret the tone of my question: *Get to the point.*

"Ah …" he started, rubbing the back of his neck uncomfortably. "One of my buddies from law school just called, and they're all going down to Atlantic City for the night. I was going to go with them and stay over, but I just remembered that I have this compliance conference tomorrow …"

"And you'd like me to cover it for you," I finished.

Mark blushed. At least, I think he did. His fake tan made it hard to tell.

"Yeah … I would have asked someone else, but this place is pretty empty now. I already tried John, but he said he has a deposition tomorrow."

I believed Mark when he said that I was his last resort. It took me years to build my reputation as the office grump, but I had finally pulled it off at the relatively young age of thirty-one. One of the perks of my unofficial title was that it was rare for coworkers to come nosing about looking for favors. Unfortunately, Mark's dopiness, coupled with his desperation, was enough to make him immune to my lack of charm. But I refused to give in so easily.

"I have a deposition tomorrow, too," I told him, which was actually true. Granted, it was scheduled to start in the afternoon, so there was really no reason I couldn't cover his appearance in the morning and then head to my deposition afterwards, other than the fact that I didn't want to. Unfortunately for me, Mark came prepared for my rejoinder, as evidenced by the hint of a smirk that touched his lips at my response.

"Yeah, I checked your calendar before I came in," he said quickly. "Your deposition starts at 2:00, right? In midtown? My conference is in Queens at 9:30, so it should be perfect. You can go straight to your deposition from court."

Afterwards, I would think of a half-dozen excuses I could have offered to get out of covering Mark's appearance. *I need to prep for my deposition in the morning*, or, *Sorry, but I have a motion due Wednesday that I have to finish*. Hell, Mark was so dumb that I probably could have told him I had an appointment with my gynecologist and gotten away with it. But it was late, and my mind at that hour was sluggish at best. With a reluctant sigh, I reached for the file, which Mark was more than happy to pass off to me.

"Thanks, Doctor!" he said. "I owe you. And the appearance should be easy. Nothing's really going on in the case."

I came to realize the following morning, as Justice Marder's rant-induced spittle sprayed my face, that Mark's assessment—*nothing's really going on*—was entirely accurate. What Mark left out was that a lot *should* have been going on. Much to my embarrassment, I learned (along with the judge) that Mark had blissfully ignored nearly every directive that Justice Marder had given him at the last court conference—an act of gross negligence that I was paying for through public humiliation.

Of course, I was tempted to interrupt the judge's tirade by screaming, "It wasn't me! This isn't my case!" But I knew that excuse wouldn't fly. I was in court as a "proud" representative of the law firm of Sanders, Martucci & Lyons, and when one of us misses a deadline, as far as the court is concerned, we *all* missed the deadline. Still, in that moment, it seemed unfair that I was the only one from my firm being drenched in judge spit.

"Do you know what this is, Counselor?" Justice Marder demanded, waving a piece of paper at me.

"Yes, Your Honor. It is an order," I replied, feeling even more absurd at being forced to become an active participant in the judge's performance. A snicker from somewhere in the gallery behind me confirmed that my embarrassment was warranted.

"Yes, it *is* an order. That means you are legally obligated to comply with it. Did they teach you that in law school?"

"Yes, Your Honor."

"I'm so glad," the judge sneered sarcastically, drawing a few laughs from the horde of attorneys at the back of the room. *Keep laughing, assholes*, I thought. *Your cases will be called soon enough.* Justice Marder then proceeded, in slow, exaggerated fashion, to make a great show of putting on his reading glasses.

"Let's see ... did you respond to plaintiff's interrogatories by February 18 like I directed you to?" he asked, reading from the order.

"No, Your Honor."

"Did you supplement your document production to provide your client's work papers for the 2003 audit like I ordered?"

"No, Your Honor."

"Did you commence the third-party action that was discussed at the last conference?"

"No, Your Honor." Or so I assumed. It seemed consistent with Mark's *modus operandi* for litigating this particular case.

"Were party depositions completed by March 18 like I ordered?"

"No, Your Honor."

Justice Marder angrily slapped the order down on his bench and gave me a stare that was equal parts bewilderment and disgust. In that moment of silence, the plaintiff's attorney—my adversary—cleared his throat.

"Your Honor, if I may?" Justice Marder finally took his eyes off me and waved my counterpart on impatiently. "I have called defendants' counsel repeatedly regarding these issues, but no one has ever called me back. I even sent a good faith letter about two weeks ago in the hope that these matters could be resolved before this conference, but I never received a response. I had been dealing with a Mark Foster, who I understood to be the associate handling the case. I believe that this is my first encounter with ..." He stopped and looked at me.

"Dave Randall," I muttered, wondering where this windbag was going with all of that. It then registered that he was trying to *help* me, and I felt a stab of gratitude at that unexpected act of kindness. It is relatively rare in the world of litigation. It was alien enough to me, at least, that I almost couldn't identify it even when it was right in front of my face.

The judge glowered, mulling his options. He had clearly been enjoying lambasting me in front of a packed courtroom, but the revelation that I was not the correct target for his rage seemed to knock the wind out of his sails.

"This is what we're going to do," he said, finally. "You are going to give them all of these documents in the next two weeks—by May 3. Do you understand?"

"Your Honor," I started, and the judge froze in shock at receiving a response that was anything more than a chastened head nod. I tried to adopt a contrite face, but it felt unnatural, like I was merely pushing out a pouty lip while fluttering my eyelashes. "I apologize for our disregard of your last order. I am confident that we will not need a full two weeks to complete all of this. We can certainly have all of these documents sent to plaintiff's counsel and in his hands by this Friday."

The judge stared at me, shocked. So did my adversary. I can't imagine they had ever seen an attorney argue in court for a *shorter* deadline to complete a task. But I didn't mind a tighter discovery schedule since I planned on throwing this file back on Mark's desk the second I returned to the office. I figured that by inserting me into this mess, he had more than earned a few late nights of putting discovery responses together. I maintained my best earnest expression and waited for the judge's answer.

"Fine," Justice Marder snarled. "You get him this stuff by Friday. And I strongly suggest you do not ignore *this* order. Do you understand me, Counselor?"

"Absolutely, Your Honor."

As soon as the judge finished scribbling out an order, I took a carbon copy, pivoted, and exited the courtroom, ignoring the various smirks lurking in my periphery. It was one of the rules I had embraced regarding court appearances: *Get out as soon as you get a ruling you can live with.* Only bad things can happen when you dawdle. It was a solid maxim, and one that had served me well in the five-plus years I had been litigating. In fact, if I were to rank my rules regarding court appearances, that particular one would have come in a solid second, only behind *Don't speak at all unless you have to.* I liked *that* particular tenet so much that I actually adopted it in my personal life as well.

I hurried out of the courthouse and lumbered down the steps to the street. I later recognized that I *should* have waited for that other attorney to thank him for his help in keeping me from getting completely steamrolled by the judge. But, of course, I didn't. The path to acting like a decent human being was, in general, something I could only see with the gift of hindsight.

I crossed the street and headed toward the paid parking lot where attorneys running late for their own court appearances were still lined up in their cars, impatiently waiting to pass off their keys to an attendant. One such attendant, overwhelmed with the backup, hurriedly took my ticket and did a double-take after glancing at it, which was followed by a death stare in my direction. It was the second such look I had received that day, and it wasn't even 10:15. "So, it was *you*," he growled in an accent I couldn't place.

Before I could open my mouth to respond (likely with nothing more than a confused *uhhhhhh* ...), he cut me off.

"You didn't leave your key! We had to move your car to another garage because it was blocking all the other cars here!"

That's impossible, I thought. *How could he have moved my car if he didn't have the ...* My hand instinctively went to my pants pocket, and I felt my key ring with my car's keyless starter attached.

Oops. I pulled out my set of keys and grinned sheepishly. "I'm still not used to this thing," I offered lamely. The attendant remained uncharmed.

"Come on," he barked, striding toward a van without bothering to check that I was following. I shuffled along behind him like a child and, at his prompting, sat in the passenger seat. He hopped in and, after throwing a quick look of disgust at my struggle to connect my seatbelt, drove off through the back streets of Jamaica.

I didn't bother trying to engage in small talk. Instead, I focused on how this ride would end. *Do I tip him?* As if reading my thoughts, my surly driver announced: "Fifty-dollar surcharge for not leaving your key." I took out my wallet and was relieved to see that I had exactly sixty-two dollars, which would cover the surcharge plus the base rate of twelve dollars. It also rendered moot my concerns regarding the propriety of a tip under the circumstances. I tried to take solace in the fact that the attendant was already so annoyed that my stiffing him on a tip was unlikely to have any material impact on our relationship.

We finally arrived at a dark garage where my car sat alone in the driveway near the street. "Thanks—" I started. My driver stared straight ahead, clearly trying to will me out of his life. I was all too familiar with that look, although I wasn't used to being on the receiving end of it. With a sigh, I handed over three twenties and two mangled singles and then hustled out before he realized I had given him the exact amount owed, sans gratuity.

Everything felt off when I entered my car. As I readjusted my car seat and mirrors (*was the guy who drove it here eight feet tall?*), I realized I had a slight conundrum. It was almost 10:30, and if I made the forty-five-minute drive back to my office, I'd have fifteen minutes to kill before having to leave for my 2:00 deposition in Manhattan. On the other hand, if I went straight to the city, I'd end up with over two hours to spare there. Not loving either option, I decided upon the latter, reasoning that I could use the extra time to study a bit for my deposition. Aside from filling a cardboard box with a bunch of random documents I *might* decide to use during my questioning, I really hadn't prepared at all. Earlier in my career, I tried to justify this lack of preparation as a conscious strategy: *Stay ignorant! Make the witness educate YOU!* Over time, I became more honest with myself and accepted that my "stay ignorant" policy was really just a flimsy pretext for run-of-the-mill laziness.

It was nearly noon by the time I parked my car in midtown and lugged my cardboard box full of "evidence" to the street. *Time to cram.* I found a Starbucks and ordered a Venti Iced Caramel Macchiato with the hope of finding a quiet table at which I could study. Unfortunately, as I sipped my tub of lactose, I noticed there was absolutely nowhere to sit in the packed café. I tried to leave, but I couldn't quite figure out how to simultaneously carry both my drink and my unwieldy box. With a sigh, I forced myself to chug my iced coffee just to free up both hands. After I disposed of the plastic cup, I took my box back out to the street. I was in the same exact position as I had been minutes earlier, only now I also had to contend with the very real threat of diarrhea. I think I just enjoy a good challenge.

Before long, I gave up on finding an indoor venue to prepare, and I settled for a bench in a small park. It was less than an ideal place to get ready. The breeze threatened to steal any documents I plucked out of my box to review, and it was a struggle to jot down notes on my legal pad without a solid surface to lean on. Also, and perhaps most difficult of all, I was sharing my bench with a homeless man screaming profanities at no one in particular. "Those shitheads" seemed to be his primary target, but I don't think I was included in that category. I got the vibe that he somewhat enjoyed *my* company.

I eventually gave up trying to prepare and embraced the prospect of just sitting and relaxing in the sun for a few hours. My stomach was making alarming noises, but I figured I would be ok if I skipped lunch. At some point, I apparently learned to tune out my companion's rantings because he managed to wander away without my realizing it. Once I had my bench to myself, I tried to at least mentally prepare for the deposition.

The case was a boring one, even when compared to the other accounting malpractice lawsuits that I handle. The extremely short version was that an accountant—my client—made a mistake on a tax return that resulted in the IRS demanding nearly $250,000 in back taxes, $64,000 in interest, and $10,000 in penalties. Everyone, including my client, acknowledged that he made a mistake in preparing the return. If the plaintiff had hired an intelligent attorney, it would have been an easy case to settle.

But, as these things tend to go, the plaintiff instead hired an ambulance chaser named Michael Terkle who was completely unfamiliar with the law relating to professional malpractice claims. So, even though it was well-settled in New York that back taxes and interest are not recoverable components of damages (making the case worth nothing more than the remaining $10,000 in penalties), the only settlement demand we had received prior to the deposition was for a cool million, which was, not-so-coincidentally, the policy limits of my client's errors and omissions insurance. At the most recent court conference, I asked Terkle how he could justify such a high demand. He scoffed and asked rhetorically, "Do you have any idea what a Manhattan jury will do to your guy at trial? An accountant who admits that he fucked up?" I didn't answer but thought to myself that it was also unlikely that a jury would fall in love with his client, a guy who made his small fortune producing porno movies.

By the time 1:45 rolled around, I had accomplished pretty much nothing. Ignoring the growling sounds from my stomach, I stood up and made my way to Terkle's office with my useless box of useless documents. I was somewhat surprised—and sickened—when I arrived at his chic office, which was on the fortieth floor of a high-rise looking out over Central Park. I had been under the impression that Terkle was practicing law out of the back of a used van. I headed to his office suite and was greeted by his receptionist—a tall, skinny blonde in her mid-twenties whose bored eyes couldn't quite bring themselves to look directly at me. She had me take a seat ("Mr. Terkle is on a *very* important phone call right now") and await his pleasure.

Twenty minutes later, Terkle emerged from a back room, smiling apologetically. "So sorry for the delay," he said. He arched an eyebrow at my box of documents. "Planning on a long one?"

"We'll see," I muttered, and he frowned. I certainly had no intention of conducting a long deposition. Despite my asinine box, I didn't think I'd have more than an hour of questions. If I finished by 3:00, there was an outside chance I could beat rush-hour traffic on my way back to Long Island. Still, I wanted to leave him with the uncertain potential of a six-hour deposition ahead of him; it pleased me to plant that seed of doubt in his mind.

I imagine that seed grew into something more substantial when, despite my best efforts, the deposition ended up lasting over five hours, caused almost solely by my scumbag of a witness refusing to answer just about every question I posed to him, even the routine introductory ones:

Q: What year did you graduate from college?

A: I don't understand the question.

Q: How can you not understand that question?

MR. TERKLE: Objection. He stated he does not understand the question. Can you rephrase?

Q: Did you go to college?

A: You mean as a student?

Q: Yes. Were you ever enrolled as a student in college?

A: What do you mean enrolled?

And so forth.

I did what I could to move it along: I made my objections, I threatened to move for sanctions. At one point I demanded that we call the court to address the witness's obstinance, but the judge ended up yelling at *me* for wasting his time. All the while Terkle sat impassively, his poker face betrayed by his eyes sparkling with amusement at my mounting frustration. Finally, after five hours of questioning, I wrapped up the deposition, having established nothing more than that my client was hired by the plaintiff and screwed up the tax return.

It was after 8:30 when I arrived back at my one-bedroom apartment in Malverne, Long Island, which sat above my landlord's house. I had neither the energy nor the inclination to make dinner, so I stripped out of my suit, grabbed a half-empty bag of Cool Ranch Doritos, and plopped on the couch to watch the Mets game, already in progress. It was an ugly combination of poor hitting and fielding on the part of both teams and fittingly went into extra innings with the score tied 1-1. I tried to stay up to watch the end, not so much out of any emotional investment in the outcome as much as a desire to put off going to bed. I knew that once I fell asleep, my next sensation would be waking up to a brand-new day of the same old crap. Shortly before midnight, with the game in the fifteenth inning, I lost my battle with consciousness and drifted to sleep on my couch.

The day had been lousy. Even sadder, it had not been particularly atypical, at least from my perspective. But in time I would come to appreciate that was the day everything changed.

April 19, 2011, was the day that my friend John Manta became God.

chapter one

When most people think of "friends," at least in the male-male context, they might think of going out for beers, or catching a ballgame, or maybe even a weekend fishing trip. John and I didn't do any of that. Our friendship was atypical. In fact, we might not have satisfied a lot of people's definition of the word "friends" at all. We did not interact socially outside of work. We never talked on the phone, and our rare text messages were purely utilitarian in nature—things like, "I'll be out tomorrow. Check my mail?" If one were cynical, one might be inclined to characterize this "atypical friendship" as a mere workplace acquaintanceship. But one would be wrong.

John was a third-year associate at Sanders, Martucci & Lyons when I started in September of 2005—my first job out of law school. It was a mid-sized firm in Garden City, Long Island, consisting of roughly seventy attorneys, which took on all sorts of insurance defense cases at cheap rates. "Cheap" being a relative word, of course. I don't imagine that many landscapers or baristas would whine about only making $220 an hour.

My employment at SM&L was a touch bittersweet for me—probably more bitter than sweet. I had done well in law school, having graduated sixth in a class of nearly three hundred. My stellar grades easily landed me a number of interviews with the highest-profile firms in Manhattan. Unfortunately, as impressive as my law school transcript was, my interviewing skills were not. It wasn't *what* I said during those interviews—I knew the stock answers that interviewers were looking for. The problem stemmed from *how* I delivered those rote responses. To be more specific, when asked, for example, what drew me to pursue a career in litigation, I would give a trite speech regarding my appreciation for the law with the artificial passion and sincerity you would expect from the host of an infomercial. I also suspect that I was regularly betrayed by my face, which I'm sure conveyed something along the lines of "I'm here because I want to make money and I don't know what else to do with my law degree."

When the dust finally settled, I had secured a single job offer, which I accepted immediately out of a fear that it would quickly vanish. My starting salary was $52,000—roughly a third of what many of my former classmates were making at various firms across Manhattan. I arrived for my first day of work at SM&L with the enthusiasm of someone who literally had nowhere else to go. But I set out to make the most of it, at least on that first day. My determination historically had a very short shelf life.

I thought I had a fairly good idea of what my job would entail before I started. The practice of law is one of those professions (like police work and the medical field) that has been romanticized in cinema, television, and literature. I figured I had seen enough movies and read enough John Grisham novels to have at least a *rough* idea of what my day-to-day life as an attorney would be. Granted, I did not think I would necessarily be trying a case in my first month (although *Legally Blonde* suggested it was at least a *remote* possibility), but I did naively envision starting out by supporting senior partners as they prepared for trial, oral arguments, and all the other sexy stuff lawyers get to do, all the while being groomed to one day take on such responsibilities myself. I was all kinds of stupid back then.

On my first day, after I filled out my HR paperwork, I was introduced to a chubby senior associate named Todd Solman who was tasked with showing me around the office and setting me up with my first assignments. Todd's rosy cheeks, coupled with his thick dark hair, slicked straight back, reminded me a bit of Babe Ruth.

The layout of SM&L placed the attorneys in the perimeter window offices, with paralegals and secretaries filling up cubicles in the bowels of the floorspace. Todd whisked me around the circumference of the floor, taking me from office to office, attorney to attorney, and repeatedly introducing me as "the new guy." He didn't bother presenting me to any of the secretaries or paralegals, who tracked my parade around the office with stolen peeks and conspiratorial whispers amongst each other.

Each of my introductions was nearly identical: small talk about where I went to law school, half-hearted jokes about waiting for the bar exam results, followed by a dismissive "Well, welcome aboard!"

After the sixth consecutive "Welcome aboard!" I whispered to Todd, "I feel like I'm on a cruise ship."

Todd looked confused. "Why?" he asked. I shook my head—*never mind*—and made a mental chalk mark to memorialize another blown first impression.

When we finished my introductory tour, Todd took me to a long, narrow conference room in the center of the office. The back wall was lined with over a hundred white boxes, fifteen columns stacked seven high, which made the tight room feel even more suffocating. On the conference room table sat a neatly laid out legal pad flanked by several pens, along with a small electronic device I did not recognize.

"Welcome to the practice of law!" Todd announced, gesturing theatrically at the wall of boxes.

I instinctively took a half step toward them and stopped. "I don't understand."

Todd smiled, and not in a kind way. More of a patronizing *sucks-to-be-you* smile.

"This," Todd proclaimed, "will be your life for the immediate future, and your first step into your legal career."

"Oh," I replied, still having no idea what was going on.

Todd ambled to the table and pulled out the chair nearest the legal pad and other supplies. He gestured at me to sit, so I did. Todd then waddled to the far end of the room to pick up a box, which he struggled to carry back to where I was sitting. With a loud thud, he dropped it on the floor beside me.

Simpering again at my bemused look, Todd explained. "We are involved in a substantial legal malpractice case arising out of an antitrust lawsuit against one of the largest pharmaceutical companies in the country. I'm sure over time you'll get up to speed on the facts of the lawsuit, but that's not really important right now. What *is* important is that the plaintiff just produced over a hundred thousand pages of documents, which are in all of these boxes. We just got these documents back from the printer, where we had them Bates-stamped. We need—"

"Excuse me," I interrupted. "What is a 'Bates-stamp'?"

Todd looked surprised. "Oh. The pages are each numbered in the lower right so that we can reference them. See?" He took out a sample page from the box he had dropped next to me and pointed out a small six-digit number in the corner.

"Ah, of course. *Bates-stamps*." I was embarrassed at my ignorance over what appeared to be a routine term of art. I had never, until that moment, heard of the phrase at all.

"Yes. Well." Todd picked up a pen and hastily drew a table on the legal pad, with columns labeled "Bates range," "Date," "Author," "Recipient," "Description," and "Nature of Privilege." I looked over the empty table blankly, afraid to ask another stupid question.

"As I was saying," Todd continued, "we are in the midst of a pretty complex litigation. And we will need to catalog all of these documents for our future use. You don't have to do it by hand; you can just dictate it onto a tape and have a secretary type it up." Todd pointed at the unfamiliar electronic device on the table, which I assumed to be some type of recorder.

"I'll admit, it's not a fun job," Todd added, "but it's an important one. And someone will have to go through these documents. Hey, at least it's good billing, right?"

It was around that time that my brain finally processed what Todd had been saying, and I realized that I was expected to catalog over a hundred thousand documents. *I was number six in my class!* This was idiot's work. Even worse, it was idiot's work that looked like it might take me several months to finish.

"I have to catalog all of this by myself?" I asked, hoping to make it sound more clarifying in nature than a complaint. Todd, to my surprise, looked downright tickled by the question.

"No. Of course not!" he said with an evil grin. He walked around to the far side of the conference room to dial the telephone. After a moment, he spoke into the phone, "Hey, John; this is Todd. Can you come meet me in conference room four? Great, thanks."

After he hung up, Todd turned back to me. "I'm getting John Manta over here to work on this with you. John's a third-year associate—a very bright guy. But he's a little ..." Todd cut himself off, weighing his words carefully before continuing. "He can be a little insubordinate at times. The partners let him get away with it because they think he might have Asperger's. Or at least that's what I've heard."

I didn't know what Asperger's was, so I nodded my head in feigned understanding.

A few moments later, John Manta came into the conference room. He was in his late twenties, a couple of years older than I was, with dirty-blonde hair and a lanky build that did not suggest any hint of a physique. Unlike all the other associate attorneys I had met that morning, who were, to varying degrees, dressed to impress, John's outfit seemed to be purposefully designed to technically comply with a dress code while simultaneously displaying a defiant middle finger at the spirit behind it. His scuffed shoes did not seem to go with his black suit at all, and that clash was further exacerbated by a faded brown belt. His blue-and-white tie might have been appropriate but for a heart-shaped coffee stain toward the bottom of it. I glanced at Todd to gauge his reaction to John's outfit and saw that he was visibly disgusted.

"Didn't you have a court appearance today?" Todd demanded.

John shrugged. "Yeah, but it was just a preliminary conference across the street. I just filled out a form in the basement and got out of there. Never even saw a judge."

Todd chewed a lip thoughtfully. I surmised that Todd had a few years of experience on John, but I wasn't sure if he had the authority to reprimand him. That seemed to be the same question Todd was asking himself as he studied John, clearly annoyed but not quite bold enough to give it voice. Deciding against pressing the issue, Todd shook his head, exasperated.

"John, this is the new guy, Dave Randall. You must have been in court when I took him around the office earlier."

"Hi," John said, somewhat shyly and without looking at me.

"Hi," I replied, putting out a hand. After a moment's pause, John reluctantly shook it, awkwardly dropping it after one pump.

The three of us stood there in painful silence for some time. John did not ask me any questions, nor did he offer any small talk. He also gave no hint of wanting to welcome me aboard. When the lull became unbearable, I threw a look at Todd, hoping for a lifeline. But Todd seemed to relish John's discomfort and continued to study him with a small enigmatic smile.

John, sensing Todd's amusement, frowned and started to back away, saying, "Anyway, I should get going ..."

But before he could reach the door, Todd spoke up. "Do you remember a couple of the partners mentioning last week a massive document production coming in that had to be cataloged?"

John paused. "Vaguely. What about it?" He looked up and noticed the wall of boxes lining the far end of the conference room. "Ahhhh ... fu- ... C'mon. You cannot be serious."

Todd threw a tight-lipped smirk at John. "It won't be so bad. You've got the new guy here to help you."

I nodded encouragingly, but John didn't see it. He wasn't taking his eyes off of Todd.

"Look, we have paralegals for this kind of thing," John snapped. "I'm a third-year associate—there's more important stuff I should be working on than spending a month cataloging a document dump!"

"Like what?" Todd replied, trying to muster up every bit of authority he thought he had. "The partners specifically requested that I get you involved in this project. And to be frank: you are *significantly* behind in your billable hour requirements for the year. You should be *happy* that I gave you such an easy assignment to bill the hell out of!"

John stared back with his lips pursed. I was somewhat amazed that John appeared to be literally biting his tongue. Todd, for his part, seemed pleasantly surprised that John was not pushing back, as if he had been expecting a fight. His confidence in his authority growing, Todd clapped John on the back and said, "I gave Dave the gist of the assignment, but I'm trusting you to make sure he does this right." After John still didn't respond, Todd added, "Look, this is a real opportunity for you to show some leadership and impress the partners. You should really make the most of it." Todd left the room, leaving me alone with John.

.   .   .   .   .

Our first day together was awkward, if not icy. John sullenly sat at one end of the long rectangular table in our cramped conference room, mindlessly shuffling a stack of papers with no real purpose. I sat at the other end, hustling in my review and cataloging of document after document, eager to make a strong first impression for once in my adult life. Unfortunately, my efforts were largely wasted. John, the only one present to even potentially note my strong work ethic, seemed unimpressed. He would arch a cynical eyebrow at me whenever I completed a box, but he otherwise didn't comment on … well, anything. He spent most of that first day just flipping through the same stack of papers, lost in his own head.

At times I tried to draw him out in conversation, whether it be through small talk (*How long have you been at the firm?*) or overly earnest practical questions (*So where's the best place to go for lunch around here?*). John's responses typically took the form of a not-so-subtle sigh, followed by a perfunctory answer calculated to invoke as few syllables as possible (*Three years. Deli across the street.*). I left for home that first day a little after 6:00 with the impression that John was somewhat of an asshole. John was still sitting at our table when I departed, staring into space while absently flipping through the same papers he had held all day.

I was hopeful upon arriving at the office early the following morning that John would have snapped out of his funk, but that optimism was quickly dashed. When I entered the conference room, John was already sitting at his end of the table with the same lost expression on his face. He acknowledged my arrival with the barest of head nods and resumed staring into space, holding the same stack of papers as the previous day, which I figured to be a prop in the unlikely event someone popped in to check on our progress.

I should stress that I am not, by any means, the type of guy who feels a need to force chatter if I am stuck with another person. If I was in an elevator with someone, I wouldn't have batted an eye at the prospect of riding quietly together. Hell, I generally preferred it. If John had at least gone through the motions of being civil, and we ended up working all day with an organic absence of conversation, that would have been just fine with me. But John had imposed an awkward silence upon our small conference room that even I, introvert that I was, found unbearably suffocating.

"Good morning, John!" I said brightly. John blinked in annoyance.

"Morning," he muttered, not bothering to make eye contact with me.

"Another fun day ahead of us, huh?" I offered lamely, trying to maintain a sunny disposition. John closed his eyes and took a deep breath, looking physically ill at this small talk. Clearly not wanting to give me any ammunition to keep our "conversation" going, he threw me a forced smile and looked away, retreating back into his own head.

But I was determined not to let him escape. I simply could not deal with another day of moping on his part. "So, do anything fun last night?" I asked.

"Nope."

"What'd you end up doing?"

"Nothing."

I waited for something more but didn't get it. I didn't know what else to do; this type of forced conversation was well outside of my own comfort zone. Defeated, I replied listlessly. "Yeah, me too. I didn't do anything."

Despite my best efforts (which really didn't amount to much), silence once again descended on our room. I gave up on drawing John out of his shell and heaved the box I had started yesterday onto the table in front of me. I vowed not to try to engage John anymore. *If he wants to spend his day sulking, that's his prerogative,* I thought. In grim fashion, I set about getting to work, too disgusted with John to even look at him. But after five minutes, I glanced up to see what John was up to. I was surprised to find that instead of staring into space, John was looking at *me*.

"What …" John spoke slowly once he and I made eye contact. I jolted in surprise—this was the first unprompted thing John had said to me since we met. "So what did your 'nothing' look like?"

I wasn't even sure at first what he was referencing. I stared back at him, trying to discern if he was mocking me. I couldn't detect any bad intentions on John's part. He seemed genuinely curious and, even stranger, somewhat fearful of my response. Not knowing what else to say, I told him the truth.

"On my way home, I picked up three slices of pizza and a couple of garlic knots. I had dinner on my couch, flipping through the channels while I ate. I eventually stumbled across an episode of *Golden Girls* on some weird channel, and I got drawn into it. Turns out that I had jumped into the middle of a *Golden Girls* marathon, and I ended up staying up past midnight watching it all. That was my night: pizza and *Golden Girls*. You?"

John's lips twitched, the first hint of a genuine smile I had seen from him. He looked more relaxed, and I puzzled over how my answer could have been *comforting* to him.

"Let's see," he said, stretching in his seat. "My 'nothing' involved getting back to my basement apartment around 8:00, making frozen mozzarella sticks, and then falling asleep to *Back to the Future, Part 2*, which was playing on … TNT, I think? I woke up around midnight, made my way to bed, and eventually fell back asleep. And now here I am." John paused, rubbing his chin thoughtfully.

"In full disclosure," he added in a serious tone, "I should mention that my recap left out the masturbation. I didn't think it was necessary to get into that."

He stared at me calmly, waiting for my reaction. I wanted to laugh, but he added that bit of information so matter-of-factly that I wasn't sure *what* type of retort he was looking for from me. I had the feeling he was testing me in some odd way, so I considered my words carefully before responding.

"It's ok," I finally said. "I left that part out, too."

John nodded, looking mildly satisfied. *How did he think I'd react?* I wondered. *Did he think I was going to faint at his reference to masturbation? Did he picture me running to Human Resources to tattle?* It irritated me that John seemingly thought I would be put off by his saucy language.

"And just to clarify any potential confusion," I added, as John raised a questioning eyebrow at me, "I should make it clear that the masturbation portion of my evening was completely unrelated to the *Golden Girls* marathon."

John's cheeks spasmed, but he managed to maintain a straight face. "Yes, thank you for clarifying. I was actually confused about that."

"No problem," I replied, also trying not to grin.

"And, in any event, I wouldn't have blamed you in the slightest if they had been related," he added.

"Yeah?"

"Yeah." John nodded gravely. "That Blanche." He shrugged in an exaggerated *what more do I have to say?* kind of way.

I snorted, and John, unable to keep his serious facade going, let loose with a laugh that was harder and longer than was probably warranted. I suspected that his moments of levity at the firm had been few and far between.

And as dumb as it sounds, with that exchange, the ice between us thawed almost entirely. I started rifling through my documents and John, to my relief, finally started working on his own box, humming softly to himself. After a moment, I placed the song as the *Golden Girls'* opening theme: *"Thank you for being a friend."* I chuckled, but I didn't say anything. I still didn't completely understand what I had said or done to set John at ease, and I was afraid of saying anything that would ruin it.

John surprised me a few hours later by asking if I wanted to head down the street with him to a deli to grab lunch. I agreed. Aside from Todd, John was the only person at the firm with whom I had any substantial interaction. At the deli, I ordered chicken fingers and fries. John got a salad, but he was polite enough not to draw attention to my unhealthy selection. I thought we would take our lunch back to the office, but John threw me for a loop yet again by sitting at a table set up on the street.

"It's so nice out," he explained. "We're not likely to get many more days like this before autumn kicks in."

I sat across from him and we ate together in a comfortable silence that was nothing like the suffocating stillness that had assaulted me the previous day. I had, by that point, managed to pick up on John's revulsion to small talk, and since I couldn't think of anything profound to say, I ate my dopey chicken fingers quietly. John didn't seem to mind at all.

After a few minutes, a group of well-dressed men and women walked up toward the deli. They looked vaguely familiar to me, and as they passed us, one of them—an attractive blonde woman in her early thirties—spied me and John sitting together. She didn't acknowledge us at all. Instead, she chuckled and whispered to her colleagues, who turned to look at us. Laughing, they all made their way inside. John continued to eat his salad without showing any sign of seeing the group.

"Don't they work with us?" I finally asked.

John didn't respond, and for a moment I wondered if he even knew what I was talking about. But then he said, "Yes."

"They were laughing," I said. John heard the question in my statement.

"They aren't used to me having lunch with someone. I usually just eat at my desk." He stabbed a grape tomato with his fork and stuffed it into his mouth.

Before I could ask another question, John hit me with one of his own.

"So, Dave, why did you come to work here?"

My immediate instinct was to give the rote answer that I gave at interviews: *Well, I have a very strong passion for litigation, and your firm has an excellent reputation in many of the practice fields that I find interesting, and ...* But I knew from the way he looked at me that John wasn't looking for a canned response, so I told him the truth.

"When I was in college, my dream was to join the FBI. I'm not sure where that came from. Certainly in part from *The X-Files*. Part from *Silence of the Lambs*. But regardless, I just got it in my head that that's what I would do. And after looking into it a bit, I learned that it's much easier to get into the FBI with a law degree. So after I graduated, I went to law school with the plan of maybe working for a district attorney's office for a couple of years and then applying to the agency."

I paused, giving John a chance to question or comment. But he didn't. He just gave me a tight nod to continue.

"I ran track in college—the 400 and long jump. It was a small liberal arts school, so the athletics weren't what you'd see at a top Division 1 university. But I was in pretty decent shape, which was useful since there is a physical test for the FBI. They test your speed, strength, endurance ... there's a bunch of things you have to do as part of the application process, but it would have been easy for me. I had been training for it for years, and I continued to stay in shape while I went to law school. Well, one night, during the summer after my first year of law school, I was playing basketball at the park. Just a pick-up game. At one point, I went up for a rebound, and this asshole took my legs out from under me. He claimed afterwards that he was just boxing me out, but he was behind me, you know? It was a dirty play. Anyway, I fell hard and landed flat on my back. It knocked the wind out of me and I ended up with a lump on my head, and I thought that was the worst of it. But the next night, I went to the track to do sprints, and my lower back randomly tightened up and I came up limping. I went to the doctor, who sent me to a specialist, who had me get an MRI, but none of them could figure out what was wrong. And it didn't go away, even with time. I just couldn't run anymore."

I paused again, giving John a chance to chime in, but he didn't try to speak. He just patiently waited for me to finish my story.

"It didn't take long for my dream of the FBI to die. But I was still in the middle of law school, with no real backup plan, so I finished and got my law degree. I did pretty well in law school, too. But when it was all said and done, the only place that wanted to hire me was SM&L. So here I am."

John processed this in silence. I stared at him, waiting for a response, but he just nodded his head in acceptance and continued to pick at his salad.

"Well?" I finally demanded. John sighed and placed his fork on the table.

"What?" he asked. "You want to know what I think?" At my terse nod, he shrugged. "If you had a cat stuck in a tree, and you set up a ladder to get him, but the cat jumped down on his own while you were climbing, would you say, 'Fuck it—I'm already halfway up' and keep going up the damn thing?"

"No," I muttered, somewhat resentfully. It was a point that had occurred to me plenty of times in the past two years, but it irritated me to have John realize it right away. The events that brought me unenthusiastically to SM&L reminded me a bit of Newton's first law of motion: *Every object in a state of uniform motion tends to remain in that state of motion unless an external force is applied to it.* I was on the trajectory of becoming a lawyer, and I just stayed on it for no real reason. Of course, the flip side to Newton's law could also apply to me without much shoehorning: *An object that is at rest will stay at rest unless a force acts upon it.* Even on the second day of my legal career, I already felt less like an object in motion than an object that was going nowhere.

"I get your point," I added. "But it's an easier issue to diagnose than it is to cure."

John shrugged, seemingly indifferent. "If you say so."

"Besides," I said, looking to change the subject, "I hate cats. I wouldn't be climbing a ladder for one in the first place."

John rolled his eyes, amused. "(a) It was just an analogy, and (b) how can you not like cats? They're so much better than people!"

I pretended to shudder. "It's the way they look at you. I feel like they're always seeing right through me. Creepy."

John, having finished his salad, stood to throw away his container. I followed his lead and asked, "What about you?"

"Hmmm?"

"You apparently think I'm an ass for working here. But what about you? You don't seem to like this firm at all."

John laughed. "Oh, God, no! It's awful!"

"Then why do you stay?"

John mulled it over before smiling. His grin tried to convey a callous indifference, but I detected more than a hint of sadness lurking beneath it.

"Where else would I go? Why, if I wasn't working here, I imagine I'd just be doing some other horseshit."

chapter two

My first moment of awareness on April 20, 2011—the morning after John attained Godhood—was pulling into a parking space in the lot behind the SM&L building. My mind snapped to life with a jolt once I realized I had arrived at work. I had no memory of waking up, getting ready, or driving to the office. It was unnerving. I thought back, trying to remember any particular detail from the time between when my alarm went off and when I pulled into the parking lot, but I couldn't. Sure, I could *imagine* how it went, having made essentially the same commute for the past five-and-a-half years: wake up at 6:45, fool around on Facebook for fifteen minutes or so, shower, shave, throw on a button down and a pair of khakis, hop in the car by 8:00, and arrive by 8:25 or 8:28, depending on whether I made the light at Hempstead Turnpike. I *knew* I must have done all of those things that morning, but I had no independent memory of them. I remained seated in my car for a few moments, trying to make sense of this development. *Are my mornings now controlled solely by mindless reflexes emanating from my spinal cord, with my brain sitting out?* I wondered. *Will this eventually become my entire day? My entire life?*

That sobering thought was interrupted by a rapt tapping on my window. I rolled it down and was caught off guard when my secretary Donna crammed her head in, giggling.

"Why'd you roll down the window, silly?" she tittered. "Aren't you going to come into work today?"

Right. I raised my window, nearly decapitating Donna, who was studying the cluttered backseat of my car with equal parts revulsion and fascination. I turned off the engine, got out, and took the box of documents from the prior day's deposition out of the backseat. Donna waited and studied my actions moon-eyed, as if I were performing a particularly amazing magic trick.

A plump woman in her middle years with wispy, unstyled blonde hair, Donna was one of the better secretaries at my firm in that she knew, more or less, how to type. That notwithstanding, I still dreaded (and actively avoided) engaging her in any type of social interaction. When she was first assigned as my secretary several years earlier, I made the mistake of routinely asking her, just to be polite, how she was doing. This, more often than not, prompted a long sigh from Donna, followed by a reluctant "hanging in there," which in turn was followed by a long story about whatever ailment was bothering her that day, and finally concluded with "one day at a time, I suppose." I eventually learned that it was safer not to inquire as to Donna's well-being but rather to simply assume that she was doing shitty.

But Donna's moods only knew black and white, with no room in the middle for any shades of gray. On those days she wasn't walking around dejected, she absolutely bounced around the office, peppering her coworkers with unfiltered personal questions. Of course, since she was *my* secretary, I was often on the receiving end of those inquiries. "How come I never hear about you having a girlfriend?" "Are you eating right? I couldn't help but notice that you've gained some weight." "Are you and John an item?" Dealing with Happy Donna was as painful as dealing with Sad Donna, and I only took note of her moods to the extent that they impacted my strategies for avoiding her. When all else failed, John and I had a backup plan in place that involved me subtly emailing him if Donna was in my office with no sign of leaving. John would then phone me, and I would answer with apologies to Donna. "Oh, I'm sorry," I would coo to her as I reached for my ringing phone. "I have to take this." And out she went. Usually.

I immediately realized that morning that I was dealing with Happy Donna. The key for handling her in such a state, I had learned through trial and error, was not to allow her to get a foothold into any conversation. Any substantive response on my part would simply fuel a further round of intrusive questions. Thus, I put on a coy face, recited an unenthusiastic "good morning" to Donna, and made my way toward the building with the box of documents jostling against my hip. Donna, eyeing my burden, followed behind.

"That's a big box you got there!" Donna exclaimed after we reached her limit for handling uncomfortable silences.

"Yup!" I grunted. I limped, trying to create the illusion that the box was heavier than it actually was. *This is too cumbersome for me to make small talk*, my body language said. But Donna was not fluent in body language.

"Looks heavy," she ventured after another long pause. Donna simply could not stomach more than three seconds of quiet.

"It is," I said as I exhaled. "Would you mind carrying it for me?"

Donna forced a laugh, and what it lacked in actual mirth, it more than made up for in volume. As we approached the building, Donna dashed ahead to hold the door open.

"The least I can do!" she said as I entered. *No shit*, I thought. We made our way to the elevators, and Donna pressed the "up" button before I could reach for it. "You're lucky I got here at the same time as you!" I flexed my face in a parody of a smile as we waited for the elevator to come down to the lobby.

Here comes the talk about the weather. But Donna surprised me.

"You know, your little buddy was out yesterday," she said.

"Who?" It was a dumb response. John was the only person in the office that I voluntarily talked to.

Donna laughed. "You know! Your buddy—John! He was out yesterday, and apparently he didn't even bother to call in!"

"Really?" I hated to tip my hand and show interest in a Donna story, but I couldn't help it. As much as John hated work, I couldn't remember him ever taking a sick day. I tried to imagine how John would handle it if he was thrown into a scenario where he had to take an unexpected day off. I *thought* he would call in, but I couldn't be sure. John was a naturally gifted attorney who was valuable to the firm, but he did like to occasionally test the partners to see what he could get away with. Which, as it turned out, was quite a lot. John often told me that he was given a long leash because the partners continued to believe he had Asperger's, but I always thought his legal talents were the bigger contributing factor. Attorneys at my firm are either normal and mediocre, or, less common, good and weird. Bigger and better firms inevitably snatched up all the attorneys who managed to be skilled and otherwise unremarkable. John was as strange as he was gifted, and the partners realized that in order to fully take advantage of his abilities, they would have to put up with a fair amount of oddness on his part … which John was more than happy to exploit.

"Oh, it was quite the tizzy yesterday!" Donna continued. "John apparently had a deposition scheduled here, and he just didn't show up at all! Everyone was waiting for him! Eventually, Sal had to go in himself to cancel the deposition. Boy, was he mad! It sure was irresponsible of John not to show up, don't you think?"

I grunted noncommittally as we both stepped into the elevator. I had forgotten about John's deposition. Sal Martucci was the head of our practice group. More importantly, he was the managing partner of the firm. If he had to cover a deposition because John was AWOL, *that* was a big deal. It was unlikely that the abnormally long leash that applied to John would cover such a transgression.

The whole thing struck me as odd. While I could picture John skipping work when he was the only one who would be hurt by that dereliction of duty, I could not imagine John inconveniencing others by acting irresponsibly. As much as he groused about his job, I had never known him to allow his piss-poor attitude to negatively impact anyone else. It was strange, and I had a lot of questions. Still, I had no desire to give Donna the satisfaction of gossiping further about John.

"Why would he just not show up for work?" Donna asked.

Please, just shut up. "Not sure," I said curtly.

"Don't you think that's peculiar?"

Not as peculiar as you, you windbag. "Maybe."

We finally reached our floor, and Donna hopped out of the elevator with a smile.

"Have a great day!" she exclaimed.

I gave her an insincere smile of my own. *Don't tell me what to do.*

Donna and I parted ways in the lobby. I nodded a curt hello to our eighty-year-old receptionist Dorothy (who was, incredulously, ignorant of *The Golden Girls*) and trudged toward my office. Along the way, I spotted Mark Foster, sporting an even more orange tan than earlier in the week and leaning casually against an office doorway. When I approached him, I realized the office entrance he was lounging in belonged to one of the firm's younger associates: a tall, attractive, dark-haired woman named Madison, only about two years out of law school. Madison, I understood, had basic "book-smart" intelligence, but on the few occasions I had spoken to her, I realized that she was so dull that she almost crossed back over into the realm of interesting. *Almost*, but not quite. John and I ended up next to her at a happy hour two months earlier, and her response to every joke we made to each other was to blink rapidly in confusion as if we had switched to a foreign language mid-conversation. After we explained to her (repeatedly) that we were joking, she proceeded to force a laugh. Not out of any sense of merriment, but merely because that was what she understood to be the appropriate response to a joke. It was weird.

I couldn't imagine any guy voluntarily subjecting himself to talking to Madison unless he was hitting on her. Mark's body language—a doorway lean that would have only seemed appropriate in the context of the original *Miami Vice* series—supported my hypothesis. I smirked and fished a sheet of paper out of my box.

"Morning, Mark. How was AC?" I asked once I reached him.

Mark grimaced at being interrupted in his flirtation.

"It was cool, man," he said, glancing coolly at me. "Anyway—"

"Awesome!" I slapped the document against his chest, surprising him. "So, that's the order from the conference I covered for you yesterday. Judge was annoyed. You have a bunch of stuff due this Friday."

Mark seemed to have forgotten that I had covered a conference for him the prior day. He studied the order, trying to comprehend its meaning. I noticed his lips subtly moving as he read.

"What … what is due on Friday?" he finally asked, giving up on trying to make out the judge's sloppy handwriting.

I shrugged. "Basically everything. All responses to outstanding discovery. There's quite a lot of that, as I understand it."

Mark's orange face turned white. "It's all due in two days?"

I gave another apologetic shrug. "Yeah, sorry. I did my best to get you more time, but the judge wasn't hearing it." I threw an exaggerated look of helplessness at Madison, who laughed vapidly. I frowned, confused, and then I realized that her inability to detect when I was joking had prompted her, out of an abundance of caution, to just laugh at everything I said. I made a mental note to pass that development along to John the next time I saw him.

Leaving Mark to puzzle over his quandary, I picked up my box and awkwardly carried it further down the hall toward my own office. It was, with surprise and, even more so, annoyance, that I discovered Todd sitting at my desk, looking smug at having caught me off guard.

How long was he waiting there just to surprise me? I wondered. I plopped my box of documents down and remained standing, even though there was another open chair on the other side of my desk available. It seemed more dignified to hover over Todd than sit like a guest in my own office.

"Morning," Todd said. He smirked at me.

"Morning."

Todd studied me for a moment, showing all of his teeth in a forced smile. I shifted my weight under his gaze, questioning my decision to remain standing.

"So, *Half-Day Dave*," Todd finally said, continuing to maintain his infuriating grin. I had no idea what he was talking about.

"I have no idea what you're talking about," I said aloud.

Todd barked a laugh. "Come on. You were out all day yesterday. I know you just had that straightforward deposition in the afternoon. You probably finished by, what, 3:30? But you didn't come into the office afterwards." He leaned closer, lowering his voice conspiratorially. "Hey, it's fine. I'm just busting your chops. Hell, I used to do the same thing back when I was an associate."

Todd had been named a partner the prior month and rammed that fact into every conversation as much as possible. Still, I knew that Todd was still trying to determine the extent of the power he wielded as a newly raised partner, and that he would likely back down if challenged. With that in mind, I circled around to the back of my desk. Todd looked alarmed but didn't move.

"Do you want me to sit on your lap?" I asked casually. Todd tried to cover up his annoyance with a laugh and moved to the other chair across from my desk. I took a seat, which was warm with the memory of Todd's ample backside. *He must have been sitting here for a while*, I realized. I tried not to think about whether Todd might have farted in my chair.

"Look," I explained, "I didn't get out of that deposition until close to seven, and it took me over an hour to get home. So, like I said, I don't know what you're talking about."

Todd looked skeptical. "A five-hour deposition? Wasn't this that routine accounting malpractice case?" He noticed the box at his feet and kicked it with his toe. "Are these the exhibits?"

I nodded.

"Why the hell did you use so many documents? Were you just trying to kill time?"

"I thought I might be able to impeach him on some points," I said, overly defensive. "Look, you can review the transcript when it comes in, if you want, and tell me how you would have managed to wrap up that deposition in an hour and a half. I don't see how it could have been done, but you've been practicing much longer than me."

Todd waved off my comments. He loved to criticize, but calling him out on it always made him uncomfortable. It ruined his illusion of being the "cool" boss.

"I'm just busting your chops," he repeated. "Your deposition isn't why I'm here." Todd paused dramatically, folding his arms. "Did you hear that your boy John played hooky yesterday?" He waited.

I leaned back, feigning a lack of concern. It was clear that Todd was thrilled at John's absence, which didn't surprise me at all. At his best, Todd couldn't stand John, and after what John had done at the last firm happy hour, Todd's attitude toward John bordered on murderous.

"I only learned a few minutes ago that John was out yesterday," I said carefully. "I haven't heard from him one way or another, so I don't know where he was. Did anyone try to call him?"

"Of course," Todd said, affronted by the silliness of my question. "No answer. We left him a few voicemails, but he didn't bother to call us back."

"Huh."

"*Huh?* Why do you sound surprised? He's never made a secret of loathing this place. Is it really so shocking that he would be so unprofessional?"

I wanted to tell Todd that it *was* surprising, because as unconcerned as John was about his own career, he would never allow that indifference to inconvenience another. I wanted to explain to Todd that since John had a deposition yesterday, it was not in his nature to just skip work and leave a mess for someone else to clean up. But above all, I did not want to have to explain *John* to Todd, who was convinced that he was the paramount judge of character in the firm. So I said nothing.

"I am somewhat surprised that you haven't heard from him," Todd said. "*We* all thought that you, at least, would be able to explain what John is up to." His emphasis on "we" left no doubt as to who he was referencing: the firm's partners.

"Sorry to disappoint you. But I haven't heard from him."

Todd grunted, as if he might or might not believe me.

"What if something happened to him?" I asked. "I don't think you guys should be beating him up over this until you figure out what his deal actually is. Hell, he could be dead for all we know."

Todd started to laugh and abruptly stopped when he realized how inappropriate it was for him, a partner, to laugh at the prospect of an associate's death. "You're right. We *don't* know his story. But after having worked with John for over eight years, I think it is much more likely that he simply reached his breaking point and gave up on this firm and less likely that he is lying in a ditch somewhere."

"Please." I scoffed. Todd raised an eyebrow at my insubordination, but I ignored it. "John was still here, preparing for his deposition, after I left at 7:30 on Monday night. Does that sound like someone who was planning on abruptly quitting the next day?"

Todd remained unconvinced. "That's a perfectly reasonable thought if we were talking about someone rational. But we're not, Dave. We're talking about John."

I again suppressed the urge to defend John, who stood much higher in my esteem than Todd did, despite Todd's beliefs to the contrary. It then struck me that our debate was entirely academic. Eventually, John's story would come out, one way or another, and there was no reason to argue with Todd about those hypotheticals.

"I'll tell you what," I finally said, eager to end the conversation. "I'll go over to his place after work and try to figure out what is going on."

Todd chuckled at what he perceived to be my naiveté. He slowly got out of his chair and wordlessly made his way out of my office. From the hallway, he paused and looked back at me.

"I can't wait to hear what you find," he said drily before walking toward his own office. I didn't have a chance to respond to Todd's parting remark. It was just as well since I didn't *have* a response.

I couldn't even guess what I'd discover at John's home, but, unlike Todd, I found myself dreading to find out.

chapter three

It occurred to me that evening as I drove the twenty minutes to John's apartment in East Meadow that the day had served as an efficient summary of the various relationships John had developed at the firm during his eight-plus years of employment. I spent the workday trying not to think about what could have happened to John, but that became impossible in light of the barrage of coworkers rotating through my office, convinced that I had an inside scoop on John's whereabouts. After those visitors learned that I was as clueless as they were, the conversations quickly fizzled and died. No one could extinguish an unwanted chat the way I could. But even in the narrow windows before those exchanges ended, I could easily gauge how the various factions in the firm felt about John's disappearance.

The support staff—secretaries, administrators, the guys in the copy room—all clearly loved John and were genuinely concerned about what had happened to him. John's secretary, a lovely woman in her late fifties named Gloria, told me that she had stayed up all of the previous night praying for his safety and had even made a special trip to her church to light a candle for him. I told her that the partners generally suspected that John was just playing hooky, and she snorted and made a crude jerking off gesture with her fist that seemed at odds with her otherwise pious nature. "Those idiots don't know him like we do," she said in a lowered, conspiratorial tone. "He wouldn't just not show. Something happened to him." Other secretaries popped their heads into my office and articulated similar beliefs, which only fanned my worries.

The attorneys at Sanders, Martucci & Lyons, on the other hand, treated John's absence as idle gossip and laughed off any suggestion that his no-show was anything but volitional. Associates were generally more candid with me in their assessments of John, citing his appearance and general apathy toward litigation as evidence of his unprofessionalism. Even a few partners came by to mock the situation. One partner, Marty, jokingly expressed surprise that I was in the office because he figured that I would be with John on some beach in the Caribbean.

The sharp divide of attitudes toward John, while interesting to watch play out over the course of a single day, was not the least bit surprising to me. John never made any effort to hide the way he felt about people. I couldn't imagine anyone at our firm ever having to think, "I wonder if John Manta likes me." There were no secrets as far as that went.

It was well-known throughout the firm that John had endeared himself to the support staff and vice versa. It irritated several attorneys—mostly those jealous that they did not receive the same degree of love and respect from their own secretaries (even the ones who were lucky enough to get a Starbucks gift card from their boss at Christmas). But anyone who stayed at the firm long enough was bound to witness examples of John going above and beyond for various members of the support staff, whether by giving a secretary a ride to and from work while her car was in the shop or bringing in a box of Munchkins for the college kid in the copy room on his birthday.

One Thursday evening roughly two weeks prior to John's disappearance, I wandered through the mostly empty office to visit the men's room only to discover John in the copy room sifting through several collated piles of documentary exhibits. He was accompanied by Ruth, a grandmotherly secretary in a different unit than ours. John threw me a grin upon catching my confused look from the door.

"Ruth has to get this motion out tonight, but the shitheads she works for only finalized it fifteen minutes ago," he explained. Ruth stopped sorting through a pile of papers to giggle and slapped John good-naturedly. "There are fifteen parties to be served, so I'm helping her get the sets of motion papers together," he added.

As he spoke, Todd, who was on his own way to the bathroom—he always annoyingly seemed to be on the same pee schedule as me—stuck his head into the room. He surveyed the scene and grunted in disapproval.

"I hope you don't think this is billable," he said coolly to John. John slapped his hands to his cheeks in mock-shock, a perfect imitation of Macaulay Culkin applying aftershave in *Home Alone*, which prompted Ruth to stifle another laugh. Todd scowled and left, continuing his way down the hall. John proceeded to extend his middle finger in the direction of Todd's path and slowly moved his hand as if it were magnetically drawn to Todd, walking unseen behind the wall on his way to take a piss. Ruth playfully slapped John again.

But as much as John was loved by our firm's non-attorney personnel, he was generally derided by the attorneys. It was hard to feel too badly for John in that regard; he made no real effort to hide his disdain for them.

I didn't learn the full extent of John's animus toward his fellow attorneys right away. John would later explain to me that he mostly kept his opinions to himself in the early days of my employment because he did not want to taint my own view of our coworkers. But it wasn't too difficult to get at least a hint of how John felt about them. Most of my polite comments to John about colleagues I had just met, which usually did not amount to anything more than some version of "she seems nice," were met with a noncommittal shrug. In time I would come to learn that after starting a new job, it takes a fair amount of time to get the lay of the land and to be able to pick out the duds from the quality humans. But SM&L was my first real job, and when I started, I was just a dumb twenty-five-year-old. As such, notwithstanding John's claim that he was acting altruistic in trying not to prematurely skew my view of the firm, I suspect that he was simply waiting for me to educate myself before talking to me with his standard candidness.

My first opportunity to view the firm as John did arose a few weeks after we finally finished our cataloging project (which took over a month). I was in my office trying to look busy despite not having any real work to do. The strategy I developed in this regard involved intently playing *Minesweeper* on my computer with a furrowed brow that suggested to anyone walking by that I was in deep concentration on something important. While playing one of those games, I received an unusual call from Sal Martucci summoning me to his office. I hastily grabbed a pen and legal pad and power-walked down the hall. Music—specifically, Bruce Springsteen and the E Street Band—got louder and louder as I approached Sal's office, and once I reached his doorway, it was downright deafening. I stood there meekly for a few minutes, waiting for Sal to notice my arrival, but he was in full rock out mode: eyes closed, nodding his head along to the music, and singing off-key. Not knowing what else to do, I stood there like an idiot, waiting for the song to end.

After what seemed like five different sax solos, the song mercifully ended. Sal looked up and expressed surprise at finding me in his door. "Come in, come in," he muttered. There were three chairs and a couch in Sal's oversized office, but all of them were filled with redweld folders relating to a case that was going to trial shortly, so I stood awkwardly in front of his desk.

Sal dug through a mess of documents in front of him and found a skinny file, which he handed to me. "About time you started getting some cases," he said. "An answer is due Friday. Get me a draft to review before then." He turned toward his computer and started to play a new song. With horror, I realized that that was the extent of the direction I was going to get from him.

"Oh!" I said. Irritated, Sal paused his song and looked at me. "I've never drafted an answer before."

Sal waved his hand impatiently. "Well, I don't have time to show you!" he said. "Go ask Danielle how to do it." Before I could respond, the music had restarted, so I slinked away.

I didn't know Danielle well. In fact, aside from my introduction on the first day, I couldn't recall ever speaking to her. I knew she was a senior associate who seemed to keep mostly to herself. With her golden blonde hair and bright blue eyes, she would have come off as very pretty were it not for the fact that her facial expression permanently looked as if she was in the midst of smelling a particularly egregious fart.

After a fair amount of searching, I found Danielle's office on the opposite side of the floor from where I sat. Although most associates' offices were littered with stray papers and files, Danielle's was immaculate. Aside from a stapler and a cup filled with pens, her desk was completely empty. Her computer was set up against a wall, and when I arrived, Danielle was engrossed, primly clicking her mouse with her back to the door. I hesitantly knocked.

"Yes?" Danielle asked without turning around, continuing to click away. I wasn't comfortable addressing the back of her head, but I soon realized that was the best I was going to get.

"Oh … hi," I stammered. "Sal gave me a new case, and he said I should see you regarding how to go about drafting an answer."

Danielle's head cocked slightly, but she still didn't turn around. "Oh did he?"

Is that rhetorical? I wondered. "Yes. He did," I said, feeling moronic.

Danielle continued to click her mouse. A glare from the window kept me from seeing her screen, but I couldn't imagine what would warrant all of the clicking she was doing. I thought it unlikely that Danielle, as I had been doing earlier, was spending the morning playing *Minesweeper*.

"Do I *look* like I have the time to show you how to draft an answer?" she asked calmly. I was fairly certain that *was* rhetorical, so I muttered something unintelligible and backed away. Danielle didn't acknowledge my departure. She continued to click her mouse in furtherance of no clear purpose.

Discouraged, I carried my new file back to my office. Along the way, I passed John, who was idly gossiping with a secretary named Margaret who was normally quite intimidating but, like most of the secretaries, had a soft spot for John. John gave me a friendly nod that turned into a frown. With a quick goodbye to Margaret, John followed me into my office and closed the door behind us.

"What's up?" he asked, concerned. I didn't think I was advertising my annoyance, but John had always been perceptive when it came to sniffing out others' misery.

"I just got my first case from Sal," I said. "I'm supposed to draft an answer by the end of the week, but Sal said he was too busy to show me. He told me to ask Danielle how to do it, but she just brushed me off as well." I sat and tossed the file for my new case onto my desk.

John sat down in the other chair in my office and stroked his chin thoughtfully. "Oh, I see. Well, how do I put this …" John paused, deep in thought, and took a long breath. "Danielle is an awful person," he finally said, as if it were the most profound statement he had ever made.

I was caught off guard by his matter-of-fact tone, and I barked a laugh despite myself. John grinned, emboldened by my response.

"On the one hand, you should take solace from the fact that she's like that to everyone," John said. "Nothing to do with you, so don't take it personally. On the other hand—" John paused. "Well, it's a bit scary that we work with someone who is like that to everyone."

"What is her problem?" I asked.

John chewed his lip thoughtfully. "It's the same problem a lot of people here have. They think they're important. But they're not. None of us are. I mean, we are an insurance defense firm. If we do a good job on a case, what happens? A multi-billion-dollar insurance company ends up paying $20,000 on a case instead of $50,000. Yippee."

John paused, waiting for an argument from me. When none was forthcoming, he continued.

"I suspect a lot of the attorneys here know this, so they need to overcompensate to make themselves feel more important than they actually are. You'll go insane if you worry about it, so I suggest you learn to just laugh at them."

John sounded sincere, but what he was saying rang somewhat false to me. After a moment, I was able to put my finger on it.

"You don't think what we do is important?" I asked, and John nodded. "Then why do you spend so much time here? It seems like you're in the office every night past 7:00. Why devote all that time and energy on something you consider to be insignificant?"

John beamed at my pushback.

"They pay me, and in exchange, I work hard. Usually. That's just having a decent work ethic. It doesn't mean that I think I'm doing earth-shattering work. I'd be an idiot to think that."

John reached for the skinny file on my desk relating to my new case—my only case—and began rifling through it. While I waited, he pulled the complaint from the redweld and quickly scanned it.

"Yeah, you'll have to answer this one. I don't see a pre-answer motion to dismiss here." John said it reluctantly. I could tell he was disappointed at reaching the same diagnosis as Sal. He would have loved to find a defense that slipped through Sal's cursory review. "Anyway, answers are easy to write. You just have to make a copy of this complaint and make notations after each paragraph. 'A' for admit, 'D' for deny, 'DKI' for when you are denying having sufficient information to either admit or deny. You don't have to type the answer up yourself; you just give the marked-up complaint to your secretary, and she'll know what to do with it."

John proceeded to explain to me the remaining details relating to drafting an answer. It took him four-and-a-half minutes. I timed it. When he finished his explanation, I thanked him profusely for his help. John waved me off, but I could tell he was pleased at finally having an opportunity to pass along his knowledge.

And yet, even after that experience, John still wouldn't divulge to me his opinions about others in the firm. "It would be dickish of me to taint your opinion before it was fully formed," he would explain. Yet, John had no issue with *confirming* my suspicions regarding Danielle. So, with that in mind, I set out on a bizarre type of scavenger hunt where I sought out experiences with my coworkers that would give me some sort of insight into their character, or lack thereof, at which point I could float my impressions by John.

Later that afternoon, I poked my head into the office of the associate next door to me—a short, prematurely balding man named Jason—to ask if he had a sample Notice of Examination Before Trial that I could use as a template. John had explained that I would need to serve one with my answer to preserve priority of deposition and ensure we could depose the plaintiff before our own client was questioned. I thought my innocent request to Jason would serve as sufficient pretext to determine if the guy was normal or an ass.

It didn't take long to find out.

"An EBT Notice?" Jason asked rhetorically. He leaned back in his chair and rubbed his chin. "Yes, I *could* give you an example to use. But how would that help you in the long run? You need to learn *how* to draft these types of documents for yourself. You can't just rely on others to always have an example for you to work from."

He paused to let the profundity of his statement sink in.

"I suggest you check the library. It should have form books that will be able to guide you."

He turned back to his computer without waiting for me to respond and intently started reading an email that had just come in. I left, more elated at my discovery of another asshole than disappointed in his lack of help, and went straight to John's office.

"Jason is kind of a jerk, huh?" I blurted out. John, who had been typing an email, was caught off guard by my sudden appearance and pronouncement, but he quickly recovered with a grin. John appreciated conversations that got to the point without meandering through fields of small talk.

"Oh yeah. Mediocre intelligence, which he tries to hide through a professorial tone. Not a bad guy *per se*, just somewhat of a horse's ass."

"Why do you say 'mediocre intelligence'?" I asked, curious. John paused, struggling to think of an example.

"Well … you know how grammar snobs will typically correct you if you say something like, 'Me and my friend are going to the store'? Well, Jason has taken that to the next level in that he seems to think the word 'me' is always incorrect. If you read his appearance memos, you'll notice it. They are filled with crap like 'In court, the plaintiff's attorney handed his discovery demands to myself,' or 'The judge asked myself if we intended to move for summary judgment.' It's a weird hybrid of pretension and stupidity." John scrunched up his face, reflective. "I may have been overly generous in describing his intelligence as 'mediocre.'"

One by one, I stalked the other attorneys in the office and reported my assessments to John. In fairness, there *were* decent human beings amongst our colleagues, and I noticed the "nice ones" were generally those who did not seem to harbor any lofty career ambitions. The associates who were clearly eyeing the road to partnership were more inclined to be dismissive, condescending, or just outright mean.

"Oh, Susan is incredibly narcissistic," John confirmed when I asked about her. "Her ability to shoehorn her own accomplishments into any conversation is unparalleled. Has she mentioned to you that she's a Mensa? Only twice? Well, you haven't spoken to her enough yet."

"Frank IS slimy," John told me on another occasion. "Do you know Eddie Haskell from *Leave It to Beaver*? That's Frank. Total kiss-ass to the partners, but he has all sorts of schemes going on that he thinks no one knows about. He's actually doing *per diem* work on the side behind the partners' backs. So if he has to cover an appearance out in Suffolk County, you know he probably has at least three other unauthorized appearances that he is handling for various solo practitioners. Raises all sorts of conflicts issues, but he doesn't care. Just a chance to make some extra money. Luckily for him, the partners here are too blinded by his sucking up to notice what he's up to."

The attorney who managed to irritate John the most, though, was Todd. I really didn't mind Todd, at least compared to many of the other self-involved associates I'd come into contact with. Unlike most of my colleagues, Todd had the ability to entertain my questions with at least a nominal amount of patience. I'd later find out that Todd's occasional assistance wasn't entirely altruistic, in that he was telling anyone who would listen about how much unbillable time he had spent "training" me. "It's an investment," I once overheard him tell a partner in a modest tone. "It helps the firm in the long run, so I don't mind."

I think it was Todd's ability to fool almost everyone else in the firm as to his true motives that put him at the top of John's list of annoying attorneys. "The others … at least they don't hide what they are," John complained to me. "But Todd, he's just so—*fake.*"

I shrugged. "Why do you care?" John didn't seem to have any career ambitions of his own. I couldn't understand why he was so offended by Todd's seemingly successful strategy to advance through the firm.

"It's the principle of it," John muttered grimly and, in my opinion, somewhat lamely. John didn't offer any further explanation, and I didn't press him on it. I couldn't disagree with John's criticisms of Todd. They were all valid. But I just couldn't manage to get as worked up about Todd as John did.

Unfortunately for John, although he and I were both in Sal Martucci's practice group, Sal more often than not couldn't be bothered with the day-to-day aspects of running a team. Thus, most of John's assignments came from Sal's right-hand man: Todd. John's attitude clearly rubbed Todd the wrong way, and Todd gradually took to expressing his frustrations with John through crappy assignments, condescending reviews of John's work product, and other petty acts. John was not in a position of power, so his resistance to Todd manifested itself, out of necessity, in a much subtler fashion.

One of John's biggest pet peeves was Todd heavily revising his writing, even when it was unwarranted, simply to establish dominance as the alpha male. Aside from occasional complaints to me about it, John accepted this heavy hand on his work stoically and without comment. Still, the indignity of it all burned deeply within him.

One day, John drafted a motion to dismiss on a low-exposure legal malpractice case in which our client was one of the most well-respected litigators on Long Island and, more importantly, a close friend of Sal. John finished a draft of the motion about a week before it was due to be filed with the court, but before he passed it along to Todd to review, John called me into his office.

"Check this out," he whispered gleefully, showing me an email to the client that read: "I attach an initial draft of the motion for your review. Given the relatively quick turnaround, this has not yet been reviewed by the senior associate on the case, but I wanted to give you as much time as possible to weigh in." With an evil chuckle, John clicked the *Send* button.

I shrugged. "So what?" John's smile only got wider.

"Wait for it."

Several days later, John received a highly edited version of the motion back from Todd. John enthusiastically forwarded that draft to the client as well, noting that it reflected the revisions made by the senior associate in charge. John bounced about the office with excitement the remainder of the day, although I still didn't understand why.

"Wait for it!" was all John would tell me.

"It" happened later that day when John was summoned to Sal's office. John told me afterwards that the client had called Sal, furious that a senior associate had deemed it necessary to revise a perfectly fine motion in order to make it fundamentally *worse*. The client went on to demand that the case be re-staffed with a partner (although he insisted that John stay on as the day-to-day associate). The end result of that conversation was that Sal took on the case himself, working directly above John, with Todd cut out of the loop entirely.

"Gee, I hope I didn't cause any trouble by sending him my version directly!" John later told me he had proclaimed to Sal, who waved off his concern before blasting The Four Seasons out of his computer speakers.

Todd was badly embarrassed by the entire exchange, but what could he do? He could hardly complain about no longer being able to sabotage John's work. Thereafter, Todd largely left John alone to handle his cases as he saw fit, although his resentment toward John did not abate in the following years. If anything, it intensified.

I knew Todd had been waiting for the chance to finally stick it to John and that he thought he had finally found it when John no-showed for work. It troubled me, as I drove out to John's home to check in on him, that the only two probable outcomes to my investigation were both negative: (a) that something had happened to John, making it impossible for him to get to work or call in, or (b) that John had no legitimate excuse, and I would end up giving Todd the ammo he needed to ruin John's career.

The sky was pitch black when I arrived at John's house, or, more specifically, the house in which he rented a basement apartment. I had never been inside his home, but I recalled where he lived from the several occasions I had picked him up to drive to court together. It had been almost two years since I last carpooled with John, and I nearly forgot which house was his. It was only his dirty Nissan Murano, parked in the street, that confirmed I had found his home.

I didn't know what to make of the fact that John's car was there. It seemed to rule out the possibility that he had bailed on his life to drive off toward the sunset. Still, there didn't appear to be any lights visible through the narrow windows that I assumed looked into John's apartment. Although no one seemed to be in the basement, a flickering light at a ground level window suggested that John's landlord was home and watching tv.

I struggled to recall where the entrance to John's basement apartment was located. There was no entrance visible from the sidewalk, but the house was flanked by two identical white gates. After drawing a blank as to where he had emerged on those few occasions I picked him up, I veered toward the right gate.

It was short enough for me to peer over, and in the dark I could just make out a set of steps descending to a basement door.

Bingo. I opened the gate as quietly as I could and went down those steps. The door to the basement had an opaque window at the top, but again, no light was visible behind it. Once my eyes adjusted a bit to the dark, I noticed a doorbell on the side of the door, which I pressed. After waiting a moment, I pushed it again. Nothing. Lacking any other plan, I pressed it again. And again.

Do I just leave? I wondered. It was a discouraging thought—I hated the idea of having driven all that way for nothing. *One more try.* But as I was about the press the bell yet again, a voice behind me slurred in a singsong voice, "Wassup, man?"

I turned and saw a young man, sporting a St. Louis Cardinals hat and a hipster beard, standing at the top of the steps and holding a half-empty glass of beer. I realized my incessant bell-ringing could probably be heard throughout the entire house, but the man didn't look annoyed. Rather, he looked mildly curious. And drunk. He looked very drunk.

"Oh, hi," I said. "Are you John's landlord?"

The man took a gulp of his beer and closed his eyes, savoring the taste. "Friggin' … yeah man." I waited for him to continue, but he just rocked slightly in place.

After a few moments, I said, "My name is Dave. I work with John."

"Cool, man." John's landlord took another sip of his beer and took his time in swallowing it. His methodical sipping reminded me of a snob tasting wine. "So good …" he finally murmured reverently. "Westvleteren 12. It's brewed by monks. Only available at the monastery. You want some?"

"No, but thank you." I found myself oddly touched that this stranger was willing to share his special monk-beer with me, and I almost regretted not taking him up on his offer. It was a strange feeling. I typically felt bad about being forced to socialize.

"I was looking for John. We work together, but he hasn't shown up for the past two days."

"John's a cool guy, man," the landlord said. I realized he wasn't really paying attention.

"I'm sorry, Mr. …?"

"Hande." The landlord hiccupped. "But you can call me Tim. 'Cause … my name is Tim Hande."

"Well, here's the thing, Tim. John's car is out front. But his apartment looks dark, and he wasn't answering his door. So I was a little worried that something might've happened to him."

I could see Tim struggle to focus.

"You want to go in?" he suddenly asked. It seemed odd that a landlord would just let a stranger into his tenant's apartment, but I decided to roll with it.

"If that's ok?" I ventured. "I'll just take a quick look to make sure nothing is wrong."

"Cool, man." Tim shook off his sleepiness and came abruptly to life. "Follow me!"

Without waiting, Tim strode away from the basement steps, went through the gate and made his way to the front door of the house. I jogged to catch up and followed him inside. As he led me through his living room to an interior set of stairs descending to the basement, Tim sung nonsensically to himself: "Shoo be doo!!!! Boo boo!!!!!" Tim, finding a second wind, energetically bounded down the steps, two at a time, and gestured to a closed door at the base of the stairwell.

"In here, man," he said. I entered, and Tim, randomly and without preamble, scampered back up the stairs, leaving me alone in John's apartment. I felt along the wall near the door until I brushed against a light switch. I hesitated in turning it on, suddenly fearful of finding John's corpse strewn out on the floor. Holding my breath, I willed myself to flick the switch …

… and found nothing but an immaculate apartment.

The cleanliness of John's home initially jumped out at me in that it seemed at odds with John's generally sloppy appearance. I heard footsteps above, and I realized the fact that John was renting was probably what had prompted him to keep his apartment so spotless. I imagined that the state of John's home would be drastically different if he owned it himself.

As I surveyed the small apartment, I heard the pounding of footsteps as Tim raced back down the stairs. "Shoo booo booooo!!!!!" he sang as he entered the apartment, his beer mug refilled. Abruptly remembering the possible "dead tenant" scenario, Tim stopped singing. "Did you find anything?"

"No," I replied. "The apartment is empty." But as soon as I finished speaking, I heard a faint scratching sound emanating from the bedroom. I threw a puzzled look at Tim, who did not notice it; he was too busy taking a long sip of his almost black beer. I walked slowly toward the bedroom. "John?" I called.

There was no response. I quickly found and turned on the light switch next to the bedroom door, but the room was empty. Just a neatly made bed, a dresser, and a nightstand. And then, again, I heard a soft noise, but I could not place its origin. I looked in the closet, which was bare aside from a few hanging shirts. "Huh," I muttered. Not knowing where else to look, I got down on all fours and looked under John's bed. It was silly—there was about a six-inch gap between the floor and the box spring that no one John's size would ever be able to fit into. Of course, when I looked under the bed, there was no one there. But in the shadows, I saw a hint of movement.

Moving over to the other side of the bed, I reached under it and felt the furry throat of a purring cat.

"John has a cat?" I asked over my shoulder as I laid on the floor. Tim, who had snuck up behind me, chuckled to himself.

"Oh! Friggin' … that's just Peaches!"

"John has a cat named Peaches?" I reached under the bed and gently pulled out the small animal, who instantly went limp and did not resist.

"Oh yeah! You know, a few years ago I found this kitten by our garbage cans, looking for food. John was coming out to go to work around that time, and he was all worried about it. He was always a little strange like that. He managed to grab it and bring it inside. I told him my wife was allergic, but he said he just wanted to feed it and find someone else to take care of it. Who knows if he ever even looked for someone to give the cat to? Either way, he ended up just keeping the damn thing. I told John he'd have to get rid of it if my wife started giving me shit about it, but she never did. I don't even think she knows about it." He took another long swallow from his glass. "So fuck it," he added solemnly.

I studied the cat in my arms. He was gray except for a white underbelly. Nearly invisible stripes—really just slightly different shades of gray playing off one another—colored his face and tail. His round face was unafraid as he stared back at me, a model of serenity. I supposed he would be considered somewhat cute for a cat, but mostly he was unremarkable. Just a good-looking stray that was lucky enough to find a home. I think it was the first time I had ever held a cat, and I wasn't quite sure if I was doing it right. I patted it on the head, the way a school teacher in the 1890s might have patted a particularly gifted student, and, to my surprise, the cat started purring loudly.

"Peaches likes you," Tim said.

I continued to awkwardly pat the cat. "Why is he named Peaches?"

Tim shrugged. "Damn if I know. Because John is weird?"

As I stood in John's vacant apartment with his landlord, lightly smacking his cat on the head, it hit me that I was at a loss as to what to do from there. "I don't think John is here," I said, stating the obvious. Tim rubbed his head thoughtfully.

"Friggin' … That is odd, with his car being here. Maybe he got a ride from some friends and is taking a trip somewhere? Or maybe he has a girlfriend within walking distance? I doubt he'd leave his cat alone for too long." He finished off his beer with one long gulp.

I was inclined to agree, but then I noticed John's cell phone, wallet and keys sitting on his nightstand. *Why would he leave them behind?* I wondered. I did not have a clue as to what it meant. *Was he kidnapped?* I kept my thoughts to myself, so as not to worry Tim. Not that he looked particularly distressed. He was looking back toward the stairs, trying to calculate how to escape for another refill.

"Well," I said, "it doesn't look like anything happened to John here, so that eases my mind a bit." Peaches had fallen asleep in my arms. "But even if John left for somewhere, I feel weird leaving his cat here alone with no one having any idea when he will be back."

I paused, waiting for Tim to volunteer to watch Peaches. After a few wordless beats, I reluctantly added what was seemingly my only other option. "Maybe I should take Peaches to keep an eye on him until John gets back?"

Tim, at that point, was struggling to keep his eyes open. "Cool, man," he muttered. I have no idea if it even occurred to him that he was potentially letting a complete stranger steal his tenant's pet. "I'll tell him you have the cat when I next see him." Without any goodbye, Tim left the apartment, and I heard him amble back up the stairs. I waited for him to come back down with a fresh beer, but he never did. I was apparently meant to see myself out.

I didn't have a carrier for the cat, so I had no choice but to just let Peaches loose in my car as I drove home. As I started the engine, I worried about Peaches panicking and clawing at my face as I drove, but those fears quickly dissipated. Throughout the drive Peaches sat tall in the passenger seat, obviously enjoying the experience. At times, he placed his front paws up against the door so as to get a better view through the side window. My experiences with cats up until that point were few and far between, but this struck me as odd behavior. I didn't dwell on it, though, because Peaches' inexplicably reserved demeanor was something of a "gift horse" for me.

I stopped at a 7-Eleven on the way home to buy cat food and litter, the latter of which I poured into an old lasagna tray I never used. Peaches quickly settled in at my apartment, and as I lay in bed that night, puzzling over what could have happened to John, the skinny cat with a disproportionately chubby face draped himself across my throat and quickly fell asleep. When I woke up the next day with a stiff neck, Peaches was still there, purring loudly.

I reported to Todd and others at work that morning that although I had gone to John's apartment to check up on him, I didn't find anything. But that wasn't quite right. I had inexplicably found a pet.

Named Peaches.

•   •   •   •   •

"Closure" was a concept I was obviously familiar with but never fully appreciated until John's mysterious disappearance. I waited the next day for him to miraculously reappear, and when he didn't, I convinced myself that he would do so the following day. This continued for some time, with my hope experiencing diminishing returns on each successive day. Several of the partners regularly checked in with me to see if I had ever heard from John, and when I told them I hadn't, they each assured me, with grave solemnity, that they would keep his job open until he resurfaced and had an opportunity to explain himself. Even Todd, who had initially mocked John's disappearance, eventually became uncomfortable with the length of his absence and took to avoiding the topic altogether. I could not make sense of John vanishing, but the thought that something bad happened to him also refused to settle in my head. Against all logic, I wasn't worried for him.

After a few days, Tim Hande reported to the police that John was missing. A pair of officers came to the firm one Monday and spoke with a number of people. Everyone they spoke with apparently mentioned our friendship, because I was soon encouraged, quite strongly, to accompany those officers to the station to discuss the situation. I think the fact that Tim had told them I visited John's apartment shortly after he vanished made the police somewhat eager to chat with me. The two officers grilled me pretty hard about what I had done at the apartment ("I just looked around"), what I had touched ("Nothing really"), and what I had taken ("Just his cat"). I don't think they ever seriously regarded me as a suspect, but they did take the time to ask me about my whereabouts from the time John first disappeared. I gave the officers a breakdown of my comings and goings during that time period, and I pretended not to notice when they exchanged amused looks at each other as I described my lack of a life.

During this time, I learned a lot of basic information about John that had managed to elude me over the course of our friendship. But in a way, it wasn't so strange; John had always been averse to anything approaching small talk, but small talk, with all of its faults, is a solid way of learning a person's basic info. Still, it surprised me to learn that he didn't seem to have any friends outside of work. He had no close family, his father having left when he was in elementary school and his mother passing away shortly after John graduated law school. It embarrassed me that I was apparently John's best friend, yet I knew so little about his life.

I got wind that the police eventually suspended their investigation, having exhausted any potential leads. They wrote it off as John simply running off for a new life, although the investigating officers, like me, had trouble reconciling that theory with the wallet, keys, and cellphone left behind in John's apartment. I overheard someone in the office speculate a few weeks later that he left those items behind because he was completely abandoning his old identity, perhaps to run off and live in the woods, á la *Into the Wild*. Of course, what happened to John was all of the gossip at work for *weeks*—everyone had an opinion or theory that they felt compelled to share while stopping in the kitchen for a cup of coffee.

I was not directly exposed to any of this. People treaded very carefully around me, treating me like I was a widow whose husband had drowned at sea. Often, I would walk into the kitchen filled with gossiping secretaries who instantly hushed upon noticing me, only to throw me sympathetic looks as they dispersed. The partners, without specifically alluding to John, offered to reduce my workload, at least for the short-term, to give me time to "deal with things." I took them up on their offer, more out of a sense of laziness than anything else.

The fact is, John had been a good friend to me, and if I had known for sure that something had happened to him, I would have mourned accordingly. But my mind couldn't process the uncertainty of John's fate. I simply didn't know how to feel about it, so I felt nothing. It barely registered with me when John's office was emptied, and his nameplate was replaced with that of a newly hired associate. So, while my coworkers walked on eggshells around me, there really was no need. I numbly accepted the fact that John was gone, and I would never see him again.

But, of course, I was wrong.

chapter four

It was the summer of 2012—over one year after John's unsolved disappearance—and I was getting impatient. But I was too invested to back out.

It seemed like a sound plan at first. I had a brief due to be filed with the Appellate Division the following day, which meant that our papers had to be sent to the printer via overnight delivery by that evening. Once the printer received our brief the following morning, they would bind it together professionally and file it with the court in the afternoon. After working frantically on the brief all week, I, at long last, had a "final" version ready to go about an hour before it had to be shipped out. But when I raced the newest draft over to Donna to make the last round of revisions, she was on the phone with her back to me. It took me about two seconds to realize that it was a personal call, and I immediately felt annoyed.

The brief related to an appeal that particularly concerned me, as it involved Michael Terkle, who I couldn't stand, and his worthless accounting malpractice suit. Or, at least, I had thought it to be worthless. Against my expectations (and, to my knowledge, roughly one hundred years of legal precedent), Terkle managed to win summary judgment against my client for a monetary award of $324,000, plus prejudgment interest of 9% per year going back to 2003. This result did not stem from any brilliant lawyering on Terkle's part. Just my lousy luck at being assigned a judge who was completely ignorant of this area of the law and who also hated my firm for reasons unknown to me.

I despised Terkle, and I was determined to get that lousy order overturned. I thought the appellate court would tear the trial judge's decision to shreds, but I was still nervous. I hadn't thought there was any chance I could lose the case in the first place. I was proud of the argument I had crafted for the appeal, and I was eager to get it on file with the court.

It was just a matter of getting Donna off the phone to type up the damn thing.

"So I said to her, 'Hey, just because YOU chose to have a baby doesn't mean I should have to bend over backwards for you!'" Donna was saying into the phone when I first reached her desk. "Well, no, I didn't LITERALLY say that out loud …"

I cleared my throat to get Donna's attention, but she didn't seem to hear me. That was when I decided to wait until she noticed me hovering impatiently behind her. I imagined her flustered reaction at looking up to see me standing there stern-faced, prompting her to quickly hang up and apologize for keeping me waiting. The thought was deeply satisfying, so I crossed my arms and waited for Donna to catch me in her peripheral vision.

Ten minutes later, I was still standing there, feeling more and more idiotic, while Donna continued to gab on the phone.

"So the doctor said he doesn't know WHAT the cause of the pain is. Which concerns me even more than if he did, to be quite honest with you." A deep sigh. "And now I suppose I will have to get ANOTHER opinion! Not that I consider 'I don't know' to be much of an opinion, mind you."

I gradually came to terms with the fact that Donna, left to her own devices, would never notice me. Throwing all tact out the window, I took the draft brief I was holding and flung it unceremoniously onto her desk. Donna jumped, startled, and gave me a glare. "Hold on a second," she said into the phone. To me, coldly, "Yes?"

She didn't end the call, I wondered in amazement. My impatience upgraded to anger.

"That's the brief we have to get out tonight. I wanted to make sure you saw it. My last round of edits is in there, but you will probably have to regenerate the table of contents and the table of authorities."

"That's due tomorrow," Donna told me, continuing to cover the mouthpiece of the phone. I took a deep breath to control my rage.

"Due to be *filed* tomorrow. It has to be overnighted to the printer tonight. And since FedEx's last pick up is in less than an hour, I thought you might want to get to it." I didn't try to mask the scorn in my voice. "After you finish what is obviously a *very* important phone call, of course."

It pleased me to see Donna finally appreciate the time crunch she was in. "I have to go," she whispered into the phone before hanging up. Taking the brief, she snapped at me. "You could have let me know this had to go out in an hour!"

She's blaming me????

"Keep your damn personal calls to your own time, and I might have had a chance to!" I strode away before she could respond. When I was a safe distance down the hall, I risked a peek over my shoulder. Donna was rapidly flipping through the latest draft I had left, gauging the amount of work that was ahead of her. I took solace in the stress she was showing. *Welcome to my world, Donna.*

As I watched my secretary, I heard Sal scream out my name from his office. "DAVE! DAVE!" Sal didn't believe in calling associates on the phone once he got to know them. He certainly did not believe in getting out of his chair to speak with subordinates. With rare exception, his method was to simply bellow a name until that person appeared before him.

When I entered Sal's office, he looked uncharacteristically serious. No music was playing, and Sal, holding a conspiratorial finger to his lips, quickly gestured for me to close the door. Years ago, such a summoning would have left me apprehensive and racking my brain for what I might have done to incur Sal's wrath. But in the year since John had vanished, I had become a model citizen in the office. I was one of the first to arrive in the morning, almost always the last to leave at night, and a paradigm of surgical focus in between. My billable hours were on pace to be at least two hundred above those of my closest competitor, Mark Foster. Several partners, including Todd, had commented upon my post-John transformation.

"If we had known you would have been this type of attorney once John wasn't around to distract you, we would have fired his ass years ago," Todd stated at my last year-end review, which even caused Sal to nod in agreement. I was mildly offended by the implication that John had been somehow holding me back. But I knew they weren't entirely wrong. I *had* become a remarkably efficient attorney in John's absence.

Thus, as I sat in Sal's office, I was confident that I was not the cause of Sal's somber mood. I gazed impassively at him until he found his words. After much fidgeting, Sal finally said, "I'm sure word will get around this place pretty soon, but I wanted to give you a head's up that we are letting Todd go."

I managed to hide my surprise. As far as I was aware, Todd had been thriving since he made partner. Of course, my impressions in that regard were based almost entirely on what Todd had told me.

"May I ask what happened?" But before those words were fully out of my mouth, I knew why Todd must have been fired. I was flooded with memories of

John's last happy hour at our firm, which was held just a few weeks before his disappearance.

Our firm held monthly after-work get-togethers as a matter of course—"forced friendship," as John cynically called them—but the unofficial theme of that particular cocktail hour was to congratulate Todd on making partner. The event was held at Conita's, a wine bar across the street from our office. All attorneys were expected to attend, but John insisted to me beforehand that he had no intention of going. "My lunch is sitting funny as is," he told me. "It can't handle the sight of Todd's self-aggrandizing." Despite my best efforts, I couldn't convince John to come.

Which is how I found myself that evening stuck at a tight table between Madison and Mark. If I didn't know better, I would have sworn they had made a bet with each other beforehand as to which of them could manage to have a more vapid conversation with me. Madison took an early lead by describing to me, in excruciating detail, the training program she was using to prepare for her next marathon. But Mark stormed back, regaling me with a ten-minute story about the deposition he just finished with a "hot as hell" court reporter. "Doctor, I tell you— I kept it going an extra three hours just so I could stare at her more." Thankfully, he didn't look for a fist bump at the end of his story.

I was surprised when, halfway through my second beer, I spotted John sheepishly walk in. John rolled his eyes at me and grabbed an open seat at the opposite end of our table. After a minute, my phone vibrated with a text from him: *Danielle caught me sneaking out.* :(

I tried to think of a graceful way to move my seat to join John without coming off as rude to Mark or Madison. I couldn't think of a clean exit, but after realizing I was indifferent to both of their opinions, I abruptly stood up, taking my beer with me. But I froze and sat back down once I saw Todd appear at John's end of the table.

Todd had, up until that moment, sat proudly at another table dominated by partners. His arrival at the associate table highlighted Todd's complete embrace of the notion that the night was being held in his honor. Todd made his way around the associates' table like a host looking after his guests or a bride and groom making the rounds at their wedding reception and accepted a series of congratulations from various associates with a false sense of modesty. John, for his part, ignored Todd and pretended to be engaged in *Sports Center*, which was playing on a television above the bar.

"Oh, thank you, thank you," Todd murmured in response to the various congratulations bestowed upon him. "I had to work my butt off to get here, but it was definitely worth it."

John, who had just received his beer from the waitress, snorted in derision. The bar was noisy, but somehow, Todd heard it. He gave John a strange look before turning back to the rest of the table.

"You know," Todd said to several eager associates, "the real question is who will be the next one up for partner. Now, from a seniority standpoint, it should be John." He clapped a meaty hand on John's shoulder, and John recoiled from the touch. "But the thing is, billable hours are a big consideration for making partner. So John's really going to have to step up his game in the next few years if he wants to be considered."

I noticed Mark nodding in agreement, which prompted Madison to also bob her head. The other associates in the vicinity started to look bored and seemed eager for Todd to leave so that they could resume talking amongst themselves.

John, in exaggerated fashion, contorted his body to escape Todd's touch.

"Billable hours? You think that matters? Billable hours?" John asked disdainfully. The disinterested group of associates, sensing a confrontation, suddenly became reinvested in the proceedings at the far end of the table. Todd reacted to John's question as if it were the dumbest he had ever heard.

"Of course! I've been the top biller amongst associates for the past five years! Last year I billed over 2,500 hours! And when I made partner, I was assured that my billables were a significant part of why I was selected."

Like a crowd at a tennis match, the associates' heads collectively turned back to John, waiting for his rejoinder. The lone exception being Madison, who inexplicably began counting on her fingers. John paused, uncomfortable with being the center of attention. I thought he was going to slink away and leave the matter alone. But then he made eye contact with me and smiled, knowing that at least one person in the vicinity was on his side. Resolve strengthened, John sat up taller and barked a laugh.

"Wow!" John exclaimed. "Twenty-five hundred hours! That's impressive!" John took a long sip of his drink before continuing. "What would be even *more* impressive was if you actually performed all of the work that you had billed for." John winked at me, which several associates caught. I slunk down in a cowardly attempt to distance myself from John.

If Todd had any inkling as to what John was alluding, I am sure he would have just gone back to his partner table. But, perhaps feeling invincible by his recent promotion, Todd was not inclined to back down.

"I have no idea what you're talking about," Todd said with a condescending smile. He moved to reapply his hand to John's back, but John was too quick. He eluded Todd's alpha male slap and, with a hop in his step, made his way down the long table full of associates.

"Ah!" John cried out, gathering the attention of the entire table. To my horror, I noticed that John's outburst had also caused a handful of partners at the neighboring table to look over. "Do any of you know Todd's trick for billing hours? No? Well, this is how it works." John was now at the head of the table, with Todd glaring across at him from the opposite end. John waited to make sure everyone was listening, but he needn't have bothered. There were no side conversations at that point.

"You know how most judges don't hear oral argument on motions?" John paused dramatically. "Well, our boy Todd here will bill multiple hours preparing for oral arguments on motions, and even 'appearing' at oral argument, when no appearance is actually held. It's brilliant, in a way, because if an insurance company or client is reviewing those billing entries, they would have no idea whether a particular motion was orally argued unless they looked up who the specific judge was and checked that judge's individual rules. Which, of course, they would never do."

All eyes swiveled back to Todd. Somehow, his smile didn't falter.

"That is ridiculous," Todd started. "I have no idea where you came up with that, but—"

"Oh!" John interrupted. "I can tell you where I got it from. I look at bills. Like that Kallman case, where the plaintiff moved for leave to appeal to the Court of Appeals? Which doesn't hear argument on motions? I saw you billed over ten hours preparing for that oral argument and four-and-a-half hours for the argument itself. Funny, though—I don't remember you driving up to Albany on that return date." John looked back at the other associates, who were all hypnotized by this exchange. "I mean, anyone here can look up your billing entries. This isn't even debatable."

Todd finally gave up on the illusion of maintaining a sense of ease. "Just because I am better at capturing my time than you does not give you the right—"

"'*Capturing time*'?" John's voice dripped with disgust, as he suddenly slapped the table in anger. "That's just lawyer talk for billing fraud. And if they—" John nodded curtly at the table of partners, who were collectively too stunned to move. "If they want to reward you for your ability to generate income for the firm by simply making shit up, that's their prerogative. But for you to come over here and brag about how *hard* you work … you're just deluding yourself."

John drained what was left of his beer and dropped his empty mug on the table with a loud *thud*. "So, kids," he said, winding down, "I suppose the lesson here is not to waste too much time trying to do good work. And don't concern yourself with working too strenuously. That won't get you anywhere. Just do what your Uncle Todd does and make shit up. It's easier and apparently a *hell* of a lot more effective!"

I don't know what kind of reaction John was expecting. Maybe all of the associates standing up on the table to cheer for him? Perhaps Todd diving across the table, knocking over drinks and appetizers, to choke him out? But if he were honest with himself, the reaction John should have expected is exactly what happened: awkward silence.

There is something of an unwritten rule that attorneys do not call out other attorneys for their billing practices. That rule was probably derived from a concern shared by almost all litigators of inviting scrutiny into their *own* billing habits. John, being one of the few (along with me, I'm proud to say) who did not exaggerate his billable time, clearly did not have that fear. But almost everyone else present had a tendency to pad their hours, at least to some extent. Billing an hour for something that really took forty minutes, things like that. And yet, simply fabricating billing entries was a whole other level of fraud. Hence, the collective state of shock following John's tirade was just the result of no one feeling comfortable enough to join in John's condemnation of Todd and, yet, not wanting to publicly defend Todd's actions.

I thought the silence would continue forever. John did not seem to feel the tension around him; he looked more stunned by his own outburst. The long, uncomfortable pause was mercifully ended when Todd sighed loudly and picked up his drink from the table.

"John," Todd said, "I really don't see the point of staying here and debating you on this. But I think you should really worry more about your own career than what others are doing." With that, Todd shuffled back to the table of partners.

At our own table, no one had much to say. Sarcastically, Mark said, "Well, that wasn't at all awkward!" which earned a couple of half-hearted laughs, but John didn't acknowledge any of it. He pivoted and, in a daze, wandered off toward the bar, away from our party. I followed him stealthily, trying not to draw any attention to my departure.

"What the hell was that?" I hissed at John when I caught up to him.

A lot of the energy John had worked up seemed to have left him, but he was still defiant. "I was just calling that turd out on his horseshit," John murmured.

"Are you *trying* to get fired?" I asked, rhetorically. When John didn't respond right away, I realized it was actually a legitimate question.

After thinking it over for a moment, John finally shrugged, indifferent. "I'm not going to get fired. At least, not for this. I mean, is Todd going to go to the other partners and ask them to fire me for calling him out on his billing fraud?"

"Todd's not an idiot, despite what you think," I responded harshly. "If he wants to sabotage your career, he can do it without advertising that it's because you pissed him off today."

John did not look remotely concerned at the possibility. He just looked tired. Wearily rubbing his temples, he glanced back at the partners. "I know my career isn't going anywhere. The system is set up so that the cheaters can advance, and people who do legitimate work are left behind. And I'm not willing to do what it takes to move ahead in this place."

I couldn't help myself. "Why not?"

John looked me straight in the eyes. "*Nothing* is worth doing if you have to give up even a fraction of your soul in the process."

It was not the response I was expecting, and I couldn't help but laugh. "God … since when are you so pious?"

John looked hurt, but that look quickly gave way to one of annoyance. Rolling his eyes, he snapped at me. "Fine. You want me to rephrase? 'Don't do things that make you have to act like an asshole.' Is that any better, Dave?" With that, John took his beer and made his way back to the table.

And so, a little over a year later, I was not surprised as Sal explained to me that Todd had been let go for what Sal described as "discrepancies" in his billing practices.

"Todd has apparently been billing for appearances and oral arguments that did not actually take place," Sal concluded solemnly, as if he only recently learned that Todd had been doing that.

No shit, I thought. Thanks to John, Todd's creative billing practices were known firmwide, although the partners had fought hard to maintain the illusion that they were unaware of it. After all, Todd's inflated bills were bringing in extra revenue—why *wouldn't* they keep their heads in the sand?

"Oh, wow!" I feigned shock, which Sal seemed to appreciate. "That is crazy! But ... why now?" Sal's eyes narrowed slightly, and I knew he could see the real point of my question. *Why is he being fired now for something that everyone knew he was doing for at least the past year?* Sal paused before answering, mindful of how his response might impact him down the road.

"Todd apparently had one case where he was billing for all sorts of oral arguments and appearances that did not exist," Sal finally said. "Todd's bills looked fine at face value, and the insurance company would never have gotten wind of what Todd was up to but for the fact that they were also the insurer for one of the other defendants. Apparently, the adjuster on our end started talking to the adjuster handling that codefendant's claim, and they came to realize that we were—or, I should say, *Todd* was billing for court appearances that the other firm wasn't referencing in their bills. It didn't take them long after that to realize that Todd had been bullshitting them for some time."

Sal pivoted in his chair dramatically and began gazing out of his window. I followed his stare, but he only had an unremarkable view of our parking lot.

"It took a lot of work on my part to convince that particular insurance company that what Todd had been doing was an aberration, that it was not reflective of our firm's practices. Of course, they made it very clear to us that if they were going to continue to give us business going forward, Todd would have to leave. So, of course ..." Sal turned his chair back toward me and shrugged.

"You may be wondering why I'm telling you all of this," Sal said. Of course, I was. "The fact of the matter is that, as embarrassing as this is for our firm, it could be a great opportunity for *you*. You see, Todd had a significant book of business that we need someone to take over. Many of the partners here are already clamoring for it. But it's my call who gets it."

Sal leaned in and pointed dramatically at me.

"I think you're ready to take over that responsibility. You have worked with Todd for years, and, frankly, I think you're a better attorney than he ever was. I don't see why there has to be any dip in the quality of our work if you were to take Todd's place. Granted, it will be a lot of extra work for you, but I know you can handle it. And I'll make sure you have a couple of junior associates under you so that you aren't wasting your time with the day-to-day nuances of those cases. And if you can show that you can handle these types of partner-level responsibilities—why, it will just make it that much easier to put you up for partner down the road."

I maintained a neutral face, but my mind was racing. My first thought was of John and how he would have mocked me mercilessly over getting worked up at the possibility of making partner. But it wasn't that hard for me to suffocate that line of thought. John had been gone for over a year, and his influence over me had significantly waned during that time. As such, my excitement at this opportunity was largely guilt-free ... and yet, a deep-seated instinct kept me from immediately committing to Sal's proposal. It didn't seem to matter, as Sal was not looking for an instant response.

"You need to think long and hard about where you would like your career to go from here," Sal said. "This is a great opportunity for you, but if I'm going to push for you, I need to know you are one hundred percent on board. Think about it. We'll talk again soon."

•　　　•　　　•　　　•　　　•

I walked slowly back to my office, deep in thought. Along the way, I noticed the Human Resources manager cleaning out Todd's office, taking his framed diplomas off the wall and placing them, along with assorted chachkies from his desk, into several cardboard boxes. *They don't even trust him enough to let him clean out his own office,* I marveled. A couple of secretaries, including Donna, were huddled together in the hall, whispering furiously to one another. I overheard Donna. "Has Todd been fired? He was one of the attorneys I work for—do you think that means that *I'll* be fired next? Oh, God; what is going to happen to me?" I made a mental note to give Donna hell for standing around gossiping if she hadn't already finished revising my brief.

But when I returned to my office, a final version of the brief was on my chair, awaiting my signature. I quickly signed it without bothering to check if Donna had properly made all of my edits and stepped back into the hallway to hand it back to her. Before she could say anything, I quickly ducked back inside my office, closing the door behind me. I collapsed into my chair, thinking hard about what Sal had said. If I was going to stay at the firm for the long term, there was no reason I shouldn't do everything in my power to try to advance to partner. It was really a no-brainer. There was no reason why I couldn't have just accepted Sal's offer on the spot. But … I didn't. I wasn't sure why.

My thoughts were interrupted by the increased volume of secretaries gossiping on the other side of my door. Word of Todd's departure had quickly spread through the firm, and everyone seemed to be congregating outside of my office, for some unknown reason, to compare notes. I heard one woman remark in a shrill Long Island accent that she had seen me huddled in Sal's office shortly after Todd was dismissed. "I never trusted that guy!" exclaimed another secretary in response, and I wasn't sure if she was referring to me or Todd. Not that I really cared.

That growing snowball of gossip was going to keep me from getting any work done. I wasn't too concerned about that; the brief that had just been finalized had been the only pressing item on my agenda for the day. But more than that, I wanted time to think in peace regarding what Sal had told me and what it meant for my career. I glanced at the clock—it was almost 5:00. I opted to take a quick walk to get a bit of peace. Fifteen minutes outside, and then I'd come back to work for a couple of extra hours.

I took the stairs in lieu of the elevator to avoid our nosy receptionist and emerged on the street in front of the building. I could not recall ever having gone for a walk with no destination in mind—at least not in my adult life—and I wasn't sure of which direction I should go. I settled on south, just to feel a bit of sun on my face.

As I walked, I tried to focus on my conversation with Sal. There was really nothing for me to think about; he laid out the path to me becoming a partner at the firm, which is something all attorneys strive for. All I had to do was say yes. I would take on some additional responsibilities, but nothing I couldn't handle. I knew I would maintain, if not grow, Todd's old book of business, and there was no doubt in my mind that, within a year—two, at most—I would be a partner.

And then?

The question came unbidden, and it irritated me that it was exactly the sort of thing that John would have asked had he still been around.

"And then I'll make more money, be more respected …" I whispered aloud, but I couldn't finish the thought.

To what end?

The follow-up question once again caught me off guard, and I grimaced in annoyance. I was disgusted with myself for even internally debating this.

"Look, it's a JOB," I muttered hoarsely. A woman walking toward me gave me an odd look, finally alerting me to the fact that I had been talking out loud. *No one LIKES to work*, I continued mentally. *Being a partner at a law firm, that's something to be proud of.* My internal voice didn't respond, but my answer still felt hollow.

As I came near a section of the street that crisscrossed with railroad tracks, I pushed any lingering doubts out of my head. Above all else, I was tired of overthinking my life. It was a great opportunity, and any doubts I had were, I realized, just part of an inherent character flaw that inserted fear where it wasn't needed or wanted. *You can't lose if you don't play*—that pathetic mentality. I abruptly stopped walking and pivoted with the intent of beelining back to the office to accept Sal's proposal, demonstrating that I was fully committed to the responsibility that he was willing to entrust upon me.

As I turned, I bumped into another man, who had apparently been walking directly behind me. I muttered a vague apology and stepped around him without making eye contact.

"Not a problem," the man said kindly, sounding amused, and I froze.

It was John.

chapter five

"John."

It was all I could muster at that moment.

John didn't immediately respond. He stood calmly, studying me with an irritating, all-knowing grin. He looked mostly the same as I remembered him, which wasn't too surprising. But there were subtle differences that took a moment to place. *Healthier,* I finally realized. *He looks healthier for some reason.* John had always been skinny, but he now looked like he had a real physique under his t-shirt and jeans. His skin, which I remembered having its share of acne, razor burns, and other minor blemishes, was entirely clear and, surprisingly, slightly tanned. It looked as if he had spent the past year working out and relaxing on the beach.

Once my initial shock dissipated, anger swept in to replace it, primarily directed at John's mischievous smile. *You vanish for a year without telling me where you were—without telling ANYONE where you were—and you think it's CUTE?* As if reading my mind, John's grin broadened, and his eyes twinkled with amusement. I suspected that he was waiting for me to ask about his mysterious disappearance, so, of course, I vowed to disappoint him by not asking anything relating to where he had been.

"Oh … hey," I said coolly.

John's smile didn't falter. If anything, it grew even bigger. "Hey," he said. We stood in silence, although John seemed immune to the notion that our reunion was anything out of the ordinary.

Just as I approached my own breaking point, John pointed across the street at a small café. "Do you have time for coffee? We should talk."

I frowned doubtfully and made a show of looking at my watch, but John didn't notice. Without waiting for my answer, he darted under a traffic light that had just turned in his favor. I briefly entertained the possibility of not following him, purely out of spite, but my curiosity overpowered my vindictiveness. And so, after a beat, I hurried along behind him.

John made his way to a coffee shop that I often passed on my way to get lunch but had never entered. He held the door open and, with a flourish, theatrically gestured for me to go inside. The shop was small—just a couple of rectangular tables lined up against the wall, across from a counter—and it was surprisingly empty. I wrote it off to the time of day, coupled with the Starbucks across the intersection that seemed to be drawing all of the late afternoon coffee drinkers in the vicinity. Still, there was no one behind the counter—no working staff at all, as far as I could see. I wondered if the shop was actually closed and someone had just forgotten to lock up.

At my hesitation, John took a seat at a table near the front window, and I tentatively sat across from him. As I was about to express my doubt as to whether the place was even open, a middle-aged waitress emerged from a back room, bringing John a black coffee and a cappuccino for me. She dropped the drinks off quickly, smiled, and left before I could even thank her.

"That was a bit presumptuous," I muttered, absently stirring my cappuccino with a spoon. John took a sip of his coffee and shrugged.

"That's what you would have ordered, no?"

"Well, yes."

"Then just enjoy your cappuccino."

John drank his coffee, seemingly oblivious to my discomfort. I sampled my drink, expecting it to burn my mouth, but it was the perfect temperature, and I took a more meaningful swallow.

I was bursting with questions, but I remained determined not to give John any satisfaction in that regard. John, for his part, seemed content to just enjoy his coffee in peace. It was a maddening stalemate.

"So, how are things?" I finally asked, fully mindful of John's aversion to small talk. I thought John might volunteer some substantive answers in response to that innocent query, but he didn't take the bait. He merely shrugged noncommittally.

"Well, things are happening at the firm," I volunteered. "In fact, Sal just told me a few minutes ago that I may have a partnership in the near future." *If John doesn't want to talk about himself, screw him.*

John was indifferent to my news and rolled his eyes. "I know," he said, sounding unimpressed.

He already knows? It was possible that John had remained in contact with one of his secretary acquaintances and that this unknown informant tipped him off in the past few minutes. But that raised the question of how that person could have even learned about my private conversation with Sal. I decided it was more likely that John was feigning knowledge, just to stifle any excitement I might have had. *Petty.*

John, infuriatingly, did not elaborate. He remained wordless and still, continuing to imbibe his drink as if he did not have a care in the world. Given the frequency of his sips, I was surprised to notice, when he returned his cup to the table, that it was still nearly full.

We continued to sit, saying nothing, and I was reminded of my first day at SM&L when John and I were sequestered together in a claustrophobic conference room, cataloging boxes of documents. I managed to somehow draw John out of his shell then, but I did not have the energy to go through that exercise again. My temper began to slip and, after chugging the rest of my cappuccino, I quickly stood.

"Look, John, you said you wanted to talk, but you're not talking. And I really have to get back to work. I'm glad you're alive and all, but—"

"Please sit down, Dave," John interrupted quietly. He met my eyes and I sat.

John studied me, weighing his words. Finally, he said, overly formal, "I understand you are taking care of Peaches. I thank you for that."

The cat? He wants to talk about the cat?

"Sure, no problem. He's a good cat." Something occurred to me. "I suppose you'll want him again now that you are back from … wherever." I tried to sound nonchalant, like I was indifferent to his answer, and I think I largely succeeded.

John mulled that over. "No," he finally replied. "I think you should watch him for a while. If you don't mind."

I caught myself before I let out a sigh of relief and shrugged. Looking around the café, I saw it still remained free of any other customers or staff. There was no sign of the waitress who had brought us our drinks.

"I know you're wondering where I've been," John said, finally addressing the elephant in the room. I scoffed, knowing full well it was an immature response.

"Don't flatter yourself," I lied. John arched an eyebrow, and I relented. "Sure, I'm curious. A lot of people wondered where you were. We were worried about you. And if you want to tell me why you vanished, and where you've been, go ahead. If not, that's fine, too. Either way, I've got to get back to the office soon. I have shit to do."

John took a deep breath and, for the first time since our reunion, he looked mildly troubled.

"This is surprisingly hard for me, Dave," John said slowly. "So please bear with me. If I simply *told* you what had happened to me, you wouldn't believe it. I mean, I could *make* you believe it, but I really don't like doing that kind of thing."

That made no sense to me, so I said nothing.

"I believe," John continued, "the only way for you to understand what happened to me is if I *show* it to you." He paused and pursed his lips, deep in thought. I still had no idea what he was talking about.

"So show me," I snapped impatiently. John shook his head sadly, like I did not understand what I was asking. Which I didn't.

"It will be intense," John warned. "Yet nothing I can tell you now would prepare you for it, anyway. You'll survive—that much I can promise you. But you'll be changed."

"Survive what?" I started to ask, but the question vanished into the ether as John's eyes narrowed and reality dissolved around me. And at that point, I saw everything. I felt everything.

Everything.

Omniscience is a difficult concept to describe. I mean, the *theory* of omniscience, of knowing *everything*, is straightforward. But what that actually *means*—our minds are simply not designed to grasp the notion of infinite knowledge.

Imagine every bit of matter, or anti-matter, that ever existed or will ever exist. Every vacuum of space in between. Every sun. Every planet. Every black hole. Every speck of dirt, every molecule of gas. Every lonely hydrogen atom spiraling lazily through space. Imagine that being part of you. There is literally nothing in existence that you are not one with. *Nothing.*

All of this is simultaneous. You are both an atom forged in the Big Bang and a chunk of ice floating between galaxies billions of years later. You are a long-extinct tree while you are also a speck of dust drifting aimlessly through space. You are subsurface lakes of frozen methane on planets on the far side of the universe and, concurrently, a bike strewn across the lawn of a 1970s suburban home in Michigan. Anything you can imagine, at any moment in time, at any place within the realm of reality—that is you. Even the stuff beyond your imagination. You are all of that as well.

Time and space have no meaning to you. You are both so large that the entirety of the universe is a marble that you can hold in your palm and so small that the space between subatomic particles in a single molecule seems to approach an incalculable infinity. The dawn of creation through its end is a flash, and each individual moment lasts forever.

Your gaze is infinite. You see all. You hear all. Yet, your focus is inescapably drawn to the tiny specks in creation that constitute Life. These traces are so small that they are, for all intents and purposes, nothing. Still, this *nothing* draws your attention more than the totality of the remainder of the universe.

Start with a person. Any person who ever existed; it doesn't matter. Now imagine being one with them. Every fleeting thought that person has, you are privy to it. Everything that person ever feels—the pain of a skinned knee, the subtle tickle of a cool breeze, the joy of a first kiss, the overwhelming sensation of that person's first breath and their last. Every hiccup, every itch, every indescribable sensation that person experiences in the course of a lifetime. You live it all as if it were your own.

But it's beyond even that. You understand every essence of that person's being more than they ever could themselves. Deep emotions that lie dormant in the subconscious—you can read those as clearly as if they were typed in front of you. Memories that seemingly vanished as quickly as they were created—you can access them all. There is not a molecule, not a rogue electron, not an electric charge in that person that you do not experience, and cannot define, with one hundred percent clarity.

When John exposed me to omniscience, I ceased being Dave Randall. I was a terrified teenage girl on the verge of giving birth alone in a forest in medieval England. I was a general dying on the battlefield in feudal Japan. I was a fisherman in Ancient Rome perfectly content to spend the day singing to myself at sea. I was even Todd, bristling with embarrassment at being called out in front of my peers by a wiseass associate. I was everyone who has or ever will exist. It is tempting to describe that number of people as "countless," but it's not. It's a fixed number, and one that isn't all that large in the grand scheme of things. Life is such a rare and precious gift, but so easy to take for granted.

Of course, that degree of understanding extends not just to humans: dogs, cows, cats, birds, dinosaurs, trees, insects, amoebas—any life form that exists, existed, or will exist. You are one with them all. Every stimulus, every response, and everything in between that any living creature in the universe ever experienced, or ever will experience. They are all yours.

You are a tree subtly tilting toward the sun to the south. You are a hamster determinedly running nowhere in a wheel. You are a baby calf crying at being torn away from your mother after only a scant few days of life. You are a blue jay instinctively burying an acorn to which you will never return. You are all of this and more—so much more.

I cannot say how long I remained in that state. As I said, time had become a meaningless concept to me. But at some point, as I swam in that state of Oneness, I recognized that I wasn't merely sharing an awareness with the universe. I had *become* the universe. And I instinctively knew that I had the power, through will alone, to *change* reality as I saw fit.

I gathered myself to mold reality to my will …

… and I felt a drowning sensation as I was abruptly reinserted back into Dave Randall. With no preamble or warning, I found myself once again sitting in an empty coffee shop, gasping for breath, across from John. I clutched at the table desperately, as if it were the only thing keeping me grounded to the planet.

I looked up helplessly at John, unable to speak. John gauged my reaction, not unsympathetically, and seemed satisfied with whatever it is he saw. While I watched on, powerless to talk or move, John took a twenty-dollar bill out of his pocket and tucked it neatly under his empty cup. He then stood up and turned toward me. It took all of my strength to tilt my head up to follow him.

"Dave, I've become God," he said. And he said it without emotion; he was simply stating a fact. "This is something I'd like to discuss with you, but I know this will all take some time for you to digest. We will talk again soon."

He turned to walk out the door and paused. Looking back over his shoulder, he said, "Please keep taking care of Peaches."

And with that, John left the coffee shop.

chapter six

This will all take some time for you to digest. That was certainly one way of putting it.

I have no memory of getting home, but I must have, somehow, because when my mind reasserted itself to a nominal degree, I was facedown in my bed with twilight peeking in between the curtains. I felt hungover as my brain commenced a hard reboot. What I had seen and felt was something the human mind was never designed to experience. I now know that I only came out of that experience with my sanity intact through divine intervention. Even so, I knew that it would be a fair amount of time before I was ever right again. Hell, I instinctively knew that I would *never* be completely "right" again, whatever that is.

Time to digest. A fair assessment. My body lay motionless, rendered useless as all of my brain power was devoted to processing what I had just experienced. I tried to recall the specifics, *any* specifics, of my dance with omniscience, but those details remained just beyond my reach. Even if the particulars eluded me, the *experience* of what I had gone through was permanently affixed to my soul. I could not characterize that occurrence with anything other than the vocabulary of a three-year-old.

Big. The concept of infinity is, generally speaking, a direction and not a destination, yet I had managed to reach that non-existent finish line as my awareness expanded to touch the entirety of reality. "Big" was woefully inadequate to describe that experience, but that was the word I repeatedly whispered to myself as I lay in my near-catatonic state. "*Big ... big ...*" Of course, it is impossible to think of "big" without drawing your mind to—

Small. We all convince ourselves that our lives, and what we do with them, are important, to varying degrees. Whether it be a PowerPoint presentation to a roomful of investors, a doctor performing open-heart surgery on a patient, or a father teaching his child to ride a bike, it is human nature to view reality through a prism that establishes meaning. Once that prism is removed, though, as it was for me, it's easier to observe that our "reality" is but a speck of a speck of a speck of a speck. We are *so small* as to essentially amount to nothing. And this isn't solely a matter of size. It's also an issue of—

Short. If they are lucky, a person might get ninety or a hundred years of life. Less so if they are unlucky. Compared with the billions of years that the universe, in its current form, has existed, let alone the infinite weight of the future, this is nothing. Not "practically" nothing, mind you. *Nothing* nothing. Because beyond the "blink and you'll miss it" flash of what we think of as life, time is—

Long. Really, really long. Again, something that will not surprise anyone as a theoretical proposition, but it will threaten to destroy the essence of your very being if you improbably manage to experience that longness firsthand, as I did.

And what does one do when hammered with the certainty of being a nothingness speck that momentarily flickered into existence? I didn't know. So I continued to lay facedown in my bed.

At some point, I nodded off to sleep, where I was tormented by nightmares drawn from the details of my brush with Godhood, which lay dormant in my subconscious. Dreams where I plummeted helplessly through the vacuum of space or burned at the heart of a dying star. Dreams where I was a single-celled organism being devoured by another. Dreams of being drawn inexorably into the depths of a black hole. I was mercifully ripped out of one such nightmare by the sound of scratching at the side of my bed. With great effort, I managed to roll over to see Peaches sitting on the floor looking up at me, wide-eyed and innocent. I blinked at him, disoriented, and he reached out to boop me on the nose with his paw.

"Right," I said hoarsely. "You're due a meal." I glanced out the window and saw a single street light surrounded by a field of darkness. My alarm clock showed 2:15 a.m. "Past due."

I got up to feed Peaches and instantly felt better upon performing even a mundane part of my old life. The blinders that John had ripped off me began to reassert themselves as I struggled to open a can of cat food, and I momentarily surrendered to the notion that there was nothing more important in the universe than for me to open that can. Peaches brushed against my legs, a mixture of excitement and impatience, and I realized that he would agree with that point of view.

Peaches happily devoured his meal, which I watched with an absurd sense of pride at being able to provide it for him. It then hit me that I was expected to go to work in a few hours. The thought of drafting a mundane motion to compel the production of medical records was horrifying after what I had just gone through. I needed time to think, or, at least, to heal. One does not process the entirety of existence in a single night.

I opened my laptop and sent a quick email to Sal about being sick. I vaguely alluded to food poisoning, knowing Sal's squeamishness would prevent him from pestering me with any follow-up questions. I realized right before I hit *Send* that food poisoning would only buy me a day or two, which I sensed would be insufficient for my purposes. I added a few other colorful symptoms that I knew would turn Sal's stomach, no questions asked. I figured I could upgrade (or downgrade) my condition later in the week as needed.

With Peaches fed and my job put on hold for at least a couple of days, I was finally free to think. *To digest*, as John put it. I briefly considered trekking to the top of a mountain to meditate. What I had to consider seemed to warrant that level of gravitas. But the thought of leaving my apartment, let alone climbing a mountain, was too daunting, and instead I just went back to bed.

I laid there for some time, drifting in and out of sleep. In the morning, I woke up with drool on my pillow. I stared at the small blob of wetness, and I recalled that I had, in my moment of omniscience, shared a degree of intimacy and understanding with the liquids comprising that collection of saliva that was infinitely greater than that shared by a couple who had been married for over sixty years. As I stared at the wet stain, I tried to recall being a part of it, but that memory remained just out of my reach, like a word stuck on the tip of your tongue.

Peaches once again snapped me out of my daze, bopping me lightly on the head to be fed. I again got up to feed him, only to beeline back to bed, where my mind struggled to adapt to this new reality with John as God.

John. Of course, he dominated my thoughts during the days following our meeting in the coffee shop. My life during that week consisted of lying in bed thinking of what John had become, with intermittent interruptions to feed Peaches or clean his litter box. When my own hunger became too much to bear, I would find something in my apartment—a few slices of bread, a half-rotten banana—to hold me over. But I did not leave my apartment at all during that time.

Which is not to say that I felt any degree of comfort in my home. I was well-aware from my encounter with John that he could *hear* each and every one of my thoughts as easily and clearly as if I were dictating them to him. I struggled *not* to think about John, knowing he was listening in, which, of course, only resulted in my thinking about him all the more.

John's omniscience troubled me greatly and manifested itself in a variety of ways. As one example, I found myself shyly "covering up" when urinating, as if that would make a difference. I went days without going "number two," mortified by the thought of John seeing me in such an undignified state, and when my will finally eroded in that regard, I would only do so with the lights off (as if John's night vision was subpar). I knew it made no sense, but I couldn't shake my shyness while aware that John could see—and *was* seeing—every single thing I was doing. Suffice it to say, this also resulted in the swift end to my masturbation habit.

One day, after a week of lying in bed with Peaches, during which time I ignored my phone and emails, my doorbell rang. I briefly considered ignoring that as well, but I had been in hiding long enough that I couldn't discount the possibility of someone just entering on their own to make sure my corpse wasn't rotting on the floor of my apartment.

Sunlight blinded me when I opened the door, and the world turned to orange. Even after I blinked a few times to get some life back into my eyes, the person at my door still seemed to glow like the sun. When my eyes finally adjusted, I realized the issue was less about my vision than Mark Foster's newest tan.

"What up, Doctor?" he exclaimed at seeing me, but his face fell once he took in what a mess I had become. I hadn't shaved or showered in the past week, and I imagined I smelt somewhat ripe. It's generally hard to smell yourself, but I instinctively tucked my nose toward my armpit and sniffed. It was unpleasant. Like a hybrid of a men's gym locker room and a bag of stale Cheetos. I was also aware I looked somewhat malnourished from a week of scavenging from the unhealthy scraps I could find in my kitchen.

Mark stared at me, his mouth moving noiselessly. He looked like a man realizing, after it was too late, that he had signed up for a job that was well beyond his ability to perform.

"Hi, Mark," I said. Or tried to say; it came out as a choked whisper. My vocal cords were a little rusty from my week of isolation.

"Are … you ok?" Mark was staring at a particular spot on my cheek. When I touched it, a small piece of cat food fell out of my week-old beard. Mark and I both stared at the blob of tuna on the ground between us in joint fascination.

"I'm …" As I started to speak, a flicker of a memory made its way across my consciousness and vanished before I could grasp it. All I could recognize was that the memory was not my own but, rather, one of Mark's that managed to lodge itself in my head from my brief taste of omniscience. I had once, if only for a moment, been privy to the entirety of Mark's existence. I had heard all of his thoughts, felt all of his pains. Been in the tanning bed with him for each one of his sessions. I had known him better than he would ever know himself. Those memories remained frustratingly beyond my grasp, and the orange man in front of me remained largely a mystery. Yet, it was a reminder that Mark was a human with his own set of thoughts and emotions. Granted, I should not have needed reminding as far as that went, but I did.

Mark shuffled uncomfortably, and I realized that I had been staring at him. "I'm fine," I said quickly, and Mark nodded doubtfully.

"Ok, cool," he said. "Cool. I'm sorry to bother you, but some of the partners asked me to check in on you. They've been trying to call you, and …" Mark trailed off, looking frazzled. I hoped he was more eloquent in court, but I doubted it.

"People are just wondering how you've been doing. You've been out sick for a week and no one's heard from you." He forced a smile. "A lot of people were afraid you were pulling a John on us."

I blinked at Mark blankly, and Mark somehow managed to look even more uncomfortable.

"I was told to tell you that although the firm is pretty lenient about days off, sick leave, whatever you call it, if you need to be out any longer at this point, they will need a doctor's note from you."

Mark paused, pleased at having delivered his message and completing his task.

"What time is it?" I suddenly asked. It was bright outside, but I hadn't paid attention to clocks in days.

"Huh?" Mark stared vacantly at me. I smiled, or tried to, and mimed pointing at a wristwatch.

Mark's face brightened, realizing he was equipped to answer that easy question, and checked his phone.

"It's 1:30. Lunchtime." Mark looked back at his car. "I should be getting back. I'll let everyone know that you're … alive. So, do you want me to tell the partners that you'll submit a doctor's note?" Dr. Mark had clearly decided that I needed more bedrest. I disagreed.

"No need," I replied. "I'm coming back with you. Just give me ten minutes to shower and shave."

Mark blinked slowly, trying to process what I had just said. "You're going back ... with me?" he asked, rather dumbly. I nodded.

"What's wrong with your car?" he asked.

"It's in the shop." I had faith that Mark wasn't smart enough to recognize it parked in the street ten yards behind him. Mark sighed and once again checked the time on his phone, this time with a bit of impatience.

I really wasn't looking to annoy Mark by making him wait for me, although his irritation was somewhat of a fringe benefit. The main reason I didn't want to give Mark a head start back to the office was to keep him from spreading tales regarding the dirty, half-crazed Dave he found quarantined in a sad, dank apartment. I knew I cleaned up nice (relatively speaking), and my arrival back at the office would undermine any gossiping Mark was inclined to engage in.

I left Mark to stew on the stoop while I shot back upstairs to shower and shave. It would have been polite to invite Mark in to wait, but I'm glad that social grace eluded me. It would have been a pity if Mark Foster, of all people, had been the first human, other than myself and my landlord, to enter my apartment.

I felt exponentially better once I cleaned myself up. My interaction with Mark, putz that he was, also cheered me immensely. If my life was a meaningless nothing, it was comforting to be reminded that there were plenty of other meaningless nothings sharing the planet with me. And as much as it pained me to admit, the visit from Mark scratched an itch that approximated "loneliness," which I didn't even realize was there until after the fact.

Mark chewed his lower lip thoughtfully when I reemerged, washed and clean-shaven and looking professional in a pair of gray slacks with a light blue dress shirt. I suspect it dawned on him that my dapper appearance would undermine what was, in his mind, a pretty juicy piece of gossip.

"I'm ready, Jeeves!" I proclaimed happily. Mark scowled and gestured to his car. I pretended as if I were going to sit in the back and laughed when Mark panicked and insisted that I take the front passenger seat.

Mark sped out as if we were in a great rush. When I realized Mark was still sulking over the indignity of chauffeuring me back to the office, I rolled down my window and closed my eyes, letting the scents of summer serve as the entirety of my sensory input. Summer to me always smelled like clipped grass, and those odors brought me back to my childhood. It was the first time in over a week that

I could last more than a few moments without thinking about John becoming God.

When we were five minutes from the office, I opened my eyes and noticed a florist shop coming up on the right. "Stop up there," I commanded, and Mark pulled over. He seemed angry with himself for instinctively following my order. Before he could ask a question, I hustled out of the car and into the shop. I emerged a few minutes later with a bouquet of sunflowers. Mark raised a questioning eyebrow.

"For me? You shouldn't have," he said sarcastically.

"No, not for you," I replied. *You're much too ugly to deserve flowers*, I mentally added, although I felt guilty for the thought.

Mark found an open spot near the office to park, and I hopped out with my flowers before he could turn off the car. Mark hurriedly cut his ignition and chased me into the building, determined to get what he perceived as his due credit for bringing me back to the fold. I didn't break my stride, but I also didn't make any effort to keep Mark from catching up. In a few minutes, it wouldn't matter.

We went up the elevator together. Mark winked at me in a last-ditch effort to build some camaraderie before we entered the office.

"Wow, you seem much better than you did a half hour ago!" he said.

"I feel better," I responded truthfully.

The elevator doors opened and we stepped into the lobby. Dorothy, sitting at the reception desk, smiled when she saw me emerge. "Welcome back!" she cried, and I nodded at her politely. Mark stopped to talk with her, but I kept walking toward my office. I could faintly hear Mark in the background discussing the story of how he found me. The last thing I heard him say was something about how I was "living in my own filth." I ignored it and kept going.

I went straight to the outer ring of offices, and the various attorneys and secretaries in the hallway stopped to stare at my entrance. One of those secretaries was Donna, who studied me with genuine concern. I was touched and approached her.

"Hi, Donna." I handed her the bouquet, which she accepted with surprise. "You've been a great secretary to me—much better than I deserve. So thank you for your hard work."

"Oh!" she said, at a loss for words.

"They're sunflowers," I added lamely. She nodded. "Well, anyway, I hope you feel better soon," I said to her, assuming she had some ongoing ailment, since she always did.

Donna started in surprise. "You've heard about my rash?" she asked.

I forced a sympathetic smile, pivoted, and made my way up the hall toward my own office. Once I reached it, I paused in the doorway. *There's really nothing in there that I need*, I thought to myself. With a shrug, I continued toward Sal's corner office. When I was five offices away, I could make out Bob Dylan singing. As I got even closer, that whisper gradually turned into a deafening roar. I stuck my head in and saw Sal singing along with his eyes closed, happily ignorant of how out of tune he was. When he finally opened his eyes and noticed me standing there, Sal raised a finger, cautioning me not to speak until the song had played itself out. Closing the door behind me, I took a seat in the chair opposite Sal's desk and waited patiently while Sal gyrated and sang, eyes closed.

After a few minutes, the song ended. As the last note faded away, Sal sighed and turned his attention to me.

"Feeling better?" he asked bluntly.

I nodded and opened my mouth to speak, but Sal cut me off before I could utter a syllable.

"Good. We need you here. Your timing couldn't have been worse. We never had a chance to address that matter we discussed before you got—what is it you had? Ah, it doesn't matter. But the other partners are putting pressure on me to decide what is going to happen with that book of business. And I keep telling them ..."

As Sal continued to speak, I found it more and more difficult to focus on what he was saying. An almost imperceptible, arrhythmic tapping from somewhere in the room bore into my skull and managed to overpower Sal's speech. I tried to subtly look for it, but I needn't have worried—Sal's eyes were closed as he continued to wax on about something. And then I found it: a small green fly banging against the window to my right. Just stubbornly hitting that surface over and over again, trying in vain to get outside.

I again felt a subtle brush against my memory, and I was reminded that I had once partaken in the life of that fly. I was there for its birth. I was there when it somehow, inexplicably, ended up trapped in this corner office. And I had shared its frustration as it hammered against the glass, wanting only to get back outside but being prevented from doing so by an invisible barrier beyond its understanding.

And, presumably, I had been one with the fly when it inevitably died in this office.

Sal was still talking—something about his cousin back in Italy—and didn't notice when I got out of my seat and made my way to the window. Up close, the green fly looked exactly the same to me as every other green fly I had ever encountered. I tried to imagine what aspects of that fly made it different from its brethren. There had to be something, if you looked close enough. But I could not see anything unique about it as it bashed its head against the windows, like so many other flies in that predicament had done before.

Quickly, but gently, I cupped my hands around the insect, forming a temporary sphere. I could feel the fly bouncing about, trying to make sense of this even more restrictive prison. I resigned myself to a dozen or so fly bites on my palms.

"I'm sorry to interrupt," I said abruptly. Sal's mouth clamped shut and his eyes popped open. He looked at me by the window, then at the empty seat I had vacated, before looking back at me. *Does he think I teleported?* I wondered idly.

"But I'm quitting," I added. I could feel the fly settle down in my hands. Sal was taken aback, but he quickly recovered.

"What do you mean, you're quitting?" he demanded. I thought it over.

"I mean I'm no longer going to come here to work. And you'll stop paying me." I paused. "But I suppose you can keep paying me, if you like. That part is really up to you."

Sal was caught off guard. He had never seen this type of snark from me. Early in my career, I was meek but hard-working Dave. I had more recently become, at best, a hard-nosed litigator and, at worst, a sycophantic careerist. This was likely the first time I spoke to Sal without any fear of the repercussions.

This must have been what it was like for John when he was here, I thought.

Sal was an experienced litigator, probably the best in the firm, and he had spent his career learning to think quickly on his feet before unpredictable judges. He calmly gestured to the empty seat in front of him.

"Please sit down, Dave. Let's discuss this."

I glanced at the chair and couldn't see any upshot to debating Sal on his terms.

"No, but thank you." I nodded at my cupped hands. "I have to go help this fly get outside."

Sal was, once again, caught off balance. I have no doubt he would have torn me to shreds in any sort of civilized negotiation, but I had stumbled across Sal's weak spot. He couldn't handle the weirdness I was exhibiting.

But I had never felt so comfortable.

While Sal's head was still spinning, I waltzed toward the door. It finally dawned on Sal that I wasn't just giving my notice, but, rather, that I was about to leave *for good*. He became angry and quickly moved to block my exit.

"Is that what you've been doing this past week?" Sal finally spat at me. Literally. I felt some hit my cheek. I tried to wipe it off with my shoulder, as my hands remained occupied. "Have you been taking off to interview with other firms?"

I laughed.

"Oh, God no!" I replied and wondered if John would mind the sacrilege. "I'm done with the law."

"What do you—" But Sal didn't finish the question. I could see he had given up on me. He ambled back to his desk and sat, defeated.

I had always been, to varying degrees, scared of Sal as the firm's eccentric yet respected authority figure. And so, it had been liberating to finally talk to him without any fear. But in that moment, I saw him as just a sad old man unable to process why I was uninterested in a career that had been so satisfying to him. He had pushed for my advancement, and I had thrown it back in his face.

"Look, I appreciate everything you've done for me here," I said sincerely. Sal waved me away with an impatient gesture. "I just … I just can't do this anymore. My reports are all up to date, so whoever takes over my cases should be able to get up to speed on their status by just—"

"Good luck to you, Dave," Sal interrupted coldly. "I hope you know why you're doing this."

I started to speak, but Sal clicked his mouse and The Four Seasons flooded the room through his computer speakers. I managed to open the door with my elbow and left, still holding my fly, which, as far as I could tell, had yet to bite me.

I strolled down the hall, pausing to glance in at my messy office and its wall lined with diplomas and framed certificates of admission to various jurisdictions. I idly wondered what would happen to them: would someone try to appropriate the frames? Or would they just throw all of my belongings into a dumpster in one fell swoop? Neither scenario bothered me.

Further down was a nook that led to a set of stairs that most in the firm were too lazy to use. I wanted a clean escape without any awkward goodbyes, so I stealthily made my way to that stairwell and skipped down two flights to emerge in the parking lot behind the building. *That was so easy*, I marveled. That notwithstanding, I felt as relieved as Andy Dufresne must have felt upon putting Shawshank behind him.

I felt a pinch in my hand, and I was reminded of the unwitting accomplice to my escape. "Fine," I whispered, opening my hands. The fly sat still for a moment, disoriented. Then it jumped off and quickly vanished from my sight.

When I shared an awareness with the fly, I wondered, *did I witness him getting back to the outside world with my help? Was that the future I saw? Or did I change it just now?* I started to get a headache as I ran through all of the permutations, and I let go of those questions to embrace an even more difficult one:

Now what?

Well, the first step was to get home. And since I had hitched a ride to the office with Mark, I was looking at a six-mile walk back. But I wasn't dreading it. I had a lot to think about.

I headed south, tracing the route of my commute for the past seven years. The first few blocks were familiar to me, but after walking for ten minutes the terrain seemed almost alien. I passed restaurants that I had never once took note of on any of my drives to or from work. I saw a post office that I had apparently passed almost every day without noticing. I was even surprised to learn, shortly after crossing into Hempstead, the next town over, that I had been regularly driving past an African-American Museum while completely ignorant of its existence.

As I walked, marveling at a reality that had been hidden in plain sight, I tried to contemplate what next to do with my life. It was liberating to be free of a career that had ultimately proved unsatisfying, but I could not surrender completely to that feeling of a weight removed from my chest. *This is the easy part*, a voice in my head whispered. *It's easy to get rid of the garbage. But, now, how are you going to fill that void?* I did not have any answers to that question.

My focus soon turned to the last words Sal had said to me: *I hope you know why you're doing this.* It is only one three-letter word, but *why?* is a question I had managed to avoid for most of my life. A question I *should* have been asking for years but had not. My life undoubtedly would have been very different had I ever posed that simple question to myself.

Why are you going to law school? Let's see ... I don't want to enter the workforce, and this seems like a way to put that off for another three years. And hopefully, when I finally do get a job, a law degree should help me earn a higher salary.

Why do you want a higher salary? Hmmmm. So I could buy more stuff, take nice vacations, have a nicer place to live ...

Why do you want more stuff? Ok, that one stumped me.

Why did you spend so many years working for that firm? Well, gotta make money somehow. Just to live, eat ...

Then why did you spend so many days working deep into the night, leaving you too exhausted to have any life outside of work? That's what was expected of me to make partner and advance at the firm ...

Why did you want to make partner? Everyone else seemed to think it was important, so why not?

Those were all terrible answers. Even worse, they were all *truthful* answers. Facing this harsh reality made me realize that my life hadn't been forged by anything that I actually *wanted* but, rather, was just a byproduct of following the path of least resistance. John had tried to tell me that on my second day of work, and I did listen to him. Just not to the extent of being motivated to change anything. The penalty for that was seven years I would never get back.

I could have made the walk home in less than two hours, but my pace was unhurried. I regularly paused to study sights I should have noticed long ago. At one point, I stopped for nearly an hour to stare at ants scurrying about an anthill on a thin slice of turf between the sidewalk and the street. There was a pattern to their seemingly chaotic movements that I could not decipher. Again, I was struck by the feeling that the answer to that riddle was lying dormant in my subconscious from my short swim in omniscience, but it remained excruciatingly just beyond my reach.

And so, it was dusk once I finally arrived home at my apartment. My legs were sore from the walk, but I felt refreshed. As soon as I came through the door, Peaches sprinted to me and rolled aggressively, displaying his belly in his trademark style of begging. I laughed, rubbed his stomach, and grabbed a can of cat food from the closet. Peaches hopped up on the counter to supervise while I prepared his meal.

"Good news and bad news, Peaches," I told him, pouring the contents of the can into a bowl. "And they are both the same: I'm now unemployed."

Peaches, focused on his food, ignored me. I placed his bowl on the ground, and he quickly got to work devouring its contents.

I hadn't decided what to do long term, but I was determined not to waste what was left of my life working just for the sake of working. I glanced about my apartment. It wasn't much, but it was still expensive. Just an inescapable consequence of living on Long Island. I then realized that without a job on Long Island, I had no reason to linger there.

"I'm thinking it might be time for a change of scenery, Peaches," I said. Peaches didn't disagree—he just continued to eat his dinner. And as soon as I voiced that intention aloud, I knew it was the right thing for me to do. I felt an immediate impatience at the prospect of delaying a new chapter in my life any more than I had to.

"Hey, Peaches. You up for a road trip tomorrow?" I asked, bending down to pet him.

Again, Peaches didn't object. He just happily continued to lick his bowl clean.

chapter seven

I often find myself wondering how others would react to what I went through—witnessing and experiencing the limits of the universe and the totality of existence, if even only for a single moment. It's hard for me to imagine that there is a person out there who could go through that type of ordeal and think, "Wow, that was cool! Anyway, time to get back to working on that presentation for the big budget meeting next week!" It would be *impossible* not to change your outlook of the world—and, more importantly, your life—after being exposed to literally everything.

The overall theme to my personal metamorphosis in the weeks after my meeting with John was ridding myself of everything that I deemed to be unimportant. And, except for Peaches, that was pretty much all of it. But without anything meaningful to insert into the vacuum left after my life-purge, I suppose the result was somewhat inevitable.

I became a bit of a hippie.

This was not a conscious choice on my part. It was a series of decisions, each completely rational at the time, that added up to my embracing something of a bohemian lifestyle. Telling "the Man" to take his corporate law job and "shove it" was a good start, but it was only a beginning.

One of the stranger side effects of my experience was becoming, overnight, a vegetarian. In that brief moment John opened my mind to the limits of reality, I had been one with all of life. I could not, and cannot, recall the details of that brush with omniscience, but I *do* remember feeling in that moment what it was like to be a "lesser" lifeform, whether a snake, a pig, a bird, or an amoeba. It was a moment of connective intimacy and empathy that no two *humans* ever experience together, and I managed to share it with an armadillo, amongst other things.

As noted, the details of my brief dance with Godhood generally eluded me, but there were occasions when those memories threatened to burst out of my subconscious. One such moment occurred when I casually took a package of ground beef out of my fridge that was threatening to go bad. I suddenly felt like I had been punched in the stomach by the memory of being a terrified cow in line with its brethren, as it was ushered into a slaughterhouse. I raced into the bathroom and vomited—mostly bile because I wasn't eating much in those days. I knew then I would never be able to touch meat again. I wasn't even sure if *dairy* would ever make its way back into my life. I was a bit concerned about starving, given that I didn't like vegetables, either, but I figured in a worst-case scenario I could live off spaghetti and tomato sauce until the end of my days.

But it was more than just a change in attitude and diet. To completely nail down my inadvertent transformation into a hippie (albeit a relatively clean-cut one), when Peaches and I fled Long Island, we ended up in Woodstock.

Again, it wasn't planned. I woke up with the sunrise on the morning after I left SM&L, eager to start a new life, which I could not do until I wrapped up the old one. I stuffed a few t-shirts and a couple pairs of underwear into a backpack, threw Peaches' cat food into a plastic bag, and looked around my apartment. It was filled with furniture, clothes, a couple of TVs … but I didn't see the point in keeping any of it. After a moment's thought, I disconnected my smallest television and carried it out to the trunk of my car. I didn't know where I was going, but I couldn't rule out the possibility of wanting to tune in to a Mets game down the road. I also reluctantly threw a freshly pressed suit in the backseat, although I could not envision a scenario where I would ever need to wear it again.

I hardly ever interacted with my landlord, who lived in the first level of the house below my apartment. Once a month, I would slide an envelope containing my rent—cash being his preferred form of payment—under his door. Every few weeks or so, we crossed paths out front and exchanged polite but disengaged nods. That was the extent of our relationship, even though I had lived there for over seven years.

As such, my landlord, a dull-looking man named Jim, was very surprised to see me when I knocked on his front door after loading up my car with my meager possessions, plus Peaches in his cat carrier. Jim looked as if he had just woken up and had not yet started getting ready for work.

"Hey, Jim," I said. He blinked in confusion.

"I hate to do this to you, but I have to move out right away. As in, right now." Jim continued to blink at me in befuddlement. I was eager to get on the road and lacked the patience to wait for him to finish waking up.

"Most of my stuff is up there, but I don't have time to move it out. You can keep all of it though. There's a laptop, my big tv ... good stuff."

Jim started to speak, but I plowed ahead before he could get a word out.

"And you should have my security deposit from when I moved in. You can obviously keep that for your troubles. And I just paid my rent two weeks ago for the rest of this month, which you can keep. So hopefully you're making out somewhat."

I glanced longingly over my shoulder at the car. Peaches wasn't visible in his carrier on the passenger seat. I then realized I had forgotten to crack a window for him and cursed my stupidity.

"Look," I said, "I'll throw in an extra $300." It was all the money in my wallet. "But I really have to go *now*."

Jim blinked again. I considered increasing my offer to a grand, assuming I remembered to bring my checkbook, but before I could say anything further, Jim nodded and held out his hand. I shoved the contents of my wallet at him.

"Nice knowing you," Jim said. "You were a good tenant."

It was the most he had said to me since I had moved in years ago. Not wanting to end our relationship on that out-of-character note, I gave him a curt nod and walked briskly toward my car. My lousy negotiating skills had already continued to plague me in my post-legal career, but it did not bother me. Not one bit.

"Sorry I didn't open a window for you," I said to Peaches as I got into the car. Peaches shuffled about uncomfortably in his carrier and offered a plaintive cry.

"You were in here for ninety seconds," I scolded him. "No need to be a baby." But Peaches continued to paw unhappily at his carrier and showed no signs of letting up.

"Come on, buddy," I cooed in a softer tone. Peaches continued to struggle. "Obviously this is only for a little bit. You're usually sleeping now, anyway. Just take a nap for the drive." Still, Peaches showed no intention of sleeping in the near future. He continued to cry and pace about his carrier, looking increasingly claustrophobic.

I sat with my car idling, afraid to start driving. Peaches was normally an incredibly docile cat, but the prospect of riding with him in that agitated state was not sitting well with me. Even after I waited for several minutes, Peaches continued to display obvious displeasure at being cooped up.

"Peaches?"

Peaches, paw raised in mid-swipe, stopped to look at me through the mesh of his carrier. The only other occasion I had driven with Peaches was the night I found him at John's apartment, when I was forced to ride with him loose in the car. He didn't go crazy then, and I was hopeful that experience was not a fluke.

"If I let you out, do you *promise* to be good?"

Peaches put his paw down and calmly stared at me. I took that as a sign of assent.

"Dammit." I reached across the car and opened the door to the carrier. Peaches eagerly hopped out onto the floor of the car. After some awkward maneuvering, I managed to get the empty carrier into the backseat, after which Peaches jumped back into the passenger seat and sat tall. No sign of panic whatsoever.

"Huh," I murmured, shrugging. "Whatever. Are you ready now?"

Peaches gave me a level look that suggested that *I* was the one holding up the road trip at that point.

"Alright." Throwing one last look at Peaches, who continued to look relaxed, I shifted the car into drive and cruised down the road, with no particular destination in mind.

•   •   •   •   •

During my career as an attorney, I was not what you might call "a social butterfly." I had no real friends outside of work, and, aside from John, no friends *inside* of work. My dating life consisted of occasional Match.com meet-ups that *almost* never led to a second date and *never* led to a third. On the rare occasions that I took time off from my job, I would generally just spend a week sleeping in until noon and devote the remainder of my time catching up on various television shows. So, while I am not frugal by nature, my lack of anything resembling a life did not even give me the option of conducting an exorbitant lifestyle.

There is, nevertheless, something to be gained by being a hard-working loser. And that *something* in my case was a decent nest egg in my savings account. Thousands of dollars that accumulated simply because I had no opportunities to spend them. More than enough money to settle down for a while to try to figure what to do with the rest of my life.

I drove out of Malverne with Peaches riding shotgun. I headed north toward the Throgs Neck Bridge for the simple reason that it was the shortest path to getting off of Long Island. Driving aimlessly, I quickly found myself on unfamiliar roads in the Bronx that turned into unfamiliar roads in Westchester County. Soon, I was a half hour north of New York City, or what Long Islanders refer to as "upstate." I felt no urgency, and it was wonderful.

There was no pattern to my route. I sought to avoid traffic when possible and took exits whenever I became sick of any particular road. At some point, I found myself on a narrow bridge crossing the Hudson and nearly crashed while staring for too long at the beautiful river and valley far below. After driving for another hour on a random collection of back roads, I noticed that I was running low on gas. Spotting a station further down the road, I pulled in and turned off my engine. I was clueless as to where I was at that point, other than being somewhere between New Jersey and Massachusetts.

"Hungry?" I asked Peaches. He rolled over in his seat and exposed his belly to me. Laughing, I reached into the backseat to grab a small bag of kibble. I dumped a handful onto the passenger's seat, and Peaches went to work on them.

I remembered to crack open a window before getting out of the car and walking into the small store to pre-pay for the gas. A skinny young man behind the cash register stood with his back to me, watching a television with great interest. His head blocked the tv, but I thought I could make out the recognizable twang of Dr. Phil. I was about to clear my throat to get his attention, but, remembering that I wasn't in any rush, I decided instead to wait until a commercial.

"Sometimes you make the right decision, sometimes you make the decision right," Dr. Phil intoned gravely through the television. From behind, I saw the young attendant nod his solemn agreement. I quietly shuffled away, not wanting to intrude on such a profound moment in that man's life.

Toward the side of the small store, I noticed a bulletin board filled with various papers, most of which were perforated at the bottom for easy access to a contact phone number. My eyes ran over the board: ads for acupuncture, yoga sessions, and pottery classes, amongst others. It was my first clue that I had stumbled into hippie country. But then I glimpsed a brief bulletin advertising a small cottage that was available to lease. The monthly rent was half of what I had been paying for my tiny apartment on Long Island. It came with a yard—a luxury

I had done without for the past several years. And, most importantly, it was furnished, which seemed to be a good thing since I hadn't brought any furniture on my impromptu road trip. I had been so eager to get on the road that morning, I didn't stop to contemplate where I would be sleeping that night.

Why not? I took out my cell phone and dialed the number written repeatedly across the narrow tabs at the bottom of the page. A man's voice answered almost immediately.

"Hi, I'm calling about the cottage for rent?" I said it as a half-question.

"Ah, yes," the man said. "How can I help you?"

"I'd like to rent it."

"Wait, what?" the voice responded, sounding utterly confused.

"The cottage you're renting. I'd like to have it."

A long pause.

"Don't you even want to see it first?" the man asked.

"It seems perfect. Can I move in today?"

The man mulled this over.

"I can pay a year's worth of rent in cash up front," I added. "And security if you need it, but I'm pretty a pretty docile tenant."

The man mulled a bit more.

"I suppose I can meet you at the house ... see if you like it ..." He spoke slowly, as if he were looking for a flaw in that plan.

"Excellent!" I responded. "I'll be there in twenty minutes!"

The man sounded like he was about to protest but decided against it.

"Ok. Twenty minutes. I'll see you there. Is it just you?"

"Kind of," I said. "What, exactly, is your policy with respect to cats?"

Twenty-five minutes later, Peaches and I were the newest members of the Woodstock community.

•   •   •   •   •

I woke up early on that first morning after I moved to Woodstock and decided to explore the area. I headed east down my street, directly into the rising sun. After walking for nearly a mile, I came across a trailhead. Although I was only wearing a beat-up pair of sneakers that were unsuitable for hiking, I impulsively made my way up the gravel trail, which wound its way into the mountains overlooking the

Hudson Valley before gently looping back to the starting point. After I finished the five-mile hike, I was exhausted, dehydrated, and exhilarated.

I set out again for that hike the next day (this time with a water bottle and a more appropriate pair of hiking boots that I picked up in town the prior afternoon), and it was an entirely new experience having some familiarity with the path. The day after, I went out again, and yet again the day after that. I vowed to move on and find another trail to hike as soon I became bored with that one—when there was nothing left to it to surprise me.

That day never came.

Each time I tackled the trail, there was something new for me to find. A quaint, isolated house that could be seen in the distance from the peak. A heart-shaped stone along the path that had somehow escaped my attention on my first several hikes. A nest at the top of a tree, barely visible from the trail, which was aggressively guarded by a red-tailed hawk. I challenged myself on each trek to discover something fresh. It was a very easy test to pass, once I reminded myself to open my eyes and actively *look* while I hiked.

After a week, I started to feel guilty at leaving Peaches in the morning to go on my daily hikes. The last thing I saw whenever I left the house was Peaches, sitting saucer-eyed in disbelief that I was leaving him yet again. Those guilt trips wore me down, and I started to think about possible solutions to my dilemma. An answer finally struck me while doing online research at the library when I came across a pet stroller that was available for purchase. It was designed to hold small dogs, but it could also comfortably fit a cat. The trail was steep at times, but the stroller looked rugged. I was *relatively* confident it could handle the hike.

It took a few days for the stroller to be delivered, and once it arrived, I took Peaches on a short test run around our neighborhood. He loved it. He peered excitedly at all sorts of birds, squirrels, and people through the various mesh windows in his new transport. When we finished our walk and returned to the cottage, I unzipped the top of the contraption to let Peaches out, but he refused to leave it. In fact, he slept in that stroller the entire night. I took that as a sign that he was up for a more ambitious hike.

I escorted Peaches in his stroller through the trail the following day. It was strenuous pushing him uphill for long periods of time (and having to physically carry the stroller during one particularly steep stretch), but I enjoyed the exercise. Peaches, for his part, seemed to love staring out at the constantly changing scenery. The other hikers I passed seemed confused by my bringing a cat in a stroller on my hikes, but they generally remarked about how cute and well-behaved Peaches was.

One morning, though, after about a week of taking Peaches along, he abruptly started crying in his stroller and scratched to be let out before we could even start our hike. I had no desire to drag Peaches up a mountain against his will, but his sudden change of attitude was perplexing. It reminded me somewhat of the morning I had left Long Island for Woodstock, when Peaches demanded to be let out of his carrier. He had been satisfied on that day once I let him out to sit freely in the car, but this new terrain wasn't a safely enclosed vehicle.

"You want out?" I asked. Peaches continued to chirp and bat at the zipper holding his stroller shut.

I looked around. No one was near us. Peaches had been an indoor cat as long as I had owned him, but I didn't think he would run away if I let him out. Although I wasn't quite sure *what* he'd do.

My hand moved toward the zipper of the stroller and stopped.

"Peaches, I'm sorry—I can't do this. This is crazy."

Peaches whimpered miserably in response.

I sighed. "Dammit."

I kicked down the foot breaks at the bottom of the stroller, locking it in place. Unzipping the front, I grabbed Peaches' face and held it close to mine.

"Please, *please* do not make me regret this." Peaches stared back calmly with unblinking eyes.

I lifted Peaches and placed him gently on the ground, ready to give chase when he ran off. But he didn't. He merely stretched and looked back at me over his shoulder. *What are you waiting for?* his look said.

"Huh," I said to myself. "Ok then."

I started to walk, pushing the now-empty stroller. Peaches fell in next to me, keeping pace and never once threatening to bolt. He bounded along happily, his tail standing straight up.

From then on, Peaches was permanently attached to my hip as my hiking companion. We would occasionally pass other hikers, who laughed when they saw Peaches accompanying me like an extremely well-trained poodle. Every so often, Peaches drew the attention of a wandering dog, which would bark and attempt to give him chase. But Peaches was never afraid. On those occasions, he simply hopped up to my shoulders and patiently waited for the dog's owner to come take control of it, at which point he would jump back down to the ground and throw me an impatient look to recommence our walk.

When we returned home after our hikes, I developed a habit of settling on a bench on my small back porch to read while Peaches alternated between exploring our backyard and curling up next to me to nap. When it became too dark outside, we'd head in, where Peaches tended to fall asleep on my lap while I read until I passed out on the couch myself.

I could not say if my daily schedule of hiking and reading constituted "a life," but it still felt like so much more than the totality of my legal career. But as much as I longed to, I knew I couldn't keep up that routine indefinitely. My savings had earned me, at most, only a few years' worth of lazing about. Still, I knew I wasn't in a position to tackle anything substantial at that time. My mind was still healing from my last encounter with John.

John had shown me everything, but, in the process, he had also stripped me of everything that I thought I was. It was difficult to focus on building myself back up while so many questions I had for him remained unanswered. But I took solace in the fact that John had promised to speak with me again; I knew it would be impossible for me to exit my holding pattern until he did.

And so I hiked. And read.

And waited.

chapter eight

Peaches and I continued our practice of hiking in the morning and lounging about the remainder of the day for over a year with few deviations. Granted, there were stretches during the winter when the mountain snows made hiking impossible. On those days, Peaches and I would have to content ourselves with wandering about the town of Woodstock, which was really only a few blocks long. It turned out that Peaches was equally adept at staying by my side in a village setting. The sight of a man and his cat casually strolling through a town would normally be shocking, but the bar for abnormality happens to be exceptionally high in Woodstock.

During that year, I also took to volunteering at a nearby farm sanctuary twice a week, which provided my only real opportunity for human contact during that time (although my closest relationships at the farm were with a muck rake and goat shit). Otherwise, Peaches and I continued to wait for a meeting that could take place any day or could be decades away, for all I knew. John had been somewhat vague as to when we would next speak.

It was very easy to lose track of the calendar when my schedule was nearly identical each and every day. I was surprised one morning toward the end of winter to receive a call from my mother, retired in Florida, singing *Happy Birthday*. She sounded somewhat offended when she realized I had managed to lose track of my own birthday. Several months later, I was shocked at night by the sound of gunfire in the air, until I realized that the Fourth of July had also snuck up on me. Thanksgiving almost passed me by as well. Had I not happened to go to the supermarket the day before and encountered two women nearly coming to blows over the last can of cranberry sauce in the store, I likely would have missed that holiday, too.

That particular Thanksgiving ended up being a gorgeous autumn day, falling perfectly on that narrow strip between cold and warm that constitutes *brisk*. I went out that morning in my preferred attire—jeans and a plain t-shirt—well aware that it might have been my last opportunity to get away with wearing that outfit outdoors for at least several months. As Peaches and I made our way to the trail, I figured that the holiday could work in our favor. Even though the day was a ten, Peaches and I had the path to ourselves because everyone else was presumably spending quality time with their family. I was actually doing the same; Peaches just happened to be more mobile than most grandparents.

As we climbed the trail that we both, at that point, nearly knew by heart, my thoughts turned, as they so often did, to John. I was focused on the question I had most often asked myself: why *John* had been chosen to become God (assuming there was a decision in that regard). I, of course, held him in high regard. He was undoubtedly selfless, smart, and kind. But not to the point that I ever thought he was in line for sainthood. I was sure there must have been someone, in the history of mankind, more qualified for the position.

Comparing John's qualifications against anyone who has ever lived, or would *ever* live, was daunting, to say the least, so that morning I focused on a more manageable question. Assuming John was "chosen" …

… why was he picked over *me?*

John and I saw eye-to-eye on most issues. Granted, John was more outspoken than me (once he managed to be drawn out of his shell). He was also much more personable (unless he disliked a person, in which case he was decidedly *less* personable). But these did not strike me as qualities that should determine Godhood.

In the years we worked together, John and I only had one major disagreement that reflected any substantial difference between our respective character. It took place the week between Christmas and New Year's, only a few months before John vanished. That week was historically slow at our firm, with most of the attorneys taking off for the handful of days between the two holidays (at least those who were not frantically trying to meet a billing requirement by the year's end). John and I were included amongst the few at the office that week, and we spent a fair amount of time together, coming up with excuses not to do our jobs.

On Thursday afternoon, John burst into my office without preamble and collapsed into the chair in front of my desk. I was working through a tedious complaint for a new case that had just come in, but I put it aside.

"It just occurred to me that I don't have any plans for New Year's Eve," John announced. He always got right to the point. "So I need to go find a new video game to pick up. Any suggestions?"

"Ummmmm … do you have *Red Dead Redemption*?"

John rolled his eyes. "Obviously."

I thought it over more. "The *Mass Effect* series is pretty awesome. Ever play that?"

John pursed his lips thoughtfully. "I've heard those games are good."

"Ok, cool." I picked up the complaint I had been reading, hoping John would take the hint.

He did, but instead of taking it, John chose to call me out on it. "Oh, am I bothering you?"

I placed the complaint back on my desk. "No. Sorry. That was a bit dickish of me." John raised a questioning eyebrow. "I just got a new case—the carrier sent it directly to me because they couldn't find a partner here this week—and it's already freaking me out. It's going to be a messy one. So I'm just a bit stressed."

John wordlessly held out a hand, asking for the complaint. I reluctantly passed it across the desk to him and sat impatiently while John read it to himself.

It was a complicated accounting malpractice lawsuit. The gist was that the CFO of a relatively small manufacturing company had been cooking the corporate books for a number of years, trying to make the business look more profitable than it actually was, with the goal of luring investors. The scheme worked—for a while, at least. But eventually the math caught up with the CFO, and the company had to file for bankruptcy and fend off a number of claims from defrauded investors. Our client was an accounting firm that had performed a number of compilations and reviews (which are less involved than full blown audits) for the company and failed (at least according to the complaint) to detect the CFO's financial chicanery. The trustee of the bankruptcy estate was now suing our client for malpractice based on the claim that a non-negligent accountant would have caught and stopped the CFO's fraud and that the company would not have gone bankrupt but for that negligence.

The 120-page complaint was substantially more detailed than that summary, but John flipped through it so quickly that I questioned how much of it he was actually processing. After a few minutes, he threw the complaint back onto my desk.

"You have a pre-answer motion to dismiss there," he remarked casually.

I scoffed. "How do you figure? There are going to be issues of fact regarding whether we deviated from the standard of care. We're going to be dealing with conflicting expert witnesses that will likely keep us from winning summary judgment. This is going to be a mess. No way we are winning on a pre-answer motion."

John smiled at my tirade and crossed his legs, patiently waiting for me to collect myself. I exhaled and leaned back in my seat, fully aware that John was about to go into one of his professorial lectures. I knew he couldn't be rushed, so it was with great effort that I resisted the urge to tap my pen impatiently.

After a dramatic pause that bordered on parody, John finally asked, "Are you familiar with the doctrine of *in pari delicto*?"

"Sure," I replied. "I learned all about that in law school. Isn't that Latin for 'pears are delicious'?"

John chuckled. "It means 'in equal fault.' It prevents someone who is mutually at fault from suing another for wrongdoing. It's why most breach of contract disputes between prostitutes and their johns are settled out of court."

I processed that information but still did not see the relevance to my case.

"You have a CFO who was somewhat of a naughty noodle, right?" John asked. I nodded. "As an officer of the company, his wrongdoing is imputed to the entire organization."

"Sure," I interjected. "But our plaintiff isn't the business. It is the trustee of the company's bankruptcy estate."

John grinned enigmatically, waiting for me to connect the dots. Then it dawned on me.

"But ... the trustee stands in the shoes of the company when he sues on behalf of the estate," I added slowly. John gave a quick encouraging nod. "The CFO's wrongdoing is imputed to the trustee as well!" I finished. "That's brilliant!"

John shrugged. "I didn't come up with that. The Court of Appeals came down with a decision a few months ago dealing with this exact issue. *Kirschner v. KPMG*, I think it was. I remember reading about it when it was published. You can find the decision on Westlaw, I'm sure. It's probably the only case you'll need for your motion to dismiss."

"This is awesome, John. Thank you."

"No problem." John stood up. "A partner probably would have alerted you to that precedent at some point, anyway." John hesitated. "Or maybe not. We work for a pretty shitty firm."

John turned to leave, but something was tickling my brain. Before he could exit my office, I blurted it out.

"What about the Sullivan case?"

John froze in the doorway.

The Sullivan case was one of John's. It involved an elderly couple, the Sullivans, who owned a small business together. After the husband, who handled the company's finances, passed away, the wife learned that he had been keeping the business afloat with a series of corporate credit cards and business loans premised upon misinformation and fraudulent applications. It was a business that was destined to fail but was artificially kept alive through a series of disingenuous transactions. It fell to the widowed wife, after her husband's death, to fight on behalf of the company against its various creditors, which also sought to pursue her personal assets in light of her deceased husband's fraud. The wife, in desperation, sued the only other professionals involved in the business: the company's accountants, who prepared the corporate tax returns for the past decade. Our firm was retained to defend those accountants through their professional liability insurance.

I only knew of the case because I attended its court conference several weeks earlier when John had a conflict—a deposition in an unrelated case scheduled that same day. Covering John's court appearance was easy; I merely had to report to the court that the parties had reached a settlement, and that the action would be discontinued shortly.

The amount of that settlement was $250,000.

"Wouldn't the *in pari delicto* defense have applied to your Sullivan case as well?" I asked. John slowly closed the door and sat back down in front of me.

"Same facts, right?" I added. "The husband's wrongdoing is imputed to the business. The business sues the accountants. That should have been an easy motion to dismiss, no?"

John carefully weighed his response.

"Do you want my official answer or the truth?" he finally asked.

I braced myself. "Why don't we hear both?"

John ignored my snarky tone.

"My *official* answer is that I was, until after the settlement was finalized, blissfully unaware of the *Kirschner* decision or the defense of *in pari delicto* or anything else that would have constituted a valid defense in that lawsuit. I saw the case going to trial, at which time the jury would collectively burst into tears for the poor, sympathetic widow, which is why I recommended an aggressive settlement strategy to the insurance company. They agreed with my analysis and authorized me to settle the case for up to $250,000. The widow, as it turns out, was a fierce negotiator, and it took *all* of my settlement authority to get a deal in place."

John paused. I dreaded my next question.

"And what is the truth?" I asked softly, eyes closed.

"I thought she deserved the money." John said it so simply, so matter of fact. I wasn't sure I heard right.

"You lost the case on purpose?" I was dumbfounded.

John scrunched up his face. "Well, a settlement isn't really a loss. It's more of a tie. But, yes, I suppose you can say I tied on purpose."

I felt nauseous.

"John, you had a defense that you ignored to screw your client!"

"No," John insisted. "*Not* to screw my client. To help *her*. And trust me: no one is losing sleep over having to pay that $250,000. Our client only had to pay their $5,000 deductible. They aren't going out of business from that."

I ignored him.

"What you did," I said, "is a *major* ethical violation."

"Really?" John asked innocently. "How so?"

I stammered; it was such a stupid question.

"How about Disciplinary Rule 7-101?" I snapped. *"Representing a Client Zealously?"*

"Oh, that." John contemptuously waved my citation away. "That's not important."

"What do you *mean* 'that's not important'?" I nearly shrieked. "We took an oath of office when we were sworn in that you just took a shit on!"

"And what's more important to you, Dave?" John asked coldly. "Helping a poor widow when the opportunity presents itself, or following a code of conduct that you were forced to adopt as a prerequisite to obtaining a law license?"

"It's not your *job*, John! You're not a judge; it's not for you to decide how a case turns out. We have courts and laws for that."

"You know what I think?" John sneered. "You don't really give a shit about these rules. You just want to cling to something that absolves you of any personal responsibility. That allows you to keep your head in the sand while proudly insisting you're an ethical lawyer, and you don't ever have to saddle yourself with the guilt for missing the larger picture."

I refused to back down. "That's not true. These rules exist for a reason. You think *I'm* missing the bigger picture? What about you? Don't you think society would turn on lawyers—more than it already has—if it knew we were just disregarding the rules of ethics whenever we thought the ends justified the means?"

John stared at me, shaking his head sadly.

"Fine, Dave. If that's how you feel, go ahead and report me."

He stood up to leave.

"Dammit, John!" I exclaimed, offended. "I'm not going to report you!"

"Why not?"

"We're friends, asshole! But I'm allowed to think this is fucked up!"

John's smile was bitter. "Disciplinary Rule 1-103: a lawyer with information raising a substantial question as to another lawyer's honesty, trustworthiness or fitness as a lawyer has an affirmative duty to report such.' As you said, Dave, these rules exist for a reason. Get to it."

My mouth was agape, but I had no response. I slumped back in my chair, defeated. John, who had braced himself for a verbal spar, softened when he saw that I was not going to fight back.

"Look, Dave, I don't mean to bust your balls. You're a good guy, and you do what is right, which is more than I can say for most of the dickheads around here. I'm just suggesting that even when it's easier for you personally to stick to the playbook, it's sometimes worth throwing it away. In this case, you're violating the rules for our friendship—which I really do appreciate, by the way. Similarly, I violated the rules to help out an old woman who would have ended up destitute if I didn't take matters into my own hands. The lines we're each willing to cross aren't identical, but the important thing is that our lines don't exist to help *ourselves*. We both ignore the rules when it serves a higher purpose. And that's not a bad thing."

John left my office, leaving me to think on what he had said. But twenty seconds later, John poked his head back in my doorway.

"But seriously: please don't report me, ok?" he pleaded. "You can call it a belated Christmas gift, if you want."

John darted away before I could respond.

We didn't speak again before the long New Year's holiday weekend. When we returned that first week of January, neither of us alluded to our fight. Our interactions were initially tentative and meek, and only after both of us realized that the other did not intend to bring up our disagreement were we able to settle in and relax around each other.

But I thought about that day often, and more so after learning that John had become God. I knew from the first week I met him that John was smart—brilliant, in fact—but, I figured that intelligence should not be a prerequisite for a job that includes omniscience as a perk. Bravery likewise does not seem to be an important attribute for a being that is omnipotent.

So what makes one candidate for Godhood better than another? *Wisdom?* It's a pretty answer, but "wisdom" isn't so easily defined. In fact, I still question the wisdom of John purposefully losing a case (or, at least, intentionally *tying* a case) to benefit a sympathetic plaintiff, but his decision in that regard demonstrated *something.* As to whether that "something" amounts to anything more than just a different perspective, I felt ill-equipped to rule.

My thoughts were interrupted once Peaches and I reached the top of our mountain. The trail briefly flattened out before it descended back down the far side of the peak. The summit itself was an open area with glorious views that stretched for miles over the entire wooded valley below. We had not passed a single person on the way up, but now, at the top, a lone man stood with his back to us. He seemed, at least initially, to ignore our arrival. Instead, he was focused on studying the land beneath him. It may not have been his creation, but it was certainly his inheritance.

John had apparently deemed it time for us to resume our talk.

chapter nine

We stood there in silence. John did not seem in any hurry; he patiently surveyed the landscape, occasionally closing his eyes and tilting his face toward the sun as if savoring its touch on his skin. I, too, waited silently. It seemed unwise to interrupt God.

I don't know that I could have spoken up had I wanted to; my thoughts were such a jumble. John had told me that he and I would speak again, so I knew that at *some* point he would re-enter my life. The *manner* in which he would reappear—that was something I could not have even tried to guess, but I had been expecting something more grandiose than merely running into him while out on a hike.

"I can come back, if you'd prefer," John finally called to me over his shoulder. He slowly turned in my direction, wearing a mischievous grin. "I'd be more than happy to have a choir of a thousand angels herald my entrance while I descend from the clouds on a white unicorn. If that's your thing."

My immediate, reactionary thought was, *This asshole is mocking me.* My next thought was, *Oh, shit. John is reading my mind.* That was immediately followed by, *Oh, shit. John just heard me think of him as an asshole.*

John laughed. Hard.

"Alright, alright; I'm turning it off," he said. "No more mind reading. Your thoughts are your own, whenever we chat. I'm not going to be your genie, but I can do that much for you at least."

I knew, intellectually, that the man in front of me was not the same John I had befriended at Sanders, Martucci & Lyons roughly eight years earlier. I also recognized that this "man" was not human at all but, rather, an omnipresent being that had merely adapted his old form to speak to me and, presumably, to put me at ease. It also occurred to me that I *should* be terrified, speaking directly to God.

But those intellectual reservations refused to take root. I saw the same John I had known for years, so I instinctively spoke to him as I would have before he attained Godhood.

"What do you mean 'turning it off'? You're omniscient, right?" I asked, walking slowly toward him.

John shrugged.

"Well … yes. I *can* know everything, see everything. When I want to. But I don't *have* to always know everything. Sometimes, it is worth keeping myself a little ignorant. This conversation would be really boring otherwise. At least for me."

A hint of a smile touched John's lips.

"Being able to dial down omniscience is helpful in other contexts, too," he said. "For example, I really have no interest in watching you play with yourself, Dave. Or listening in while you go to the bathroom. No offense."

I could feel my cheeks getting warm, and John laughed again at my blush. As he snickered at my discomfort, John's eyes fell upon Peaches, who was licking himself clean behind me. John beamed.

"Peaches!" he cried, crouching down and putting out a hand. Peaches happily bounded to John and rolled onto his back, exposing his stomach. John enthusiastically rubbed Peaches' belly, and even over the sound of the wind I could hear loud purring.

In hindsight, I might have treated John more like God if he had *acted* more Godlike. But he conducted himself in the same way he always had with me, and it didn't even occur to me to fall to my knees in worship under the circumstances. I wasn't quite sure *how* to behave, but everything about John's behavior signaled that this was to be an informal affair, so I played along.

I felt a need to say something while John knelt alongside Peaches, vigorously tickling him. "Why did you name him 'Peaches'?" I asked. That had puzzled me for some time.

John stopped his petting and threw me a quizzical look.

"You have a chance to speak with God and THAT is your first question?" he asked, incredulous.

"Apparently." I felt the blush reasserting itself. John had clearly established the upper hand in our conversation, but I wasn't sure it was possible to outwit God. John shrugged at my response.

"Ok. You want to know why I named him 'Peaches'?" He pinched the cat's cheeks playfully and, looking deep into Peaches' eyes, said in a baby-talk voice, "because he has such a peachy face!"

Peaches continued to purr and roll about gaily.

I watched the bizarre scene unfold, unsure of what to say next. John detected my unease. Or perhaps he divined it—I wasn't sure how strictly he adhered to his "no mind reading" promise. In any event, he stood up and adopted a more serious demeanor.

"So, how are you doing, Dave?" he asked. From anyone else, it would sound like small talk, but from John—from *God*—it was a real question.

"I'm fine," I replied. "At least, I think I am. You gave me a lot to mull over, the last time I saw you. But I'm much happier now than I was then."

John nodded solemnly but didn't speak. I realized he was looking for more from me.

"I think I now have a … healthier perspective on things. There was a lot of bullshit in my life before. I see it now, even though I think you've been trying to get me to see it for years. But I think I got most of the nonsense out of my life."

John nodded again. *Go on.* I took a deep breath.

"What I am wrestling with now," I said, "is figuring out how to fill those holes. But what you showed me the last time we spoke, it made me appreciate—it made me *know* just how small, how nothing I really am. How even this—" I gestured to the wide-reaching view surrounding us—"is nothing. I've always had some basic understanding of how big the universe is, and how short my life will be in comparison to the rest of existence. It's just that now, my knowledge of how insignificant I am isn't an abstract theory. I've witnessed my nothingness firsthand. And whenever I try to imagine what to do with my life, I can't avoid the inescapable conclusion that whatever I do will ultimately be small and meaningless."

John nodded thoughtfully.

"And so you spend your days climbing up and down this mountain with my cat," John said quietly.

"Apparently," I said with a shrug.

John turned away and looked back toward the sun. He nonchalantly reached his right arm up toward it, as if he was stretching, and made a fist. He turned back to me and opened his hand, revealing a small sphere of fire hovering in his palm. John gestured with his chin for me to take a closer look.

"You're now bigger than the sun, Dave." John spoke softly, glancing meaningfully at the small dancing ball of light in his hand. "Does that make you feel any more important?"

I instinctively glanced up at the sky and saw the sun still sitting there. John rolled his eyes.

"Give it eight minutes or so," he said. "Man—don't you remember anything you learned as a kid about the speed of light? But trust me, this is the sun. And it's tiny compared to you. Does that make you feel better about yourself?"

I stared in horror at the miniature star in John's hand. It was easy for me to be lulled into a sense of false complacency around John every now and then. John plucking the sun out of our solar system was not one of those moments.

"What? No! I don't feel any different." I backed away, panicked. "Please, put it back. I'm pretty sure we need that."

John gave a self-satisfied bob of his head and closed his hand. "Trust me," he said. "No one will ever realize it was gone."

John opened his hand, which was now empty. He quickly turned his two hands over and back, a blackjack dealer ending his shift. Despite John's reminder of the principles of physics, I stole a glance at the sky and was relieved to see the sun exactly where it should be.

John started to walk slowly, as I stood, transfixed. He didn't go far—just a slow amble around me with his hands clasped behind his back. A professor about to begin a lecture to his class. Peaches, curious, followed John in his circular route.

"Tell me what you own," John finally said.

I blinked in confusion at this non sequitur.

"You're God. You know what I have. Right?"

"I want to hear you say it." John stopped pacing and folded his arms across his chest expectantly.

Alright. With no idea where this was going, I ran a quick mental inventory of my meager possessions.

"Let's see," I said. "I got rid of most of my stuff when I moved up here. I have my car. I brought a small tv up with me to watch Mets games. I purchased a fair number of books in the past few months. I have some clothes, and—"

"Wrong."

I froze when John cut me off. He walked toward me with two purposeful strides and pinched my shirt sleeve.

"This shirt isn't yours. Those shoes aren't yours. This view," John gestured around him, "isn't yours. At any given point in time, there is only one thing that is truly and indivisibly yours. And that is the Moment."

John paused, watching to see if I was processing this. His point, quite frankly, sounded a bit trite, but I did not say so aloud. My face might have betrayed me because John proceeded to further explain.

"You lament that you feel small. Well, you were just bigger than the sun, and you didn't feel any different. You seem to think that anything you do will ultimately be meaningless. Again, why is this moment, right now, any less important, any less *meaningful*, than a moment that will occur millions of years from now? Besides, you have it backwards: your actions are not meaningless. *Everything* you do has the potential to alter any given moment, for good or bad. And since moments are all that you, or anyone, really has ... well, that is not a power that you should be so ready to discount."

John blinked and bent to scratch Peaches behind his ears.

"I don't mean to lecture you, Dave," he said. "I would just hate if my act of showing you a glimpse of my ... existence caused you to undervalue your own self-worth. That wouldn't be fair to you. And I think you have a lot to offer as far as helping others improve their own moments. But, right now, I don't think you're really living at all."

I blinked in surprise. "What do you mean? I'm so much happier now than when I was practicing law."

"You managed to get rid of a lot of crap," John conceded, kneeling besides Peaches. "But what you're feeling is not so much happiness as the relief of no longer having to carry around the weight of needless burdens. Sure, you're carefree for now. But when you're really living, there is something in your life that you are afraid, at some level, of losing. And I don't sense any fear in you."

I instinctively glanced down at Peaches. He had become my best friend in the past few years, but John was right. I didn't have any fear of losing him. That wasn't coldness on my part. I just instinctively knew I didn't have to worry about his well-being.

"Look," John said. "You cleared away the rubble. That's a solid first step. But it's *only* a first step. You're in a position now to build a life—a *real* life. I think you should take it."

John shrugged, as if he didn't care if I took or ignored his advice.

"Your back is better," John added, seemingly apropos of nothing. And he was right, although I didn't realize it until he pointed it out. The pain in my lower back that I had felt since law school was no longer present. It had gradually diminished to the point of non-existence, and I hadn't even recognized it.

"Is that something you did?" I asked. John shook his head.

"No, that was all you. A year-plus of rehab—climbing up and down this mountain—straightened you out. And you're only thirty-three years old. You are still young enough to apply to the FBI, if you're so inclined."

It was true. I recalled that the FBI entertained applicants up to the age of thirty-seven. I certainly felt healthy enough to tackle, with a bit of training, the physical rigors of the application process. But it was difficult for me to even remember what had drawn me to that potential career in the first place.

"I don't think that would be fulfilling to me anymore," I said, unable to articulate my feelings on the issue any more than that. John tilted his head, and I could hear his unspoken question: *So what would be fulfilling to you?* "I don't know what would be," I said.

John smiled. "You'll figure it out. And that's not pep talk. That's a fact."

I had nothing to say to that, so I just walked to the edge of the cliff and looked down. I could make out parts of the trail leading up, but not a soul could be seen below. John seemed to enjoy his privacy when he spoke with me. After a moment, John stepped to my side and looked out.

"Was this your agenda?" I asked softly, not making eye contact. "To get me on some sort of 'right' track?"

John likewise answered without looking at me. "No. There is actually something I need your help with." I started to ask the obvious question—*How can I possibly help God?*—but John shushed me with a raised finger. "But first," John said, "I need you to understand a bit of what I am. What I've become. I'm sure you have questions for me. Ask away."

Of *course* I had questions. I had so many questions, I didn't even know where to start. Fortunately, John didn't seem in any rush to leave, so I started with an easy one.

"When did this happen?"

"April 19, 2011. The morning after my last day at SM&L."

I ran some quick math in my head.

"So you have been God for about two-and-a-half years?"

John, face scrunched, bobbed his head and wobbled a hand in front of him. *Kinda.*

"In a way, but not really," he said. "It's more complicated than that. You see, I don't really exist within time anymore."

"Uh—" I started. And then I remembered that moment where John had given me a taste of omniscience. Occupying every particle of the universe, feeling each moment of existence not as a sequential ordering but, rather, as a blended amalgam that was well beyond the ability of a human mind to decipher. I nodded. "Right. You're outside of time." While I had a vague recollection of the state of being described by John, it was still difficult for my mortal brain to fully grasp the implications of it. He noticed my struggle.

"I know; it's a tough concept to wrap your head around, but you're better equipped than most to get it. Think of it this way: Imagine you're reading *Harry Potter and the Prisoner of Azkaban* ..."

I felt my cheeks go warm, yet again. I had just finished *Prisoner of Azkaban* roughly two weeks earlier, and I had since put it at the top of my list of favorite books. I was still working up the nerve to pick up *Goblet of Fire*, as I feared being disappointed by the sequel.

John ignored my embarrassment and continued.

"You would start at the beginning and work your way to the end. Time progresses more or less chronologically in the book, but it is unconnected to you, the reader. Time can advance three months in the story while for you, in the real world, it may just be a matter of seconds. Likewise, you could put the book down for a year, come back to it, and be right at the same point in the story as you were when you left it. Hell, you could even read the story by starting at the last chapter and work your way backwards, essentially going backwards in time in the Harry Potter universe. Granted, it'd be a weird thing to do. But you *could* do it."

John paused to see if I was following. I gave a subtle nod, and he continued.

"Now, imagine you had access to a story that sets forth everything that has ever happened, or will ever happen, in this universe. And also imagine you have the ability to edit that story however you see fit, using nothing more than your will. You could go back to the beginning and revise the dawn of creation. You could jump to a random section and rewrite the laws of physics, if you felt like it. You could go back and erase Hitler from existence, and then just sit back and watch how the story played out. And yes—you could even insert yourself into the story if you wanted, which is, for the purposes of this analogy, pretty much what I am doing right now in speaking with you directly. Anything can be changed if you will it. Time is irrelevant."

John stopped again, making sure he hadn't lost me. I waved at him impatiently to continue.

"So, to keep this analogy going, April 19, 2011, was the day I was plucked out of 'the story' as a character and given access to it as … an author? An editor? Someone outside of the narrative, in any event. And once I was removed as a 'character,' time lost all meaning for me. I don't live in any particular moment; I see them all. Simultaneously."

It was a bit demoralizing to think of myself as a mere character in a story, but John's analogy did help to paint at least a fuzzy picture of what he had become.

"What did you do once you were 'plucked out'?" I asked.

"Well, to be clear, I wasn't *physically* 'plucked out.' It was like this: on the morning of April 19, 2011, I woke up with an awareness of … everything. Everything that was. Everything that ever would be. You know what that was like; I shared that experience with you last summer. So I'm sure I don't have to explain to you how jarring that transformation was."

I assured him that he did not.

"I don't know how long it took because I was existing outside of time at that point," John said, "but I eventually realized that I wasn't merely aware of all existence—that I was one with the universe—but that I could manipulate reality however I wished."

John paused to let that sink in.

"What did you do then?" I asked softly. John chuckled to himself.

"Oh, I thought about doing all sorts of things. Flying around like Superman. Going back in time to talk to history's greatest hits. Weird sex stuff. Hell, I briefly considered reincarnating myself as a baby born in Queens who grows up to be bitten by a radioactive spider. But those were just the remnants of impulses I would have had as a human. They quickly passed."

I recalled that John had been a big Spider-man fan. Then something occurred to me.

"Todd was fired after you became God. Was that your doing?"

John grimaced, ever so slightly. "Todd." He paused, as if undecided whether to savor or spit at the name. "I used to really hate that guy, you know? It was bizarre—my feelings toward him were so much more than what was justified. He was a bit of an ass, but nothing unique about him in that regard. Some people just have a knack for rubbing others the wrong way. It's like soulmates, if you replace love with annoyance. And Todd had the ability to irritate me to the very depths of my soul."

John bent down to lift up Peaches. Stroking the cat's chin, he continued. "But where I am now, I can see everything that made Todd *Todd*. He was really overweight in elementary school, and his classmates put him through absolute hell for it. His mother was overbearing, but his father did nothing to hide his disappointment in his son. Todd spent a lot of nights as a kid awake in bed, hearing his parents fight with each other about *him*. Do you know what that's like for a little kid? Listening through a thin wall as your parents scream at each other and believing you were the cause of it?

"Of course, I didn't know any of this back when I was going out of my way to annoy him. How could I have? And even if I had, I'm not sure if that would have changed how I felt about him. Maybe there would have been a tinge of pity beneath my contempt? I'm not sure. But the point is that Todd is as far from perfect as he is far from evil. He is largely a product of where he came from. There were times in Todd's life where he managed to rise above his past and become a better human being than he might have otherwise been. And there were times when his crappy childhood clamped itself firmly to his ankle and dragged him down."

John dropped Peaches back to the ground and looked off. I wondered whether John even remembered my original question.

"I see so much of that, Dave." John spoke in a hushed tone, and I struggled to hear him above the wind. "Bad decisions. Moments of weakness from people who aren't bad themselves, but who act out of anger, or pride. Pick your favorite sin. Granted, there is genuine evil out there, but much less than what you'd think. No, most of it is just bad, misguided decisions."

"But to answer your question: No, I did not arrange for Todd to be fired. He managed that on his own. Like I said, he made bad decisions."

I felt somewhat relieved by the fact that John had not been exploiting his position to exact revenge on those who had ever rubbed him the wrong way. I figured that if *Todd* was safe, no one else should really lose sleep over the thought of a vengeful God. But that begged another question.

"Ok," I said. "You didn't interfere with Todd, and you didn't resurrect yourself as Spider-man. So what have you been doing?"

John's lips tightened in brief annoyance, but he quickly let out that tension with a sigh.

"Let's come back to that one. What else would you like to know?"

It was frustrating. I had no shortage of questions for John, but in that moment I struggled to articulate *any* of them. *I should have made a list*, I thought bitterly.

"Why did this happen to you?" I finally asked.

John shrugged.

"Beats me." He smiled slightly at my puzzled expression.

"Look," he said. "Go back to my analogy from earlier. And imagine the story that is the universe being laid out in a Word document on a random computer. After I was removed as a character, I was given a chance to edit that document—that story—as I saw fit. I assume someone created the story before I came along, but there is no evidence of who, or what, did so. I didn't make the universe, even if it is now mine to manipulate however I want. I have no idea who my predecessor was, or why I took things over. And to be honest, I'm not entirely sure I *want* to know."

"Why is that?" I asked.

John looked directly at me. "I'm not sure I want to know what could have caused God to abdicate this post. But I have my suspicions."

John took a seat on a rock. Peaches followed, again rolling at John's feet. John reached down absently to tickle him, and Peaches grabbed onto John's hand with his paws. When he resumed speaking, John's voice was tinged with uncharacteristic bitterness.

"You asked earlier what I have done since I was appointed God. Well, the answer is nothing. I haven't done a damn thing."

John's eyes flickered down toward Peaches below him. "Nothing that would materially impact the world at large, at least," he added. "And I'm not even sure what I *should* be doing. So I'm just sitting on my ass, doing nothing but watching. And although I have evolved beyond the reach of 'boredom,' this existence can be a bit … unfulfilling."

John continued sitting on his rock, staring off at nothing in particular.

"I don't understand," I said. "You could do anything."

"Yeah." John shrugged. "But it's not nearly as exciting as you might think."

I scoffed. "Excitement aside, you are in a better position than anyone in the history of the universe to make things better! You can end wars! Cure diseases! Eliminate pollution! And all you would have to do is will it! Right?"

"I could," John said as he stood. "I could have every terrorist organization in the world conga-line their way to the nearest U.S. military base to surrender. I could have every murderer at large gather together to cook meals for the homeless. But why stop there? I could set up the homeless—hell, set up everyone—in gorgeous homes on the beach, with perfect weather, where no one ever had to work, and everyone got everything they ever desired. No one would ever fight, no one would ever get sick, and no one would ever age, let alone die. It would take zero effort for me to make that happen. A universe filled with happy puppets, bouncing along merrily on strings that I alone am holding. Is that what you think I should do, Dave?" John's voice remained calm, but I thought I could detect a hint of frustration as he spoke. Or was it regret?

"That's a bit disingenuous, John." John's lips twitched in annoyance at my lawyerly tone, but I ignored it. "I don't see why this has to be 'all or nothing.' You can make things better without completely depriving humanity of its free will. There are kids starving around the world; surely you can help them without creating that universe of happy puppets you just described. There are diseases, natural disasters—"

John shook his head emphatically.

"No. I told you earlier that you should strive to cherish each moment as if it is the only thing you have, because it is. But that's not true for me—I don't see snapshots. I see the entire tapestry. What you're describing is putting a couple of bandaids on this particular moment, for ... what, exactly?"

At seeing my bewildered expression, John pointed west without taking his eyes off of me.

"There is a twelve-year-old boy on a bike in a suburb outside of Cleveland right now. His name is Alex, and he's wearing a helmet and otherwise riding his bike responsibly. But in exactly one minute, he will be struck by a car and he will die. I could stop that from occurring—I could just put a thought in the driver's head to slow down slightly and the accident won't happen. I could have Alex pause to tie a shoe. There is an infinite number of ways I can stop this."

I found myself counting down in my head—*fifty-five, fifty-four*—as John paused, unconcerned.

"Well do it!" I snapped fervently. John continued as if he had not heard me.

"Alex would live, grow up. And the world would be changed forever."

Thirty-two, thirty-one ...

"I don't just see the future, Dave. I see the outcome of every scenario where I feel inclined to put my thumb on the scale. I'm not looking at a line—it is a web of infinite possibilities, and I can steer existence along any strand that I choose.

"So let's say I save Alex. He grows up to be a quality human being. He starts a family and raises a son who also goes on to become a good man. That son, in turn, has a daughter, who becomes a great doctor when she is older. Her skills allow her, early in her career, to save the life of a teen from almost certain death."

He will not allow this boy to die, I silently prayed.

Seven, six ...

"Twelve years later, that teen she saved will break into a home and murder a family of five."

Two, one ...

"John!" I shouted.

John closed his eyes and waited a beat.

"And now that family will live," he said softly.

I stared at John in shock. Peaches seemed to sense my horror and rubbed himself against my calf in sympathy.

"How could you—" I started, unable to finish as my throat clenched.

John shrugged.

"You think I'm a monster, and, frankly, I can't blame you. But you have to understand that I don't see things as you do. You are trapped in this moment, and I understand why your instinct is to maximize its potential. 'Make things better *right now.*' The thing is, I can see how *all* of the moments, or even how potential, hypothetical moments, connect to one another. And sure, I can steer things along a wondrous path, where pain and loss are minimized. But is that the point of life? Just to avoid sorrow? Because, if so, we may as well just embrace that happy puppet scenario I described earlier."

I remained traumatized, unable to speak. John's face was unreadable.

"I have, for reasons unknown to me, inherited this story that is writing itself. The characters are making their own choices, and I am not willing to deprive them of that freedom. No matter what. I am also not willing to completely rewrite this story just to help a couple of characters live a few extra years, or to trade one life for another. As such, I'm wrestling with the question of what my role is. What *should* I be doing? Am I meant to merely observe?"

John added quietly, "Am I even necessary at all?" He turned to look at me. He showed no hint of the wisecracking friend who had greeted me earlier.

"I have a lot of respect for your judgment, Dave. I really do." John broke off his eye contact with me and looked away. "I hope you will reflect on my dilemma and offer me your thoughts the next time we talk."

And with that, John vanished. Peaches ran to the area where he had been standing and sniffed about, confused. I was confused myself, albeit for a different reason.

John was unwilling, or unable, to meet my eyes when he alluded to speaking with me again. It was years before I learned why.

•   •   •   •   •

The next morning I went to the library and did a search on a public computer. It did not take me long to find an obituary for a twelve-year-old boy named Alexander Bennett who lived outside of Cleveland. Alex was a goalie on his travel soccer team and played the trombone in his middle school band. He was survived by his parents and his eight-year-old sister.

chapter ten

Empathy. The ability to vicariously experience the feelings or thoughts of another. In theory, it is so simple. You only need to ask yourself: *How would I feel if I were experiencing what that person is going through?* Some manage to live their entire lives without showing any capacity to empathize. Even sadder are those who *do* have the ability but manage, at some point, to shut it down.

People like me.

I first stumbled across the concept of empathy in fourth grade at a religion class my parents enrolled me in, seemingly for no other reason than to get me out of the house for one afternoon a week. Although the "religion" part of that class never quite took root, I managed to take a number of ancillary lessons to heart. I recall one day being introduced to the concept of *"Do unto others as you would have them do unto you,"* derived from Jesus' Golden Rule. After our teacher, Mrs. Meier, translated "unto" for a group of nine-year-olds, my classmates nodded their collective heads in appreciation of that maxim. But something about that basic rule troubled me, even though I had trouble articulating my objection.

"What if I want to be treated in a way that is different from someone else?" I asked. Mrs. Meier raised an eyebrow, not fully understanding my question.

"I mean …" I struggled for an example. "Say that Joe really likes big parties, so he throws me a huge party for my birthday. But I don't like parties, so I don't throw one for Joe on his birthday. We would both be disappointed, right?" The rest of my small class tittered at my weak hypothetical. Fortunately, Mrs. Meier was able to catch my drift.

"Well," she replied. "I think it mostly relates to bigger things. No one wants to go hungry, so if you have a chance to feed someone that is starving, you should do so. No one wants to be cold, so you should go out of your way to help people who are homeless. I don't think Jesus was implying that everyone necessarily wants the same exact things out of life."

She then changed topics, but I still wasn't satisfied with her explanation. Why make a rule that didn't apply to *everything*, especially without explaining *when* the rule should be applied? And so, after that class I did the sacrilegious: I mentally rewrote scripture. Unsatisfied with the existing version, I vowed to follow an *improved* directive: *Do unto others as they would <u>like</u> to be treated.* This revised version adequately addressed the lame example I had given in class, but it carried its own set of baggage. Specifically, it required everyone to inherently realize what others wanted. *Maybe that's why Jesus dumbed it down?* I wondered at the time.

Still, I was determined to give my improved version of the Golden Rule a shot. I took to silently studying everyone in my life—parents, teachers, friends—to try to divine how *they* wanted me to treat them. So, when I came downstairs in the morning for breakfast, I made a point of brightly announcing "Good morning!" to my mother, who would happily respond in kind. I ignored my father—not out of malice, but because I knew he preferred not to be interrupted as he read the paper. Once at school, I developed the habit of asking my teacher, Mrs. Hemmingway, how her night was after realizing that she was lonely and eager for an opportunity—*any* opportunity—to discuss her life (which seemed to consist of an unappreciative husband and a trio of unruly dogs). By contrast, my gym teacher, Mr. Winters, responded harshly the one time I made a personal inquiry to him, and I thereafter vowed to keep things strictly professional between us.

I managed to maintain my empathetic nature for a few years, which was pretty good considering my short attention span. Unfortunately, my project to decode the subsurface feelings of others came to a swift end with the onslaught of puberty and, a few years later, the emotional toll of high school. I no longer had the luxury of spending energy trying to ascertain how to make others happy; my goals were reduced to basic self-survival. Further, any remnants of my old empathetic self were knocked out completely once I reached law school, where it was every man (or woman) for himself (or herself). And when I finally entered the workforce as a full-blown lawyer, I had evolved into something that little nine-year-old Davey Randall would have detested.

My point being that although I *had* the ability to empathize with others, it was something that I grew away from as I continued to develop as an attorney—and as an asshole. Changing into an asshole was sadly effortless. It was an easy river to float down, and I worried about how difficult it would be to swim back upstream.

John had asked me to reflect upon what he should do with his newfound Godhood. Initially, I was confused by this assignment. He presumably had access to the greatest minds and the deepest philosophers in the history of the world, not to mention future geniuses who have yet to be born. But he asked *me* to help him determine the reason for his existence. *Why?*

That was just one of the questions I wrestled with following my meeting with John at the top of the mountain. And so, I set out to do something I would have once considered implausible: I tried to empathize with God.

At first, I picked up a cheap black and white notebook from Staples to record my thoughts and take notes on the assignment John had given me. I scribbled a few casual reflections in it before being hit by a grandiose thought: I was memorializing my observations and impressions from meetings with *God*. Many throughout history sacrificed entire *lives* in an attempt to be closer to the Almighty, and yet, for me, the opportunity to literally *talk* to God had fallen in my lap. It even struck me, in one not-so-humble moment, that my writings could someday form the basis for a new part of the Bible. A $1.49 notebook seemed inadequate for such an undertaking, so I decided to splurge and purchased a classy journal made of faux-leather.

In the back pages of the journal, I tried to transcribe my two meetings with John, post-Godhood, as best as I could remember them. Our most recent meeting was relatively easy to detail with what I believed to be a fair degree of accuracy. But my initial meeting with John at the coffee shop proved more difficult to memorialize. Aside from the significant amount of time that had passed between that meeting and my journal writing, the other hurdle I faced was that I hadn't even appreciated the profundity of that meeting until *after* the fact. I summarized what I could remember about that exchange (including a description of my brief dance with omniscience, to the extent that any of those memories remained intact). There was a difference between those two meetings with John that I couldn't place—something profound. But it did not come to me, no matter how much I went back and reread my account of those two encounters.

The earlier sections of my journal were devoted to my attempt to solve the puzzle John had laid out for me. Each section tackled a different question or issue for me to reflect on. I labeled each topic as if it were a point heading for an appellate brief. Old habits die hard. And so, the very first page was headed with the same question I had been contemplating on my way up the mountain before I last spoke with John.

POINT I: WHY WAS JOHN CHOSEN TO BECOME GOD?

The act of John becoming God was too arbitrary, too absurd, for me to seriously entertain the possibility that he was randomly selected. There was something about John that made him up for the task, at least in the eyes of his predecessor or whatever appointed him.

How is John different from the rest of us? I wrote beneath that heading. He was always an odd duck, but there is no shortage of weirdos in the world. I tried to imagine what I would do if granted omnipotence and omniscience, and there was a lot. It was impossible to imagine *anyone* not taking full advantage of those types of powers upon becoming God. And yet, John had not. According to John, he did nothing of note (although there was an open question as to what he considered to be *not* of note).

Was that it? Was John selected because it was known he would do nothing?

I decided against it. If doing nothing was a virtue, why was John picked at all? Why have someone maintain the position of God only to sit idly by? It was a question that would continue to haunt me for some time. But, lacking any further insight into that topic, I jotted down: *John can demonstrate restraint.* After a moment of staring at that notation, I scribbled next to it: (*But does restraint necessarily mean doing <u>nothing</u>?*)

I had nothing to add to that area of inquiry. In fact, I didn't know if I would ever come up with a completely satisfactory answer to that question.

POINT II: WHY DOES JOHN HAVE TO SPEAK TO ME AT ALL?

John is omniscient and can see not only every thought that I ever had, but every thought that I would *ever* have. If I were ever to come up with a satisfactory answer to John's problem, shouldn't he already be aware of it?

Unlike my first question, I was eventually able to apply some logic and come up with at least half an answer to that apparent contradiction. One night, when I was curled up on the couch with Peaches, I jotted the following in my journal:

- John can see every aspect of the future;

- I would not have contemplated the purpose of John's existence if he had not spoken to me about that issue;

- John would not have had an occasion to hear my thoughts (present or future) on that issue unless he spoke with me about it (particularly given his apparent refusal to interfere with matters of free will);

- Only by speaking to me did John set me on this path.

It was a near-satisfactory answer, but it begged another question. Since John can see all aspects of the future, if I ever solved his riddle, he should already know it. At the bottom of that same page, I added:

Why is it necessary for John to speak to me again? Nothing I can tell him will ever surprise him.

It would be years before I added anything further to that page.

POINT III: WHY DOES JOHN HAVE TO SPEAK TO *ME*?

I emphasized the last word of that heading to make it clear that the question was a narcissistic one: *Why me?* Specifically, John had access to literally every mind that ever existed or would ever exist. John could easily grab Einstein, or Stephen Hawking, or JK Rowling, or another genius who wouldn't be born for centuries to have a chat about his conundrum. But he grabbed *me*. There was only one answer I could think of, which, again, told me nothing:

I knew John before he became God.

Why, if at all, was *that* significant? I didn't know. But it was the only thing that distinguished me from most everyone else who would ever walk upon this planet.

POINT IV: WHY DOES JOHN SEEM UNHAPPY WITH HIS GODHOOD?

John seemed genuinely pleased to see me during each of our meetings, but there was an underlying sadness about him. Perhaps not sadness—John seemed to have evolved beyond such a petty emotion. But he did communicate that his new existence was a bit unfulfilling.

Was that it? Perhaps it was just my own refusal to accept that being God could be unrewarding, but there seemed to be more to John's dissatisfaction than what he described.

A plausible theory struck me one snowy night while I lay restless in bed. I had been unable to sleep, partly because my mind was racing and partly because Peaches was hogging my pillow. I thought it unfair to move him when he looked so comfortable. Besides, he *was* there first.

While I stared at my ceiling, I mentally cycled through my catalog of John stories in the hope of obtaining a deeper understanding of what he had become. At some point, I almost dozed off when a dormant memory floated up to the surface.

It involved an associate in our group named Diane. I rarely thought of her, given her quiet nature and the fact that she only worked at our firm for about two years, early on in my career. Many partners in the firm managed to go through the entirety of Diane's tenure without ever even learning her name. She was as unremarkable as she was unobjectionable.

Diane's sole defining trait at the firm was her love of weed. Granted, she never came out and discussed this at work, but Diane somehow earned a reputation as the office stoner. I wasn't equipped to make that sort of diagnosis myself, but others who were more knowledgeable on the topic repeatedly confirmed this to me. At least for a time. Toward the end of her run at the firm, it became evident that Diane had given up smoking. The pieces fell together shortly thereafter when it also became obvious that Diane was pregnant. As she got closer and closer to her due date, Diane's cases were gradually reassigned to the other, less fertile members of our team to watch over while she was out on maternity leave. We all reluctantly accepted this bulk increase in work, not that we had any real choice in the matter.

Two weeks before her due date, Diane had nearly wrapped up all of the loose ends on her case list. The lone exception was an appellate brief she was drafting for a case that was scheduled to go to trial within the next six months. The appeal was a loser, but the client apparently wanted to force the issue, if only to use the appeal as leverage to negotiate a reasonable settlement. Diane, uncharacteristically, slaved over that brief for days, even though she was in a perfect position to pass it off to the poor associate tasked with babysitting that particular case (which so happened to be John).

The brief was due only a few days before Diane's due date. However, on the morning of the day that the brief had to be sent out, Diane didn't show up for work. A frantic call from her husband later that afternoon clarified that Diane had gone into early labor. John was in a tizzy.

"What should I do?" John asked Sal. "The brief hasn't gone out yet."

It was a sign of John's panic that he felt compelled to talk to Sal while he was blasting his music. John typically refused, as a matter of principle, to engage Sal while he was distracted.

Sal, who had been rocking out to *While My Guitar Gently Weeps* at max volume, shrugged.

"It's done, isn't it?" he asked loudly, not bothering to turn down the music. "Sign the damn thing and get it out. We're going to lose anyway, right?"

John wanted to protest, but he knew that was really the only option. So, even though he was not yet familiar with the case or the appeal, John blindly signed the damn thing and got it out.

Then a funny thing happened. The appeal turned out *not* to be a stinker after all. Stoner Diane, powered by whatever angels keep watch over pregnant women, managed to write a brief that convinced the Appellate Division: First Department to overturn nearly thirty years of precedent relating to the continuous representation doctrine, resulting in the case being dismissed on statute of limitations grounds a few short months before trial. It wasn't *Roe v. Wade*, but it was a huge decision in the realm of professional liability litigation. The New York Law Journal published the decision in its entirety, with a separate article explaining the ramifications of that decision (and acknowledging John's role as counsel of record).

And John got all of the credit for it. It drove him absolutely nuts.

The day the article came out, various partners popped into John's office to offer their congratulations. John repeatedly explained it was Diane's appeal, and that he had only signed the brief because of her early labor. By the end of the day, his nerves were completely frayed from deflecting credit.

"You're being too hard on yourself," I told him. "You wrote the reply, you argued it. You deserve a fair share of the credit."

But John shook his head.

"No. Did you read the decision? They almost quote verbatim what Diane wrote in her brief. My reply, my argument didn't change any minds. This was her win."

The following day, John contacted the clerk's office to see if the decision could be amended to reflect Diane's name, but he was told that since he was the attorney of record who signed the briefs, there were no grounds to add another attorney's name. He also called the New York Law Journal, but they, too, saw no reason to change their story given that John had signed the papers.

John did not give up. He sent around a firmwide email explaining that Diane had drafted the brief that served as the basis for the court's decision, and that he only signed it because she went into labor. That email was somewhat awkward, in that it was sent nearly a week after the decision was published and long after everyone at the firm had already forgotten about it. John also called Diane, nearing the end of her maternity leave, to apologize for usurping her credit. Diane, having bigger issues to contend with, told John not to worry about it. But he did. From that day forth, he steadfastly refused to sign another attorney's work product. If an attorney was out sick on the day one of their motions was due, John was known to drive to their house and drag them out of bed to sign the papers. He even did this for Todd on one occasion, much to Todd's annoyance. Even though there were not many lines John was unwilling to cross if a situation warranted it, that one became abundantly clear: John aggressively and furiously refused to infringe upon anyone else's credit.

That memory lingered as I was rudely awoken by Peaches walking across my throat to settle in on the opposite side of the bed. I groggily turned on my lamp and opened my journal, which had been resting on my nightstand. I flipped through the pages to find Point IV. Aside from the heading, the remainder of the page was blank.

I wrote two sentences directly below the words *WHY DOES JOHN SEEM UNHAPPY WITH HIS GODHOOD?*

The first was: *John doesn't understand how he obtained it.*

That sentence was followed by a double-stemmed arrow—a "therefore" in the language of mathematics—which connected it to three additional words:

It feels unearned.

·   ·   ·   ·   ·

There were two additional matters that weighed heavily on me in the months following my talk with John, although neither made it into my journal.

The first was Alex Bennett. It seemed wrong to trivialize his death by listing it in my notes as some sort of clue, but that didn't stop me from thinking about it. After I became aware that John had become God, I regularly read stories about death in the news. But even when I allowed myself to wonder why John would allow those negative occurrences to happen, I never *blamed* him for those tragedies. Yet, hearing him announce, in advance, that a child would die and acknowledging that he could prevent that death with no effort whatsoever—that was different. I understood, intellectually, that if he prevented that particular demise, there would be no reason he shouldn't stop *all* deaths. And I also accepted that John doing so would change the entire meaning of life. I knew John as a good, kind person, and I assumed those traits carried over into Godhood. It was impossible to think of him as a murderer; that ran contrary to everything I knew about him.

Still, none of that kept me from replaying the moments leading up to Alex's death over and over again.

The second matter that consumed my thoughts related to John's assertion that he had not done anything to materially change the world. That rang hollow to me. John, through his conversations with me, *had* touched the world. I was on a different path than the one I would have followed but for his interference. If I were in a story that was writing itself, John had diverted the narrative the moment he invited me to grab that cup of coffee with him.

But John didn't state that he left the story untouched. He merely said that he had not done anything to "materially alter" the future, the implication being that even after his talks with me, *I* would not do anything to *materially* alter the world. It was a tough position to argue against, given that my life had become a repetitious pattern of hiking and reading in solitude with my overachieving cat. Even after seeing the expanse of the universe and speaking with God on multiple occasions, I had not done anything to even hint that I could be an agent of change.

At least, not yet.

chapter eleven

Not many towns in America with five-figure populations have managed to become household names, but Woodstock is one of them. Made famous by the 1969 Woodstock Music and Arts Fair, which ironically took place nearly sixty miles away in the town of Bethel, Woodstock is a town familiar to pretty much every child in America by the time they reach high school. Woodstock sits approximately two hours north of New York City, making it an easy day trip for the millions who live in the metropolitan area, as well as the millions more residing in the suburbs of Long Island, New Jersey, Connecticut, and Westchester County. The "town" area of Woodstock is quite small, consisting of one main strip (Tinker Street) and its several offshoots.

Given the foregoing, it was not at all uncommon for me to run into someone from my old life on those occasions that I ventured down Tinker Street with Peaches. Those were usually non-events since I was quite skilled at slinking away, undetected, before that damning moment of eye contact. But even when my ninja-like ability to avoid unwanted social interactions failed me, those conversations never lasted long. I knew how to prematurely kill small talk with my arsenal of awkward silences and body language that not-so-subtly begged for a swift end to the exchange of pleasantries. But on one occasion, the arrival of a remnant from my past had a feeling of serendipity about it, and I chose not to run from it.

It was early March, a little over three months after my last conversation with John. My savings had not yet depleted, but they had gotten low enough to where I had at least mild concerns about sustaining myself long-term. And beyond that, my routine of journal writing, hiking, and reading was no longer enough, in and of itself, to satisfy me. I was starting to feel restless.

On that particular Sunday, I stopped by the vegan café in town after my morning hike to pick up an order I had placed. I was never sure how the restaurant would react to my bringing a cat inside, and I was too shy to ask, so I left Peaches outside just to be safe. He usually didn't have any trouble attracting a family to play with him while he waited.

In the restaurant, I headed to the counter to ask for the order of spaghetti and wheatballs that I had called in. A waitress apologized and explained that it wasn't quite ready. I glanced out the front window and saw two high school girls gleefully rubbing Peaches' belly on the patch of grass in front of the restaurant. I shrugged and sat down to wait at one end of the counter.

The counter wasn't long—it only fit three stools. A bearded man sat by himself at the other end, two seats down, staring into his bottle of beer. It was a somewhat unusual sight. Although the café served beer, it wasn't a "bar" in any sense of the word. I figured that most of the patrons who ordered a beer did so with a meal and didn't just pound drinks at the counter (let alone in the middle of the afternoon).

I glanced at the man, who looked familiar. After a moment, I placed him.

"Excuse me, but are you John Manta's old landlord?"

The man looked at me with no hint of recognition.

"Yeah, man," he said in the same singsong voice I recalled from our last meeting. He turned back to his beer.

"Your name is Tim, right?" I pressed. "We met before. I'm John's friend. You let me into his apartment." Tim's eyebrows scrunched in confusion. "You let me take his cat?" I added tentatively.

It was unclear if Tim remembered me—he *had* been drinking a lot that night—but if not, he decided to at least fake it.

"Oh, hey, man," he said casually, nodding at me. "I remember you. Your name is … Xavier, right?"

"No, it's Dave." *Xavier?* I wondered.

"Oh, right, right." He took a long drink from his bottle.

"So what brings you up here?" I asked. Tim rolled his eyes.

"Friggin' … the wife wanted to come up here with the kids, so here we are."

I glanced around the restaurant. I didn't see any sign of his wife or kids. Tim noticed my puzzled look.

"Oh, they're out buying tie-dye t-shirts or some other hippie shit. I'm just killing time waiting for them." Tim paused. "You know, there's not really a lot of good bars in this town."

"Yeah, sorry about that," I responded drily. Tim missed my sarcasm and shrugged.

"It's cool." He took another sip of his beer. "You're friends with John, right? Did they ever find that guy?"

"No," I replied. "They didn't." I put a slight emphasis on "they." It made it feel less like a lie.

Tim shrugged again.

"Too bad; he was a good guy. You were a lawyer with him?" I sensed Tim was finally starting to remember our first meeting, at least a bit.

"I used to be. But I'm not an attorney anymore."

Tim downed the remainder of his beer and gestured to the waitress for a new one.

"Founders All Day IPA. So good," he murmured, staring reverently at his empty bottle. "It's a sweet find for a non-bar like this." Abruptly, he remembered that I was still there. "Not an attorney, huh? What are you doing now?"

That was an uncomfortable question, so to stall, I gestured for the waitress to bring a Founders for me as well. She quickly plopped a second bottle on the counter, which I tasted. Tim was right: it *was* a solid beer.

"I'm not really doing anything now," I finally said. "I knew I didn't want to be an attorney anymore, but I'm still not clear on what to do next. I'd like to do something that makes a difference—or, at least, could *potentially* make a difference."

Tim angled his bottle toward me. Once I realized what he was up to, I awkwardly clunked my own against it.

"Cheers to that, man," Tim said. "That's what I was thinking when I became a teacher." Tim took a long swig of his beer and belched. "I'm friggin' awesome at it," he added.

Teacher. The word struck a chord in me. John had told me that I had the potential to help others attain meaningful moments, and teaching seemed like an ideal vehicle for pursuing that goal. Did I have what it took to be a good one? Thinking back to my childhood, the one common denominator separating those teachers who failed their students from those who succeeded seemed to be the amount of effort they put in. *I can control that much, at least*, I thought.

"You know, I've thought about becoming a teacher," I told Tim. I didn't mention that I had only started thinking about it ten seconds earlier.

"Yeah?" Tim asked. "Any particular subject?"

Tim was peppering me with questions faster than I could plan my new career. But it didn't take me long to provide a truthful answer.

"I think elementary school is where I'd like to end up." Kids tend to grow more rigid as they get older, I figured. I imagined younger children to be more malleable. Whatever wisdom I had earned over the course of a life that was predominantly lived poorly, I had a hunch that it would be more readily received by students who did not yet have to contend with puberty.

"Oh, man!" Tim slapped his forehead. "Do you live up here?" At my curt nod, he said, "I have a cousin, Ed, who works about a half hour from here! Ed Gallagher. He's a principal at Pinewood Elementary. You should totally go talk to him!"

I *nearly* rejected the offer out of habit, but then I paused. It *was* a possible direction, which was something a directionless person, such as I was at the time, should cherish. Moreover, whenever leads just happened to fall in my lap, I always harbored a deep suspicion that they were somehow steered by John, whatever he claimed about not interfering in our world. I did not lightly ignore such moments.

"Should I give him a call?" I asked Tim.

Tim waved me off. "Nah, he's a chill guy. Just swing by and say you want to talk to him. I'll give him a head's up that you're coming—the dude friggin' loves me."

At that moment, the waitress brought my bagged lunch to go. I paid for it, as well as my impromptu beer. After a moment's thought, I also paid Tim's tab, and I was only mildly surprised to find he was already five beers in. I surmised that the odds of him remembering to call his cousin on my behalf would be slightly improved if I left him on a generous note.

"Thanks for the help. I'll check in with your cousin tomorrow."

"Yeah, man; no sweat. I'll text him later. And thanks for the beers." Tim downed his bottle. "Hey, you still watching that cat?"

I was caught off guard by the non sequitur. "Yeah. I am." I looked outside and saw a ten-year-old girl cradling Peaches as if he were a baby. *He's such a ham.*

"Cool, man. I'm glad. You know, I never saw John get worked up about anything, but he friggin' loved that cat. I'm sure he'd be glad knowing he's ok. Holy shit, did he love that cat!"

•　　　•　　　•　　　•　　　•

The next morning, I pulled up to Pinewood Elementary wearing a suit I had not touched in nearly two years—not since my last court appearance. It felt looser than I remembered, which was a pleasant reminder that daily hikes were a healthier alternative to sitting on my ass, pounding K-Cup coffees in a fluorescently lit office. I was nervous; it had been almost ten years since my last job interview.

The school was set off the road and surrounded by forest on three sides. As soon as I stepped out of my car, I felt far-removed from the rest of the world. It seemed an ideal environment for learning. And teaching. I wondered whether this type of peaceful school was atypical, and I struggled to recall any details relating to the elementary school I had attended as a child. All I could remember was that it was situated next to a wastewater treatment plant that seemed to serve as the impetus for a significant number of fire drills.

I entered the building and paused to watch a line of about twenty students, who looked to be in third grade, dutifully follow their teacher down the hallway. It looked like they might be heading to gym. I was pleasantly surprised at the diversity of the class and how behaved they all were. The lone exception was a heavyset child at the tail-end of the line who went out of his way to repeatedly step on the sneakers of the smaller student in front of him as they walked. It brought back painful memories of being bullied as a child, and even worse ones of situations where *I* had been the bully.

Once the students filed past me, I found the administration office and ducked inside. The two women occupying the office, who had been engrossed in conversation, both froze comically to stare at me as I entered.

"Hi, I'm here to see Mr. Gallagher?" My eyes darted back and forth between the two women, not knowing which one, if either, was in charge. They exchanged a silent glance, and, after a beat, the older of the two walked up to me and eyed my suit up and down, confused.

"Is he expecting you, Mr. …?" she asked hesitantly.

"Oh, I'm Dave Randall. And yes, I think he's expecting me." I gave it a 50-50 shot that Tim Hande had remembered the text he had promised to send on my behalf.

She gave me another searching look, and then, without a word, made her way to an open door at the far end of the office and stuck her head through. After a minute, she reemerged.

"Mr. Gallagher is not sure what this is about," she told me. Her friend tried to hide a smirk. Some people just seem to love watching men wearing suits be put in their place.

Tim, you idiot, I thought bitterly. *And after all those beers I bought you.*

"Oh, I'm sorry." I tried to negotiate a graceful exit. "A mutual friend was supposed to have set up a meeting for me. I can come back at another time."

The woman looked mildly amused at my deference.

"That won't be necessary. Mr. Gallagher says he has a few minutes to speak with you. Just head back that way." She nodded toward the door on the other side of the office.

"Oh, great! Thank you so much."

She wordlessly watched as I made my way around her desk to the back of the room.

Ed Gallagher's office was not terribly large, but it was neat. The one exception was the desk, which was covered in various papers in a pattern that presumably only Mr. Gallagher could decipher. I decided that was a plus in his column. Most of the biggest jerks I'd met during the course of my legal career maintained immaculate desks.

Mr. Gallagher was dressed respectably, wearing a pair of tan khakis with a red polo shirt—a more casual look than I was expecting. I'm also, under most circumstances, not a fan of mustaches, but Mr. Gallagher made the look work for him. He looked to be in his early fifties, perhaps fifteen to twenty years older than me. His face as he greeted me was kind, but a slight crevasse in his brow seemed to ask, *Who the hell are you and what are you doing here?*

"It's a pleasure to meet you," I said. "Thank you for taking the time to meet with me."

Mr. Gallagher politely shook my hand and gestured for me to take a seat in front of his desk. Sitting down across from me, he said, "Likewise. And you are …?"

Before I could respond, a cell phone on the desk vibrated. Mr. Gallagher picked it up and, after a quick glance at it, smiled ruefully.

"A text from my cousin saying a guy named Xavier was coming in this morning to talk to me about a job." He met my eye. "Are you Xavier?"

"No. Well, kind of. My name is Dave. I know your cousin Tim Hande, but he seems to think my name is Xavier for some reason."

Mr. Gallagher arched an eyebrow. "I can tell you two are really close," he remarked sarcastically. That put another plus in Mr. Gallagher's column. I enjoy a good wiseass.

"Well, he's my friend's former landlord, and I've only met him a few times. But I ran into him yesterday and mentioned that I was looking for a job, and he recommended reaching out to you." Mr. Gallagher continued to stare at me impassively. "He said you were a really cool guy and that I should just stop by informally," I added weakly.

Mr. Gallagher rolled his eyes. "Of course he did. Do you have a resume?"

"Yes." I took a copy out of my briefcase and handed it across the desk. After reading it for a moment, Mr. Gallagher's eyes shot back up.

"You are aware, Mr. Randall, that this is not a law firm?"

"Yes," I replied, feeling absurd. "But I am interested in making a career shift and becoming a teacher, preferably at the elementary level. I was hoping you might be able to help me. Or at least maybe point me in the right direction."

Mr. Gallagher closed his eyes, deep in thought.

"If you don't mind my asking," he said, "what prompted you to give up being an attorney? I'm sure you made much more than what any of our teachers are making here. Hell, I'm sure you even made more than what *I'm* making now. The summers off aren't worth *that* big of a pay cut."

I instinctively trusted this man who I had just met and decided to be as honest with him as I could. I briefly summarized the events that had led to my abandonment of the practice of law and moving up to Woodstock, carefully omitting all parts of my story that would make me come off as a lunatic. So, although I did not mention John or his newfound status as a deity, I alluded to developing a greater appreciation for life and a need to do something more important than litigating on behalf of insurance companies and their insureds.

"I would just like to do something where I can make a difference," I concluded. "I made a lot of thoughtless decisions in my life that brought me to a place where, well, I wasn't happy with who I had become. And I'd like to try to help kids avoid some of the mistakes I made, and I feel that teaching would put me in a position to do so."

I didn't know if my speech moved Mr. Gallagher, but I felt better after vocalizing it. It was refreshing to advocate for something I actually believed; a large chunk of my legal career was dedicated to spinning various lines of crap while struggling to maintain an earnest face. It was a strange but rewarding feeling, articulating a position without quickly feeling a need to shower.

Throughout my story, Mr. Gallagher had maintained steady eye contact with me and listened thoughtfully. He did not interrupt me once, and he waited a few moments after I finished before commenting himself.

"Do you want to guess why I became an educator?" he finally asked. I was hoping it was rhetorical, but, after an awkward silence, I realized he wanted me to throw out a theory.

"To help children?" I ventured lamely.

Mr. Gallagher chuckled and reached for a framed photo on his desk. He spun it around to face me, and I saw it was his wedding photo. It looked to be around twenty-five years old. I noticed that Mr. Gallagher had maintained his mustache even back then.

"Nope. It was for her." He tapped on his wife's face—an impressive feat considering that he was holding the photo away from himself. She was very pretty in a "girl next door" kind of way. Her eyes revealed a kind-hearted nature, the kind of woman who would be willing to put up with a mustache for decades. "I had started talking to her in undergrad, and I didn't have any plans as to what I was going to study myself. After I got wind that Liz was planning to major in education, I coincidentally decided that I, too, would become an education major."

He paused and smiled to himself.

"And a few years later, I found myself with a teaching degree … and a wife. And trust me: I was much more excited about the wife than I was about becoming a teacher."

I grinned along at the story, although I wasn't sure where it was leading.

"This is my point: I didn't have any grandiose thoughts of transforming children for the better when I came into this field. My sole motivation was to get a particular girl, which worked out for me. But once I started teaching, there were students that I connected with, and others that I could not reach, despite my best efforts. And I think that because I came in without any real preconceptions, I managed to focus on the lives I was able to steer, however slightly, down a better path without experiencing a sense of failure as to all the students I couldn't help. But I worked with colleagues who seemed to envision brightening every single life they touched, and those were the ones who were more susceptible to burning out once their success rate dipped below one hundred percent."

"Your motivations for becoming a teacher aren't wrong," he said. "And I don't believe you should temper your expectations for what you can accomplish. Swing for the fences—why not? But I suspect that, if you pursue this career, you will find that opportunities to improve young lives are often impeded by bureaucratic nonsense, or that you'll simply be faced with students that you can't connect with for whatever reason. That should not turn you off. Because when opportunities to make a positive impact *do* present themselves, however rare they may be, the good teachers are the ones who seize them."

I took his message to heart. My experience in entering the practice of law had been tainted by my own unrealistic expectations. But that had been a completely alien world to me. By contrast, I had spent over a dozen years of my early life exposed to teachers; I felt adequately equipped to recognize the impact a great one could have on students.

"Fair enough," I told Mr. Gallagher. He nodded and smiled a bit sadly.

"Anyway, lectures aside, I have good news and bad news for you," Mr. Gallagher continued. "The bad news is that I can't hire you, even if I had any openings. You're going to need some further education and licensing to be eligible to teach at the elementary school level."

I nodded, disappointed but unsurprised.

"But the good news," he added, "is that there are programs for people like you—professionals looking to change fields into the realm of education—that will allow you to become certified to teach without starting from scratch. Teach for America is one I can think of offhand …"

He turned to his computer and typed away. It took some time as his typing style was hunt and peck. Eventually, a printer next to his computer spurted to life. Mr. Gallagher handed me the print job, which, I realized at first glance, was literature on Teach for America.

"I believe you'd have to commit to two years," he said while I flipped through what he had handed me. "And they'd assign you to a low-income area that is in need of good teachers. But they would help you get whatever certifications you need, and you'd be able to teach—and get paid—right away. Anyway, it's just a thought."

He shrugged, in a *that's-all-I-got-for-you* kind of way. I continued to sit there, somewhat uncomfortably, until I realized that that was the end of my impromptu interview. I stood up and extended my hand, which Mr. Gallagher enthusiastically shook.

"Thank you for all of your help," I told him. "I really appreciate it. And I'm sorry for just barging in like this. It was just—I was looking for information online, and everything I saw seemed so contradictory. When your cousin mentioned speaking to you, I jumped at the chance to talk to someone knowledgeable in person." I didn't add that the extent of my online research was spending a half hour that morning conducting Google searches on "how to become a teacher."

Mr. Gallagher waved off my apologies.

"Don't worry about it. We have, fortunately, a school here that pretty much runs itself. I welcome any good-natured distraction that makes its way to my desk."

As I walked to the door, Mr. Gallagher called after me.

"And for what it's worth, I appreciate your motivation for wanting to become a teacher, especially when you were already so far along in a completely different career. I would be very interested to hear how things develop for you."

He wrote down his email address and phone number on a scrap of paper, which I took and stuffed into my pants pocket. I assured Mr. Gallagher that I would keep him updated on how my new career developed.

And so, I did.

chapter twelve

When I arrived home early in the afternoon following my meeting with Ed Gallagher, I flipped idly through the materials on Teach for America that he had printed for me. I was on the fence whether it was worth pursuing. Hell, I wasn't even sure if *teaching* was the right path for me. I was stuck in a paradox I had encountered often following my brush with omniscience. On the one hand, I had seen firsthand that life was too short to waste any time on unworthy ventures. On the other, I also knew life was also too short to waste time deciding what was or was not an "unworthy venture."

A page in my Teach for America packet detailed the application process. I noticed that there were five deadlines to apply throughout the year, starting in September and running through early March. After that, applicants had to wait until the following year for the cycle to start up again. The March deadline jumped out at me, but I couldn't place its significance. I mentally ran through the list of my relatives' birthdays to see if there was a match, but I came up dry. But then, it dawned on me that the reason that particular deadline was tickling my brain was because *today* was that day. Meaning that if I didn't apply within the next few hours, I would have to wait another six months to do so.

I let out a low, exasperated moan. Peaches, who had been sleeping next to me on the couch, lifted his head to glare at me with groggy eyes, only to lower it after deciding he wasn't that interested in what I was up to. After allowing myself a minute to wallow in a pool of indecision, I thought to myself: *Screw it. I'm going for it.*

Still in my "interview" suit, I hurried to the car and made the short drive to the public library. Fortunately, there were several unused computers available. After signing in, I quickly navigated to the page for Teach for America's online applications. From there, it was a race against time: could I complete my application and the accompanying essays before the library closed at 5:00 p.m.? The answer, as it turned out, was *barely*. My essays, frantically drafted, were passable, although I knew they would not win me any awards. My focus in crafting those quick blurbs was more on proper grammar (and avoiding typos) than substance. I couldn't imagine anyone wanting an elementary school teacher who mixed up *to, too,* and *two.*

Shortly after 5:00, I staggered out of the library, dazed and a bit unclear as to the next step in the application process. When I got home and revisited Mr. Gallagher's print-outs, I was surprised to see that according to the schedule, I should be contacted for an interview within the next several weeks. To my shock, that actually happened, and my interview took place later that month. From there, the process continued to fly along, as I was contacted in mid-April and asked if I'd be interested in teaching a fourth-grade class downstate in the Bronx. I was given time to decide, but I didn't need it—I said yes immediately. And thus, in a span of less than two months, I became a teacher.

Kind of.

I also learned that I was expected (*i.e.*, required) to attend a six-week training course over the summer in New York City. I knew it would be a hellish commute to and from the training, but I figured I could put up with anything for a mere month and a half. As such, once that training started, I woke up at 4:00 a.m. each morning, and by the end of that first week, I was already wondering whether getting up before the sun did was something to which I would ever become accustomed. Before leaving each morning, I gave Peaches the option of spending the day inside the house or being put out. Peaches, it turned out, had an uncanny ability to predict the weather, as the handful of days he elected to stay outside ended up being the best of the season.

The training was intensive, but I enjoyed spending time learning about a field I thought I had understood but clearly didn't. I was exhausted at the end of each daily session, but, even so, I mustered up the energy every day to make the two-hour-plus commute home, solely because I had to. I adopted a habit of picking up a bite to eat on the long drive back, which allowed me to go to bed upon arriving at home. It was usually dark by that point, and I regretted losing a summer of hiking with Peaches, although we tried to make up for it on weekends.

Even though spare minutes were a rare commodity during that time, I stayed true to my word and remained in touch with Mr. Gallagher. At first my emails were short and tentative, since I was not really sure how interested in my career Mr. Gallagher truly was. It was a symptom of my low self-esteem that I assumed he really had *no* interest but only gave me his email address out of a sense of politeness. Thus, my initial email to him was brief and to the point: *I was accepted into the Teach for America program. Thank you again for all your help.*

But Mr. Gallagher always responded to my emails, regardless of how short they were, with enthusiasm and with a bevy of questions that necessitated a longer response from me. Over time, my guardedness dissolved and my correspondence gradually morphed into memoirs that chronicled my transition into the education field. I always looked for a sign that I was annoying Mr. Gallagher—an overly long delay in responding to an email, or a curt acknowledgment—but it never came. As cynical as I was, I came to accept that Mr. Gallagher *enjoyed* hearing from me.

It felt nice.

And then September rolled around, and I was finally expected to *teach*. I'm not sure what I had been expecting, but whatever it was, it was substantially easier than the reality I faced. That first week was a disaster. I could feel, as if it were a physical reaction, that class of thirty students lose more and more respect for me as I floundered to create a compelling lesson, and I feared that even if I eventually managed to get my act together, it would be too late to win them back. I didn't know what I was doing wrong, but each passing day, the growing disconnect between me and my students became harder to ignore.

Toward the end of that initial week, while teaching a lesson on multiplication, I posed a basic math problem to the class. I was answered with thirty bored stares, and I nearly burst into tears.

"Anyone?" I pleaded. The defeat must have registered on my face, because a student—one of the bolder boys named Marques—seemed to take pity and raised his hand. I eagerly pointed toward him.

"Mr. Randall? Why do you talk to us like we're in kindergarten?" The others in the class tittered, and I knew instantly that however much I wanted to deny the accusation, he had touched upon a valid criticism.

"Have I been doing that?" I asked aloud. Almost all of the students nodded, and a handful giggled again. I was flabbergasted; I had no idea I was talking down to them like that. *Was I unknowingly doing baby talk?* It was mortifying. I didn't know what to say. I felt like a complete horse's ass.

"I'm sorry," I said. "I did not realize I was doing that." Marques shrugged, and I knew I had to say more.

"Look. Teaching is new to me. I'm trying to learn as much as you guys are. So if I'm doing something ... odd ... please feel free to call me out on it, as respectfully as you can, at least. And in the meantime, I'll try to talk to you all like you're adults."

"Does that mean we can call you David?" one girl called out. Her classmates laughed, as did I.

"No!" I said firmly, smiling. I wouldn't have minded if they did, but I had a hunch the school might take issue with that practice. "Let's stick with Mr. Randall for now." Everyone laughed again.

"But that goes both ways," I added quickly. "You can't leave me up here feeling like an idiot while everyone pretends they don't know the answer to a simple math problem. So will *someone* please answer it so we can move on to something more interesting?"

Amidst all the laughter, several hands went into the air, which was really all I cared about.

Things went relatively smoothly from that point on. I thought long and hard before each class about what types of lessons would have gotten through to me when I was a young student and which would have bored me to the point of counting ceiling tiles. Determined to do more than spend the day talking *at* the class, I began concluding math topics with team-based quiz games where the students' competitiveness managed to overcome any ingrained apathy toward numbers. I punctuated a history lesson about the American Revolution with selected songs from the *Hamilton* soundtrack (which, unfortunately, led to a phone call from an annoyed parent after I forgot, until it was too late, that Hercules Mulligan drops an F-bomb in *Yorktown*). In addition to assigning mandatory reading, I worked with each student to ascertain their personal interests so that I could help them track down books that they would be able to read simply for enjoyment. Even if I didn't manage to inspire every student to learn to the best of their ability, I was pleased with the dynamic I eventually crafted in the classroom.

Still, notwithstanding Mr. Gallagher's prior warning to me, I found myself wondering at times as to the impact I was having on those young lives. We had fun as a class, but I questioned the extent to which my efforts lasted beyond the end of the school day, let alone whether my lessons would maintain any weight once the school year came to an end. I came to realize that teaching was largely an act of faith in that there is rarely instant gratification, and the best I could hope for was to plant a seed or two that might grow into something worthwhile after I was long removed from the picture. It was a trust fall exercise, and it took significant willpower to stifle my natural cynicism long enough to take that plunge.

I hardly had any free time during my two years with Teach for America to obsess over John or the assignment he had entrusted to me. My days were spent teaching (or dealing with the brutal commute to and from the city), and my evenings were filled with college courses in furtherance of obtaining a master's degree and other certifications that would allow me to continue teaching even after my Teach for America commitment was completed. Peaches was fortunately able to keep himself largely entertained during this period and didn't seem to suffer at all from my limited availability. In any event, I *always* made time on weekends for the two of us to go on our hikes.

Toward the end of my run with Teach for America (at which point I was largely comfortable with my role as a teacher), the John-related questions that filled my journal began to reassert themselves and once again started to gnaw at me. One such topic included why John needed to speak with me again, even though he was aware of every thought I ever had or *would* ever have. It seemed pointless and illogical, no matter how many ways I tackled the issue. I wondered if I might be too close to the problem to see it clearly; it was plausible that I was overthinking the entire thing. Curious as to how children would view this scenario, I decided one lazy Friday afternoon in May to workshop the question with my class of fourth graders in the form of a riddle.

"Here's a story," I said to my class. I noticed a few students in the front were prepared to take notes, and I told them to put their pencils down. "This won't be on any test," I added. That admission quickly revealed itself to be a strategic error, as I immediately observed a few students in the back stop paying attention entirely. I chose to ignore them.

"Long ago, two children—a boy and a girl, who were brother and sister— lived in a land that was ruled by a wizard who could do *anything* and knew *everything*. He could travel through time, he could fly, he could see into the future. You name it, he could do it. Well, one day, the wizard kidnapped the boy, and when he did, he told the girl, 'I will come back in one year's time, and if you can tell me something I don't know, I will give you your brother back.' The girl thought long and hard over the course of that year, but she, like everyone else in that area, was aware of the wizard's infinite powers and knowledge."

A boy in the front of the class raised his hand.

"Yes, Blanyi?"

"Is the wizard God?"

"No," I replied adamantly. The last thing I needed was a parent complaining that I was teaching religion in a public school.

"But isn't God omnis …" Blanyi struggled with the word.

"It's not God," I insisted. "He's a wizard. With a long beard and everything."

"God has a beard …" Blanyi muttered.

"Not God!" I snapped. Blanyi shrugged, and I continued.

"Anyway, the girl thought long and hard about what she could possibly tell the wizard that would surprise him. But the wizard knew the thoughts of every person in her village, even thoughts they had not yet had. The wizard could recite the words of every book ever written, and even those of stories that had not yet been created. The wizard knew exactly how many grains of sand were on the beach near the girl's village, how many leaves were on all of the trees in the nearby forest, and even how many stars were in the universe."

I then turned it over to the class.

"Does anyone have any ideas for helping the girl get her brother back?" I asked. A number of hands shot up, but those tiny hands turned out to represent questions rather than answers.

"Can the wizard shoot out lasers from his eyes?"

"Yes."

"Can the wizard turn himself into a shark?"

"Yes."

"Can the wizard spin himself around really fast?"

"Uh, sure."

"Can the wizard turn himself into a bagel?" Laughter from around the class.

"I guess, if he wanted to." I started to fear that the conversation had derailed.

"Does the wizard know the answer to 1,128,948 times 4,328,223?"

"Yes."

"You said the wizard can read people's minds?" This question came from Chelsie, a tiny girl with large glasses sitting by the window.

"Yes." I started to point to another raised hand but paused when I saw Chelsie had a follow-up question.

"Even the girl's mind?" Chelsie pressed. I started to instinctively respond "yes," but I hesitated. I recalled a detail from my last meeting with John that had not been accounted for in the story I had crafted.

"Well, he *can* read her mind. But when he meets with her, he doesn't do so out of politeness." *If this wizard was so concerned about politeness,* I wondered, *why did he kidnap the boy in the first place?* I wished I had spent more time coming up with a tighter analogy to share with the class.

The class groaned and objected at my explanation, but not for the plot hole that had occurred to me. Rather, a number of students called out "no fair!" because I was "changing the rules" on them. Several started yelling out at the same time, but I could not make out those answers over all the noise. Once I managed to quiet everyone down, I called on Chelsie again.

"That's easy then!" Chelsie declared. "When the wizard shows up, she just has to tell him what she's thinking about at the time! If he's not reading her mind, it will be something that he doesn't know!" A few other students nodded their heads in agreement and whined that they hadn't been called on to solve the riddle.

I frowned, deep in thought as I tried to apply Chelsie's conclusion to my own scenario. If John spoke with me again and kept his promise to stay out of my head while we spoke, would that create the type of blind spot that Chelsie suggested? I continued to assume that John was privy to my thoughts at all times—past, present, and future—when he wasn't talking to me, but I had never really thought about what happened *while* he spoke to me.

I tried to dumb it down. If I were to think to myself at some point in the future *pickles are delicious,* John would already know it. But what if I had that same notion as he was speaking to me and John was honoring his commitment to not read my mind? Would he still know in advance that I would mentally give that positive review of pickles? If so, it seemed such would defeat the entire purpose of him staying out of my thoughts while we talked.

Something about my two meetings with John, after he became God, had nagged at me, but Chelsie's explanation illuminated what I had been missing. In my first meeting, when John was presumably privy to my thoughts, he seemed, in hindsight, downright inhuman with his all-knowing smile—like an actor going through the motions in a play he had already performed countless times. By contrast, in our second meeting, where John had agreed to "turn off" his ability to intrude on my thoughts, he had been incredulous at my question relating to Peaches' name. He had winced at sensitive questions I asked him. Although he didn't come out and say it, John had shown various signs, subtle as they were, of being surprised during our discussion. Small signals that seemed decidedly ungodlike.

I glanced at the clock; the school day was nearly over.

"I think Chelsie solved the riddle," I announced. Chelsie beamed, and others muttered amongst themselves about the puzzle being "cheap" and "not fair."

"Mr. Randall," Blanyi called out with his hand raised. I gave him a quick nod. "That was a pretty terrible story."

"I know," I admitted. *Whatever.* "Have a great weekend, everyone." The bell then rang as if on cue.

When I got home that afternoon, I found my journal and opened it to Point II ("Why does John have to speak with me at all?"). The page was mostly blank, leaving plenty of room to add a few notes:

If John inserting himself into "the story" to talk to me changes the narrative, and he stays out of my mind while we talk, he might not be able to see those thoughts (whatever they may end up being) in advance. There should be a narrow window for me to surprise him.

I knew that even if this revelation was meaningful (a highly questionable assumption), it would not be unknown to John. I wasn't deluding myself; there was no way for me to pull one over on God. I continued writing.

Of course, that window will only exist if John allows it. The fact that I reached this conclusion means that John is aware (and had been aware) that I would do so. But although it is impossible for me to "trick" John, if he adheres to his own rules, then the next time he talks to me I should theoretically be in a position to tell him something that could change his mind about his role in the universe.

I paused again, wondering what that "something" could be. Logically, I assumed it was impossible for me to figure that out before I next spoke with John, since he would then be aware of it in advance. Eyes closed, I rubbed at my temples as I felt a headache coming on. Trying to get my head around Godhood and the seemingly circular logic that went with it was exhausting.

I added a few more lines at the end of that entry: *If I could figure out something to say in advance of our next conversation that would change John's mind, he would already be aware of it and there would be no need for us to talk at all. Thus, the only possible way to change John's mind regarding what to do with his Godhood, assuming he adheres to his promise not to listen in on my thoughts, is to figure out something groundbreaking while we are in the midst of talking.*

Pounding headache aside, I was relatively satisfied with this analysis, and I vowed to be extremely accommodating to Chelsie the next time I graded one of her tests. But in reviewing my notes, I realized that the answer I had reached unavoidably led to a *new* question, one I could not answer, which I scribbled at the bottom of the page:

How, exactly, does one prepare for an epiphany?

•   •   •   •   •

Toward the end of my two-year commitment to Teach for America, I received an email from Mr. Gallagher describing how several of the teachers at his school were set to retire that summer. He casually mentioned that he had to get to work on filling those vacancies and wondered if I would have any interest in applying. It took me no time to express that I *was* interested in the position. I loved teaching in the Bronx; the experience had exceeded all of my expectations. Still, the commute, which touched upon two hours each way, had been wearing me down, and I longed to settle down in the Hudson Valley region of New York. Fortunately, thanks to my relationship with Ed Gallagher, it didn't take me long to lock down a position as the newest fourth grade teacher at Pinewood Elementary.

I reflected often that summer before starting my new job on the progress I had made in the past several years. I had found a career that gave me a sense of purpose and meaning—at least as much purpose and meaning as a speck in the universe like me might be expected to attain. It was easy for me to paint a satisfying picture of the rest of my life: teaching during the day, going for walks with Peaches in the evenings and on weekends, and reading in bed until I fell asleep. It wasn't the type of thrilling existence anyone would feel compelled to make a movie about, but I was prepared to embrace it with open arms. I figured my journey was complete, and that the mundane but rewarding life I had crafted was my reward.

These dreams of a fulfilling, albeit minimalist, existence now strike me, with the gift of hindsight, as being incredibly naive. But you have to keep in mind: this was all before I met Abby.

chapter thirteen

Teaching is a profession that most people probably think they understand. After all, pretty much everyone has spent a dozen or so years, early in life, watching teachers do their thing. Refresher courses on the subject are also quite easy to come by thanks to incessant *Saved by the Bell* reruns. But even after I had been a teacher for several years, there still remained plenty left to surprise me about the profession. And one of those surprises was that most young teachers like to drink. A lot.

Almost immediately after I started work at Pinewood Elementary, colleagues would grab me on a Thursday to ask if I was going to happy hour. I always politely declined, offering one lame excuse after another, only to go home, take a short hike with Peaches, make a quick dinner, and read until I fell asleep. The stories I would hear on Fridays about those happy hours tended to shock me: stories of the art teacher vomiting after one too many shots, make out sessions between oddly paired coworkers, and shouting matches that were quickly forgiven or forgotten by the next morning. It was fun to hear the gossip on Fridays, but I didn't feel like I was missing out by not being there to witness the magic firsthand.

One Thursday in November, about two-and-a-half months after I started working at Pinewood, another teacher named Paul grabbed me in the hallway at the outset of one of my break periods. Paul was only a few years out of college and seemed to be in denial about it.

"'Sup, bro?" It was clear from his tone it wasn't a real question, so I just nodded politely.

"You coming out tonight?"

I was caught off balance, as I had never, to my recollection, really spoken with Paul. I was surprised by his invite, and I didn't have any of my usual deflections at hand. He pounced upon my non-response.

"It'll be a good time. You should come. We work with a fun group of people, but it's hard to tell in this setting." He gestured around him at the empty hallway. "I don't think I've seen you come out yet. It'll be fun."

Again, I hesitated. I had always written off Paul as an idiot, but I realized he was showing me his version of kindness. After my experience four years earlier where I had shared a consciousness with everyone alive (and more), it had become much more difficult for me to cling to my negative impressions of people. It was a touch bittersweet. I had become a softie at the age of thirty-six.

"Maybe I'll come out for a drink," I finally said.

Paul nodded his head in approval and extended a closed fist, which I reluctantly pounded. I tried not to wince at the explosion sound he made as he withdrew his hand with a flourish.

"You'll have a good time," Paul promised. "I'll find you after school and make sure you don't get lost on the way over."

Before I could respond, we were both distracted by a commotion at the far end of the hallway. Two fifth graders were fighting, although, after a moment, I realized it wasn't much of a "fight" at all. Matt Prince, a tiny bespectacled student who was closer in size to an average third-grader, was pinned to the ground by Patrick Conley, who was as large as he was mean. I generally wasn't afraid of ten-year-olds, but if there was one in the school who could manage to intimidate me, it was Pat. Pat wailed on Matt with a series of wild punches. Matt's mildly successful defense took the form of rolling up in the fetal position.

Paul, moving before I could fully register what was happening, sprinted down the hall and pulled Pat off of Matt. I snapped out of my trance and followed a few steps behind and, upon arriving at the scene, helped Matt get to his feet. His glasses had broken in the scuffle, but aside from a few scratches on his face, he didn't look to be injured. Matt, in a daze, adjusted the broken glasses on his face and exhaled, and a waterfall of blood fell out of his nose.

"Dammit!" Paul snapped. Both students instinctively reacted to hearing a teacher curse and stared at Paul with wide eyes. Paul ignored them and instructed Matt to pinch his nose closed while holding his head back. As I stood there uselessly, Paul led Matt off toward the nurse's office.

"Take him to Gallagher!" Paul called over his shoulder. Turning around, I noticed Pat attempting to sneak away on his toes, as if he were a cartoon burglar. I rolled my eyes and caught up to him in a few long strides. Pat froze when he felt my hand on his shoulder.

"Mr. Conley. Care to take a walk with me?" I asked, trying to sound cooler than I was.

"No," he answered sullenly. *Tough shit*, I thought, but since I couldn't think of an appropriate verbal rejoinder, I didn't respond.

I led Pat to the administrator's office adjacent to Mr. Gallagher's office, and I was surprised to find that the door to the principal's office was closed. I could hear faint shouting through the door, although it didn't seem to be Mr. Gallagher doing any of the yelling.

"He's in with some parents right now," one of the office assistants explained, glancing curiously at Pat sulking beside me.

"I have a ruffian here to drop off." I nodded toward Pat, eager to be relieved of my burden.

"Well, you'll just have to wait," she replied. "I don't know how long he'll be."

I sighed and glared down at Pat.

"You know, this is supposed to be my break period," I said. I tried to keep any hint of a whine out of my voice. Pat shrugged, unsympathetic.

There were several open seats along the wall near the door in the office, but I opted to lead Pat back out to the hallway. I took a seat on a bench in front of opaque glass windows that separated the hall from the administrator's office. At a curt gesture from me, Pat sat at the other end of the bench, leaving a large gap between us. We both stared straight ahead in silence, each of us reflecting on the various injustices that led us to that shared moment of misery. The wall opposite from where we sat featured a mural painted by a class of third-graders depicting various animals in a desert landscape. Stylistic differences between the animals suggested that each student in the class had been tasked with a different creature. One student, apparently aware of his or her lack of artistic talent, tackled the relatively easy-to-paint snake, yet still managed to make it barely recognizable. Another, more ambitious student did quite a nice job with a camel, even after increasing the degree of difficulty by opting for two humps. My favorite animal, by far was a giant cheetah, even though it didn't quite fit the overall theme of the project. I didn't judge. If I had the ability to paint cheetahs with that level of skill,

I would also make a point of shoehorning one into any piece of art I was tasked with creating.

Pat and I continued to sit in silence. I wondered how long it would take for Mr. Gallagher to end his meeting so that I could divest myself of that surly kid and resume my break. I glanced sidelong at Pat, who caught my look and seized it as an opportunity to claim his innocence.

"That actually wasn't my fault, if you even care." He folded his arms defiantly.

I shrugged. "As a general rule, when you're twice the size of someone, and you're caught straddling and punching them, it's hard to play the martyr card." I wasn't sure if Pat understood, and I didn't really care, but he resumed staring sullenly at the exaggerated desert landscape in front of us. I dutifully rejoined him, casting my eyes over the wall. I noticed a fat bird, perhaps an owl, inexplicably perched atop a cactus. It had an eerily human-looking face that reminded me a bit of my old colleague, Todd.

Todd. I wondered what he was up to. It was hard to imagine him leaving the practice of law. *Perhaps he had a relative in the field that took him in?* The legal community can seem very small at times, and gossip about misbehaving attorneys tends to spread like wildfire. It certainly would have been hard for Todd to join another firm without some sort of "in." I tried to summon sympathy for him but couldn't. Like John had said, Todd was just a victim of his own poor decisions.

But still, John had also indicated that a lot of the "bad" in Todd derived from factors outside of his control. Being bullied as a child, rough parents … I knew Todd had not been a slave to that trajectory any more than anyone is bound to their circumstances in life, but it did put him at a decided disadvantage.

I stole another glance at Pat at the far side of the bench. I had once, for a moment, shared every experience he ever had or would ever have. Closing my eyes, I tried to summon a single memory that would give me any insight into why a boy like him would feel the need to pummel one of the most harmless kids in school. But any remembrances in that regard lurked just beyond my reach and continued to elude me.

I decided I would have to fly blind.

"When I was a kid," I started, and Pat jumped in surprise. I gave him a second to collect himself and began again. "When I was a kid, I was tall for my age. I think I was something like 5'10" in sixth grade and all of 130 pounds. Granted, I only grew another two inches or so after that, but, for a while, I was a certified bean pole. I was one of the first kids in my class to be hit with puberty, so I also had a sad little mustache for a while—at least until it occurred to me that I needed to start shaving."

"Is this going to be a lecture?" Pat interrupted. "I don't want to talk to you."

"You don't have to talk," I replied in an indifferent tone. "You just have to listen. Or you can sit there and not listen. I'm really not asking you to do anything here." I met Pat's eyes and held the look. While engaged in my staring contest with a child, I heard the *clip clop* of heels making their way down the hall toward us. I continued to gaze calmly at Pat as a woman passed us in my periphery and entered the administrator's office. Only after the door to the office closed again did I continue.

"Sixth grade was rough after leaving elementary school. Yeah, elementary school was easy. It was fun. Kids are nice there." I paused, and my eyes flicked meaningfully toward Pat. "Usually," I added. Pat shifted uncomfortably, and I assumed that he was still listening to me. "But when I got to middle school, those seventh and eighth graders were *mean*. They were just looking for easy targets. And what better target was there than a tall skinny kid whose mustachioed face peeked out of every crowd he was in?" Pat chuckled at the image. I wish I could say it didn't hurt my feelings.

"I was awkward, too. Years later, I would grow into my body and become a decent athlete, but then? I was constantly tripping on stairs or just over my own clown feet. The older kids loved to knock books out of my hands in between classes and kick them around the hall while I scrambled to pick them up. I remember that happening one afternoon in front of our gym teacher. He just looked at me in disgust and said that I needed to learn to stand up for myself before going back into his office. Another time, on Halloween, I made the mistake of going to school in an Elvis costume, with fake sideburns and everything. A monster eighth grader, who I am convinced was held back at some point—he looked like he belonged in high school—this kid punched me in the stomach before classes started and knocked the wind out of me. After I slumped to the floor, he ripped off my wig and sideburns. Later that day, I saw him in the main hallway wearing them himself, calling out, 'Look at me! I'm Elvis! I'm Elvis!'

"Yeah … sixth grade was a really crappy year for me."

Pat was torn. On the one hand, I could tell he *really* had his heart set on ignoring me. But on the other, it's not often a student gets to hear a teacher talk about what a loser he was as a kid. Even though he refused to look at me, it was clear that Pat was hanging on to every word I was saying.

"I was pretty miserable back in those days. One of the few bright spots for me was lunch. It was all sixth graders in there—kids I had known since kindergarten. I was part of a group of four friends that sat together. The leader of our pack was this guy named Frank, but we called him Frankie back then. Frankie kind of took charge of us. He really did have natural leadership skills, to his credit. But he also had a mean streak. The rest of us went along with it, I think mostly just to avoid getting on his bad side and ending up in his crosshairs.

"Anyway, there was another lunch table that was filled with students from our school's LIC program. That stood for 'Learning Intervention Center,' or something like that, but the schoolwide joke back then was that it meant 'Learning Is Complicated.' They were the more challenged students, and Frankie *loved* to torment them. He'd eat only half his lunch just to have ammo to throw at that table when no teachers were looking. The rest of us eventually caved in and followed Frankie's lead, like we always did. We'd spend time at lunch writing cruel parody songs about those LIC kids, and other tables would laugh as we sang them loudly. I don't even know if the LIC table fully appreciated what was going on, and I felt bad about what we were doing, for obvious reasons. But the scary part? I also felt good. It felt nice to be the hunter instead of the hunted for at least one period of the day.

"One Friday after school, a group of us were at the field behind the school throwing a baseball around. All of a sudden, one of those LIC kids—I think his name was Chris—came out of nowhere on a bike and rode through the middle of us." I don't know why I pretended in that moment to have forgotten the boy's name. It was Chris Reyes. "He was obviously slow, but Chris's real claim to fame related to his inability to control his snot: he was constantly dripping everywhere. And on this occasion, where he randomly showed up amongst us on a bike, he had a long train of snot flying behind him like it was a banner. It was utterly disgusting. Some of us laughed, and others of us wanted to vomit. But Frankie was there, and he got angry.

"Chris rode through the lot of us once without incident, but he seemed to enjoy the reaction that his arrival had caused. So he circled back, snot streaming in the air, singing a song I couldn't recognize. He was surprisingly fast on his bike—too fast for any of us to catch. And Frankie knew it. So rather than face the indignity of trying, and failing, to chase him down, Frankie used the only ammo he had—his baseball glove—and flung it at Chris. And he missed, badly."

Pat, though silent, had initially seemed defensive, waiting for the story to be tied back to him so that he could deny its relevance. But as my tale meandered on without any moral, Pat began to relax a bit and simply listened.

"I made the mistake of laughing when Frankie missed," I continued. "Frankie glared at me right away, and I was scared—terrified, even—of ending up the target of his rage. I did the first thing I could think of to get the attention off of me. I shouted, 'This is how you do it!' and I flung my own glove at Chris as he came around for his third pass.

"The glove hit the front wheel of the bike and got caught up in the spokes. The bike lurched forward, and I remember Chris flying over the handlebars. It was like slow motion, watching him leave his bike and falling face-first into the ground. His face was a bloody mess when he got up. He even lost a tooth." I paused, feeling ill at the memory.

"What did you do?" Pat asked.

"We ran. All of us." I remember hesitating, knowing the right thing to do was help that poor kid, but ultimately giving in to my cowardly instinct to pick up my glove and flee with the rest of my friends. "When we finally got a few blocks away, we didn't discuss it at all. And then someone made a joke about it. I don't remember what it was, but it got a big laugh out of the rest of us. Just one of those big 'let out the tension' laughs." I trailed off again, making Pat impatient.

"Well? Did you get in trouble?" he demanded. I blinked, surprised at the question.

"No," I replied. "Chris never told on us." I wondered if the guilt would still have stayed with me all my life if he had. Getting away with it scot-free left me feeling a karmic imbalance that I could not shake.

I stayed silent. Pat's face scrunched in confusion, trying to figure out the purpose behind the story. Then he gave up.

"What was the point of that?" he demanded.

I shrugged. "I don't know. We were sitting on this bench together waiting. It felt awkward to me, so I figured I'd kill the time with a story."

Pat didn't know what to do with that. He stared at me like I was a lunatic and raised two impatient hands, palms up: *Well?*

"Fine," I said. "You need a point laid out for you? Well, part of it should be obvious: I picked on that poor kid because I felt lousy about myself and wanted to drag someone down to my level of misery."

Pat opened his mouth, ready to protest that whatever served as the impetus for his attack on Matt, it had nothing to do with poor self-esteem. I cut him off.

"And no," I added. "I'm not saying you beat Matt up because you feel bad about yourself. I have no idea why you did it." Pat's mouth snapped shut with an audible *click*.

"And maybe you're not even sure why you did it," I said. "But someday, like me, you'll be smart enough to look back and figure out why it happened. Maybe you'll even feel bad about it when you do. But I suppose this is my point: whatever you do *now*, you will own that. Forever. You may wake up one day and decide to become a saint. You may turn yourself into a completely different person. But the best you can do is go forward. There's no going back. What you do now isn't like a chalkboard you can wipe clean. It will never stop sticking to you."

"So, young Patrick, it's like this for me: I'm stuck with a ton of guilt because I was an idiot and it took me years to even *want* to be a better person. But you're young; it doesn't have to be that way for you. So, sure: I have no idea why you felt compelled to slap Matt around. But if you don't either, you should try to figure it out soon. Because you *will* figure it out eventually, and you may not like the answer when you do. But the longer it takes you to do so, the less time you'll have to fix it. And every bad choice you make up until that point will stick to you like glue."

Pat stared at me, and I knew that I had gotten through to him. But that illusion dissolved after a few moments as Pat's lips curled into a sneer.

"Whatever," he shrugged indifferently. "I wish I could have seen you getting beaten up in an Elvis costume." He forced a wicked laugh.

I resisted the urge to strangle him. *I poured my heart out to you, you little shit.*

The door to the administration office banged open, and an angry-looking couple stormed out, whispering ferociously to each other. I managed to collect myself as they marched past us.

"Whatever indeed," I announced, defeated. "Let's go see the warden."

I led Pat back into the office, where Mr. Gallagher, looking exhausted, was standing with two secretaries, recounting his hostile meeting with that set of parents. He sighed when he saw me enter with Pat.

"Take a number, Mr. Randall," he said wearily, rubbing his temples. I looked about in surprise and noticed a pretty young woman seated against the wall who had been just out of my view. She was dressed smartly and sat perfectly erect—a model of good posture. Her hair, somewhere between blonde and brown (*the color of straw*, I would later think, unpoetically), was parted neatly on the side and fell to her shoulders. *I'll bet she has really elegant handwriting,* I recall thinking inanely at the time. I surmised that she was the woman who had passed us in the hall several minutes ago while I was trying to intimidate a ten-year-old child.

The woman jumped up when she realized that Mr. Gallagher was implicitly referring to her.

"Oh!" she cried out in a lilting voice that seemed as if it belonged in an animated Disney movie. "Mr. Randall was here before me; he was just waiting in the hall. You should see him first!"

The woman sat back down, seemingly embarrassed at being the subject of everyone's focus following her outburst. Her light blue eyes danced about, as if begging someone else to say something to take the attention off her. Mr. Gallagher shrugged, indifferent as to which of the two of us had priority, and glanced at Pat.

"Let me guess: Pat was fighting?" he asked, and I gave a quick nod. Without looking, Mr. Gallagher pointed behind him at his office, and Pat reluctantly plodded through the door. I had the sense that this was a dance the two of them had performed often. With a head nod, Mr. Gallagher directed me out to the hallway. On my way out, I stole one last glance at the woman, who had resumed her position of sitting perfectly upright, staring straight ahead. Mildly disappointed that she hadn't sought to steal a glance at *me*, I walked out to the hall where I filled Mr. Gallagher in on what I had witnessed with regard to Pat punching Matt. When I finished my summary, Mr. Gallagher nodded curtly.

"Thanks, Dave. I'll take it from here." I moved to head back to my classroom, but, after a few steps, I paused.

"Who is she?" I blurted out. Mr. Gallagher froze, and a small smile, which I could just make out under his mustache, touched his lips. His brow furrowed as he weighed his response.

"We are getting a new second grader next week who is visually impaired," he finally confided to me. "She will need orientation and mobility lessons throughout the week, so we will be having an itinerant teacher come in periodically for those. I was just about to meet with that teacher to discuss the logistics. Her name is Abby Petersen."

•　　　•　　　•　　　•　　　•

True to his word, Paul found me at day's end and offered to let me follow him on the drive to the bar, which was about ten minutes outside of our school's district.

"Gets awkward when a parent inadvertently walks in on happy hour, you know?" Paul explained to me. Without much enthusiasm, I followed Paul's car, even though Paul's practice of speeding through every changing light had me half-convinced that he was trying to lose me. Paul did not bother to wait for me in the lot and had already entered the bar by the time I parked my own car. As I forced myself to walk to the front door, I could make out the tumult of eighties rock music and the screams of my normally serene coworkers.

One beer. I told myself. *Nurse one beer and then you can sneak out.*

I steeled myself and went inside.

chapter fourteen

Twenty minutes later, I was trapped.

The pub was narrow—there were only a few scant feet between the bar itself and the opposite wall. The various teachers from my school, getting drunker by the minute, had congregated at the side of the room near the exit around a digital jukebox, which had been commandeered by someone with a twenty-dollar bill and an intense love of eighties rock. I had taken a seat at the bar on the periphery of that social circle, close enough that my colleagues wouldn't think I was shunning them, but not so close as to ensnare me in the debauchery.

Unfortunately, my positioning had resulted in a crowd of intoxicated coworkers blocking my exit. I hadn't even been there a half hour, but I already regretted coming. Try as I might, I couldn't think of an effective way to sneak out without drawing attention to myself. I was in no mood for dealing with any awkward goodbyes. And so, I sat at the bar, ordered another beer, and plotted my escape.

At one point, I began to mentally pray. *John, I have never asked you for anything since you became God. But if there's anything you can do for me here ...* But my silent plea went ignored.

What if I fake getting an important call? I thought. I played it out in my head: I would yell loudly into my cellphone that it was too noisy, followed by a frantic walk to the exit with my phone pressed to one ear and a finger pressed to the other to block out background noise. *It has a shot ...* But then I remembered where I had parked; my car could be seen right outside the window, about ten feet from where the rest of the herd had gathered. *Everyone will see me drive away. Is it worth getting a dozen questions tomorrow morning about why a phone call caused me to urgently flee?* Down by the jukebox I heard someone cry out, "Body shots!" A few moments later, I could barely make out through the crowd a woman lying face-up on the bar, shirt raised to expose her navel, followed by peals of laughter. *Maybe I can just leave my car and walk home?*

I was so intent in plotting how to best slip away that I didn't detect the woman who took the seat to my left. I'm unsure of how long she tried to get my attention; my head was too far up my own ass to notice her.

"Hello again!" she said loudly in her song-like voice.

I looked up, surprised, at the mirror behind the bar and saw that Abby, the woman in the office earlier that day, had managed to sneak onto the bar stool next to mine. Her posture remained immaculate, and I found myself transfixed by the image of the two of us sitting side by side in the mirror.

"Hello, there," I finally said to her reflection. Abby's face scrunched up in confusion, and then she also turned to face the mirror, leaving us both staring straight ahead.

"I feel like I'm in a spy movie," she said, smiling at my reflection. I grinned and, after a moment's thought, adopted an overly casual face. Continuing to face the mirror in front of us, I circumspectly slid a napkin down the bar toward Abby. Abby, catching on, deftly picked it up and subtly stuffed it into her sleeve.

"Burn after reading," I murmured.

"I will," Abby replied softly, not looking at me. Then, breaking character, Abby laughed and threw the napkin back onto the bar.

"It was wet," she explained. She glanced suspiciously at the napkin and looked mildly disgusted. "I think someone may have blown their nose with it."

Oops. Eager to change the subject, I said, "I didn't have a chance to introduce myself before. I'm Dave Randall."

"I know." Abby blushed, having given away the fact that she had made an inquiry regarding my identity, as I had with her. "My name is Abby."

I decided to throw her a bone.

"I know."

Abby smiled, relieved, and held up her glass of beer.

"Nice to meet you … again," she said, and we clinked our glasses together.

We sat there mutely, and for one of the first times in my life, I cursed my inability to make comfortable small talk. I tried to think of something, anything, to fill the void. But I became tongue-tied in my panic at trying to summon the magic words that would keep Abby there a bit longer, and the silence continued. Fortunately, even if Abby detected any awkwardness on my part, she still didn't seem eager to leave. Leaning forward, she looked past me toward the mob of teachers preparing for another round of shots.

"I suppose those are my new coworkers," she observed.

"Mine, too," I replied, thankful that my tongue still worked. "I only started a few months ago."

"Well, it *seems* like a fun group," Abby noted diplomatically, albeit without much conviction.

I shrugged.

"They're mostly good people, although this setting isn't quite bringing out the best in them."

A high-pitched scream caused us both to turn our heads abruptly. A petite first grade teacher had been picked up and placed on Paul's broad shoulders. She laughed and yelled to be let down, but Paul, in exaggerated fashion, pretended that he couldn't hear her. The group reacted as if it were the funniest thing they had ever seen. Abby and I both relaxed when we realized the shriek had been a false alarm.

"How did you manage to end up here?" I asked, gesturing around the room. "I thought you only had a brief meeting with Mr. Gallagher today?"

Abby sighed. "One of the guys over there invited me. That man with the woman on his shoulders." Paul still hadn't let his passenger down; he kept playfully threatening to walk under the ceiling fan while she laughed and batted at his head. "He was waiting to talk to Mr. Gallagher when my meeting ended, and I spoke to him for a few minutes. He invited me to this happy hour. I'm new to the area and haven't been out much since I moved up here, so I said yes."

It made sense. I imagined that Paul would have gone to check in with Mr. Gallagher regarding Pat and the fight after he finished up in the nurse's office with Matt.

An uncomfortable thought then hit me.

"Did … did he invite you as some sort of date?" I realized it was a rude question as soon as it came out, but Abby didn't seem to mind. Instead, she shuddered theatrically at the notion.

"God, I hope not," she said. "If so, he's a pretty lousy date. Do you come to these happy hours often?"

"This is actually my first one." I grinned. "I was invited by the same guy. And he's been a terrible date to me so far as well."

As Abby giggled, I noticed her glass was nearly empty, so I ordered another round for the two of us. When our drinks came, Abby tilted her glass toward me in appreciation before taking a small sip. Then her face grew serious.

"I have a confession, Dave."

I had no idea what she was talking about, so I just smiled stupidly.

"Earlier today when you were talking to that tough kid in the hallway—I heard all of it. I didn't mean to eavesdrop! But I was sitting in the office, and the two of you were talking in the hall, just on the other side of the glass behind me."

I shrugged. "It's fine. It wasn't a big deal."

Abby looked relieved that I wasn't angry. "Thank you. And for what it's worth, I thought it was really sweet what you said to him."

Sweet? I thought. *I look like the biggest jerk in that story.*

"I'm glad you enjoyed it. But I don't think it made a difference with him."

Abby frowned. "Why would you say that?"

"Oh, he was just the same smartass afterwards as he was before."

Abby rolled her eyes. "Are you kidding? No kid in that position would *ever* give you the satisfaction of knowing you got through to them. But he was listening. I could tell that much even through the glass. And I guarantee you that he'll think again about what you said. Maybe it won't change him, but I would bet it does, at least on some level."

I sipped my beer. Abby's prediction sounded a lot like the seed planting theory I had developed during my Teach for America days. I contemplated whether it was possible that my talk with Pat could one day grow into something meaningful.

"Maybe you're right," I said. "I can be overly cynical at times. I try not to be. It's just … a few years ago I switched careers and came into this profession hoping to make a difference. I was warned not to set my sights too high at the time, and I try to be a realist, but sometimes—well, sometimes I wonder how much of an impact I really have on the students."

Abby cocked her head inquisitively. "What did you do before this?" she asked.

"I was an attorney." Abby, in the midst of drinking her beer, feigned a spit take, and then laughed at her own antics.

"Just kidding!" Abby quickly turned serious again. "Why did you stop?"

I could have made something up, but I knew preemptively that I'd feel lousy if I lied to someone who, I could tell off the bat, was a genuinely nice person. But there was more to it than that. I was baffled by Abby choosing to sit with me while I lingered alone, and more so by the fact that she seemed to be *enjoying* my company. As pleased as I was with this development, I felt like it was unearned. That's why, I suppose, I felt the need to test Abby by laying it all out with as honest an answer as I could muster.

"I'd spent most of my adult life as an attorney, but it was turning me into somewhat of an asshole," I said. "Not the kind that goes out picking fights with the elderly, or anything like that, but I was someone who did not enjoy or appreciate life as much as I should have. But one day, a few years ago, I had an experience that made me want to become a better person. After taking time off to reflect on the lousy human being I had become, and what I wanted to be, I decided to pursue a career in education. And sure, that decision generally feels like it was a step in the right direction. Still, there are plenty of times when I can't shake the sense that I'm just pretending to be a better person, and I wonder how different I really am from the asshole that I used to be."

Abby chewed her lower lip in silence as she studied me. I wondered if she was able to make any sense of what I had said.

"You're not an asshole, Dave," Abby finally said in a quiet but firm voice. It was strange, hearing the profanity come out of her innocent-looking face. It felt as misplaced as if Princess Aurora had casually dropped an F-bomb after pricking her finger in *Sleeping Beauty*.

"How do you know?" I asked, trying to make it sound light. "You've only just met me."

"True," she conceded. "But I've known assholes. And the thing about assholes is, they generally don't spend time worrying about whether or not they're assholes."

I felt my cheeks grow warm. It was pathetic that merely being told I wasn't an asshole was enough to make me emotional. But the sentiment would not have touched me so had it come from anyone else. I sensed that Abby was a kind and authentic soul, and any validation from her carried substantially more weight than it would have from other sources. Suddenly fearful of getting too affected—I figured it would derail the conversation if I broke into tears—I tried to change the subject.

"I feel like we are both overusing the word 'asshole,'" I said. "We may have to retire it for the night."

Abby, grinning mischievously, feigned concern. "Well, won't that make it really hard for us to describe what is happening over there?" She nodded toward our colleagues, who were circled around a fifth-grade teacher trying, and failing, to do "the Worm" on the floor to an unfamiliar Michael Jackson song.

I didn't have a rejoinder aside from grinning at Abby. I had not had an opportunity to engage in anything approaching "banter" since John was still human, and I had not realized how much I had missed it. Abby had mentioned being new to the area herself, and I figured that she, too, was deriving something from our conversation that had been absent from her life.

I realized abruptly that I didn't know *why* Abby had moved to the region, or really much of *anything* about her. She had patiently let me talk about myself, and I was too lousy a conversationalist to ask anything about *her*. Grateful that I had realized my faux pas before it was too late, I politely asked Abby to tell me about herself. "Oh!" she replied, as if pleasantly surprised by the mundane question. And that was when Abby showed me that as good and patient of a listener as she was, if she felt comfortable enough and was presented with the opportunity to do so, she can *talk*.

A *lot*.

I learned that Abby, like me, had grown up on Long Island, and that she was the middle of three sisters. She had initially pursued a career in education, but after working for several years as a reading teacher, she decided to go back to school to become an Orientation and Mobility teacher, which generally involves helping students with visual impairments develop strategies for independent traveling. Abby noted gleefully that her coursework in this regard at one point involved her being dropped off blindfolded in the heart of Manhattan, tasked with getting back to her school's campus. She worked for several years in the New York City public school system, helping younger students with visual impairments learn to navigate their schools and older students take on more challenging travel tasks (*i.e.*, using a white cane to detect obstacles, learning the transit system, learning to listen for auditory clues at street crossings, etc.). Although there was a lot about New York City that Abby loved, she felt she was more of a country girl at heart, and when the opportunity to take on a new job and move upstate presented itself earlier in the year, she jumped at it. She was currently renting a one-bedroom apartment, which she loved for how clean and modern it was, but simultaneously hated for its "no pets" policy. She had not had much of a social life since the move and somewhat guiltily admitted that after going straight to the gym from work, her nights were mostly spent watching reality tv and true crime shows and struggling with over-ambitious cooking projects from cookbooks that she acknowledged might be a tad beyond her skill set.

Mind you, all of that information flowed out of Abby in response to my basic inquiry: "Tell me about yourself." Abby did not need a syllable of further prompting from me once she got going. She spoke animatedly, her eyes dancing as key points were punctuated with emphatic hand gestures, and I found it impossible to avoid being swept in by her enthusiasm, even when she touched upon subjects that would, under other circumstances, bore me (such as her reality tv habit). It was apparent that Abby had been waiting some time for an opportunity to spill out her life story, and I was more than happy to be on the receiving end. As a fringe benefit, Abby's long rant gave me a chance to look at her for prolonged periods without coming off as creepy (or so I hoped). My initial characterization of Abby as "pretty" had upgraded itself to "beautiful" the longer I spoke with her.

Only after Abby finally ran out of breath did she seem to realize that she had been talking for fifteen minutes, non-stop. "Well," she concluded, after pausing to collect herself, "long story longer, that's how I ended up here!"

"Wow." I had received so much information in bulk, I wasn't sure how to even follow up. Abby's eyes twinkled at my befuddlement.

"But enough about *me*," she said. "Tell me more about you." She gestured toward the pack of drunken teachers, some of whom were finally showing signs of dispersing. "I'm getting the vibe that this isn't your idea of fun. So what is?"

"Oh, man; I'm dull. On weekends, I typically just sit around reading or go for hikes."

"Really?" Abby seemed intrigued. "Where do you hike?"

"There is a trail down the road from my house. I've hiked that just about every day for the past few years—at least as much as I am able to."

"You hike the same trail over and over again?" Abby looked slightly confused, and I felt the need to explain further.

"Do you remember how I told you that I used to go through the motions with life? Well, it got to the point, back when I was an attorney, where I would drive to work on autopilot. I eventually managed to get to my office without actually *seeing* anything, at least not in any kind of way that registered. I tended to look through everything, like it was all transparent. So when I found this trail, I vowed to hike it until there was nothing new on it for me to appreciate. Now, every time I climb up that mountain, I challenge myself to see something that I haven't noticed before. And I haven't failed yet. So that trail for me represents a reminder to live life with eyes and ears opened and not take anything for granted. That's why I climb that mountain as much as I can."

Abby mulled that over in silence. I noticed that her glass was nearly empty, and I feared we were coming to the end of our conversation.

"That seems like a compelling reason to climb up and down a mountain," Abby finally said. I wasn't sure if she bought into my premise or was merely being polite. "Is it a pretty hike?"

"I think so. I'm sure I would've moved on to another trail by now if it wasn't."

Abby stared down at her mostly empty glass, almost looking shy. "Well, I'd love to see it someday," she said quietly.

I finished my beer in one swallow and braced myself for rejection.

"You're free to come with us whenever you'd like," I ventured.

"Us?" Abby asked sharply, looking up at me.

"Oh, I forgot to mention: I hike with my cat. He's named Peaches." Abby stared at me as if I had two heads. "He's a good boy," I added unhelpfully.

Once the shock wore off, Abby smiled broadly.

"This," she said, "I have to see."

·   ·   ·   ·   ·

That Saturday, Abby met me and Peaches at the trail head. Even wearing hiking boots, shorts and an old t-shirt, with her hair held back in a short ponytail, Abby still managed to look prim and proper. She smiled when she got out of her car and saw me waiting for her, but absolutely melted when she saw Peaches milling about beside me. She squealed and knelt next to him, offering a cautionary hand for him to sniff. Peaches took one whiff, liked whatever it is he detected, and instantly rolled over to expose his belly to Abby.

"I wasn't completely sure you were serious about the cat!" she said to me, rubbing Peaches' stomach vigorously as he purred.

"I would never lie about something like that," I said. "Shall we?"

We headed up the trail, with Peaches taking the lead. I could tell Abby was in shape and exercised often, but after about fifteen minutes of hiking, she was breathing heavily. We stopped at a clearing and drank water out of bottles I had been carrying in my backpack. I even poured some into a small bowl I brought along so that Peaches could rehydrate as well.

"Did you find it yet?" Abby asked. At my confused look, she added, "You told me that you find something new and beautiful every time you come to this trail. Have you found it?"

"Oh," I replied. "Well, you see, I've never done this hike with another person. Just Peaches. And on the way up this mountain, the sun is generally in front of us, or to the side, so I never really noticed my own shadow. But today, there were times while you walked in front of me and your shadow seemed to dance amongst the trees and the rocks. It seemed almost magical, like a fairy teleporting about a forest. And *that* was my 'new' observation from this hike."

Abby nodded wordlessly. When we resumed our gentle climb up the mountain, I noticed her occasionally stealing glances over her shoulder, subtly smiling at her shadow.

A few hours later, we finished our hike. We didn't talk much along the way; it was too taxing of a climb for casual chitchat. But the absence of conversation felt natural and comfortable. It was early afternoon when we achingly made it back to our cars, and we were both tired, dirty, and drenched in sweat. I stood about awkwardly, not wanting to acknowledge the end of our date, if it even was a date.

"That was fun," Abby said, still breathing a bit hard. "Thank you for taking me."

"Of course. I'm glad you came with us."

"So what do you do now?"

I thought about it. "Sometimes, we go into town and get something to eat. Other times, if I'm particularly exhausted, I'll head straight home to shower and read. And once in a while, if we have the energy, Peaches and I will head to the farm."

"The farm?"

I'm not normally a bold man, by any means. It had been a fun morning, and it would not have been unreasonable for me to end our time together at that point on a high note. But in that particular moment, I felt brave enough to take a risk.

"Would you like to see it?"

•　　•　　•　　•　　•

It was about a half hour drive. I was initially worried about trying to fill up any awkward silences while Abby and I (and Peaches) drove together, but my apprehension was misplaced. Abby seemed to have no shortage of what she called "her stories." Abby spotted, almost immediately, a half-empty pack of gum in a cup holder, which prompted her to tell an incredibly detailed story about a vacation her family took when she was young, during which her younger sister, Stacey, fell asleep while chewing gum only to wake up a bit later with it firmly enmeshed in her long hair. There really wasn't much more to the story than that, aside from her family's various efforts to remove the gum (all of which failed, forcing Stacey into an uncomfortably short haircut). With her animated narration, Abby's enthusiasm for the story was unavoidably infectious. When she finished, Abby once again seemed surprised and somewhat embarrassed at getting carried away. I wasn't sure how to explain to Abby the extent to which I enjoyed having her songlike voice banish the quietness that tended to follow me, so I simply smiled and told her not to worry about it.

Abby did not seem in any rush during our drive and was taken aback when I abruptly turned off the street onto a dirt road. When I reached the top of a small hill, a number of barns appeared, scattered in the distance, that were connected by a network of amply spaced, fenced in fields. A wide but shallow stream could be seen to our right running parallel to the path we drove upon. As had happened so many times before, the calm beauty of the farm made it feel as if I had been magically transported into a children's book, where farm animals talk kindly to one another in a painting-like setting.

"Where are we?" Abby breathed, trying to take it all in. She spotted a cluster of animals in the distance. "Are those goats?"

"This is a sanctuary for farm animals," I explained. "They take care of animals that typically end up as livestock and give them a safe place to live. And yes, those are goats; they're really playful. Peaches and I used to volunteer here every week or so, although Peaches tends to nap more than work. We started coming here when I moved up to Woodstock, but it's been harder for me since I started teaching. I still make time when I can."

Arriving at a small lot, I parked the car and Peaches, who had been napping in the backseat, let out a fierce yawn. I opened his door and he hopped out, but of course he didn't run off.

"Do you mind getting dirty?" I asked. Abby made a face.

"Please. I'm already filthy from that hike."

At that moment, one of the animal caretakers, a redheaded woman in her late fifties named Kristine, rolled through the small parking area in a golf cart but stopped upon recognizing me.

"Hey, Dave, I didn't realize you were coming today," she said, not unkindly. Spotting Peaches beside me, she added, "Or him."

"Sorry, Kris; it was a last-minute thing," I replied. Gesturing to Abby, I said, "This is Abby. Abby, this is Kristine—she runs the volunteer program here."

"Very nice to meet you," Abby piped in her singsong voice. Kris nodded politely in return.

"Can you use us today?" I asked, trying to look apologetic. "I know we're on the late side."

Kris snorted and waved me off good-naturedly.

"Are you kidding? We can always use more bodies around here. I just sent a bunch of college students off to clean out the pig barn. Feel free to go help them out." With that, Kris restarted her cart and sped away.

I gestured for Abby to walk with me toward the far corner of the farm where the pigs were kept.

"I hope you're not against cleaning up after pigs," I said as we walked together, Peaches flanking my other side.

"No," she replied, looking excited. "Not at all. At least, I don't think so. This will be a first for me."

"Cleaning up for the pigs isn't a bad job," I said. "They're really smart—smarter than dogs. And they typically don't go to the bathroom where they sleep. So it's a much less smelly job than, say, cleaning up after the goats. Or the chickens. The chicken coops can get funky."

Abby nodded solemnly, and we continued in silence. When we arrived at the pig barn, a half-dozen college students, mostly women, were only starting to clear out the old bedding with muck rakes. After quickly waving hello to the other volunteers, I found a pair of rakes and a wheelbarrow for me and Abby to use. Peaches hopped up on a bale of straw outside of the barn and fell asleep almost immediately. I knew he'd stay there until we finished.

As tired as she was from our hike earlier that morning, Abby attacked the cleanup job with vigor. When I took a wheelbarrow, filled with dirty straw, out to the nearby compost heap to dump it, Abby, rather than rest, would join up with another pair of volunteers to help them fill their own wheelbarrow. The entire group worked hard, and after almost two hours of labor, only a few remnants of soiled straw remained. Abby threw me a questioning look: *What now?* As I wheeled yet another full wheelbarrow outside, I gave a subtle nod toward a broom along the wall. Abby, catching my drift, took it and started sweeping until spotless portions of concrete appeared below. Other volunteers followed Abby's lead, and the entire floor of the barn was soon spotless.

"This is the fun part," I told Abby. I went outside to where Peaches continued to sleep on a stack of straw bales neatly piled against the outside of the barn. "Sorry, buddy," I told him, carefully lifting him and resettling him on the ground. Peaches looked mildly annoyed, but soon fell back to sleep against the wall a few feet away. I carried one bale inside, and one of the volunteers cut the twine holding it together with a box cutter. A few more trips, and we soon had over a dozen bales inside the barn.

"Now we just spread the straw out a bit. Like this." I kicked a brick of straw and spread it out with my feet. Abby, ignoring my inartful style, picked up her own brick and delicately pulled it apart with her hands.

I noticed one of the farm's caretakers, who had come by to check on our progress, fidgeting with a short gate at one end of the barn. I nudged Abby.

"I think we're going to get some other helpers now," I said.

"Who?" Abby asked. But before I had a chance to respond, the gate opened and a family of six pigs, who had been waiting impatiently outside for the past several hours, burst in and scampered excitedly amongst all of the volunteers. A couple of the younger pigs, which were nonetheless enormous, picked up sheets of tightly packed straw in their mouths and carried them while they chased each other about the barn. Abby, amazed, stared at the animals and giggled when a gigantic hog shoved his snout into her hand. She scratched his head, and the pig rolled over, exposing his stomach to her, much like Peaches had done earlier that morning. Squealing with delight, Abby dropped to the ground to fiercely rub the pig's belly with both hands, while he snorted with pleasure under her. A feeling of warmth filled me as I watched Abby, radiating pure euphoria, play with that family of pigs.

In the past, I had always assumed it was just a figure of speech whenever I overheard someone tell another, "I am so happy for you!" I harbored doubts relating to whether such a state of being was physiologically possible. My skepticism in that regard vanished that afternoon in the pig barn when I felt Abby's happiness so clearly that I could claim it as my own.

Abby and I were both exhausted but elated when the job was finished and everyone had reluctantly stopped playing with the animals. Peaches was also somehow tired, even after his afternoon of napping, so he allowed Abby to carry him as we walked back to the car together. The sun sat low in the sky, and I knew it would be dark within the hour. Abby seemed too tired to regale me with any of her "stories," so we spent most of the walk lost in our respective thoughts about the day that we had spent together.

"You told me why you hike," Abby finally said, breaking the silence. "Why do you do this?"

I was surprised by the question. "Didn't you have fun?"

"Of course! But I'm curious what motivates *you* to do this."

I knew the answer, but I was unsure of how to articulate it.

"The people who run this place will tell you that these animals are ambassadors," I said, gesturing about the farm, "so that visitors can come here and appreciate the various personalities on display, and maybe think differently about what they're eating. And sure, I think that's a noble endeavor. But it's not quite what I think of when I come here."

"So what is it?" Abby pressed. I frowned, trying to find the words.

"Whenever I'm here, I'm reminded of a story I learned when I took religion classes as a kid," I said. "I'm sure this is a butchered version, but this was the gist of it: Two girls were walking one morning along a beach that was covered with starfish that had been washed up on the shore. There were thousands of them, and they needed to get back to the water before they dried out and died. One of the girls picked up a starfish and gently placed it in the surf. The other scoffed and noted, 'There are too many starfish on the beach to save them all. What difference did that make?' And the girl replied, 'It makes all the difference in the world to that one.'"

Abby petted Peaches absently while she walked next to me. As prone as she was to delve into one of her long stories, she could also be a remarkable listener.

"That's the story that pops in my head when I'm here," I continued. "I want to change the world for the better, but I'm not always sure how to do it. And it can be too daunting at times to consider the big picture. So today, we gave those pigs—who are *incredibly* lucky to begin with, in that they aren't already bacon—a clean place to sleep tonight. And even if we didn't solve all of the world's problems today, we managed to help out that family of pigs. It may not be much, but it's at least a step. It's something."

Abby, aside from slowly nodding, didn't respond right away. She gradually slowed down enough to put Peaches back on the ground, and I adjusted my own stride to accommodate her. While the three of us walked toward the sunset, Abby, without speaking, reached out to take my hand in hers. I was not anticipating the physical contact; I could not have possibly been any dirtier or sweatier, although the same could be said for Abby.

"You mentioned you took religion classes as a child," Abby remarked, continuing to hold my hand gently. At my nod, she asked, "Are you still religious?" When I didn't answer right away, she added, "Do you believe in God?"

Those are very different questions, I thought. The last thing I wanted to do was lie to Abby, so I chose to answer the easier of the two.

"Yeah," I said. "I believe in God."

chapter fifteen

Abby and I (and, of course, Peaches) hiked and volunteered at the farm again the following weekend. And then again the weekend after that. I constantly worried about inviting Abby to do it all again the following weekend, in case she was getting bored with that routine (or, even worse, bored of me). But I soon realized that Abby had at some point penciled me in for each of her Saturdays going forward, as her last words to me after volunteering were always a perfunctory and hopeful, "Same thing next week?"

In between those Saturdays, I found myself prowling the hallways of my school during my free periods, hoping to "accidentally" run into Abby during one of her lessons. I tried to decode her itinerant schedule, but it was erratic and not subject to any pattern that I could discern. One day, when I had managed to successfully track her down, I asked Abby for a clue as to what days she would be at my school. She laughed and fluttered her eyelashes mischievously, but stubbornly refused to give me even a hint of her schedule. I suspected that she was tickled by the thought of me trying to hunt her down throughout the week.

Over time, as fall transitioned into winter, it often became too cold to hike, and Abby began to invite me into her world. Thus, I found myself being the sole male member of her Wednesday night Pilates class, surrounded by women who tactfully ignored my complete lack of flexibility. Abby also seemed to own the Blu-Ray of just about every animated movie that I had ever heard of, and we spent many snowy weekends together on the couch, along with Peaches, as we worked through her catalog of movies. At one point in December, Abby offered to make dinner for me later in the week. Abby was familiar with my vegetarian lifestyle, and I was tickled to find several vegetarian cookbooks lying about her apartment when I arrived for dinner, which was a lentil-roni pasta dish with kale chips on the side.

"Did you get those cookbooks for me?" I asked, touched.

"No," Abby said with a grin. "For *me*." At my look, she added: "Come on. You didn't think I could spend every Saturday hanging out with cows, pigs, and chickens without going green, did you?"

Sometimes I tried to picture how others would view Abby and me when we were together. I imagine the tired cliché of "opposites attract" entered a few minds, at least to those familiar with both my quiet brooding self and Abby's cheerful, perky optimism. To be sure, I cannot speak to what Abby saw in me, but there was no mystery as to what attracted me to her. Simply put, her arrival in my life made me realize how much I had been missing up until then. In leaving the practice of law, I cleared away useless, hurtful rubble, and I was content for a time with living a life relatively free of pain. Abby nonetheless taught me that joy is more than just the absence of hurt. More than merely being the loss of a negative, joy is a positive force that fills a day with moments that are truly worth living. To me, that force was Abby.

I likened the experience to how I imagined the advent of cinema—specifically, that semi-famous story where a crowd fled a theater, panicked at the silent projection of a train in motion. At some point later, those individuals must have gone to see another movie, this time with an accompanying soundtrack, and realized only then what they had been missing, and what they stood to gain, by immersing another of their senses in the movie-going experience. Some things simply have to be felt firsthand before you can appreciate the gaping chasm that was once, but is no longer, there. Abby's gentle voice, whether it was communicating something profound or one of her overly detailed "stories," became one of those things that I knew I could not live without.

I learned that Abby, unlike me, possessed an effortless appreciation for beauty. When we hiked, I continued to labor in seeing and appreciating nature around us. Abby, by contrast, had a natural ability to view and cherish the world. While my gaze was narrow and discerning in its quest to capture reminders of the miracle of life, Abby's wide eyes constantly managed to catch moments that threatened to slip by me: a comical look from a cardinal at being interrupted in its song by a squirrel. An autumn leaf that vaguely resembled an angry old woman. A rock that was shaped like a heart. As I spent more and more time with her, it became easier to see the world through Abby's eyes, and I became a better person for it.

A year and a half after we first met, Abby and I were engaged. We did not see the point of a prolonged engagement or a large wedding, so we married a few months later, in August. I hoped deep down that John might bless our wedding, but there was no evidence of that. In fact, our wedding ceremony was driven indoors as a result of a torrential downpour that lasted the entire evening. Fortunately, that didn't damper our wedding at all. Our guests, limited in number as they were, all commented that Abby was one of the most beautiful brides they had ever seen, and I could tell that at least most of them meant it. Peaches, in dignified fashion, served as our ring bearer, and a video that Mr. Gallagher took of our cat making his way proudly down the aisle, ring appended to his collar, ended up going viral.

Around the time of our wedding, Abby and I closed on a small house outside of Woodstock that was not much larger than the cottage I had been living in for the past several years. We took time off for ourselves after the wedding, but we didn't go on a honeymoon. This was partially because we didn't have much money at the time, but, more importantly, we couldn't think of any place to go in the world that would be more rewarding than where we already were.

And from there, we lived.

It was not a fancy existence, but we were content. More than content—we were *happy*. After work, we went for walks, where I listened to Abby fill me in on seemingly every detail of her day. Abby could also sniff out when I was sitting on a story that warranted telling, and she was tireless in her efforts to draw those tales out of me. Other times, when Abby was tired of talking, and I had nothing to say, we'd simply sit together comfortably on our porch reading, with Peaches alternating between laps to lay in.

This is not to say that we did not have our share of issues now and then, as every newlywed couple is bound to have. Fortunately, those issues were generally small and easy to resolve and would often serve as the basis for jokes between us only a few short days later. A lot of it was just stereotypical, clichéd buffoonery on my part, like agitating Abby during the night by leaving the toilet seat up. Or getting caught not paying attention to one of Abby's many stories while trying to glimpse the score of a Mets game being broadcast on the television behind her.

Even the differences between us that could have resulted in a more serious rift proved to be fairly easy to work out. For example, during one particularly cold

February, I was crushed by the flu and spent a long and miserable weekend in bed. During that time, Abby occupied herself by getting drawn into some sort of true crime marathon on tv, with reenactment after reenactment of a criminal breaking into a house to murder an entire family. I don't know why she did it. Abby was a complete scaredy-cat when it came to horror movies. But while I spent days in bed, choking on my own phlegm, Abby was downstairs working herself up more and more to a state of abject terror.

"We need to have a gun here," she told me matter-of-factly when I finally had the strength to get out of bed.

I typically gave in to whatever Abby wanted, simply because (a) it was usually something easy that would make her happy, or (b) if I pretended to go along with it, she usually forgot about it in a day or two (such as when she asked if we could adopt our own family of goats). Her request for the gun fell squarely in category (b), so I told her "sure" and waited for her to drop it. But she didn't. The next day, she asked when we would go out to get a gun, and again the day after that. Finally, I was backed into a corner and had to fight back.

"Why do we need a gun? We don't have anything here that would warrant the effort of breaking into our house!"

"Thieves don't know that until they get in!" Abby countered. "Besides, there are people out there who will just kill for the joy of it. I've seen those stories!"

"On tv?" I asked pointedly.

"Yes," Abby said. "But based on real stories. There was this guy who was living in the walls of a family's house for *months*, and he would only come out at night to leave threatening notes. And one day—"

"We don't need a gun," I interrupted, rolling my eyes. "Statistically, we're more likely to end up shooting each other than a burglar." I opted to try a different tack. "This seems very out of character for you. You're such a sweet, innocent person. I never even suspected that I was marrying Rambo."

Abby would not back down.

"I don't need a machine gun. Just a form of protection we can keep here in a safe in case something happens." Then Abby opted to change tactics herself. "What if someone breaks in and sexually assaults me? Is that what you want, Dave? Do you want me to end up being raped?"

And that is how Abby won that argument.

In the end, we settled for a Glock 26, or, as the guy at the gun store called it, a "Baby Glock." Abby listened intently as we were shown how to load and unload the pistol, and I sullenly followed along. I had no intention of ever using the thing myself, but I suspected karma would only throw me into a situation where I needed it if I remained oblivious as to how to use it. Once I learned the basics, I planned on just storing it in a gun safe and never thinking of it again. Indeed, once we put our Glock away in a small safe under our bed, Abby seemed content. For whatever reason, the mere presence of a gun in our house, even locked away and forgotten, comforted Abby, so in the long run I considered the minor compromise of my principles to be a small price to pay.

That was the extent of our disputes in those first two years of marriage. Those minor hiccups aside, married life agreed with me. I think it agreed with Abby, too. I had spent almost all of my adult life in isolation, and I was initially worried about losing that freedom. But that "freedom" came with a price that I couldn't appreciate until after the fact: the weight of being alone. The basic pleasures to be derived from simply being able to laugh with someone, vent to someone, care for someone—as I said, those were things I didn't realize I couldn't live without until I experienced them firsthand. So, even if my marriage fell short of perfection (as all marriages are wont to do), it was close enough to perfect for me. After years of failure, I finally felt as if I were truly living the way I was meant to. And for several years, everything was wonderful.

Until, of course, it wasn't. That day arrived when Abby managed to find my John journal.

It was a crisp Sunday morning in mid-October. Abby and I had been married for a little over two years by that point, and we had already settled comfortably into our weekend routines that we largely carried out wordlessly. Our Saturdays were usually devoted to hiking and volunteering, but Sundays were for errands. Food shopping, mowing the lawn, raking leaves … we tried to wrap all of that up as quickly as we could so that we had a few hours to rest before starting up a new week of work.

That particular Sunday, though, was a bit atypical for us in that Abby had planned to spend most of the day on Long Island with her mother, who was organizing a surprise 70th birthday party for Abby's father. Abby had volunteered to help with the planning and had recently suggested to her mother that they make a photo collage to display at the party in her father's honor. Abby's mom loved the idea, and they waited for a day when Abby's father would be out of town to tackle that project together. When Abby learned earlier in the week that her father would be on a golfing trip for the entire weekend, she quickly made plans to spend Sunday with her mother.

Abby had an aversion to driving through the city (and, in particular, driving over large bridges), so she took the train whenever she visited her family. That commute involved a half hour drive out to Rhinecliff, at which point she would catch an Amtrak train to Penn Station in Manhattan. From there, it was a quick transfer to the Long Island Railroad, which took her out to Great Neck, where her family lived, in less than a half hour. She bought a ticket online for a train scheduled to depart Rhinecliff shortly before noon. I largely stayed out of Abby's way that morning as she rummaged about upstairs for pictures she could bring to add to her father's collage.

I was surprised when 10:45 rolled around and Abby still had not come back downstairs. After hearing her stomp about all morning, things had been eerily quiet for the past fifteen minutes. Wondering if she had lost track of time, I ventured up the stairs where I found Abby lounging on our bed, surrounded by various photos from her childhood.

And reading my John journal.

It had been so long since I wrote anything in it, I struggled to recall where I had last left it. In the drawer of my nightstand, perhaps. Wherever it had been, Abby found it.

Abby heard me enter the room but did not look up from reading.

"'If John inserting himself into 'the story' to talk to me changes the narrative, and he stays out of my mind while we talk, he might not be able to see those thoughts (whatever they may end up being) in advance,'" she read aloud. "'There *should be* a narrow window for me to surprise him.'"

She then looked up at me quizzically.

"Did I marry a crazy person?" she asked bluntly.

"Crazy sexy," I replied, trying to make light of what she had found. She wasn't going for it.

"This is your handwriting. And this sounds like the writings of a lunatic."

I was thankful she hadn't made it to the end of the journal, where I detailed my two meetings with John. The beginning sections were odd without any context, but the end—that's where Abby would *really* start to question my hold on reality.

I tried to assess Abby's mood. She didn't look truly concerned or angry. Mostly just curious. That was fine; I could handle curious. The minefield I faced at that moment wasn't so much Abby's mood as it was how to navigate the conversation without lying, something I had vowed long ago never to do to her.

"It's—it's no big deal," I said and instantly regretted it. My casual, knee-jerk response was actually a whopper of a lie. "I mean, it's a long story."

Abby arched an eyebrow. "I've certainly subjected you to more than your fair share of long stories. I'm sure I can handle it."

I didn't know where to start.

"Do you remember when we first met? Not outside of Mr. Gallagher's office. I'm talking about when we spoke at that happy hour. Do you remember me mentioning a life-changing experience that made me leave the practice of law?"

"Of course," Abby replied.

"Really? You never asked about it."

"I figured you'd tell me about it when you were ready. I didn't want to badger you."

"Ah. Anyway, that journal relates to what I went through."

"How so?" Abby asked. But before I could answer, her eyes jumped to the digital clock on the nightstand next to our bed. "Darn it! I'm late!"

Abby hurriedly gathered the pictures around her on the bed and stuffed them into her purse.

"Can I make it to the train in thirty-five minutes?" she asked, frantic.

"I guess we'll find out."

Abby gave me a withering look and rushed downstairs. I was somewhat relieved that she left the journal behind.

"Are you sure you don't want me to come with you?" I asked, hoping she wouldn't call my bluff.

Even as she scurried about the kitchen, looking for her keys, Abby realized I was merely going through the motions with my offer, and she laughed.

"Oh, that's so nice of you!" Abby exclaimed with mock sincerity, fluttering her eyelashes. "You'd be willing to miss Game 5 tonight to spend the day making a photo collage with me and mumsie?"

"Sure," I replied with little conviction. The Mets had somehow squeaked into the playoffs and, even more surprisingly, made it to the National League Championship Series against the St. Louis Cardinals. The magic of their season seemed to be dying, though, as the Cardinals had quickly taken a 3-1 series lead. The game starting later that afternoon—Game 5—could very well be the last game of the Mets' season, and Abby knew it.

"You're sweet," Abby said, giving me a quick kiss. "Even when you're not sincere. Enjoy your game. I'll be back tonight around 9:00. And you *will* tell me all about that book, and your life-changing experience, when I get back. Understood?"

"Absolutely. I'll tell you everything," I called out as Abby ran out the front door. And I meant it.

I really did.

chapter sixteen

Here's the story of a man named Tom Horton.

By all accounts, he lived his life as a good man. Following his graduation from Catholic high school in the late 1980s, he entered a Navy training program through which he became an Explosive Ordnance Disposal Technician, specializing in locating, identifying, and disabling explosive hazards, including Improvised Explosive Devices, or IEDs. After the resolution of the First Gulf War, he was stationed for a period of time in the Persian Gulf region, where he worked to clear sea mines and other explosives. Longing to return home to Long Island, where he was raised, he made an impromptu career change in the late 1990s, taking an entry-level job as an insurance adjuster, which he held for several years. During that time, Tom's nights were dedicated to college courses, taken in furtherance of obtaining a Bachelor of Arts degree. After a few years of study, Tom finally earned his degree in Risk Management and Insurance. From there, Tom quickly rose through the ranks of his company, becoming a manager of a small unit of adjusters, and then, a few years later, he was promoted to vice president, where he oversaw a unit devoted to adjusting directors' and officers' liability claims.

Tom had explained to friends and a few members of his church that the key force that drove him away from working as an EOD Tech was a feeling of being kept apart from his faith. Tom was raised a devout Catholic, although he acknowledged that the structure and community of the Catholic Church was something that he took for granted as a child and only came to fully appreciate while he was deployed overseas for months at a time. Thus, upon returning to Long Island, Tom vowed to become reacquainted with his faith, which he did. More than "reacquainted," in fact. He fully embraced it with all of his being.

Somehow, while he was working, taking night classes, and diving headfirst into his church community, Tom also found time to fall in love. The woman's name was Gail Mulhern, although she took Tom's last name once they married in 2002. Almost nine months to the day after their wedding, Tom and Gail had their first child—a baby girl they named Claire. Less than a year later, a second daughter was born, who was named Theresa after Tom's deceased mother. Theresa was born shortly after the school system's cutoff date of December 1, so she ended up being one grade below Claire.

The Horton family eventually settled in Manhasset, Long Island (which, incidentally, is the next town over from Abby's hometown of Great Neck). It is one of the richest areas on Long Island; indeed, it's the home of the famous "Miracle Mile" that occupies a formidable section of Northern Boulevard. Manhasset would have normally been too expensive a location for Tom to live, even with his status as vice president of a large insurance company, but Gail came from wealth, and her family helped the Hortons get settled in that prestigious locale. Tom took the Long Island Railroad to work every day, a thirty-minute commute followed by a fifteen-minute subway ride to his office in downtown Manhattan. Gail initially stayed home with the girls, but when Claire and Theresa were both old enough to go to school, Gail made a bit of extra money watching other families' children during the day.

Despite their one-year grade difference, Claire and Theresa, by all accounts, grew up as close as two sisters could be. According to one of their neighbors, Claire went through a phase in second grade where she intentionally failed all of her tests in the hope of being held back so that she could become a classmate of Theresa. That scheme didn't work, and the neighbor joked that the two girls would have had a better chance had they focused on having Theresa, one of the brightest students in her class, try to skip a grade to catch up with Claire.

The Hortons became fixtures at their church on Sunday mornings, although some noted that the women in the family did not seem to share Tom's religious fervor. Gail, Claire, and Theresa never complained about Tom's faith; they were fully supportive as far as that went. But members of their church noted that the women, unlike Tom, seemed somewhat apathetic during services.

Claire and Theresa grew up to become two of the most popular girls in school. Claire is said to have been more outgoing than Theresa, who was substantially more academically gifted than her older sister. It was further said that Theresa was the prettier of the two, although Claire (who was beautiful in her own right) tended to nevertheless draw more attention from boys due to her bubbly and outgoing personality. Those differences in their personalities became more apparent as the girls grew older. That notwithstanding, Claire and Theresa remained nearly inseparable throughout all of high school. In fact, many noted that they were often mistaken as being fraternal twins.

The Hortons grew into a quintessential American family. While other families in their community were struck by tragedies, divorces, and domestic abuse, the Hortons seemed immune to any such adversities. Some in Manhasset took to referring to the Horton family (likely with more than a hint of bitterness) as "the Cleavers." But, unfortunately, there are situations where it only takes a single push to fell a row of dominoes. Such was the case for the Horton family.

It started in the summer after Theresa graduated from high school. Claire had just finished her freshman year of college and was home with her family for the summer. Theresa was scheduled to start college in September. Tom and Gail had strongly encouraged their daughters, who had always been so entwined in each other's lives, to attend different colleges to force each of them to make their own friends and social connections, without being able to use one another as a crutch. The girls reluctantly agreed, although they hedged their bets: they ended up enrolling in two different colleges in upstate New York that were a mere half hour from one another.

In her freshman year of college, Claire ended up becoming close friends with her assigned roommate, a girl named Katie who lived in New Jersey. Claire and Katie made arrangements to remain roommates in their sophomore year of college, and they kept in touch regularly over the summer. In August, they made plans to meet up in Manhattan to see a band—a Canadian group featuring a pair of twin sisters—that was playing at a small venue on a Wednesday night. Theresa reportedly wanted to join them, but Gail took her aside and encouraged her to stay home, explaining that it was important for Claire to have quality one-on-one time with her new friend. Gail's friends would later acknowledge that this advice, however well-intentioned it may have been, ended up haunting Gail; she became somewhat obsessed with how things might have played out had Theresa been permitted to tag along. How things may have been different had Claire not taken the train into the city alone.

The concert ended around 11:00 p.m. Katie later explained that even though she and Claire had a great time at the show, it was hard for them to talk to one another, to catch up, over the loud music. As such, once it ended, Katie suggested that they go out for a drink to discuss their summers and the school year ahead of them. One drink became several, and by the time they made it back to Penn Station to catch their respective trains (Katie's being the westbound New Jersey Transit and Claire's being the eastbound Long Island Railroad), both girls were pretty inebriated. Katie's train was scheduled to depart about twenty minutes before Claire's, so, at around 2:00 a.m., the girls hugged and went their separate ways.

The 2:20 a.m. train to Great Neck was fairly dead that night. Tom and Gail mentioned afterwards that the last time Claire had gone into Manhattan at night, she fell asleep on the train ride back and woke up, disoriented, in Port Washington, the final stop on that line. That experience may have contributed to Claire's decision to stand near the train doors rather than take one of the many available seats, although that is pure speculation.

The police later determined somehow (or at least developed a strong suspicion) that Claire managed to pass out even in her upright position on the train. A passenger in that car who later came forward recalled seeing Claire being led off the train by a man at one of the stops in Flushing, Queens. This witness claimed he didn't think anything of it at the time; he assumed that Claire and the unknown man were together. He only recalled that detail at all because of how visibly drunk Claire seemed to be when she exited to the train platform, allowing herself, with zombie-like steps, to be guided by the strange man.

At some point, while she was being led down the platform stairs to the street, Claire's instincts managed to override her drunkenness. Surveillance footage, I'm not sure from where, barely managed to catch Claire's struggle to separate herself from the strange man who had whisked her away. The footage did not capture any of the man's physical details, but it showed him refusing to let go of Claire. He could be seen physically restraining her. It was reported that as the man wrestled with Claire, one of his hands could be seen, even in that grainy footage, going up the bottom of Claire's dress. That was when Claire began to scream.

There were several people on the street, even at that late hour, who later acknowledged hearing Claire yell. They all offered various excuses as to why they did not investigate the noise. One couple, walking home from a bar themselves, claimed they thought it was just obnoxious horseplay. Another claimed, somewhat incredulously, that he thought the sound of Claire crying for help was merely wild laughter. Things might have turned out differently had one brave soul stuck his or her head into that darkened stairwell. But it's all academic, because no one did.

After Claire started screaming, the theory goes that her assailant panicked and did the first thing he could think of to silence her: he stabbed her in the chest with a stiletto he had been carrying somewhere on him and hurried back up to the train platform. It's assumed he escaped the scene through another set of stairs at the opposite end of the platform. He left Claire behind, sprawled near the bottom of the stairwell, fighting for breath, but it didn't take long for her to die.

The Horton family was devastated. But rather than grieve as a family, their mourning seemed to take each of them down separate paths. Gail was the most demonstrative: she sobbed throughout the wake and the funeral and naturally drew the most attention from sympathetic well-wishers. Tom's grief was largely internalized. He often retreated alone to pray, presumably for Claire's soul. Many wondered whether Tom should have been more present for Gail and Theresa during that time, but those thoughts were only conveyed in hushed whispers. No one feels comfortable telling a parent how to mourn a lost child.

As undemonstrative as Tom was, Theresa was even more so. A few people caught her occasionally misty-eyed at the burial, but, for the most part, she carried herself through the funeral proceedings with a dignified stoicism. Anyone familiar with the Hortons knew how close Theresa and Claire had been, so no one doubted for a moment the love that Theresa carried for her sister. Friends of the family assumed that Theresa was either holding back most of her emotions in public and letting them out in moments of solitude or, alternatively, that she was simply repressing those feelings because she was in some form of denial.

After the burial, it is said that one of Theresa's aunts delicately raised this issue with her. In response, Theresa explained that while she was hurt by Claire's death and would feel her sister's absence for the rest of her life, there was nothing to be gained by ceasing to function in the wake of that grief. "Claire certainly would not want that," Theresa stressed emphatically. Tom and Gail attributed Theresa's attitude in this regard to her remarkable intelligence, which, in hindsight, may have been somewhat naive.

Given Theresa's acceptance of Claire's passing, it was not entirely surprising that she steadfastly refused to put off her college education in order to give herself adequate time to heal. "What am I going to do?" Theresa asked a couple of her friends rhetorically. "Sit around here being sad for four months? What would that accomplish?" Tom and Gail, lacking the energy to fight with their remaining daughter, reluctantly gave in to Theresa's wish to start school the following month, as originally planned.

Three short weeks after Claire was buried, Theresa began college. At first, she was convinced that the change of scenery was doing her well, and that it was helping to put her grief behind her. As noted, Theresa was a very attractive girl, and even without her more outgoing sister, it was not long before she was routinely invited to almost all of the college parties (one of which could be found practically every night). And Theresa, who had been so studious in high school, rationalized that it was healthy for her to go out and socialize, to readjust to a world without Claire. That is why she never declined any of those invites.

Theresa was never a big drinker in high school. At most, she would nurse a beer on those occasions where Claire managed to drag her out to a keg party. In college, her inhibitions shifted. At her first party, she had several beers and enjoyed feeling buzzed for the first time in her life. A few parties later, she upgraded to mixed drinks and never declined a round of shots. Theresa's alcohol tolerance was low even by college freshmen standards, but she managed to ignore any warnings from her body and push through those barriers that would inform most college freshmen that it was time to stop drinking for the night. The speculation that arose later from armchair psychiatrists was that Theresa's drive to maintain a state of inebriation at college stemmed from her running away from unprocessed grief for Claire. There may be something to that, even though, as far as I am aware, Theresa never discussed Claire or her passing with anyone at college.

Two-and-a-half weeks after she started school, Theresa was found in her room, dead from alcohol poisoning. Her roommate, who had gone home for the weekend, returned that Sunday night to find Theresa lying on the floor, surrounded by a pool of vomit, an empty bottle of vodka, and another partially consumed bottle. The roommate, who was trained as a lifeguard, made a valiant effort to revive Theresa, but it was too late. It was later estimated that Theresa had been dead for at least a day before she was found.

In a little more than a month, Tom and Gail Horton were forced to bury both of their daughters. In the wake of those tragedies, Tom dove further into his faith and, in the process, away from Gail. He took to attending multiple Masses a day, and when he wasn't at church, he sat alone, reading the Bible incessantly for solace. In looking to himself, Tom forgot there was still another devastated member of his family who needed his support.

Two days after Theresa's funeral, Tom returned home from church one morning to find Gail in bed, having overdosed on sleeping pills that were prescribed to her after Claire's death in August. Although it was obviously a suicide, Gail didn't leave a note. I suppose no explanation was necessary.

Tom Horton, in the course of a month and a half, went from having a seemingly perfect family to being alone. The loss of his family left a hole in Tom— a hole too big to remain unfilled for long.

Tom, to his credit, tried to stay positive in the wake of adversity that no person should ever have to experience. No one could have blamed Tom had his faith wavered after what he had gone through, but this did not happen. Instead, his grip on his faith tightened, and other devout members of his church embraced him in the aftermath of that series of tragedies. Tom also refused his job's offer of granting him a leave of absence, telling his bosses that he had to stay busy to maintain any sense of normalcy. Despite his best efforts, though, a seed of anger had been planted in Tom—a seed that would grow and eventually eat away at him like a cancer.

It started small. Members of Tom's church would regularly check up on him, bringing him meals and offering aid, in any way they could, to help Tom get through that difficult period. At first, Tom politely thanked them for their compassion, but his tolerance for those acts of pity waned over time. This slowly evolved into paranoia. Imagined smirks behind his back. Perceived whispers regarding how his family "wasn't so perfect after all." No matter how many "friends" were around him, Tom felt increasingly alone.

Tom mostly kept those dark thoughts to himself and only shared them, on a single occasion, with his sister, who lived in California. The anger in Tom that was bubbling just below the surface erupted one evening when Tom lashed out at a trio of women who had stopped by with a lasagna for him, screaming incoherently about how he knew they were all judging him and that he did not need their phony charity. The women, taken aback, left abruptly and reported Tom's actions to the other members of their church. Tom later apologized to those women, but, after some discussion, it was agreed that it might be best to give Tom his space. Tom's church made it clear to him that it would still be there for him with open arms "when he was ready."

Tom's increasing paranoia manifested in his professional life, as well. When he returned to work, Tom was met with a series of awkward expressions of sympathy from coworkers, to which he responded with rote and inauthentic expressions of gratitude. And then, after that initial wave of compassion, he was left alone. It was, undoubtedly, uncomfortable for Tom's colleagues to engage him on mundane insurance matters while ignoring the fact that his entire family had been struck down in a matter of weeks. I'm sure they meant well in trying not to bother Tom with issues that were relatively unimportant, but the end result was that Tom became isolated at work—an island in a sea of judging eyes that purposefully avoided him.

There was no reprieve for Tom Horton. The media had seized upon his family's story, which made Tom, as the sole survivor, something of a local celebrity. Although most publications handled their coverage with decency and respect, other outlets focused on the "sexier" side of the story. Claire and Theresa were both beautiful, "barely legal" teens, and both died alcohol-related deaths. It was unsurprising that some trashy magazines hyped their coverage with "the truth about the Long Island party girls." Even people who were disinclined to buy those types of rags saw the headlines and, perhaps unavoidably, questioned how perfect the Horton family had actually been. And, in turn, how good of a father Tom actually was. Every time Tom went out in public, or took the train to work, he felt those unspoken questions. And they burned away at him.

Tom had never felt so alone in his life. As irrational as he knew it to be, Tom was convinced that everyone who had expressed sympathy to him, however earnestly, was secretly judging him and discussing amongst themselves how Tom managed to fail so completely as a father and husband. Those thoughts took root deep inside him. What had started as hurt evolved to anger, which in turn progressed to hate, and the hole that had been in Tom was finally filled. And when that hole began to overflow, Tom acted.

The vest took him three weeks to build. Tom's prior life was devoted to dissembling and deactivating explosives, including a variety of homemade devices, but he had never before attempted to build a bomb from scratch. As it turned out, whatever scraps of knowledge Tom retained from his career as an EOD were enough.

On one Sunday afternoon in the fall, Tom wrote a short note that he left on his kitchen table before donning his vest, which he covered with an overcoat. He then walked five minutes to the station and caught the 5:29 train to Penn Station. Upon arriving in Manhattan, Tom turned around, boarding the 6:32 train back to Manhasset. It's unclear why Tom made the trip into the city only to immediately take the train back to Manhasset. There was some speculation that he wanted to wait until he was on the eastbound train, in honor of Claire's last train ride. Another theory is that it was simply a matter of Tom being unable to work up the nerve to activate his vest until the return trip.

Whatever the reason, it did not happen until about halfway through the eastbound train ride. At 6:51 p.m., Tom, sitting in the first car of the train, activated his vest, causing an explosion that instantly killed him and the other eighteen people sitting in his car. That, as awful as it was, should have been the end of it.

But it wasn't.

In the days following, Long Island Railroad officials insisted that an interior explosion such as the one caused by Tom should not have been able to derail the train. The fact that it did so was written off as a fluke—a worst-case scenario stemming from the speed of the train at the moment of detonation, coupled with the fact that the train was also on a curve in the track at the time. Experts later explained that the explosion caused a lateral rocking in the front cars that caused them to derail and spill to the left, partially obstructing the parallel set of tracks used primarily by westbound trains heading into Manhattan.

Seconds after Tom's train derailed, it was struck by the train that was speeding around that same bend toward the city. It was a glancing blow, but it was enough to cause that train to derail, too. Anyone within a half mile of the collision clearly heard the gruesome sound of metal slamming into metal. The first three cars of the westbound train spilled off the overpass, twisting toward the street below, only to be held up precariously by the weight of the rear train cars that were still on the track. In all, the explosion, train collisions, and derailments killed forty-two people and injured dozens more.

•   •   •   •   •

At 6:51 on that Sunday evening, Abby was riding the train taking her back to Penn Station, at which point she would switch to the Amtrak train to take her the remainder of the way home. She sat in the lead car of the train—a strategic decision that would result in her being directly below the Amtrak station upon arriving at Penn Station. Abby always told me that she generally felt claustrophobic in Penn Station and sought to avoid walking through it as much as she could. I imagine that Abby was staring out the window, idly watching Queens fly by below her, when her car was struck by the eastbound train, causing it to topple to the street.

They were never able to determine whether it was the initial collision or the subsequent derailment of the train that caused her neck to snap, but it didn't make a difference. All that mattered to me was that Abby was gone.

chapter seventeen

You always remember where you were, and what you were doing, when you learn that a loved one has died. It's probably something mundane that will leave you with irrational guilt after the fact. *How could I have been napping when dad died of a heart attack?* Or, *What kind of asshole is sitting around watching porn while his mother dies in a car accident?* And so forth.

In my case, I was lounging on the couch next to Peaches, watching the Mets attempt to stave off the end of their season. I was glad Abby hadn't called my bluff that morning by asking me to go down to Long Island with her, although I felt a bit selfish about it. I tried to focus on how lucky I was to have married someone who was happy to let me watch an important baseball game in peace. Abby didn't seem to realize that not all wives were like her in that regard.

The game went into extra innings, and at the end of eleven, the score remained tied 5-5. The commercial break leading into the twelfth inning was unexpectedly interrupted with a breaking news announcement addressing what seemed, at first blush, to be a terrorist attack on the Long Island Railroad that had taken out two separate trains on the Port Washington line. Abby's line.

With a trembling hand, I clicked off the television and reached for my cell phone. I tried not to panic as I called Abby, but the call went directly to voicemail. "Please call me as soon as you get this," I said after the beep, trying to keep the nerves out of my voice. "I love you." *Maybe she just turned her phone off,* I thought, reminding myself to breathe. *Or she's in a tunnel somewhere.*

Steeling myself, I next called Abby's parents, hoping that she was still with them. *No,* her mother told me. *She left for the train about an hour ago. Why do you ask?* I couldn't bring myself to voice my dark suspicions, so I muttered something incomprehensible in response and hung up. I sat, stunned, staring at my dark television, with no idea what to do. Eventually, I turned the tv back on to watch the news, hoping there would be some breaking detail about the attack that would somehow confirm Abby was fine. I called Abby's cell phone again every few minutes, but it continued to go straight to her voicemail. Shortly after the explosion, but what felt like an eternity, I received the official word: Abby was dead.

•   •   •   •   •

Time and reality sputtered once I learned of Abby's death. There were long stretches where I became completely lost within myself, only to eventually reemerge at some point in the indeterminate future, confused and disoriented.

In this regard, I vaguely recall Abby's parents telling me that they wished for Abby to be buried on Long Island and my numb acquiescence to that request. I also have a faint recollection of being directed by Abby's parents to stay with them in Great Neck through the funeral and burial. Even in my state of shock, I recognized that a motel would not allow Peaches, a deal-breaker for me, so I accepted their offer. It probably would have been impossible for me to slink away to a motel in any event; Abby's mother was adamant that this was no time for me to be alone.

By the time my mind started to reassert itself, Peaches and I were settled into the basement of Abby's childhood home. The basement, which had a small kitchen, a bedroom, and a full bathroom, had once been used as an apartment when Abby's grandmother resided with Abby's parents and had not changed since she passed away several years earlier.

Abby's two sisters, Erica being the older, and Stacey the younger, left their respective families and resituated themselves in their old bedrooms during the week following Abby's death. Erica, a vice president at a major bank, handled the logistics of the wake and funeral with brisk efficiency. It was just as well. I was in no position to do so myself. The reason for that was simple: scheduling Abby's funeral would have been tantamount to an admission that her death was permanent. And that was not something I was prepared to concede.

Erica informed me that Abby's wake would be held on Friday—a two-hour session in the afternoon, followed by another in the evening. The funeral and burial would take place the following day. Erica explained that the wake could not be held until the end of the week due to complications arising from the investigation of the train crash. I nodded sadly in response when she told me, but truthfully, I was in no rush to bury Abby. I largely viewed these funeral proceedings as annoying distractions—not out of any lack of love for Abby, but merely because they were keeping me from the more important task at hand.

Although I shared a house with the Petersens, I mostly kept myself isolated and apart from them. Even when we were all together in the same room, it felt as if I existed on a different plane of reality than the others. For while the four remaining members of Abby's family all went through the various stages of grief together, I was stuck on the first: denial. The possibility of Abby coming back was not on her family's radar, so they did not obsess over it as I did.

But unlike me, they did not know God.

And so I spent most of my time that week in my temporary basement apartment with Peaches, taking for granted that the notion of getting Abby back was not only possible, but that it was just a matter of time before it happened. Still, as firmly as I held onto the belief that Abby's death was a mere hiccup, voices expressing questions of doubt managed to find their way into my skull:

John can see and control everything. Why did he allow Abby to die?

"It doesn't matter," I muttered darkly to myself. "He can bring her back."

John let Alexander Bennett die. Why should Abby be any different?

"John cares about me. He won't allow this."

He is one with everyone and everything. Did he not care about Alex?

"It's different with me."

Is it, though? Is this why John couldn't make eye contact with me when he last bid me farewell?

"He promised last time that we would speak again. I'm sure he will fix this then."

Then what is he waiting for?

That, I did not know, and I grew antsy waiting for John's intervention. Lacking the patience to sit around doing nothing, I struggled to conceive of *anything* affirmative I might do to speed the process along. That is why, even though I knew that John was undoubtedly aware of everything that had transpired, I developed an unseemly habit of trying to get his attention while I lurked in the Petersens' basement. At first, I simply took to muttering aloud when no one was around to listen. "John? John? Please; I need your help."

After those pleas went unanswered, I remembered that John, as God, had only ever spoken with me when no one else was around. *Perhaps it's the crowded house that's keeping him away*, I wondered. Granted, it didn't make any sense; if John wanted to talk to me, he would. Yet, it was a theory I could not let go. With that in mind, I then took to sneaking away to isolated areas to call out for John's help.

One night, I escaped the house while everyone else slept and walked several miles toward Little Neck Bay. Finding a place near the water that was adequately isolated, I called aloud. "John, I really need to talk to you. Please?" I spent most of that night in the freezing cold, fruitlessly waiting for God.

"John, my wife died. Abby. I need your help. Please." This I pleaded the next morning from a wooded area I discovered a few miles to the south of the Petersens' home. When John still did not come, I went back to the house. Recalling John's love of his old cat, I brought Peaches back with me to that desolate stretch of forest and reiterated my cries for John to appear. Even with Peaches present, those calls continued to go unanswered.

Abby's family, even through the fog of their own pain, noticed my increasingly odd behavior, and each member of the family addressed it in their own unique way. Abby's mother, a sweet woman who reminded me of what Abby might have become in another thirty-five years, came downstairs at one point and explained that although they would all respect my grieving process, I needed to remember that I was not alone in my suffering. Abby's father, struggling to keep his own emotions in check, attempted to draw me out on another occasion by inviting me to come out to the back deck to split a six pack in Abby's memory. I politely declined his offer.

Erica and Stacey came downstairs in tandem to plead their case.

"You're part of the family, you know," Erica, who seemed to be used to getting what she wanted, told me with more than a hint of impatience. "You don't have to go through this alone."

"Abby wouldn't want you to suffer by yourself like this," Stacey added before bursting into tears. Of all of the family members, Stacey had been the most demonstrative with her emotions in the immediate aftermath of Abby's passing.

I tried to explain to them that I didn't mean to shun everyone by holding the entire family at arm's length, and that I was just processing Abby's loss in my own way. I don't know if they were satisfied with my explanation, but they eventually took to leaving me to my own devices in the basement, where I continued, in private, my attempts to summon John.

There were stretches during which I could pull myself away from my obsession with attracting John's attention. In those moments, I dedicated my time to watching the news and reading just about every story I could find relating to the train wreck. I stayed up all night combing the internet and flipping through the various news stations, which were dominated by coverage relating to Tom Horton's attack. Not all components of the story interested me. I would, for example, quickly change the channel whenever video of the train wreck itself was shown. I also tuned out for any discussions relating to the political ramifications of the incident.

Rather, the stories I sought out related to Tom Horton. I needed to know *why*. I needed to understand what had driven him to do what he had done. And so, for hours each day, I locked myself away in the Petersens' basement and learned all about the tragic history of the Horton family. Indeed, while that saga had been well covered by the local news even before Horton's fatal attack, the explosion resulted in those old news stories being resurrected, only this time, at the national level.

I also learned that Tom Horton, with the one glaring exception that was his last act in this world, had lived his life as a quality human being. After Horton was identified as the perpetrator of the attack a few short hours after the explosion, the media mercilessly sought out Horton's neighbors, coworkers, and friends—really anyone positioned to opine Tom's mental state in the days leading to his breakdown. Those people all offered the same opinion, albeit in different words: Horton was a good man who was dealt more pain than he knew how to handle.

This was confirmed by Horton's hastily written suicide note, which was found on his kitchen table shortly after he was identified as the cause of the train wreck. "Note" being somewhat of an overstatement, as Tom's message was a mere eight words, hand-written in sloppy cursive: *"My pain is too great to be contained."*

The media struggled to find a preexisting narrative to adopt in contextualizing Horton's actions. Some drew comparisons to Andreas Lubitz, the German pilot whose severe depression led him to purposefully crash a passenger jet into the mountains. Experts on television stressed that cases such as Horton's and Lubitz's were exceptions, and that murder-suicides are not a normal byproduct of depression (particularly when they result in extrafamilial incidents). These experts explained, albeit in more pretentious language, that self-harm is more common among people suffering from depression than outward violence. Tom Horton's case seemed to be an outlier that could not be easily reconciled with any recognized, established pattern.

I wanted to hate Horton. I truly did. But despite my best efforts, I couldn't bring myself to do so. He had gone through so much, it was impossible not to feel for him at some level—even though he had killed my wife. The most I could muster was hate for Horton's final decision. For the man behind that decision, I felt only pity. I tried to empathize with what Horton had experienced, but I came up short. I simply could not fathom lashing out at the world in the way he had. Senselessly killing all of those people. Killing Abby. It would never make sense to me. Thus, while the hours I spent alone allowed me to become somewhat of an expert as to the facts relating to Horton's attack, my understanding of Horton himself remained incomplete.

I was caught off guard when Friday, the day of Abby's wake, finally arrived. I went to the funeral home with the Petersens early in the afternoon, where we were led to a large windowless room filled with all sorts of floral arrangements. *I didn't realize Abby knew so many people*, I thought as I gazed over what looked like an indoor garden. Even if Abby's social circle was small, she had managed a near-perfect rate of success in earning the love of anyone exposed to her.

In the midst of all those flowers, I saw Abby, laid out in her casket. The last time I had seen her was five days earlier when she dashed out of our house to catch the train. It felt like a month had passed since then.

I stared at her, looking as if she were simply sleeping peacefully, and I struggled to hold my tears at bay. *Why are you drawing this out, John?* I thought bitterly. *Why are you putting me through all of this?* He did not respond.

Abby's parents, followed by Erica and Stacey, approached the casket to pray, or just to say goodbye to Abby, while I lingered behind. Again, I could not bring myself to participate; that would have been an admission that Abby was dead and, even more objectionable, that she would remain so. As the family gathered at one side of the room, I took the opportunity to turn away from them to again whisper fiercely for John. My tone became more plaintive as I begged for him to end the farce, and I jumped, startled, when I felt a hand on my shoulder. Looking down, I saw Abby's mother, who gestured toward the front of the room with her head. The other family members had dispersed, respectfully giving me room to approach.

"You should go say goodbye to her," she told me gently. I nodded dumbly and shuffled across the room.

A small kneeler was set up on the side of the coffin for prayer. I knelt, although I refused, in that particular moment, to address John. Instead, I took the opportunity to study Abby's beautiful, kind face—perhaps the one thing in my life I had never taken for granted.

"I'm so sorry you have to go through this, Abby," I whispered to her resting figure. "I'm trying to fix it, but I'm not sure how. I won't give up though. You don't deserve this." I trailed off and gazed at her face for a long moment. "You don't deserve this," I repeated softly, before standing back up and rejoining Abby's family.

A few minutes later, the area was opened to the public and the afternoon session of the wake was underway. It did not take long for the room to fill, and I was again struck by how many lives Abby had touched. Before long, the space was packed with Abby's old friends from high school and college, teachers and parents she worked with over the past several years. A number of children, from kindergarten through high school, also appeared during the wake, and I could tell from their darkened glasses and white canes that they were current or former students of Abby (or "Ms. Abby," as they referred to her when I spoke with them). Aside from my mother, who flew up from Florida, where she had retired years ago, I didn't have any friends or family in attendance. That was largely my own fault; I hadn't reached out to anyone from my past about the arrangements or even Abby's death. I had not envisioned things proceeding so far along without John's intervention.

I spent time during the wake speaking with teachers who had worked with both Abby and me. They generally knew me better than they did Abby, as her itinerant status only took her through my school, at most, a few times a week. Still, even if their only exposure to Abby had been passing her occasionally in the hall, they recalled that she would always smile brightly at them with a loud "Good morning!" One of those teachers told me bluntly that she had always thought Abby was too good for me, and that her sunny disposition seemed entirely at odds with my introvertedness. She quickly apologized, but I told her not to bother; her assessment seemed fair.

Everyone who came to pay their respects to Abby, even those who did not know me at all, tried to engage me and break what they perceived as my shocked state of grief. I managed to go through the motions and make polite conversation in response to those efforts, but my mind tended to wander to John and why he was delayed in taking action. There was only one person who managed, if only for a few minutes, to draw me out of myself: Ed Gallagher. He arrived alone, toward the end of the evening session, and looked more haggard than I had ever seen him.

"Hey, Dave," he told me, grabbing me in a fierce embrace. "I'm so sorry. Abby was an amazing person. We all loved her."

"Thank you, Mr. Gallagher," I replied. I had never been able to bring myself to call him Ed.

"How are you holding up?" he asked, peering into my eyes like a doctor assessing a concussion.

"It's …" I trailed off.

Mr. Gallagher nodded sadly in understanding.

"I know, I know. It's too much to process in such a short period of time."

He let out a long sigh and looked around the room, struggling to collect himself. Although he was stunned by Abby's sudden death, Mr. Gallagher seemed to be carrying his own set of baggage even beyond that. I gently asked if everything was ok with him. His long pause confirmed the presence of his own demons, and I wondered whether he would respond to my question at all. But then he did, and his voice was choked with emotion.

"There are two ways of losing someone," he said, staring at a blank space of wall. "It's either expected, or it's unexpected. It's really that simple. And they each come with their own set of pratfalls. If you lose someone unexpectedly, you remember them as they were, but the grief—it's like a punch in the gut. It's overwhelming. Still, when you lose someone and it *isn't* a surprise, you have time to prepare, but then you have to deal with the cost of watching a loved one die. Watch them just wither away." He paused, but I didn't interrupt.

"My point," he continued, finally able to look at me again, "if I have one at all, is that it's *never* easy. There is no ideal scenario for losing someone. It all feels impossible to handle, just for different reasons."

We stood in silence for a few moments, surrounded by the idle chatter of other attendees. Somewhere in the room, a young girl abruptly laughed and was quickly shushed by her mother.

"Who did you lose?" I asked softly.

"I—I didn't mean to make it about me," Mr. Gallagher said, embarrassed. When I continued to stare at him, he gave in. "I haven't suffered a loss. Not yet, at least. But I'm losing someone." He took a deep breath. "My wife has been fighting breast cancer for some time. She went through months of chemo, but …

We went to the doctor yesterday, and we were told that she's at stage four. The damn thing is spreading, and—"

He couldn't finish. I reached behind me and grabbed a tissue from one of the strategically placed boxes spread around the room, which I handed to him.

"Jesus," I whispered. "I'm so sorry. But you should be with her now; you didn't have to come all the way down here for this."

He waved off my concerns, dabbing his eyes with the tissue.

"Liz insisted that I come. She's strong—stronger than I ever was. Her sister and her best friend are with her now, and she told me that she needed some girl time to lift her spirits." He chuckled softly. "I think her exact quote was, 'Your mopey ass isn't doing me any good here so you may as well drive down to Long Island.'"

His laugh died as he remembered where he was, and who he was talking to.

"And it was important to me to pay my respects," he added in a more serious tone. "You're a great guy, and Abby was a sweetheart. An absolute sweetheart. It's a shame when things like this happen to the good ones."

Mr. Gallagher noticed others had been lining up to pay their respects to me, and he moved as if to leave. I grabbed his arm before he could escape and gently pulled him back.

"Can I ask you something?" I asked. "It's a bit of a tactless question."

"If there's ever a week when you can be forgiven for some tactlessness, this is it," he replied drily. "What have you got?"

"This is going to sound like an odd question, but your wife—if there were a cure for her out in the world, but you had no idea how to find it, would that be preferable to just being able to accept her fate, whatever it was?"

Mr. Gallagher seemed taken aback by the question, but I think my expression convinced him that this issue weighed heavily upon me, even if he couldn't understand why. He didn't hesitate in answering.

"Of course I'd want the option of a cure," he said. "Any hope, no matter how miniscule, beats no hope at all."

"But you could lose your mind trying to find that cure," I said. "And if you didn't, and Liz passed away because of your failure, you'd be stuck with that burning guilt in your gut."

Mr. Gallagher shook his head emphatically.

"That's the thing, Dave. It's not about me. It's about *her*. I'd damn myself a thousand times over for a shot, however small it might be, to save her."

With that, he gave me one last sad pat on the arm and drifted away. Before someone else could grab me, I took the opportunity to sneak outside and went to an isolated alley behind the funeral home.

"Please, John!" I cried into the night. "This is too much for me to handle. Just let me know what I have to do, and I'll do it. I'll do whatever you want me to do."

But my pleas continued to go unanswered.

•   •   •   •   •

The funeral was held the following morning.

My erratic sleep patterns throughout the week had caught up with me, and I felt drunk with exhaustion when I arrived at the church with the Petersens. My mind was a fog, and I found it nearly impossible to think straight. As scattered as my thoughts were that morning, there was one in particular that never left me, even for a second: *John can still make this right.*

As such, while the pastor led those assembled in prayers through the course of the funeral service, I savagely whispered my own set of invocations: "John, please. I need you. I don't know what you're doing, but please. Help me. I'm begging you, John." Even when the funeral proceeded without any divine intervention, I refused to let go of my belief that John would fix this mess eventually, and that his delay was some sort of fluke. *Whatever else happens, I know John won't allow her to be buried.* I tried to convince myself of that while Abby's casket was blessed by the pastor.

I struggled to maintain a sliver of hope after the funeral ended as I rode east in a limousine with Abby's family. "Please, John," I continued to mutter, ignoring the worried looks thrown my way by the Petersens. I distracted myself by daydreaming of John, radiating pure light as he reached down from a cloud to restore Abby to life with a single touch of his holy finger. Or perhaps Abby would sneak up on all of us from behind while we were gathered around her casket, which was revealed to be empty to the shock of all. During that drive, there were no limits to my imagination as I tried to envision the moment Abby would come back to us.

I was convinced a miracle was about to happen when our funeral procession hit random mid-day traffic. *John is slowing things down while he breathes life back into her,* I thought. But then the traffic, without warning, let up, and we made our way in due time to the cemetery.

From my vantage at the back of the limo, I could not see when the hearse carrying Abby's casket drove away from us. After stopping for a few moments inside the cemetery, our car lurched forward and parked a few minutes later. Abby's family guided me out, and I walked alongside them, muttering increasingly frenzied and incoherent requests for John to take action. I was dimly aware of a mob of people emerging from other cars to follow us, but I didn't turn to look at them.

We were led through rows of headstones until we came to a large hole in the ground next to a mound of dirt. My vision swimming, I could barely process a casket being wheeled out and inserted into an unfamiliar apparatus. I looked around, bewildered, unclear as to what was happening. Stacey, sobbing, came to my side and rubbed my back to calm me down. I was on the verge of asking her what was going on when I heard the apparatus come to life. And then Abby's casket was lowered into the ground.

That was the moment Abby's death finally hit me. There would be no last-minute intervention from John staying the burial after all. A week's worth of grief locked away in me, suppressed by the hope Abby would be brought back, erupted like a volcano, and I fell apart. With an anguished inhuman scream, I fell to my knees and wailed. Someone—I don't know who—knelt down beside me and cradled my head as I sobbed uncontrollably. I hardly processed the pastor reciting an unfamiliar prayer as Abby was lowered to her final resting place. For some indeterminate period of time I knelt there crying, only occasionally stopping long enough to catch my breath. Once I had collected myself enough to allow a semblance of sanity to reassert itself, I could no longer see the casket. Whoever had been holding my head let go, leaving me on the ground, gasping and exhausted. Through my blurred vision, I saw everyone else in the procession slowly making their way back to the row of cars. A couple of them looked back at me in concern, but most judiciously pretended as if they had not seen my spectacle.

I knelt on the ground, confused as to what I was supposed to do. Eventually the pastor came to my side and, in a calm and understanding tone, suggested that I say my final farewell to Abby. He pointed subtly with his chin toward the hole in the ground where Abby had been lowered. The pastor gave a sad smile of encouragement as I stood up and wiped away my tears with a sleeve. His expression of compassion quickly turned to confusion, though, when I pivoted and wordlessly walked back to the limo where Abby's family was awaiting my return.

I regretted not properly saying goodbye to Abby at that time. It obviously would have been the right thing to do. I hoped Abby would understand that I simply lacked the mental capacity to frame a farewell to her at that moment, as I was all-consumed by a single thought:

John has betrayed me.

chapter eighteen

We were silent as the limo drove us back to Great Neck. A tension seemed to have left everyone once the matter of burying Abby was put behind us. I felt the loss of that emotional strain myself, although it troubled me. Part of me longed to continue to resist accepting Abby's passing, even though I knew deep down that madness lurked in that direction.

Abby's sisters and father seemed afraid to look at me after my outburst at the grave site, and they sat with their heads down, lost in their own thoughts. Abby's mother, by contrast, was absurdly relieved at seeing me finally release the emotions I had been suppressing all week, and she sat at my side, occasionally patting my hand in a consoling fashion even though I had long since collected myself.

We were heading toward what had been Abby's favorite Italian restaurant for a post-funeral lunch with family and close friends. I had been to those types of lunches before, but always in a peripheral role where I felt comfortable enough to have a couple of beers and laugh over fond memories of the deceased. This would be my first after-burial lunch where I was part of the epicenter of grief, and I was dreading the experience. If I truly had to continue my life without Abby, all I wanted to do was take Peaches home and begin to process my loss.

After an hour of driving in silence, we arrived at the restaurant. Abby's mom grabbed my arm possessively and escorted me in. The entire restaurant had been reserved for us. I assumed that Erica had worked out the logistics. I was led to a table in the center of the room and took a seat next to Stacey, whose makeup had run a bit from crying all morning. I felt like I should say something reassuring to her, but I had nothing to offer, so I continued to stare blankly into space while the restaurant filled up around us.

"I can't believe she's gone," Stacey said, giving in to a need to break the silence.

"I can't either," I replied, truthfully.

Stacey sighed and looked out a giant window. The sun was shining brightly, and rays of light pierced the room.

"It was such a beautiful day today, too," Stacey added. "I feel like it was a sign of how much God loved Abby."

I felt my throat clench and choked, but Stacey, still looking out the window, didn't notice. A stream of people who had driven out to the burial continued to enter through a back entrance. I was surprised when Mr. Gallagher came in, accompanied by a pretty woman wearing a headscarf who I assumed to be his wife, Liz. *I had no idea they went to the funeral and burial,* I thought.

Liz looked pale and weak from her chemo treatments, but Mr. Gallagher seemed ready to pounce to her aid at a moment's notice. Even as he walked in, Mr. Gallagher's eyes never left his wife for more than a second or two. *That is what love looks like,* I noted. *Did I ever radiate love like that when I was with Abby?*

I tried to recall what Mr. Gallagher had told me two days earlier. *I'd damn myself a thousand times over for a shot, however small it might be, to save her.* I could tell from the way he hovered at his wife's side that he had meant every word.

All of a sudden, the room felt unbearably oppressive, and I had to get out. Staying there to eat a pasta lunch would be giving up on Abby.

"No," I muttered aloud, standing up. Stacey frowned at me, concerned.

"Excuse me." Without waiting for Stacey to respond, I walked briskly away from the table. People continued to file in from the parking lot that sat behind the restaurant, so I exited out the front to the street. Once I got my bearings, I started off toward the Petersens' house—a brisk walk that was soon upgraded to a run. My dress shoes threatened to break from the strain of my jog, but I didn't care. It was about a mile to the house, which I covered in less than ten minutes. When I finally arrived, I was sweating profusely through my suit. My feet ached and I was out of breath, but I felt lighter at my decision to continue to fight against Abby's death. Somehow.

"Peaches!" I called as I entered the basement. The cat emerged from the bedroom, yawning and stretching. I patted his side fondly as he rubbed against my calf in greeting. "We're going home."

I quickly changed out of my suit into a more comfortable pair of jeans and sweatshirt. After tossing the rest of my belongings into a bag, I carried it out to the car with Peaches following along. Without any prompting, Peaches hopped into the passenger's seat and laid down. I turned off my cell phone and drove away without delay, fearful of someone from Abby's family coming back to check on me.

My eyes felt heavy shortly into the two-and-a-half-hour drive back to Woodstock, and I was reminded once again of how little sleep I had managed that week. On more than one occasion, I was ripped out of a life-threatening doze by the sound of tires hitting the rumble strip on the side of the Thruway.

"Sorry, Peaches," I mumbled after the third such instance. "I haven't really slept in days. But don't worry. I'm still pretty sure he wouldn't let anything bad happen to you."

The sun had just set by the time I pulled onto my street. Peaches stretched and stood up, but he seemed confused when I didn't pull into our driveway. I slowed the car down as I neared our house, deep in thought, only to accelerate once again down the block.

"We're going to the mountain," I announced. Peaches didn't object, although he would have had good grounds to do so. My decision to tackle the mountain at that moment was undeniably reckless; it was dark, and I was beyond exhausted. The more intelligent course of action would have been to just go to bed and make the hike in the morning. But sleeping wouldn't have helped Abby, so I did not see it as a viable option.

The sun was long gone by the time we arrived at the trailhead. The nearly full moon provided nominal illumination, which I calculated would be enough for me to reach the summit. I was hopeful; I had long suspected, after all of my hikes with Peaches, that I could navigate the path blindfolded, if need be. Unfortunately, my confidence in my hiking abilities turned out to be vastly overinflated.

Nearly from the get-go, I found myself stumbling over unseen rocks that threatened to break my ankles on several occasions. I tripped over a log at one point, landing painfully on my shoulder. Even then it didn't occur to me to turn back. I felt as if getting to the top of that mountain was the most important thing I would ever do in my life.

Peaches, with his nocturnal vision, became my savior. He had no problem navigating the difficult terrain, and he seemed delighted by the sounds of unseen animals scurrying about in the undergrowth as we ascended. Still, as interested as he was in those noises, he did not leave my side. Step by step, I allowed my cat to guide me up the trail.

After nearly three hours of climbing, we reached the top. I had never experienced the view from the summit at night—pinpoints of light in the distance (houses I assumed), blanketed by a seemingly infinite tapestry of stars. It hardly registered with me. I was focused on making yet another plea to John. There was no rational reason I couldn't have made my pitch elsewhere, but on this mountain was the last place I saw him. The locale felt significant, if not quite holy. I could not think of a more meaningful place on the planet to reach out to John.

"John!" I called. Peaches started at the sudden noise, and I bent to scratch his head to calm him down.

"I buried my wife today. But you know that, don't you?"

There was no response but the wind. I felt a growing impatience, and I started pacing about the summit like a caged lion.

"You let her die. You ignored me when I begged for your help. And now you're apparently afraid to face me." I looked straight up into the sky. "I never thought you were a coward."

Peaches sat and continued to watch my performance.

"I guess I was wrong. Abby is now buried under six feet of dirt because of your cowardice." I felt a rage rush through me, and my voice grew louder. "I spent *years* listening to you whine about how unimportant your job was, and how much you hated being a lawyer. Well, you finally have something important to do, and you're too fucking scared to do it! You just sit back, watching the world suffer— watching Abby die—and do nothing! Not a damn thing!"

I paused to get my breath, but again there was no response. I felt a wetness on my cheeks. *When did I start crying?* I took a deep breath and tried to calm myself back down.

"But you can still fix this. You were thrown into this position for a reason. You can make the world better. Just trust yourself. You aren't meant to be doing nothing. You *know* that!"

I paused, desperately hoping for John to materialize. But he didn't. Peaches continued to sit, riveted by my actions. I couldn't think of anything else to say or do, and I felt helpless.

"You promised we'd speak again," I whispered hoarsely. "You promised …"

I trailed off, feeling foolish. I looked back dejectedly at Peaches, barely visible in the moon's feeble light, and resigned myself to making the long descent down the mountain with nothing to show for it. I took two steps in Peaches' direction, but on the third my left foot fell on a barely visible rock, causing me to stumble and fall to my right. Before I could extend my hands to catch myself, my head struck a large boulder. Consciousness drifted away, and I was too tired to hold onto it.

●　　　●　　　●　　　●　　　●

Then it was sunrise, and Peaches was batting at my nose.

It took me a moment to place where I was, and another few to recall *why* I was there. As I struggled to reconstruct the prior night, Peaches swatted at my nose again.

"Ok, ok … I'm awake," I murmured, sitting up. The side of my head throbbed, and I felt a large bump when I touched it. "Right," I sighed, remembering everything.

My body was stiff and sore after spending the night out in the open on top of a mountain. The weather had been cool, but fortunately not cold enough for me to run any real risk of hypothermia. I plucked a few gray hairs off of my tongue and surmised that Peaches had helped keep me warm by nestling against my face all night. I realized that my actions the prior evening had been particularly stupid.

"Why'd you wait so long to wake me?" I asked Peaches, scratching behind his ears. Taking a deep breath, I recognized that despite the swelling lump on my head and an overall achiness, I felt better than I had in days. For the first time since Abby died, I could think somewhat clearly again.

"Ah, it was probably the right call. I needed those few hours of rest."

I stood up and stretched. The soreness would work itself out eventually, and the bump on my head did not seem that severe. I surmised that I had not done any long-term damage with my desperate antics.

I glanced at Peaches, who was ready to head back down the trail. "I tried, Peaches," I said. "I really did. I just don't have any ideas right now." Peaches chirped in sympathy, or so I imagined, and rubbed his body against my calves.

We made our way back down the mountain, which was exponentially easier to navigate in the daylight. From there, it took me twenty minutes to drive back to our house. I felt trepidation at entering, not wanting to deal with a home that Abby was not part of. Finally, reminding myself that Peaches was long overdue a meal, I forced myself to head inside.

Our home looked exactly as I remembered it, but it could not have felt more different. I limped into the kitchen to feed Peaches, and my eyes were drawn to a grocery list Abby had affixed to the refrigerator with a dolphin magnet. I stared at it for some time—a list of items that I knew I would never go out to purchase myself—and I was only snapped out of my trance by the impatient cry of Peaches, waiting to be fed.

Once Peaches set to devouring his bowl of cat food, I went upstairs. My "nap" on the mountain was enough to restore most of my sanity, but I still felt as if I could sleep for a week. I envisioned taking a quick shower to wash off the dirt and clean out my various scrapes, after which I would collapse in bed. I knew not what would come next, but I vowed to put off worrying about that until I caught up on my sleep. I hoped Abby would understand.

I felt mildly better after I had showered and donned a fresh pair of shorts and a t-shirt. But as I stood by the bed, surveying the bedroom, a new wave of loss swept over me. So much in the room was Abby. Pictures of the two of us in various settings in a cutesy "I Married My Best Friend!" frame that she had set on her nightstand after our wedding. Her gray cat slippers, which she'd purchased in Peaches' honor, were still lined up neatly on the floor by her side of the bed. Hell, even the gun safe under our bed, holding the "Baby Glock" that Abby insisted on having in the house, reminded me of her. I didn't know how I could sleep surrounded by all of that. I could not fathom how I would ever sleep in that room again.

Seeing the bedroom, which seemed like a memorial to Abby, fanned the flickering flame inside me that refused to give up on her. I cast my eyes about the room, looking for inspiration. My eyes settled on my side of the bed, and I was hit with memories from my childhood that I had thought were lost forever. It gave me a weak idea, but it was at least something. Desperate times lead to desperate plans.

I felt foolish as I knelt down gingerly to face the side of my bed. Placing my two hands together, I closed my eyes, and then, for the first time in decades, I began to pray.

"Dear John," I intoned. "Or God. I'm not sure of your preferred title. I'm sorry about what I said to you last night. You have to understand, though: I spent so much of my life unhappy. I was so miserable, yet I still couldn't even realize what I was missing, but you helped me see it. Abby became a tremendous part of my joy, but now she's gone."

Downstairs, I could hear Peaches scratching in his litter box. I continued.

"As thankful as I am that you helped steer me to a road that led to Abby, I can't help but think you've also treated me a bit unfairly. I mean, if you never came to me and showed me what you had become, I would have been able to at least *accept* Abby's death, as painful as it would have been. But you made me believe—made me *know*—that literally *nothing* is impossible. I don't know that I can ever put this behind me, being fully aware that you can bring Abby back, but you won't, for whatever reasons you have. This will consume me. You owe me, if nothing else, an explanation. Why it is that even though you can arrange for Abby to be alive right now, you won't. Because there is no chance that I'll be able to move on without that. So please ..."

I didn't know what more I could say, so I ended it. "Amen."

I stayed in my genuflected state for a moment, eyes closed. After a beat, I felt another presence enter the room behind me. Holding my breath, I stood up and turned around to face it ...

... and was instantly driven back to my knees, the air forced out of my lungs. Reality dissolved around me to be replaced with a searing white light, which was not confined by the walls of my bedroom. That light, pulsing and all-powerful, instead appeared to stretch toward infinity in all directions. I could no longer see my bedroom, although I could vaguely feel the rug under my hands. The world I had occupied had been replaced with that burning glow, brighter than all the stars of the universe combined. It felt as if my eyes were melting as I stared into that blaze, yet even through that excruciating pain, I could not will myself to look away. In agony, I tried to scream, but no sound other than a garbled croak emerged. The mere *presence* of that radiance permeated every molecule of my being, and I could feel myself losing hold of rational thought. All I could process, even while being consumed by that searing pain, was that light. My last thought before I was completely driven to the floor was the horrific realization that whatever I was facing was no longer the John I had once known.

I was facing God.

My mind tried to grasp a hold of something, anything. I knew I could not succeed if I gave in to John's presence.

Abby. Think of Abby.

I held onto the image of her face the way a sailor caught in a tsunami would desperately cling to the ship's mast. It helped, but not much, in the onslaught of John's radiance.

What happened to him? Generating that simple thought felt like lifting a ton of bricks, and it left me breathless. *How could he have changed so much in just a few years?*

"*AS I TOLD YOU ONCE, I EXIST OUT OF TIME.*" A deafening, dispassionate voice inside my head that threatened to tear my skull apart. My hands flew to cover my ears, as if that offered any protection. I whimpered, tortured, as I continued to stare into that blinding white inferno.

He's reading my mind. The thought floated through the pain, and I remembered once working out that John being privy to my mental workings would be disastrous, even if I could not recall why that was so. All I knew at that moment was that I would fail if I allowed John to remain in my head. "*Get him out!*" screamed the tiny part of my consciousness that had yet to submit to John's presence.

"You promised—" I attempted to shout, but it came out as a weak gasp. Even those two words took all of my energy to muster. Still, John heard it. Of course he did.

"YOU WISH TO HAVE YOUR THOUGHTS BE YOUR OWN. YOU BELIEVE THIS WILL SOMEHOW GIVE YOU AN ADVANTAGE OVER ME." John's booming voice, which no longer originated from inside my head, sounded faintly amused. "SO BE IT. NOW SAY WHAT YOU WILL."

Some pressure lessened once John exited my mind, but it just felt like being crushed by a train instead of a mountain. Although I continued to hold onto Abby's memory as a desperate anchor, my senses remained scattered in the presence of that infinitely powerful light. I tried, once again, to look away, but I could not. Gasping for breath, I feebly voiced the one coherent thought I could muster. "Abby is dead."

"I AM AWARE." John's voice emanated from the light. I struggled to articulate a follow up.

"You could have stopped it," I finally whispered, struggling to lift myself, only to fail before collapsing again.

"I COULD HAVE."

I felt what was left of my will slipping further away. *Keep thinking of her ...*

I momentarily drew a blank as to who the "her" was, and then I reclaimed the memory with reserves of strength I had not known were in me. *Abby. Don't let it go.* I questioned how much longer I could continue.

Giving up on picking myself up, I weakly whispered from my prone position, "Even now, you could bring her back."

"I COULD."

Breathing itself became an impossible task. I could not think of anything to say that would move John to bring Abby back. The best I could muster with my last remaining strength was to spit out the three words that I feared would haunt me forever. "But you won't."

My question, which was really not a question, had no time to linger before John responded.

"NO."

There was not even a hint of a pause.

As I lay suffocating from John's omnipresence, I tried to formulate an argument, a compelling reason as to why John should bring Abby back, but my will had completely eroded. My mind had succumbed to that pounding light, and my thoughts were no longer my own. I had lost.

I was dimly aware of that failure, but even that thought drifted away as I lost my tenuous hold on memories of Abby, leaving me completely helpless, prone before the all-powerful might of God. I had succumbed entirely to that light, and John's parting words hardly registered as they washed over me:

"DEATH IS A PART OF LIFE. YOU DO NOT REALIZE: I DO NOT SEE YOU AS YOU EXIST IN THIS MOMENT. I SEE A BABY, GASPING FOR HIS FIRST BREATH. I SEE AN OLD MAN LYING IN BED, LETTING GO OF HIS LAST STRAND OF LIFE. I SEE ALL OF YOUR MOMENTS IN BETWEEN. BUT ABOVE ALL ELSE, WHEN I LOOK AT YOU, I SEE NOTHING. I SEE THE NOTHINGNESS THAT EXISTED BEFORE YOUR BIRTH, AND THAT WHICH WILL CONTINUE INDEFINITELY AFTER YOU ARE GONE. SO SHALL IT BE FOR YOU.

"AND SO IT IS NOW FOR ABBY."

And then John said the words that confirmed my failure, which I was powerless to challenge.

"GOODBYE, DAVE."

Abby. The name came back to me, although I remained unable to do anything with it. All I could muster was a silent prayer that Abby would be able to forgive me for failing her.

For losing her to the power of God's might.

chapter nineteen

Then, suddenly, from somewhere back in the realm of reality, I heard a noise.

At first, I thought I had imagined it. But John apparently heard it also, for his suffocating presence subsided a bit, and I regained a small ability to think. John paused in his departure, seemingly confused, and then we heard the noise again.

The sound was a question.

It was a protest.

It was a command that could drive God himself to his knees.

"Meeeeooooowwwwww!"

I managed to turn my head away from John's pulsating light and felt immediate relief that my sight remained intact. Through my blurred vision, in the doorway to my bedroom, I could make out Peaches, staring defiantly over my shoulder, with his gray ears angled back and his tail swishing ominously behind him. The hair on his back stood upright as he glared into the room. I don't know if he saw John as I did, but whatever it was that Peaches perceived, he clearly did not like it. And so, that tiny cat, who didn't weigh more than twelve pounds, proceeded to face off against God with the body language of a roaring lion.

And then, for the first time since I had met him years earlier, Peaches hissed.

"Peaches!" John exclaimed. "It's me!" I did not see John revert to his human form, but as I stared at Peaches, John—as I remembered him—rushed by me and knelt cautiously in front of his old cat. Peaches, still agitated, warily sniffed John's extended hand and then reluctantly allowed John to scratch him behind his ears.

While John reacquainted himself with Peaches, I tried to collect myself. My mind was no longer a jumbled mess once John had reverted to his human form, and I struggled to catch my breath. *Get it together*, I thought. *As long as John's still here, you have a chance.* I blinked several times until my vision cleared up.

I stood up, woozy, and balanced myself with a hand on my bed as John continued to work on calming Peaches. After a minute or two, Peaches finally rolled over onto his back in submission, and John stood to face me. Although he mostly looked as I remembered, there remained something inhuman about him. After a moment, I realized that it was his eyes that seemed off. They were the eyes of someone who had literally seen everything.

And they looked bored.

John stared at me, seemingly emotionless.

"Was there anything else?" he asked me flatly. Thankfully, it once again felt as if I was merely talking to another human, although I could not forget what I was dealing with.

"I want you to bring Abby back," I said bluntly.

John shook his head. "We've been through this. No."

"She's the best person I've ever met," I said. "She didn't deserve to die like that!"

John chuckled, but it was devoid of humor. More of a scoff, really.

"Since when does 'deserve' come into this? You have no idea how many tragic deaths I've seen involving people who lived their lives in a manner that warranted sainthood. Do you have any idea how many prayers I hear that are made on behalf of those who are at least as deserving as your Abby? What makes you different from all of them?"

I had no immediate answer. I knew I was asking for something entirely selfish, but I didn't care.

"The difference," I finally said, "is that all of those times where I was calling out to you, I wasn't praying to 'God' for divine intervention. I was asking a friend for help. At least, that's what I thought I was doing."

John had the grace to at least look slightly abashed. But then he shrugged.

"Maybe that's not so different from praying to God after all," he said. He quickly continued before I could respond.

"But I've told you before that the one line I will not cross, that I will *never* cross, is interfering with free will." John turned to look out the bedroom window. I realized with a jolt he was facing south: the direction of where the train wreck had occurred. "Tom Horton engaged in a course of conduct that ended with Abby's death. And a lot of other deaths. I wish he had not done so, but he did. I will not undo that."

"Do you really think that your purpose is to sit on the sidelines and do nothing?" I asked. "I knew what you were like before you became God; you had a tremendous heart, and you always saw the big picture, even when I missed it. I know you're meant to be more than this. You have to just trust yourself."

John remained unmoved. "Yes, I heard you say as much last night from your mountain."

Keep him talking, I thought. *You have a chance if you keep him talking.* I suddenly recalled my impromptu lesson involving young Chelsie years earlier. *Stall until you find your epiphany.*

"Is there an afterlife?" I asked.

"You don't need to know that."

I stared at John, dumbfounded, and he softened slightly.

"Look," he said. "That is not something that will do you any good to know. Abby is at peace; I can tell you that much."

I took a hard look at John, as if seeing him anew. He was not uncomfortable under my gaze, and he looked back impassively.

"What the hell happened to you?" I whispered. John arched a questioning eyebrow. "Do you even care?"

"Ah. You think I am coming off as cold." John's voice continued to sound off, like he was just going through the motions of displaying emotions. "It is not that I do not understand what you are going through. Trust me: I remember what it is like to lose someone. But we went through this before, and I told you that I absolutely will not deprive anyone of free will. Tom Horton purposefully caused many people, including your wife, to die. I will not interfere with that. Not even for you."

Something John had said tickled at my brain, but I could not identify it. As I struggled to place it, he continued.

"Hate me if that helps, Dave. Climb every mountain and curse my name to the heavens if that gets you to sleep at night. I won't mind. But I will not interfere with this world, and whether you agree or disagree is utterly irrelevant."

It was clear that John was about to leave, and I had to act.

"You just said you remembered what it was like to lose someone," I muttered, thinking out loud. John looked sharply at me, as shocked as I had ever seen him since he attained Godhood.

"What of it?" John asked nonchalantly. But I thought I detected something else in his voice. Shame? Fear?

"You remember." When John didn't respond, I snarled with emphasis. "You *remember*. That's not the way this is supposed to work. I recall that much at least from that glimpse of omniscience you gave me years ago. The details may have left me, but I remember sharing the feelings of all living things in this world. Pride, joy, sadness … *pain*."

"What is your point?" John asked, but I could see that he already knew. His eyes no longer looked bored.

"My *point* is that this pain I'm going through right now isn't something you should have to *remember*. You should be sharing it. Feeling it. But you're not."

And then I put the final piece of the puzzle together.

"Is that something you turned off, like how you turned off your ability to divine my thoughts?" My voice rose in anger. I took three quick steps across the room and shoved John squarely in his chest. He made no effort to defend himself. "Is that why you're not feeling this?" I snapped, pointing at my chest emphatically.

John remained silent, studying me. I pressed my case.

"You told me years ago that all I own is this moment. I took that to heart, John, but right now—right now, this moment sucks. And if you're not going to do anything about that, at least have the guts to share my pain! Because this belongs to you just as much as it belongs to me!"

I ended in a shout, glaring at John and daring him to deny my accusations. John calmly met my stare, but I could detect an anger lurking below the surface. I wondered, for a moment, if I would be willed out of existence or consigned to some deep level of hell for my impertinence. Time seemed to freeze as John decided what to do with me. I stood tall, too far in to back down. I could not decipher John's expression as his eyes slowly narrowed into sinister slits.

"Fine," he eventually growled, accepting my challenge. I let go of a breath I didn't realize I had been holding and waited for whatever would come next.

I could not see what John did then, but a subtle change in his expression suggested that whatever empathy switch he had deactivated had been turned back on. Perhaps in so doing he only allowed himself to share my emotions. Maybe it was broader than that, and he reopened himself to all of what humanity was experiencing. Possibly, even, every bit of life in the universe. But whatever John did, it caused a discernible difference. The variation in his expression was not pronounced—just a mere tightening around the eyes and a hint of a grimace—but I was looking for it and noticed it. Those subtle, almost imperceptible gestures revealed that I had done the impossible:

I had wounded God.

John walked slowly to the bed and sat down, as if to catch his breath. I said nothing, transfixed by his reaction.

"It was too much," John finally said softly, unable to look at me. "Even for me. It was too much. I had to turn it off."

Peaches hopped up on the bed beside John. John smiled sadly and scratched him behind his ears. I only vaguely understood what John was talking about, but I addressed it as best I could.

"I can't imagine how much it hurts, feeling *everything*. And you were always sensitive—it must have been hell on you. If I had to guess, that's probably a large part of why you ended up with this job. But it defeats the purpose if you just turn that part of you off."

John continued to stare blankly, absently petting Peaches, and I wasn't even sure he was listening to me.

"People are hurting, John," I added quietly. "Hell, *I'm* hurting. The thing is, you're in a position to help ease some of that. You were given this job because *someone* trusted your judgment—trusted your ability to make things better. *I* would trust you to do what's right, not that my opinion means anything. But you sitting around, doing nothing, shielding yourself from the pain that everyone else is going through—you're smart enough to realize that's not your purpose. You can make this world better. You just have to believe in yourself to do it."

John continued to sit, unmoving, focused on nothing in particular. When he finally raised his head to look at me, he appeared troubled.

"I know you're hurting, Dave," John said, sounding sincere. "I'm truly sorry about that. But even if you have some valid points, I cannot alter free will. As much as it hurts me, I absolutely will not cross that line. Humanity has to forge its own path."

I started to object, but John cut me off with a raised finger.

"But," he said, "you've been a great friend to me, and to Peaches. You've become a good person, which I realize sounds trite. But really, it's something. You could argue it's the *only* thing. And it's something to be proud of."

John stood up and studied me carefully. I didn't know how to interpret his expression, although he seemed to be wrestling with a decision. He glanced at Peaches on the bed, who coolly met his gaze. When John looked back at me, his face was unreadable.

"You deserve a chance," he said simply. And with that, John vanished.

I stood, dumbfounded, staring at the spot in the room where John had just been standing.

"A chance at what?" I cried out. When there was no response, I called out again. "A chance at *what*, John? I don't understand!"

Peaches' head suddenly popped up; his ears perked. Without warning, he hopped off the bed and darted out of the room. A moment later, I heard his footsteps descending the stairs. I followed, and when I reached the steps myself, I picked up on what had drawn his attention: a voice from downstairs. *John?* I wondered.

I cautiously made my way down the staircase and the source of the noise became clearer: the television was on. I was confused; that TV hadn't been on since the night that Abby died. When I walked into our living room, a beer commercial was playing loudly. *A chance at what?* It still didn't make any sense to me.

I searched about for the remote to turn off the television. I couldn't think with it blasting. I finally located it tucked behind one of the pillows on the couch, and I was about to click it off when I froze. A moment later, the remote fell from my limp hand to the floor.

"No," I whispered, transfixed by the screen.

The commercial had ended and cut back to the pre-game festivities of a playoff baseball game. The announcer's voice boomed throughout my living room.

"We're back at Busch Stadium where Game 5 of the National League Championship Series is about to get underway! The New York Mets look to stave off elimination in this best of seven series against the St. Louis Cardinals ..."

chapter twenty

The pre-game activities continued while I stared blankly at the screen. I knew I was watching something profound, but I struggled to place *why* it was significant. Then it registered: *I have seen this already.* I continued my efforts to connect the dots. *Is this a repeat? Why would they rerun the entirety of this week-old game?*

My interest in the baseball season ended the moment I first suspected Abby's death, but I did hear at some point that the Mets ended up losing the game I had been watching at the time of Horton's attack. The Cardinals would have advanced to the World Series, and the Mets' season would have ended. The World Series was presumably ongoing, not that I was following it. I could not fathom why a week-old game, involving a team that had already been eliminated, was on television.

As an unfamiliar country singer belted out the National Anthem, I dared to ask myself the crucial question: *What is today's date?* I hustled around the house, looking for my cell phone, before realizing I had left it in the car after turning it off back in Great Neck. I ran outside to the car, found the phone in a cupholder, and waited impatiently for it to power back on. Finally, a screen came to life that displayed the date forever burned into my soul: Sunday, October 18. The day Abby died.

I stared at my phone in a stupor as I walked back into the house. *This can't be real*, I thought, although, of course, there was an easy way to test it. My hand trembled as I accessed the list of recent calls on my phone, which was dominated by calls to and from Abby. *Am I hallucinating?* I tapped one of those old calls, and my phone began to call Abby's cell.

Two rings, and no answer. I idly wondered what *should* happen if you were to dial the cellphone of someone who had died a week earlier. *Should it have gone straight to voicemail?* But my thoughts were interrupted after the third ring when I heard something that I did not expect to ever hear again.

"Hey, babe. What's up?" It was Abby—so nonplussed and routine. Not a hint of acknowledgment that my world had been torn apart, only to have been miraculously restored. I was at a loss for words, and my mouth hung agape as I pressed the phone to my ear, desperately needing Abby to say more.

"Dave, are you there?" This time I managed to let out a croak, a desperate noise that only emerged out of fear of her hanging up.

"Dave?" she repeated, confused. "Look, I'm having trouble hearing you. I think we have a bad connection. But we are just finishing up here, and I plan on heading to the train in about another hour, two hours tops."

Her mention of the train was like being doused with a bucket of cold water.

"No!" I shouted into the phone.

"Oh, you're there," Abby said. She sounded distracted, as if she were multitasking. "What do you mean 'no'?"

"Oh God, Abby; you're ok," I babbled. "Do not take the train. Please? Promise me! Promise me you won't take the train!"

A long pause. I knew I was coming off like a lunatic, but I couldn't stop myself.

"Why don't you want me to take the train, Dave?" Abby asked cautiously. The tone one would use in trying to calm down a deranged person ranting and raving on the street. I had sworn long ago to never lie to Abby, but in that moment, I couldn't think of a way to avoid it. *I'll explain it all to her later*, I thought. *Just get her home safe first.*

"I … I was just at the store and I overheard two cops talking about a potential terrorist threat on the railways today. So I'll just drive down now and pick you up in a couple of hours."

I could faintly make out Abby talking to someone in the background, presumably her mother. When she came back to the phone, she sounded skeptical.

"We didn't hear anything about that down here. My mom was watching the news just now and there was no mention of that."

"Please … just … don't go on the train," I begged. "I think I heard the cops say something about keeping it from the press, for whatever reason. I don't know. But please just promise you'll wait for me to come get you. Please. I have an awful feeling about all of this."

I knew my story was weak—very weak—but I hoped that Abby trusted me enough not to push back against it. When I heard her reluctant sigh through the phone, I knew she wouldn't fight me on this.

"Fine," Abby said, sounding more confused than annoyed. "If you want to drive all the way down here to get me, I won't take the train." I turned my head away from the phone and let out a half-garbled cry of relief. I quickly put the phone back to my ear when I heard Abby continue to speak.

"It doesn't make sense, though," she added thoughtfully. "Why wouldn't the police make it public if there was a threat today? I mean, what about everyone who *is* going to take the train tonight? Do they have a plan to help *them?*"

My throat constricted, and I again lost the ability to speak. *Everyone else.* I started to sweat. *I forgot about everyone else.* My mind was a jumble, and I neglected to answer Abby.

"Are you there, Dave?"

I wanted to stay on the phone with her for hours and not let her go until she was with me again. I wanted to keep her on the line and remove any chance, however small, of her changing her mind regarding the train. The thought of losing this gift terrified me, and left to my own devices, I would not have broken contact with Abby until she was safely back in my arms. But I knew I didn't have that luxury. The mess I had to fix would require more than just a single phone call.

"I'm here, Abby. I'm sorry, I have to go." I could feel my eyes brimming with tears. "I'll see you soon though. I love you. It's ridiculous how much I love you."

"I love you, too, Dave," she replied. She hesitated. "Is everything ok? You sound a little off."

"Everything's cool," I said, wondering if that would end up just being another lie. "There's stuff going on that I'll tell you about later, but … Seriously, please do not get on that train. Any train. Stay off of all trains, and stay away from all train stations, until I see you again. Promise me."

"God, I'll stay off the damn train!" Abby laughed. I didn't join her.

"Promise me!" I repeated with a greater sense of urgency. Abby stopped laughing.

"I promise," she replied solemnly. "I swear I will not leave this house until you get here. I don't understand why, but I promise if it is that important to you. Is that good enough?"

"Yes." I hoped she wasn't merely humoring me. *It's the best I can do.* "Thank you."

"Ok, I'll wait for you." Abby paused. "Was there anything else? Otherwise, I should get back to helping my mom ..."

I didn't want to get off the phone. I wanted to stay on and make Abby tell me one of her twenty-minute-long stories that went nowhere. Perhaps a story about her trip down to Long Island, with every meaningless detail included. But I couldn't.

"Sure." My voice caught with emotion, and I cleared my throat. "I'll see you in a couple of hours. I love you."

"I love you, too, Dave."

And then she hung up.

I stared at my cellphone, and almost immediately wondered whether I had imagined that call. My finger involuntarily moved to call her back, but I checked myself. *Forty-two people will die in a few hours*, I thought. Then I corrected my math: *Make that forty-one*. Abby was in the clear, at least. Unfortunately, I didn't have the phone numbers of the other victims.

I ran through all of my options and quickly realized that I did not really have any. My first thought, likely because it involved the least amount of work on my part, was to simply call the police and report that there would be a suicide bomber in the first car of the 6:32 train from Penn Station to Manhasset. It would have to be an anonymous call—if questioned, I was certainly in no position to convincingly reveal the source of my intel. I also did not know how the police would respond to such a threat. They might increase the police presence on the train, but that would probably only result in upping the number of fatalities. Hell, even if they shut down the train entirely, Tom Horton might end up activating his vest in the middle of Penn Station to a result that was even more tragic. I reluctantly accepted that I would have to stop Horton myself.

But how?

I briefly considered the possibility of trying to knock Horton unconscious before he could activate his vest, but that seemed like a reckless plan at best. For starters, I wasn't sure I even knew how to knock someone out. The fact that I would have to render Horton unconscious while he was seated on a moving train merely increased the difficulty of that challenge. Further, to succeed, I would have to lay Horton out cold. If he maintained even a second or two of consciousness— all Horton had to do was press a button. It was not a workable plan.

Diplomacy also struck me as a fruitless option. There was no question that whatever level of inner turmoil a person requires to blow up a train and kill dozens of people, Horton surpassed it. I did not see how asking him *not* to do that, no matter how nicely I phrased my request, would change anything. Any attempt I made to charm Horton into changing his mind was more likely to end up spooking him into detonating his bomb right in my face, bringing the total number of fatalities back up to forty-two.

If I had a day or so to plan, it is possible I could have come up with a better option. But I only had a little more than two hours to catch Horton's train. As sick as it made me, I could only think of one strategy that had even a decent chance of success.

I had to kill Tom Horton.

•   •   •   •   •

I stared at the safe in my bedroom, trying to work up the nerve to open it. Abby had forced me to memorize the combination: 4, 14, 44. Chosen by Abby, the numerologist. *All of those fours will mean that the angels will be with us*, she told me at the time, only half-joking. I hoped she was right. Steeling myself, I opened the safe and picked up the Baby Glock as if it were radioactive.

I didn't know much about the gun, but I thought I recalled enough to be able to fire it. We stored the gun loaded, so I didn't have to worry about that. I stuffed the Glock into my jacket pocket and stood in front of the mirror to make sure it wasn't conspicuous. I was not up to date on New York's concealed carry laws, but I was pretty sure I was about to emphatically break them.

I had never imagined having to use this weapon. Abby's insistence on getting a gun was not borne out of any love of violence; that would directly contradict the very essence of her peaceful nature. Rather, the fact that I had a pistol at my disposal stemmed solely from Abby's practical side. *It's better to have and not need than need and not have*, she argued at one point, although it was doubtful Abby ever anticipated that my particular *need* would relate to murdering a man.

Murder. Is killing to protect other innocents considered murder? Probably not in the ethical or moral sense, but I wondered how the legal system would view my execution of Tom Horton. *He'll be wearing his suicide vest. You could justify it as self-defense.* Which, in and of itself, would raise the issue of why I was prancing around on the Long Island Railroad illegally carrying a loaded weapon. Then there was the issue of explaining how I knew Horton planned on blowing up the train.

I forced these thoughts out of my head. *Worry about that later. Take care of business.*

"Why do I have to do this?" I suddenly snapped in irritation, fully aware that John heard it. Was it some sort of test? Was I doomed to failure, with nothing changing other than the trade of my life for Abby's? *If so, it would still be worth it*, I thought, although I was honest enough to admit a preference for a scenario where both Abby and I survived the day.

Weapon in place, I next confronted the problem of getting to New York in time to make Horton's 6:32 train. Driving was possible but risky. Many Long Islanders and New Yorkers head upstate or to New England on the weekends, creating traffic havoc when they head back to their homes on Sundays, particularly in the late afternoon. Trying to drive down to New York could easily result in me sitting helplessly in a traffic jam on the New York State Thruway while those two trains collided.

The safer choice was to take Amtrak down to Penn Station, at which point it was only a few short steps to the Long Island Railroad. That was precisely how Abby had made her own way to Great Neck earlier in the week. *No; earlier in the day*, I reminded myself. I pulled out my phone to look up the Amtrak schedule and saw that there was a 4:45 p.m. train out of Rhinecliff, the nearest station, that arrived in Penn Station at 6:25. It would be tight on both ends. It was normally nearly a half-hour drive to the Rhinecliff station, but if I left right away, I'd have twenty-three minutes to make it there. Likewise, if the train arrived at Penn Station at its scheduled time, I'd be left with about seven minutes to transfer to Horton's train.

I decided to try to make the Amtrak train, figuring that even if I missed it, I could still attempt the drive to the city as a fallback option. On my way out, I grabbed a nearly empty backpack that I used for hiking, envisioning a scenario where it might become necessary to hide the gun. I was nearly out the front door when I heard a questioning *"meow."* I looked back to spot Peaches, sitting in the living room, staring up at me inquisitively.

I knew I had no time, but I had to say goodbye to him. He had earned that much.

"I'm sorry buddy, I have to run out," I told him, lowering a hand toward his face. Peaches rubbed his gums against my knuckles affectionately. "Abby will be home later to feed you. And hopefully I will be, too."

Peaches purred and continued to rub his face against my hand.

"You helped save her, Peaches. You know that, right? You saved Abby. You're a good cat." Peaches continued to nuzzle against me happily, and it pained me to pull away from him. I felt tears in my eyes for what seemed like the thousandth time in the last forty-eight hours. "Whatever else happens, you did your part. You're the best cat. There's just some stuff I have to take care of now."

I didn't allow myself to look back as I exited out the front door and raced for my car, parked on the street. As the engine sputtered to life, I glanced at the dashboard clock and did quick math: *twenty-one minutes.* At best, it would be close.

I drove aggressively out of Woodstock and hit the highway in a matter of minutes. Normally a cautious driver, I flew down the road, which was thankfully mostly empty, at a dangerous pace. I only slowed when I approached the Kingston-Rhinecliff Bridge to pay the toll, after which I quickly accelerated to speed across the bridge itself. I was making unbelievable time, but I still wasn't sure if I would make the train. It was a few short miles of backroads from the bridge to the station, and I could only hope that there were no pedestrians milling about as I took blind turns at a reckless speed.

Finally, I sped into the small parking area next to the station, nestled on the east side of the Hudson River. Almost everything had gone right for me during that drive, but despite my best efforts, it was 4:47—two minutes late. Hopping out of my car, I struggled with what I should do next. *Drive all the way to Manhattan? Race the train south to another station and try to hop on there?* But as I was mulling my options, I saw movement on the train platform: an elderly couple, waiting patiently as they looked to the north.

I bounded up the wooden stairs leading to the platform two at a time and then raced to the couple I had spotted from the parking lot. Gasping for breath, I was about to ask if the train was running late when I saw it arriving. I felt an immediate sense of relief at not missing the train, but I noted that its late arrival would tighten things up on the back end. If it had remained on schedule, it would have only left me seven minutes to switch to the Long Island Railroad once I arrived. With the Amtrak train running a few minutes late, I was looking at a much more stressful scenario upon arriving in the city. I decided that the Amtrak train was still my best option and got on board.

There had only been a handful of times where I took Amtrak down to the city. Those trips typically involved traveling with Abby to visit her family for a holiday, and I was concerned about the prospect of drinking and driving. I desperately tried to remember where on the train would place me the closest to the Long Island Railroad upon arriving at Penn Station, but I could not recall any useful details regarding the layout of the station. Hedging my bets, I settled in the middle of the train.

The train was not even half-filled, and I was glad to be able to sit alone. The Baby Glock, as small as it was, sat heavy in my jacket pocket, and I was continually braced for that moment when it inexplicably and accidentally discharged. But it never did.

The train conductor came through shortly after we departed the Rhinecliff station, and I realized with a start that I did not have a ticket. The conductor saw my horrified look, laughed, and explained that I was allowed to purchase a ticket on the train, although he gently admonished that it's generally cheaper to buy a ticket before boarding. I tried to smile at his gentle chastisement and felt a sense of relief when he moved on to ticket other passengers. After that, I could finally sit and try to relax as the train chugged along toward Manhattan. But despite my efforts to calm myself, my thoughts kept turning to the fact that I had set out to kill a man.

Why are you making me do this John? I thought, not really expecting any response. *Is this your way of not interfering with human will—have* me *fix it?* Despite my confusion, and my terror, I could not direct too much ill will toward John. Abby was alive.

As I looked out the window at the Hudson Valley rolling by, I texted Abby. *Just making sure you're still not on the train. Love you! :)* Apprehension grew when she did not immediately respond, but then her text came in: *Not on train! I promised, remember? Relax! Love you!* It eased my mind, and I was glad to get Abby's confirmation. I anticipated that, in a few minutes, I would not be in a position to think about Abby at all.

At the scheduled arrival time of 6:25, I hovered by the door, ready to sprint. We were in a dark tunnel and I had little sense of how quickly we were moving. At 6:27, the train stopped entirely, and I struggled to remain calm. But then the train began to inch forward, and, after a minute, the sight of the train platform rolled into my view from the left. As the train settled to a stop, I glanced at my phone: *6:31*. If that was 6:31 on the verge of turning to 6:32, I was done.

The train doors opened, and I flew up the nearest set of stairs. At the top, I was momentarily blinded by the lights of the Penn Station concourse, but then I noticed a sign for the 6:32 train to Port Washington directly across the corridor. Shoving my way past a tourist inexplicably taking a picture of a CVS, I raced down another set of stairs and reached the tail end of Tom Horton's train.

And the doors were closed.

"No," I whispered. I lunged toward the nearest set of train doors and pounded on the glass. "No! Let me in!" I didn't let up and continued to hammer away. A handful of people in the last car got out of their seats to see what the commotion was about. The conductor, who had been lurking at the back of the train in anticipation of collecting tickets, hurriedly walked to the door and glared at me in annoyance through the glass. I continued to slam my fist against the window, begging him to open the door, and I could see him mentally weigh the pleasure he would derive from leaving me behind against the paperwork he would have to fill out if I successfully broke the glass. With a grimace, he took out a key which he proceeded to insert into a slot outside of my field of vision, and the door opened.

"You need to calm down, buddy," the conductor snarled as I jumped in. I stood there, frozen in relief at having made the train, while he reclosed the door behind me. The train started to move moments later.

"I'm sorry," I stammered. "I know that was really obnoxious of me. It's just … my wife went into an early labor, and …"

The conductor's face lightened at that, and he held up his hands in a *say no more* kind of way. Even though I lacked any talent in the lying department as an attorney, I seemed to do much better while under real duress.

The conductor, in a much kinder tone, then asked for my ticket. Again, I did not have one, so I shoved a twenty at him and muttered something about going to Great Neck. The conductor, in excruciatingly slow fashion, proceeded to punch me a one-way off-peak ticket while lecturing me on how it is cheaper to buy a ticket before boarding.

"Thanks," I muttered, taking my ticket and heading toward the front of the train.

"And congratulations!" the conductor called after me. I nearly replied, "For what?" but then I remembered my lie. I threw him a half-hearted wave and made my way through the bowels of the train.

The train was long, and I moved through it as quickly as I could without drawing any undue attention to myself. I recalled that those passengers located toward the back of the train fared fairly well in the collision—just minor scrapes and bruises, at most. When I made it past the midpoint of the train a few minutes later, I had reached the zone where more serious injuries occurred. A few more minutes, and I approached the front of the train—the fatality area. Once I reached the first car at 6:46—five minutes before Horton detonated his vest—it no longer felt like I was on a train at all. It felt like I was riding a bomb.

I casually scanned the car, looking for Horton. As I did so, I spotted a variety of other passengers, and I was flooded with memories of news coverage relating to the various victims. A family of four sat together, wearing souvenir t-shirts from *The Lion King*, and I remembered watching a grandmother sob to a reporter about her family's fatal trip into the city to catch a Broadway show together. A young man and woman snuggled together in another row, and I recalled their faces from an article about a couple who had just gotten engaged earlier that day in Central Park before their tragic deaths. A trio of college-aged girls sat giggling together toward the middle of the car, and I relived a memorial held by Hofstra University on Long Island for the three students it lost in the attack.

The severity of my task hit me with these reminders of the stakes. My knees momentarily buckled from the pressure, but I pressed myself to walk further into the car, as calmly as I could manage.

Then I finally spotted Horton. He sat alone at the front of the car, next to the window in an empty three-seated row facing the rear of the train where I had entered. The car was only about a third filled, but Tom Horton seemed to be an island unto himself, with no one else sitting within two rows of him. It wasn't surprising—he seemed very out of it, sweating profusely in his bulky coat, staring intently out the window at nothing in particular. I knew that I looked as if I hadn't slept in a week, but Horton seemed as if he hadn't slept in *months*. I was aware of what he looked like from the news coverage, but all of the pictures I had seen displayed Horton as a clean-cut professional. The man I saw on the train looked the same at a superficial level, but his eyes looked defeated and lost. I wondered how no one else on the train could see what I saw. Perhaps they did, on some level, which would explain why no one sat within a ten-foot radius of him.

I whisked myself down the train aisle, taking great pains to stare straight ahead while the train rocked gently beneath me. It was still a few minutes until 6:51, but I thought it was possible that a suspicious look on my part could conceivably change history and drive Horton to detonate his bomb early. I did risk a quick peek at his hands, which were clasped tightly together on his lap. *No finger on a button*, I noted, counting that as a positive sign. I had been concerned about the possibility of Horton detonating his vest in some type of death throe, even after I shot him.

Horton did not stir at all as I passed and took a seat two rows directly behind him. He continued to stare out his window, and it looked as if he was muttering something fervently under his breath.

I felt for the gun and carefully slid back the rack to drop a round into the chamber. Moving slowly, I transferred the Baby Glock out of my pocket to rest it on my lap. I struggled to see Horton's visage in the reflective surface of the window. The plan was straightforward: *One quick shot to the back of his head and then put the gun on the floor and raise your hands in surrender. That's it.* Horton continued to gaze out the window, seemingly looking at nothing. With my free left hand, I stole another look at my phone: 6:48. Less than three minutes.

I could barely view a sliver of Horton's face reflected in the window, but even with that obstructed view, I saw a man who had lost everything. And, had John not intervened and brought Abby back, I saw what I might have become. I thought of my own reckless actions in the aftermath of Abby's death, and I wondered how I would have reacted had I experienced that type of loss, multiplied by three, over the course of only a few weeks. *You wouldn't have committed murder,* I thought to myself, but still, as I looked at Horton, I did not see an evil man. Just a confused one about to make a horrendous decision.

Alarmed at my softening, I mentally shouted at myself. *Look at the other people on this train! These people will* die *if you do not act!* But still, that logic could not compel my legs or my right arm to work, and I continued to sit there motionless. *Do something!* my brain screamed at muscles that had suddenly gone on strike. And then I had a realization.

I realized, well too late, that whatever it would have taken for me to kill Tom Horton, to put a bullet in the back of his skull, I did not have it. I knew I would not be able to compel myself to pull that trigger, even if it resulted in the death of me and everyone else in that train car. Which it would.

Suddenly, I was standing and moving back down the aisle, driven by an instinct that I did not understand. *Am I making a run for it?* The thought flashed shamefully through my mind. *I might have just enough time to get out of the first car.* But I did not go far. Before I could process what was happening, I found myself shoving the gun back into my jacket pocket and taking the aisle seat in Horton's row, with only the empty middle seat separating us.

He did not notice my arrival, with his eyes closed tightly as he continued his inaudible prayers to himself. It was a blessing, really: given the mostly empty train, there was no reason for me to sit next to him, and he probably would have been moved to push his detonator had he perceived my suspicious move. But he didn't, and so we sat together in silence for a few moments while the clock inched toward 6:51.

"Please don't do this, Tom." The words spilled out of my mouth, almost of their own volition.

Horton's eyes snapped open, and his head swiveled toward me. I stared straight ahead, afraid to make any eye contact. In my peripheral vision, I perceived his right hand moving to the inside of his coat. I closed my eyes, waiting for the blast that would extinguish my life. *Will I even feel it?* I wondered.

When I realized moments later that I was still breathing, I risked opening my eyes and stole a glance at Horton to my right. He stared at me, angry and suspicious, and I fought down the urge to bolt.

"What did you say?" he whispered in a gravelly voice. Horton quickly scanned the train for any other suspicious activity, with his hand never leaving the inside of his coat, and, presumably, the button that would end us all.

I closed my eyes again, trying to find the nerve to speak. "I said 'please don't do this, Tom.'" Choosing my words carefully, I added, "You're a better person than this."

"Who are you?" he snarled, backing against the window of the train like a cornered wild animal.

"I … I'm Dave." I immediately realized the feebleness of my response, and Tom, terrifyingly, became further agitated by my meaningless answer. I sat staring straight ahead like a statue, determined not to do anything that could be perceived as a threat. *Don't provoke the man with his finger on the button.* The thought grew to become my mantra.

"Are you a cop?" he asked sharply.

"No, I'm not a cop," I answered as calmly as I could. "I think the police would be handling this quite differently. Don't you?"

As Horton mulled over my answer, I heard a rumbling to my left and quickly saw out of my peripheral vision the westbound train to Penn Station speed past us. Abby's train. Or at least, what would have been Abby's train. I let out a small sigh of relief. *If nothing else, I saved them.*

But I remained unconvinced that I could save myself. Horton's eyes were wild, and I was at a loss for why he hadn't already detonated his suicide vest. It may have just been curiosity as to who I was and where I came from. *Just keep him talking. That's all you can do at this point.* After all, the strategy had worked with John earlier in the day.

Horton struggled to process my unanticipated arrival, and I sensed that his confusion was the only thing that had kept me alive to that point. But I knew it wouldn't last; he would eventually realize that whatever disorientation he felt at my intervention would be rendered moot once he pushed that button.

"Then who sent you?" he demanded, struggling to keep his voice down and avoid drawing the attention of other passengers. I wasn't ready for that question, and I paused. I intuited that if I didn't start giving substantive answers, our conversation, and our lives, were over. Suddenly, I was struck by a flash of inspiration.

"I was sent by God."

It was probably the most truthful thing I had said in the past few hours. Horton was not prepared for that response and his surprise earned me another few precious moments of life. I risked another glance at Horton and saw shock register on his face. He caught my look and quickly recovered, pressing his back against the window in a crouched position so that he could fully face me. Willing myself to suppress my terror, I adopted something of a pious look.

"You lie," Horton snarled at me. But still, he did not blow us up. An optimistic thought skipped through my mind: *He* wants *to believe.* I decided to try to fan that flame.

"I know all about you, Tom, and what happened to your family. And I'm sorry about that. I don't know if that means anything to you right now, but I really am so sorry for what you went through. That was more pain than *any* husband or father ever deserves. And I know you're a good person who did not deserve any of that. But this thing you're planning to do—it's not you. It's not who you are. And you know that's not the way to honor your family."

Horton sat motionless for a bit. I did not know if I was saying the right things, but I figured anything I said that did not cause him to push his button should be considered a success.

"What do you know of what I'm planning?" he finally grumbled. I seized the opening he left me.

"I know you think that life isn't worth living. I know you think it's unfair that so much anguish was dumped disproportionately on you, and that killing these people, and destroying countless other lives in the process, will restore some sort of cosmic balance. I know you think that your pain is too great to be contained."

Horton's head jolted at my quotation of his suicide note. I sensed him finally buying into the notion that I was some sort of prophet.

"But it doesn't have to be this way." I spoke calmly but forcefully. "You can still be a force for good."

Horton processed this in silence. He did not back away from the window or remove his right hand from the inside of his coat, but I thought I could feel him relax, albeit slightly.

"Why did He do this to my family?" he whispered hoarsely. There was no doubt, from the way Horton said "He," who he was referring to.

"I don't know, Tom," I said, shaking my head sadly. "I'm sorry, but I don't. All I know is that God has tremendous respect for our free will, however that manifests itself. Maybe what happened to your family was just an act of evil that spiraled out of control. Maybe this all falls under the auspice of 'God works in mysterious ways.' I don't understand it, and I know I never fully will. All I can say is that the gift of free will has left *you* with a choice, right now. You can choose to get off this train and do everything in your power to make this world a better place, a world that is better than the one that took Claire, Theresa, and Gail. I know that's the choice God wants you to make, but again, that is only up to you."

"Or," I said, "you can choose to feed into the evil that took your family from you." I glanced meaningfully at the area of his coat covering his hand, which I knew to be clutching the detonator. Tom Horton followed my gaze, and then, after a moment's reflection, miraculously withdrew his hand slowly from his coat. He sat there unmoving, reflecting on the monumental decision he had just made. As did I.

I have done it, I exulted to myself. I forced myself to maintain a calm facade. *I have erased Horton's attack from history.* I was so excited that I did not notice the two drunk guys coming toward us just then.

They looked to be in their early twenties, possibly college kids inebriated from a day of drinking in the city, as they wobbled down the train aisle together. It seemed as if they were looking for the first car, for whatever reason, but did not realize they were in it as they passed me and Horton. Tom Horton, fresh off of his apparent decision not to blow up the train, continued to look bewildered, and his wild expression drew the attention of those young men. The kid in front leaned in unsteadily to stare at Horton as he passed us, only to snap back with a loud hoot.

"Holy shit, dude!" he said to his friend in a whisper that could be heard throughout the entire car. "That's the guy whose family was wiped out in like a WEEK!"

"What?" his friend asked in a sleepy voice, giving us a curious look as he passed. The two of them made their way a few rows behind us and continued to talk in a loud whisper that I could clearly hear. As could Horton.

"You know! It was all over the news!" the first one insisted. He may have thought his tone was circumspect, but I'm sure half the car could hear him. "He had those two slutty party girl daughters that died. And they were fucking *hot!*"

"Shame to lose hot skanks," the second one mumbled, sounding like he was struggling to stay awake. The first laughed.

I felt ill as I sensed movement to my right. Filled with dread, I turned my head to see Horton quivering with rage, his hand back inside his coat.

"This world is beyond salvage," he hissed, eyes crazed.

And I knew I was dead.

Time slowed as Horton's hand moved beneath his coat. I felt a sense of peace; I had done everything I could, and I was resigned to what was about to happen. Abby was alive, so I did not view it as a failure. *Is this my life flashing before my eyes?* I wondered as time continued to crawl at a snail's pace. Then I heard a voice not my own in my head.

Dave. John's voice, sounding unhurried.

John? I asked mentally. The slowdown in time affected me, too, and I could not manage to move my lips.

You're in quite a pickle.

I'm aware, I thought calmly, accepting my fate. *Are you here to take me to Heaven?*

John chuckled.

Not just yet. Tell him "Romans 8:18."

What?

Just do it. "Romans 8:18." I felt John's presence abruptly leave my mind.

Then, in a rush, time reasserted itself.

"Romans 8:18," I blurted aloud, wondering what would come next.

I was clueless as to what "Romans 8:18" meant. But it caused Horton to freeze, jaw agape. He instantly looked horrified at what he had been on the verge of doing and took a few deep breaths to collect himself.

In a fierce whisper, he quickly recited to himself, "I consider that our present sufferings are not worth comparing with the glory that will be revealed in us." That reminder unearthed something deep within Horton, and he began to cry.

I didn't fully understand what had happened. Horton was sobbing into both hands, and I slowly processed that he was no longer holding that button. I sensed that the danger had passed, and I allowed myself to relax a bit.

Thank you, John, I thought. I didn't expect an answer, but I was surprised when John responded.

You were doing so well, John explained with a small laugh. He sounded proud. *It would have been a shame if it all fell apart because of those two idiots.* I felt John's presence leave my mind, and I knew I had to wrap things up with Horton.

"I think you're being tested, Tom," I told Horton while he continued to sob quietly. "But I think you're strong enough to pass this test. You can be a beacon and show everyone that you won't be defined by what happens to you, but, rather, by how you can change the world. And I know you can change it for the better. It's up to you."

Horton looked up at me with red-rimmed eyes. Sanity appeared to have firmly reasserted itself in him, but I also caught a hint of something more:

Hope.

"You've—you've given me much to think about. I …" He glanced down at his torso. "I almost lost myself. Thank you."

His hand twitched toward me, and I thought for a moment that he would try to shake my hand. Horton looked unsure of what else to say, and I was reminded of one of my old rules for appearing before judges: *Get out as soon as you get a ruling you can live with.*

"Peace be with you," I said. It seemed like a properly religious sendoff in light of how our conversation had progressed. As the words came out, I realized I meant it. "Peace be with you," I repeated.

I stood up and walked away, leaving Horton behind in the first car. I was still working my way back when the train slowed to a stop, and I realized we had arrived in Great Neck. I quickly disembarked and hurried down the stairs. Stepping into the men's room, I ducked into a stall and unloaded my Glock, stuffing the gun and cartridge into my backpack, which I threw over my shoulder. I emerged to a darkness held at bay with scattered streetlights. Horton was behind me, but Abby laid ahead.

The streets around the train station held a smattering of people who I easily dodged as I ran toward the Petersens' house, nearly a mile away. It was the second time I had made that run in the past two days, but the two could not have felt more different.

I'm not sure of how long it took me to get to the house, but I stayed at a near sprint for the entirety of it. When I finally arrived, I was panting and sweating profusely despite the cool October air. I stopped on the sidewalk when I saw Abby's silhouette behind the living room curtains. She quickly disappeared, and only when she reemerged at the front door did I realize she had watched my arrival.

"You know," she called drily, "when you said you were coming down to pick me up, I stupidly assumed you meant with the car. Do you plan on carrying me home on your back?"

She said it with a smile. A confused smile, but a smile nonetheless.

I approached her slowly and cautiously, as if she were a mirage that could disappear at any moment. When I stepped within the radius of the porch light's glow, Abby could finally see me clearly. She saw a man who had barely slept over the course of the past week. She saw a man limping with the aches and scratches caused by spending a night exposed to the elements on top of a mountain. She saw a man who was still processing the trauma of surviving an encounter with a suicide bomber.

Still, I can't imagine she ever saw me look happier.

"Jesus, Dave, are you ok?" Abby asked, taking it all in. She reached up to my face, a concerned look on hers. I allowed her to touch me, and I savored the realness of it. Before she could say a word, I pulled her into a tight embrace.

"I know you have questions," I murmured into her hair. "But please, can they wait? I have had somewhat of a day."

Abby didn't respond, but after a moment I felt her body relax, and she wrapped her arms around me. And we held each other wordlessly under the porch light for what seemed like forever, but still felt too short to me.

epilogue

I didn't realize it at first, but the world was different after that day Abby came back to me.

My suspicions were first aroused several weeks later when I ran into Mr. Gallagher during my lunch period. Mr. Gallagher typically patrolled the hallways with a quiet dignity, but when I encountered him that morning, he seemed uncharacteristically giddy. In fact, as Mr. Gallagher walked in front of me, unaware of my presence behind him, he looked as if he were on the verge of skipping. I watched as a student with a bathroom pass came toward us from the opposite direction, and Mr. Gallagher suddenly and uncharacteristically raised his hand for a high five. The young boy grinned and raised his own hand, which Mr. Gallagher loudly smacked. I laughed, and Mr. Gallagher spun around, only to smile when he realized I had witnessed that exchange.

"You're in a good mood," I noted when the student was out of earshot.

"The best, Dave. The best." He bobbed his head indecisively, wondering if he should say more. I knew he would and remained silent. Finally, Mr. Gallagher said, "I'm not sure if you've heard about my wife ..."

"Do you mean her cancer?" I blurted out. Mr. Gallagher's eyes momentarily narrowed, and I remembered that I only learned about her condition in a now defunct timeline. Fortunately, Mr. Gallagher shrugged off his confusion with a grin.

"I suppose there are no secrets in a small town. Yes, a few weeks ago we were told that her cancer had spread to stage four. She was doing chemo, but we were led to believe that the best we could hope for was to slow the spread of the damn thing, maybe relieve some of her symptoms. But she went in to see her doctor this morning to discuss the results of certain tests they had her take. She doesn't like me to go with her; she insists I'm a downer at those appointments. Well, she just called me to tell me the results: complete remission! Not a trace of cancer! Her doctors are stunned! I'm running out of here to see her now."

"Oh my God! That's amazing. They have no idea what happened?"

"None!" he proclaimed proudly. "And I couldn't care less! You can't look a gift miracle in the mouth!"

With that, he continued bouncing toward the exit. As I resumed walking toward the teachers' lounge, I pondered Mr. Gallagher's characterization of his wife's remission. A "miracle." I didn't know enough about cancer to assess the rarity of remission following a stage four diagnosis. *Is that truly a miracle, or just an example of someone defying the odds?*

I mulled over the possibility that it was the former. Could John have intervened to save Mr. Gallagher's wife? It completely flew in the face of his announced *laissez-faire* approach to Godhood. But then, so did John turning back time to allow me to save Abby, as well as the help he extended during the course of stopping Horton from blowing up that train. *Were those divine acts exceptions, or the start of something entirely new?*

I reached the lounge and took a seat by myself near the window. Ignoring my bagged lunch, I stared outside and allowed myself to wonder. *What if my conversation with John, or, more specifically, my challenge to him to reconnect with mankind's suffering, changed his mind about not interfering with the world?* I also recalled John's lament from the mountaintop relating to his perceived lack of purpose. *Is it possible that John finally found a compelling reason for his existence in the course of helping me?* If so, I could see why he would strive to maintain that sense of meaning.

In the days that followed, I began to seek out proof of other "miracles" that could lend support to my half-developed theory. To my delight, I found that once I started keeping my eyes open for them, miracles seemed to be *everywhere*.

I soon stumbled across a story of a couple who went rock climbing out west, only to somehow dislodge a large boulder above them. The stone proceeded to roll directly toward where the young woman was positioned. Video from the boyfriend's GoPro showed her throwing herself flat against the mountainside, but still in the boulder's path. The rock tumbled directly over her, yet she remained, incredibly, unharmed, as a result of a perfectly aligned indentation in the boulder that was roughly the size and shape of her own body.

I located another anecdote in the news regarding the pilot of a small plane who was drawn off course as a result of an unexpected storm, ultimately crashing into the Atlantic Ocean, miles from land. He was picked up almost immediately by a stray boat that had also deviatedfrom the standard boating lanes, into the middle of nowhere, as a result of that same storm.

A story of a woman waking up in the dead of night due to a sudden compulsion to check on her father, miles away, who arrived just in time to save his life while he lay unconscious on the kitchen floor. Another news report of a no-kill animal shelter being torn apart by a vicious tornado that struck before dawn, only to have each and every animal therein accounted for the following morning after the storm had passed. A recently evicted mother of three, leading her family to spend their first night together in a shelter, who tripped and landed on a piece of litter that was, in fact, a winning Lotto ticket worth over $800,000. Stories like these permeated every news source I could find. I wondered how many additional miracles were taking place that weren't being reported.

This spread of miracles turned out to be more than just a series of heartwarming anecdotes. Scientists began reporting changes in the weather that, inexplicably, seemed to benefit the planet as a whole—areas plagued by droughts reported record rainfall; hurricanes that seemed destined to hit land often blew harmlessly out to sea. Many species of animals on the verge of extinction suddenly and inexplicably began to thrive. The recovery rates in children's wards around the world spiked exponentially.

This is not to suggest that things became perfect. There were still innocent lives shattered by gun violence. Politicians continued to squabble over nonsense. New wars seemed to start up as quickly as old ones ended. Mankind remained its own worst enemy. But John seemed to be giving the world enough of a push to slowly shift global trends from a state of deterioration toward one of healing.

As much as I studied John's apparent handiwork, I could not ascertain any pattern relating to where and when he would act, as opposed to those situations where he elected not to intercede. All I could do was have faith that he was acting toward a bigger picture I couldn't see or understand. I also assumed that his oft-repeated respect for free will also compelled him, at times, to stay out of challenges that we were meant to face on our own.

One individual who rose to take on at least some of those challenges was Tom Horton. Nearly two years after I confronted him on the train, I came across a newspaper article with the headline "Hope Born from Tragedy," accompanied by a picture of a Tom Horton, smiling in front of his church. According to the article, Horton had managed to redirect the rage that flowed from his grief and used that energy to organize a support group for individuals and families struck by unexpected tragedies. Wives who were transformed into widows overnight by a drunk driver. Children turned orphans as a result of a plane crash that took out their vacationing parents. Horton sought out anyone thrown into a situation where hope seemed unobtainable, and he would help those individuals find it.

"I know firsthand the temptation to give up in the face of tragedy," Horton was quoted as saying in the article. "And I will do everything in my power to make sure no one goes down the dark path that nearly consumed me."

So yes, we lived in a different world after the day that John elected to send me back in time to save Abby and dozens of others by stopping Tom Horton. There have always been individuals willing to sacrifice their lives in an effort to improve things, even if only a bit, but people can only do so much by themselves. John, through a series of subtle miracles, most of which seemed to escape all but the most discerning eyes, silently provided the extra help needed to make countless lives better than they would have been otherwise.

Although, I must note, there was one particular miracle that was anything but subtle.

The night I was reunited with Abby, we returned to our home in Woodstock via the Long Island Railroad and Amtrak. Abby was initially perplexed at my acceptance of the train system given my earlier warnings against it, but I managed to convince her that the threat was gone. She was skeptical, but given the lack of any proof that there was any danger in the first place, she eventually gave in.

At my request, Abby had patiently withheld all of the questions she had for me, but as we sat together on the train, I could see them bubbling beneath the surface, ready to explode out of her. I decided to tell her as much as she could handle.

"I know you have a ton of questions for me, and that today seemed really weird," I told her as we huddled together on the train. "It's not that I don't *want* to tell you; I want to tell you *everything*. But it is all so insane, I know there's no chance you'll ever believe me." Abby started to protest, and I quickly added, "It's not a criticism of you. *I* wouldn't believe *you* if the situation was reversed. It's all completely beyond belief."

Abby pursed her lips thoughtfully. "Why don't you try me?"

I thought it over and shook my head.

"You'll think I'm crazy. You will think I'm an utter lunatic."

"Can you give me the gist of it?" Abby pressed. "If it seems like something I can handle, I'll let you know, and you can tell me all of it. And if not … well, I guess we just put it aside and move on with our lives."

I hesitated, torn between the need to share my story with her and the knowledge that however much she loved and trusted me, Abby was not ready at that time to believe what I had to tell her.

"Ok," I sighed, giving in. "I'm going to tell you the sum of it now, but I don't think you're ready to accept it. At least, not yet. There may be a day in the future, I think, when you'll view things differently. When that happens, you can just let me know and I'll tell you everything then. Deal?"

Abby thought it over, and then, with a grin, stuck out a hand. We shook hands like a pair of idiots.

"Deal!" she announced.

"Ok …" I wasn't sure where to start. "Have I ever told you about my friend John that worked with me when I was a lawyer?"

Abby's brow furrowed in thought, and then she nodded. "I think so."

I forced myself to continue. "Well, a few years ago … John became God."

Abby studied me in silence, looking for a sign that I was pulling a joke on her. I waited patiently, trying to gauge her reaction.

"Do you mean he literally became God?" she asked carefully. I nodded.

"Yes. Omnipotence, omniscience—the whole deal."

She nodded her head slowly, trying to keep an open mind.

"I think …" she began. Then she shook her head sadly. "You were right. This is more than I can accept right now."

"I know." I kissed her on the forehead. "Believe me, I know."

We did not discuss it any further the remainder of the trip home, or even in the months or years to follow. For a while, I would occasionally catch Abby studying me, as if assessing my sanity, when she thought I wasn't looking. Fortunately, that brief phase passed after Abby could not find any other symptoms of mental illness.

It was almost eleven years later before the topic came up again. During that time, Abby and I expanded our family beyond Peaches. On that particular morning, our two boys, Pete and Walt (who at the time were ten and eight, respectively), were out of the house at a day camp they attended during the summer. Abby sat at the kitchen table writing "thank you" notes in response to various birthday gifts she had received from her family earlier in the week. Abby was engrossed in each note, and she didn't notice the sun striking the face of her watch as she wrote. That reflection, in turn, birthed a small ball of light that danced along the wall next to her, bouncing in time with the subtle movements of her wrist. After that went on for a bit, Abby abruptly stopped writing and looked up at the sound of scratching. She glanced to her right and noticed Peaches playfully chasing that moving light and, at times, attempting to scramble up the wall to catch it. Abby continued to move her watch about and studied Peaches as he hopped about the kitchen. After a minute or two, she called me into the room.

"Do you see this?" she asked in a monotone voice as soon as I entered from the living room. I followed her gaze to Peaches.

"Yes," I said, uncertain what she was referring to. "He likes to play," I added, unhelpfully.

Abby did not take her eyes off the cat.

"How long did you have him before we met?" she asked.

I ran some quick calculations. "A little over five years? I'm not sure exactly."

"And how old was he when you got him?"

"I don't know, exactly. He wasn't a kitten, I can tell you that much. A few years old, at least."

"Dave, I've known you for just about fifteen years. That cat is over twenty years old, and he's bouncing around like a kitten." Her stunned face looked overwhelmed. "He's not aging."

Abby stared at me, her distraught look begging for an explanation. I gave her the only one I had.

"Peaches was John's cat before I took him. John loves that cat."

The little color that had been in Abby's pale face left completely. She wordlessly swiveled her head from Peaches to me and then back to Peaches. Blinking twice, Abby slowly stood up and went upstairs to our bedroom. Peaches seemed disappointed that his "chase the light" game had ended, but he quickly settled to sleep in a patch of sun on the floor.

Not knowing how to take Abby's reaction, I wrestled with whether she wanted to be left alone or whether I was supposed to have followed her. After several minutes passed and Abby still had not come back downstairs, I hesitantly headed up to check on her. I found her sitting on our bed reading a book—my old journal on John. I didn't know how she always seemed to know exactly where that thing was. She looked up when I entered the room.

"Tell me everything," she said.

So I did.

It took me several hours to tell my story. Abby did not ask many questions, and those that she did ask tended to focus on who John was before he became God, and my relationship with him during those times. When my throat went dry and I needed to take a break, Abby occupied herself by ferociously tearing through my journal, reading my various ramblings with a new perspective.

Abby was visibly shaken when I reached the part about her own death, and she cried softly as I described the emotional breakdown I suffered as her casket was lowered into the ground. But she would not let me stop. She insisted that she wanted to hear it all, and I did the best I could to oblige.

My voice was nearly gone once I reached the end of my story. In a raspy voice, I explained my theory that John, following my last encounter with him, had begun to actively work to make the world a better place. I described to Abby the circumstances relating to Mr. Gallagher's wife's recovery, as well as all of the other examples of "miracles" I had learned about over the course of the past decade. After I finished, I was exhausted from talking for hours on end, and I laid down on the bed beside Abby. She let me rest as she proceeded to reread my journal, page by page. At some point, I must have dozed off, but Abby was still reading when I awoke. She lowered the journal when she caught me watching her.

"Did you ever piece together why John reached out to you in particular?" she asked. I could see that she had been in the process of reading Point III of my journal: "Why does John have to speak to *me*?"

"Not really," I replied.

Abby smirked.

"I think it's obvious." She grinned mischievously, waiting for my follow up question.

"Well?" I asked, quickly giving in.

Abby held up a single finger.

"One: He didn't understand why he became God, and you wrote in here that it probably felt to John as if it were unearned."

Abby raised a second finger. "Two: You were his best friend. You knew him better than anyone else, before he became God."

Abby paused, waiting for me to see the answer. I didn't, and I shrugged. Abby rolled her eyes, exasperated, and gave me a hard shove.

"Come on, Dave! He needed to be convinced he was equipped to handle that responsibility! Only a person John respected, and who understood his character, could possibly do that. It was *you*, dummy!"

"Maybe," I allowed.

"Maybe?" Abby asked, incredulous. "Definitely! You told me that John was shy to the point of being catatonic when you joined your old firm, right?"

"Sure."

"And that after a few years, John was comfortable enough to rant in front of the entire firm about a partner's billing fraud?"

I saw where she was going, but I still resisted. "He came out of his shell," I said defensively.

Abby would not let up.

"And why do you think that was? You gave him strength then, and you gave him strength after he became God! You just can't see it because you never give yourself enough credit."

I was uncomfortable with Abby's analysis, and I tried to change the subject.

"It's a good theory," I conceded. "Better than anything I ever came up with. But can you solve the hard question?"

"What's that?"

"Why was *John* chosen to become God?"

I didn't expect Abby to have an answer—not really—but she took my question seriously. I didn't interrupt her as she chewed her lower lip, deep in thought.

"You know what I think?" she said after a bit, her eyes sparkling. "I think John is now doing what he was meant to do from the beginning. Striking that delicate balance between improving lives and respecting free will. But like I said before, you're the one who got him there by saying exactly what he needed to hear and helping him restore enough of his old humanity to drive him to act. So maybe the reason John was picked … is you. Maybe John's predecessor knew how this would play out and knew that John's friendship with you would allow him to get to where he was supposed to be."

Abby seemed pleased with her answer. It was just another example of Abby seeing more in me than I had ever managed to detect in myself. I had no response to her theory, but Abby was not looking for one. With a loving smile, Abby kissed my forehead and went downstairs to feed Peaches, leaving me alone to reflect on her diagnoses. But I didn't ponder for too long. My experience with John had left me with a multitude of questions, and I knew I was unlikely to ever get complete answers to them. But that was ok.

As I write this, I have a wife who makes me smile and laugh every day, and who managed to tap reserves of love so deep within me that I hadn't even realized they were there. I have two sons who have grown up to become better men than I ever was. I have a thirty-three-year-old cat, my oldest friend, who helped save the world by tethering God to his lost humanity. Every day, I wake up to experience moments that are filled with joy and are fully lived.

And that's more than enough for me.

about the author

When he is not writing, Daniel Maunz works as an attorney in New York City, serving as in-house counsel for a major insurance company. He currently lives in Bayside, New York, with his wife Lynne, their son Patrick, and their two cats: Admiral Meowy McWhiskers and Captain Cutie (or "Admiral" and "Captain" for short). *Questions of Perspective* is his first novel.

NOTE FROM THE AUTHOR

Word-of-mouth is crucial for any author to succeed. If you enjoyed the book, please leave a review online—anywhere you are able. Even if it's just a sentence or two. It would make all the difference and would be very much appreciated.

Thanks!
Daniel

Thank you so much for reading one of our
Paranormal Fantasy novels.

If you enjoyed our book, please check out our recommended
for your next great read!

The Graveyard Girl and the Boneyard Boy by Martin Matthews

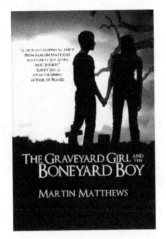

"... a compelling and eminently likable cast of characters."
–Authors Reading